Morgan Chane swam alone in the infinite, with stars above him and below him and all around him.

He wondered if anyone had ever been so alone. His parents had been dead for years, killed by the heavy gravitation of Varna. His friends on Varna were friends no longer but hunters eager to kill him. He had always thought of himself as Varnan and now he knew that he had been wrong.

No family, no friends, no country, no world . . . and not even a ship. Just a suit and a few hours of oxygen and a hostile universe around him.

But he was still a Starwolf, and if he had to die he would die like one. . . .

EDMOND HAMILTON
STARWOLF

ACE SCIENCE FICTION BOOKS
NEW YORK

All characters in this book are fictitious.
Any resemblance to actual persons, living or dead,
is purely coincidental.

THE WEAPON FROM BEYOND by Edmond Hamilton Copyright © 1967 by
Ace Books, Inc.
THE CLOSED WORLDS by Edmond Hamilton Copyright © 1968 by Ace
Books, Inc.
WORLD OF THE STARWOLVES by Edmond Hamilton Copyright © 1968 by
Ace Books, Inc.

STARWOLF

An Ace Science Fiction Book / published by arrangement with
the author

PRINTING HISTORY
Ace original / October 1982
Second printing / January 1983
Third printing / June 1983

ISBN: 0-441-78422-4

Ace Science Fiction Books are published by The Berkley Publishing Group,
200 Madison Avenue, New York, New York 10016.
PRINTED IN THE UNITED STATES OF AMERICA

THE
WEAPON
FROM
BEYOND

I

The stars watched him, and it seemed to him that they whispered to him.

Die, Starwolf. Your course is run.

He lay across the pilot-chair, and the dark veils were close around his brain, and the wound in his side throbbed and burned. He was not unconscious, he knew that his little ship had come out of overdrive, and that there were things that he should do. But it was no use, no use at all.

Let it go, Starwolf. Die.

In a corner of his mind, Morgan Chane knew that it was not the stars that were talking to him. It was some part of himself that still wanted to survive and that was haunting him, prodding him, trying to get him onto his feet. But it was easier to ignore it, and lie here.

Easier, yes. And how happy his death would make his dear friends and loving comrades. Chane's fogged mind held onto that thought. And finally it brought a dull anger, and a resolve. He would not make them happy. He would live, and some day he would make those who were now hunting him very unhappy indeed.

The savage determination seemed to clear the blur of darkness a little from his brain. He opened his eyes and then, slowly and painfully, he hauled himself erect in the seat. The action pulled at his wound sickeningly, and for a few minutes he fought against nausea. Then he reached out a shaky hand toward a switch. He must first find out exactly where he was, where the last desperately hasty course he had set as he fled had brought him.

Like little red eyes, figures glowed on the board as the computer silently answered his question. He read the figures but his brain was not clear enough to translate them. Shaking his head drunkenly, he peered at the viewplate.

A mass of blazing stars walled the firmament in front of him. High-piled suns, smoky-red, pure white, pale green and gold and peacock blue, glared at him. Great canyons of darkness rifted the star-mass, rivers of cosmic dust out of which gleamed the pale witch-fires of drowned suns. He was just outside a cluster, and now Chane's blurred mind remembered that in the last desperate moment of flight, when he threw his stolen ship into overdrive before blacking out, he had jabbed the coordinates of Corvus Cluster.

Blackness, nothingness, the eternal solemn silence of the void, and the suns of the cluster pouring their mighty radiance upon the tiny needle that was his ship. His memory quickened, and he knew now why he had come here. There was a world that he knew about in this gigantic hive of stars. He could lie up there and hide, and he sorely needed such a refuge, for he had no healamp and his wound would take time to heal naturally. He thought he would be safe on that world, if he could reach it.

Unsteadily, Chane set a course, and the little ship hurtled toward the edge of the cluster at the top speed of its normal drive.

The darkness began to dim his brain again and he thought, *No, I have to stay awake, for tomorrow we raid the Hyades.*

But that could not be right, they had hit the Hyades months ago. What was the matter with his memory? Things seemed jumbled and without sense or sequence.

Sweeping out from Varna in their swift little squadron, running down the Sagittarius Passage and crosscutting Owl Nebula to come down in a surprise swoop on the fat little planet with the fat little people who squealed and panicked when he and his comrades hit their rich towns. . . .

But that had been a long time ago. Their last raid, the one where he had got this wound, had been to Shandor Five. He remembered how on their way there they had been spotted and chased by a squadron of heavies, and had escaped them by slamming right through a star-system at full speed in normal drive. He could remember Ssander laughing and saying, "They won't take the chances we Varnans take and that's why they never catch us."

But Ssander is dead, and I killed him, and that is why I'm flying for my life!

It flashed across Chane's mind: he remembered the quarrel over loot on Shandor Five and how Ssander had got furious and tried to kill him and how he had killed Ssander instead. And how, wounded, he had fled from the avengers. . . .

The dark veils had cleared away and he was here in his little ship, still fleeing, hurtling toward the cluster. He stared at it, sweat on his dark face, his black eyes wild.

He thought that he had better stop blacking out or he would not have long to live. The hunters were after him, and there was no one in the galaxy who would give aid to a wounded Starwolf.

Chane had aimed to enter the cluster at a point where one of the dark dust-rivers divided it, and he was already passing the outpost sentinel suns. Soon he could hear the tick and whisper of dust against the hull. He was keeping out of the denser drift, and the particles were not much bigger than atoms. If, at these speeds, he met particles much bigger, they would hole the ship.

Chane got into his suit and helmet. It was a prolonged effort, and the pain of it was such that he had to set his teeth to keep from groaning. It seemed to him that the wound was more agonizing than it had been, but there was no time to look at it; the heal-patch he had put over it would have to do for now.

Up the great, dark, dusty river between the cluster stars went the little ship, and often Chane's head sagged against the board. But he kept his course. The dust might prove death for him. But it could be life, for those who would come hunting could not probe far in it.

The viewplate was blurred and vague now. It looked like a window, but it was a complex mechanism functioning through probe-rays far faster than light, and his probes had little range here. Chane had to keep all his attention on the dimness ahead, and that was hard with the wound throbbing in his side and the dark fingers always reaching for his brain.

Stars loomed up in the dust, burning like muffled torches, angry red and yellow suns that the tiny ship slowly passed. A deeper spot of brooding blackness, a dead sun, lay far ahead to zenith and became a somber star-mark that he seemed to approach with unnatural slowness. . . .

The dim river in the stars twisted a little, and Chane changed course. The hours went on and on, and he was well inside the cluster. But it was a long way yet. . . .

Chane dreamed.

The good days, the morning days, that now had so suddenly ended. The going forth from Varna of the little ships that were everywhere so dreaded. The slamming out of overdrive and the swoop upon a city of a startled world, and the warning cry across the suns— *The Starwolves are out!*

And the mirthful laughter of himself and his comrades as they went in, mocking the slow sluggishness of those who resisted: Go in fast and take the plunder and beat down those who tried to stop you, fast, fast, and away to the ships again, and finally back to Varna with loot and wounds and high-hearted triumph. The good days . . . could they really be ended for him?

Chane thought of that, and fed the fires of his sullen anger. They had turned against him, tried to kill him, hunted him. But no matter what they said he was one of them, as strong, as swift, as cunning as any of them, and a time would come when he would prove it. But for now he must hide, lie concealed until his wound bettered, and soon he would reach the world where he could do that.

Again there was a turning of the dark river, the dust rifting deeper into the cluster. More of the baleful witch-stars went by, and the dust whispered louder on the hull. Far ahead, a glazed, dim eye of bloody orange watched his ship approach. And presently Chane could make out the planet that moved lonesome around the lonely dying star, and he knew it for the planet of his refuge.

He almost made it.

II

His luck started running out when the blip of a ship approaching in normal drive showed up on the probe-screen. It was outside the dust, coming along the edge of the river in the stars. It would surely come close enough for its probes to spot him, even in the dust.

There were no alternatives. If the ship was one of the Varnan hunters, they would destroy him. If it was from anyplace but Varna, they would be his enemies the moment they identified his Starwolf craft. And they would identify it as such at first glance, for no world anywhere had ships like the hated Varnan ships.

He had to go deeper into hiding and there was only one place for that, and that was the denser drift. He took his little ship deeper into the dust-stream.

The whispering and ticking on the hull became louder. The larger particles outside so blurred his probe-rays that he lost track of the ship outside the dust. Similarly, they would lose track of him. Chane cut his drive and sat motionless. There was nothing to do but wait.

He did not have to wait long.

When it came, it was no more than a slight quiver that he could hardly feel. But all his instruments went out.

Chane turned. One look was enough. A bit of drift no bigger than a marble had holed the hull and had wrecked his drive-unit and converter. He was in a dead ship, and nothing he could do would make it live again. He could not even broadcast a call.

He looked at the now-blank screen, and though he could not now see the images of the stars he seemed again to hear their mocking whisper.

Let it go, Starwolf. . . .

Chane's shoulders sagged. Maybe it was as well this way. What future would there be for him anyway, in a galaxy where every man would be his enemy?

Sitting slumped there, in a kind of numb daze, he thought how strange it was that he should end up this way. He had always thought that it would come in a sudden blaze of battle, in some swift swooping raid across the stars. That was the end most Starwolves came to, if they went out too many times from Varna.

He had never dreamed that he would die in this slow, dull, leaden fashion, just sitting and waiting, waiting in a dead ship until his oxygen ran out.

A feeling of revulsion grew slowly in Chane's weary mind. There must be some better end for him than this, some last effort he could make, no matter how hopeless.

He tried to think it out. The only possible source of help was the ship just outside the dust-river. If he could signal them and they came to his aid, one of two things would happen: they could be the Varnans hunting him, and they would kill him; or they could be men of some other world and as soon as they saw his Starwolf ship, they would be his deadly enemies.

But what if his ship was not here? Then, they would accept him as an Earthman, for that was what he was by pure descent even though he had never seen Earth.

Chane looked back at the wrecked drive-unit and converter. They were dead, but the power-chamber that supplied energy to the converter was intact. He thought he saw a way. . . .

It was a gamble, and he hated to bet his life on it. Yet

it was better than just sitting here and dying. But he knew that he had to make his bet quickly, or he would not even have this gambling chance.

He began, slowly and clumsily, to take apart some of the instruments on the board. It was difficult work, with gloved hands, and it was even more difficult to reassemble some of the parts into the mechanism he needed. When he finished, he had a small timing-device that he hoped would work.

Chane went back to the power-chamber and began to hook his timing-device to it. He had to work fast, and his task involved bending and crouching in a very confined space, and he felt the wound in his side tearing at him like a vulture. Tears of pain blurred his vision.

Cry, he told himself. *How they'd love to know that you died crying!*

The blur went away and he forced his nerveless fingers, ignoring the pain.

When he had finished his task, he cracked the lock open and took all four of the impellers from the spacesuit rack. He went back then to the power-chamber and turned on his crude timing-device.

Then Chane went out of the ship like a scared cat, two impellers in each hand driving him out amid the stars.

He hurtled away from the little craft, with the stars doing a crazy dance around him. He had gone into a spin but there was no time to right that. There was only one thing important and that was to get as far away as possible before his timing-gadget shorted the energy chamber and destroyed the ship. Chane counted seconds in his mind as the glittering starry hosts went round and round him.

The stars paled for a moment as a white nova seemed to flare in his eyes. It went out and he was in blind darkness. But he was living. He had got far enough before the power-chamber let go and destroyed his ship.

He turned off his impellers and drifted. The men in the ship outside the dust-river should have seen that flare. They might or might not come into the dust to investigate. And if they did, they might or might not be the Varnans who wanted his life.

He swam alone in the infinite, with stars above him and below him and all around him.

He wondered if anyone had ever been so alone. His parents had been dead for years, killed by the heavy gravitation of Varna. His friends on Varna were friends no longer but hunters eager to kill him. He had always thought of himself as Varnan and now he knew that he had been wrong.

No family, no friends, no country, no world . . . and not even a ship. Just a suit and a few hours of oxygen and a hostile universe around him.

But he was still a Starwolf, and if he had to die he would die like one. . . .

The grand and glittering backdrop of the cluster stars revolved slowly around him. To check his rotation might take power from the impellers that he would later need. And this way he could scan all the starfields as he turned.

But nothing moved in them, nothing at all.

Time went by. The lordly suns had been here for a long while and they were in no hurry to see the man die.

On what seemed to him his ten-millionth rotation, his eye caught something. A star winked.

He looked again, but the star was serene and steady. Were his eyes betraying him? Chane thought it likely, but he would push his bet all the way. He used his impellers to urge him in the direction of that star.

Within minutes, he knew that his eyes had not erred. For another star winked briefly as something occluded it. He strained his eyes, but it was hard to see, for the dark veils were closing around him again. The wound in his side, strained by his exertions, had opened again and he felt that his life was running out of it.

His vision cleared and he saw a black blot growing

against the starfields, a blot that grew to the outline of a ship. It was not Varnan; the ships of Varna were small and needle-like. This ship had the silhouette of a Class Sixteen or Twenty and had the odd eyebrow bridge that was characteristic of the ships of old Earth. It was barely moving, coming his way.

Chane tried to formulate in his mind what story to tell to keep them from suspecting the truth about him. The darkness closed in on him but he fought it off, and flashed his impellers on and off as a signal.

He never knew how much later it was that he found the ship beside him and its airlock opening like a black mouth. He made a final effort and moved clumsily into it, and then he gave up fighting and the blackness took him.

He awoke later feeling surprisingly good. He discovered why when he found that he lay in a ship-bunk with a healamp glowing against his side. Already the wound looked dry and half-healed.

Chane looked around. The bunk-room was small. A bulb glowed in the metal ceiling, and he felt the drone and vibration of a ship in normal drive. Then he saw that a man was sitting on the edge of the opposite bunk, watching him.

The man got up and came over to him. He was older than Chane, a good bit older, and he had an oddly unfinished look about his hands and face and figure, as though he had been roughly carved out of rock by an unskilled sculptor. His short hair was graying a little and he had a long, horse-like face with eyes of no particular color.

"You cut it pretty fine," he said.

"I did," said Chane.

"Will you tell me what the devil a wounded Earthman is doing floating around in Corvus Cluster?" asked the other. He added, as an afterthought, "I'm John Dilullo."

Chane's eyes strayed to the stun-gun the Earthman wore belted around his coverall. "You're mercenaries, aren't you?"

Dilullo nodded. "We are. But you haven't answered my question."

Chane's mind raced. He would have to be careful. The Mercs were known all over the galaxy as a tough lot. A very high proportion of them were Earthmen, and there was a reason for this.

Earth, long ago, had pioneered the interstellar drive that opened up the galaxy. Yet, for all that, Earth was a poor planet. It was poor because all the other planets of its system were uninhabitable, with ferociously hostile conditions and only a few scant mineral resources. Compared to the great star-systems with many rich, peopled worlds, Earth was a poverty-stricken planet.

So Earth's chief export was men. Skilled spacemen, technicians, and fighters streamed out from old Earth to many parts of the galaxy. And the mercenaries from Earth were among the toughest.

"My name's Morgan Chane," he said. "Meteor-prospector, operating out of Alto Two. I went too deep into the damned drift and my ship was holed. One fragment caught me in the side, and others hit my drive. I saw my power-chamber was going to blow, and I just managed to get into my suit and get out of there in time."

He added, "I needn't say that I'm glad you saw the flare and came along."

Dilullo nodded. "Well, I've only one more question for now. . . ." He was turning away as he spoke. Then he suddenly whirled back around, his hand grabbing out the weapon at his belt.

Chane came out of the bunk like a flying shadow. His tigerish leap took him across the wide space between them at preternatural speed, and with his left hand he wrested away the weapon while his right hand cracked Dilullo's face. Dilullo went sprawling to the deck.

Chane aimed at him. "Is there any reason why I shouldn't use this on you?"

Dilullo fingered his bleeding lip and looked up and said, "No particular reason, except that there's no charge in it."

Chane smiled grimly. Then, as his fingers tightened on the butt of the weapon, his smile faded. There was no charge-magazine in it.

"That was a test," said Dilullo, getting stiffly to his feet. "When you were unconscious, and I fixed that healamp on you, I felt your musculature. I'd already heard that Varnan ships were raiding toward this cluster. I knew you weren't a Varnan . . . you could shave off the fine fur and all that but you couldn't change the shape of your head. But all the same, you had the muscles of a Starwolf.

"Then," Dilullo said, "I remembered rumors I'd heard from the out-worlds, about an Earthman who raided with the Varnans and was one of them. I hadn't believed them, no one believed them, for the Varnans, from a heavy planet, have such strength and speed no Earthman could keep up with them. But you could, and right now you proved it. You're a Starwolf."

Chane said nothing. His eyes looked past the other man to the closed door.

"Do me the credit," said Dilullo, "of believing that I wouldn't come down here without first making sure you couldn't do what you're thinking of doing."

Chane looked into the colorless eyes, and believed.

"All right," he said. "So now?"

"I'm curious," said Dilullo, sitting down in a bunk. "About many things. About you, in particular." He waited.

Chane tossed him the useless weapon, and sat down. He thought for a moment, and Dilullo suggested mildly, "Just the truth."

"I thought I knew the truth, until now," Chane said. "I thought I was a Varnan. I was born on Varna . . . my

parents were missionaries from Earth who were going
to reform the wicked Varnan ways. Of course the heavy
gravitation soon killed them, and it nearly killed me,
but it didn't, quite, and I grew up with the Varnans and
thought I was one of them."

He could not keep the bitterness out of his voice.
Dilullo, watching him narrowly, said nothing.

"Then the Varnans hit Shandor Five, and I was one
of them when they did it. But there was a quarrel there
about the loot, and when I struck Ssander he tried to
kill me. I killed him instead, and the others turned on
me. I barely got away alive."

He added, after a moment, "I can't go back to Varna
now. 'Damned Earthpawn!' Ssander called me. *Me,* as
Varnan as he was in everything but blood. But I can't
go back." He sat silent, brooding.

Dilullo said, "You've plundered and robbed and
you've doubtlessly killed, along with those you ran
with. But do you have any remorse about that? No.
The only thing you're sorry about is that they threw you
out of the pack. By God, you're a true Starwolf!"

Chane made no answer to that. After a moment,
Dilullo went on, "We—my men and I—have come here
to Corvus Cluster because we've been hired to do a job.
A rather dangerous job."

"So?"

Dilullo's eyes measured him. "As you say, you're a
Varnan in everything but blood. You know every
Starwolf trick there is, and that's a lot. I could use you
on this job."

Chane smiled. "The offer is flattering. . . . No."

"Better think about it," said Dilullo. "And think of
this—my men would kill you instantly if I told them
you're a Starwolf."

Chane said, "And you'll tell them, unless I sign up
with you?"

It was Dilullo's turn to smile. "Other people besides
Varnans can be ruthless." He added, "Anyway, you

haven't got anyplace to go, have you?"

"No," said Chane, and his face darkened. "No."

After a moment he asked, "What makes you think you could trust me?"

Dilullo stood up. "Trust a Starwolf? Do you think I'm crazy? I trust only the fact that you know you'll die if I tell about you."

Chane looked up at him. "Suppose something happened to you so you couldn't tell?"

"That," said Dilullo, "would be unfortunate . . . for you. I'd see to it that, in that case, your little secret automatically became known."

There was a silence. Then Chane asked, "What's the job?"

"It's a risky job," said Dilullo, "and the more people who know about it ahead of time, the riskier it'll be. Just assume for now that you're going to gamble your neck and will very likely lose it."

"That wouldn't grieve you too much, would it?" Chane said.

Dilullo shrugged. "I'll tell you how it is, Chane. When a Starwolf gets killed, they declare a holiday on all decent worlds."

Chane smiled. "At least we understand each other."

III

The night sky dripped silver. The world called Kharal lay in the heart of the cluster, and the system to which it belonged was close to Corvus Nebula. That great cloud was a gigantic glowing sprawl across the heavens, with the burning glory of the cluster stars around it, so that soft light and deep black shadows lay always over the planet by night.

Chane stood in the shadow of the ship and looked across the small and quiet spaceport toward the lights of the city. Those reddish lights hung in a vast pyramid against the sky. A soft wind laden with spicy scents that had an acrid background blew toward him from that direction, and it brought him the sound of a distant buzz and hum.

Hours before, Dilullo and one other Merc had been taken secretly by a Kharali car to the city under cover of darkness.

"You'll stay here," Dilullo had told them. "I'm taking Bollard with me, and no one else, to talk to those who want to hire us."

Chane remembering that, smiled. The other Mercs were in the ship, gambling. And what was there to keep him here?

He walked toward the city, under the softly glowing sky. The spaceport was dark and quiet with nothing on it but two dumpy interstellar freighters and several armed Kharali planetary cruisers. No one passed him on the road except that once there was a whizzing roar as one of the three-wheeled Kharali cars sped by. These were a city-loving people, and even those who worked the mines that were this world's wealth returned to the cities at night. The arid, flat lands stretched away, still and silver under the nebula-sky.

There was a pulse of excitement in Chane. He had visited many strange worlds, but always as one of the Starwolves, and that meant that everywhere he had been a feared and hated enemy. But now, alone as he was, who would know that he was anything but an Earthman?

Kharal was an Earth-sized planet and Chane, used to the heavy gravitation of Varna, found himself moving with a soft vagueness. But he had adjusted to that by the time he reached the city.

It was a monolithic city, carved long ago from a mountain of black rock. Thus it was a city-mountain, with high-piled galleries and windows and terraces shining ruddy light, with alien gargoyles projecting out at every level, a mammoth hive of life towering up into the soft nebula sky. Chane looked up and up, and heard the sounds from it now as a dull, throbbing roar.

He went through a great arched doorway in the base of the city-mountain. It had huge metal doors that could be closed for defense but they had not been closed for a long time and were so corroded that the reliefs upon them which picture kings, warriors, dancers and strange beasts were vague and blurred.

Chane started up a broad stone ramp, ignoring the motoway that slid beside it. At once the bursting life and roar of the place were all around him: Men and not-men, the human Kharalis and the humanoid aborigines, voices high and light, voices guttural and throaty. They jostled under the ruddy lights, with the throng now and then giving way before a hairy humanoid who brought a lowing, hobbled and grotesque beast to market. Smells and smokes of strange foods from cookshops in the galleries, the bawl of peddlers offering their wares, and over all the haunting singsong of the Kharali multiple-flutes echoing and reechoing.

The humans of Kharal were very tall and slender people, none of them under seven feet. They looked down, with contempt in their pale blue faces, at Chane. The women turned away from him as though they had seen something defiling, and the men made remarks and laughed mockingly. A young boy, gawky in his rather soiled robe, followed close behind Chane to show that even he was inches taller than the Earthman, and the mocking titters were redoubled. Other boys took up the game, and as he went upward he acquired a jeering retinue.

Chane ignored them, climbing to still other levels, and after a little time they tired of him and went away.

He thought, *This would be a dangerous city to loot. You could easily get trapped in these galleries.*

And then he remembered that he was not a Varnan any longer, that he would not again raid with the Starwolves.

He stopped at a stall and bought a cup of stinging, almost acid, intoxicant. The Kharali who served him, when he had finished, took the cup and ostentatiously scrubbed it. There were more titters.

Chane remembered what Dilullo had told them about the Kharalis before they landed.

They were truly human, of course, like the peoples of many star-worlds. That had been a big surprise for the first explorers from Earth after they perfected the stardrive . . . the fact of so many human-peopled worlds. It had turned out that Earthmen hadn't been the first, that many systems had been seeded by a star-traveling human stock so remote in the past that only vague traditions of them lingered. But this human stock had been altered in different ways by ages of evolutionary pressure, and the Kharalis were the result here.

"They consider other humans as much beneath them as their own aborigines," Dilullo had said. "They're utterly insular, and dislike all strangers. Be polite."

So Chane was polite. He ignored the mocking looks and the contemptuous remarks, even though a few of the latter, uttered by Kharalis who spoke galacto, the lingua-franca of the galaxy, were perfectly understandable. He drank again, and studiously avoided looking at Kharali women, and went on climbing the ramps and stairways, stopping here and there to peer at some odd sight. When the Varnans went on a plundering raid, they had little time for sightseeing, and Chane was enjoying a new experience.

He came into a wide gallery whose one whole side was open to the nebula sky. Under the ruddy lights, there was a small crowd of Kharalis, gathered around something Chane could not see, and there was laughter from them and now and then a strange hissing sound. He worked his way, without shoving or jostling, through the ring to see what it was they watched.

Several of the humanoids were here, hairy creatures with too many arms and mild, stupid eyes. Some of them carried leather ropes curiously looped at the ends. Two of them had such ropes tied to the legs of a winged beast that was between them. It was a semi-reptilian creature half as big as a man, its body scaled and wattled, its fanged beak striking the air in brainless fury. When it made a lunge in one direction, the rope on its other leg pulled it back. When that happened, the creature's wattles turned bright red and it hissed furiously.

The tall Kharalis found it amusing. They laughed each time the wattles crimsoned, each time the wild hissing began. Chane had seen beast-baiting on many worlds, and thought it childish. He turned to make his way out of the ring.

Something whispered, and a loop wrapped itself

around each of his arms. He swung around. Two Kharali men had taken trapping-ropes from the humanoids, and had used the clever cast-and-loop to fasten onto Chane. A burst of malicious laughter went up.

Chane stood still, and put a smile on his face. He looked around the circle of mirthful, mocking blue faces.

"All right," he said in galacto. "I understand. To you, an Earthman is a strange beast. Now let me go."

But they were not going to let him go that easily. The rope on his left arm tugged, pulling him sharply. As he reacted to keep his balance, the rope on his right arm pulled so that he staggered.

The laughter was very loud now, drowning out the distant flutes. The wattled beast was forgotten.

"Look," said Chane. "You've had your little joke."

He was keeping down his anger, he had already disobeyed orders by being here and there was no use in making it worse.

His arms suddenly flew up to horizontal, grotesquely pointing in each direction, as both Kharalis pulled simultaneously. One of the humanoids came and capered in front of Chane, pointing at him and then at the wattled beast. It was a joke that even his simple brain could understand and his merriment triggered new bursts of laughter from the blue men. They rocked with it, looking at the humanoid and then at Chane.

Chane turned his head and looked at the Kharali who held the rope on his right arm. He asked softly, "Will you let me go now?"

The answer was a sharp and painful tug on his right arm. The Kharali looked at him with a malicious smile.

Chane moved with all the speed and strength that his Varna-grown muscles gave him on this slighter world. He leaped toward the Kharali on his right, and the surging strength of that lunge pulled the man with the left rope off his feet.

Chane dived in close to the tall, startled Kharali and

thrust his arms under the man's arms, reaching upward. His hands curved out to grab the front of the Kharali's arms, near the shoulders. He put all his strength into a levering, surging embrace. There was a dull double crack, like the sound of wet sticks breaking, and Chane stepped back.

The Kharali stood, his face a mask of horror. His long, slender arms hung limp, both of them broken near the shoulders.

For a moment, the Kharalis stared silently. It was as though they could not believe it, as though a despised cur dog had suddenly become a tiger and pounced.

Chane used the moment to slide between them across the gallery to a narrow stair. Then a raging chorus went up behind him. He started running then, going up the stairs, taking three steps at a time.

He was laughing as he ran. He would not soon forget the Kharali bully, and how his face had changed from malice to open-mouthed horror.

The stair came up into a dark corridor in the rock. His eyes picked out another stairway angling off and he took it. The whole city-mountain was a labyrinth of passages.

He emerged into a broad, red-lit bazaar that seemed to run away forever and was crowded with the tall people chaffering at stalls. Behind a stall that was festooned with statuettes of blasphemously hideous little snake-armed idols, Chane spotted a narrow stair that led downward. He slid through the crowd toward it, as blue faces looked down at him in surprise.

Going up was no good; he could only get out of this place by reaching the base of the city-mountain. He had been in worse places than this, and he was not greatly worried.

The narrow stair he followed downward suddenly opened into a big room in the rock. The glowing pink lights here showed it was a little amphitheater, with robed Kharalis sitting all around its edge, looking down at a small central stage.

Three nearly-naked Kharali girls were dancing on the stage to the wailing of multiple-flutes. They danced amid glittering points of steel, six-inch pointed blades that bristled from the floor, set about fifteen inches apart. The slender blue bodies leaped and whirled, and the bare feet came down close to the cruel blades and leaped up again, and as they danced the girls threw back their long black hair and laughed.

Chane stared, fascinated. He felt an admiration that was almost love for these three girls who could laugh as they danced with danger.

Then he heard the echo of distant gongs, and a scrabble of feet coming down the stair behind them. He started to run again as his pursuers came out of the stair.

He had not thought that someone with a weapon might have joined them. Not until he heard the stungun buzzing behind him.

IV

Dilullo sat in the big, shadowy stone hall high in the city-mountain, and felt his frustration and anger increase.

He had been sitting here for hours, and the oligarchs who ruled Kharal had not yet come. There was nobody across the table except Odenjaa, the Kharali who had contacted him at Achernar weeks ago, and who had this night brought them from the ship up into the city by secret ways.

"Soon," said Odenjaa. "Very soon the lords of Kharal will be here."

"You said that two hours ago," said Dilullo.

He was getting tired of this. The chair he sat in was damnably uncomfortable, for it had been made for taller men to sit in, and Dilullo's legs dangled like a child's.

He was pretty sure they were keeping him waiting purposely, but there was nothing he could do but compose his face and look unperturbed. Bollard, sitting nearby, looked quite unbothered, but then fat Bollard, the toughest of the Mercs, had a moon face that rarely showed anything.

The lights around the room threw a ruddy glow that hurt his eyes, but the black rock walls remained dark and brooding. Through the open window came chill night air, and with it came the whispered flutes and voices of all the levels in the vast warren beneath.

Suddenly, Dilullo felt sick of strange worlds. He had seen too many of them in a career that had gone on too long. A Merc was old at forty. What the devil was he doing out here in Corvus Cluster, anyway?

He thought sourly, "Quit being sorry for yourself. You're here because you like to make a lot of money and this is the only way you can do it."

Finally, the lords of Kharal came. There were six of them, tall in their rich robes, all but one of them middle-aged or elderly. They seated themselves with ceremony at the table, and only then did they look superciliously across at Dilullo and Bollard.

Dilullo had dealt with men of a good many starworlds, though with none quite so insular as these, and he was determined not to be put into any position of inferiority in making this deal.

He said clearly and loudly in galacto, "You sent for me."

Then he was silent, staring at the lords of Kharal and waiting for them to answer.

Finally, the youngest Kharali, whose face had darkened with resentment, said harshly, "*I* did not send for you, Earthman."

"Then why am I here?" demanded Dilullo. His hand waving toward Odenjaa, he said, "This man came to me at Achernar, many weeks ago. He told me that Kharal had an enemy, the planet Vhol, the outermost world of this system. He said that your enemies of Vhol have a great new weapon which you wish destroyed. He assured me you would pay me well if I brought men and helped you."

His deliberately patronizing statement brought scowls to the faces of all the others, except for the very oldest Kharali, whose eyes studied him coldly from a face that was a spider-web of wrinkles.

It was this oldest man who answered. "Collectively, we did send for you, though one of us dissented. It may well be that we can use you, Earthman."

Insult for insult, Dilullo thought. He hoped that now that they had shown proper contempt for each other, they could get down to business.

"Why are those of Vhol your enemies?" he asked.

The old man answered. "It is simple. They covet our world's mineral wealth. They are more numerous than we, and they have a somewhat more advanced technology"—he spoke the last as though it was a dirty word—"and so they tried to land a force and conquer us. We repelled their landing."

Dilullo nodded. This was an old story. A star-system got space-travel, and then one of its worlds tried to take over the others and start an empire.

"But the new weapon? How did you learn of this?"

"There have been rumors," said the old Kharali. "Then a few months ago, a reconnoitering Vhollan cruiser was disabled by our own cruisers. There was one living officer in it, whom we captured and questioned. He told us all he knows."

"All?"

Odenjaa, smiling, explained. "There are certain drugs we have that can make a man unconscious, and in his unconsciousness he will answer every question, and not even remember it afterwards."

"What did he say?"

"He said that soon Vhol would destroy us utterly, that out of Corvus Nebula they would bring a weapon which would annihilate us."

"Out of the Nebula?" Dilullo was startled. "But that place is a maze of drift, uncharted, dangerous. . . ." He broke off and then said, with a sour smile, "I can see why you wanted to hire Mercs to do this job."

The youngest of the lords of Kharal said something harsh and rapid in his own language, looking furiously at Dilullo.

Odenjaa translated. "You are to know that Kharalis have died trying to enter the nebula, but that our ships lack the subtle instruments that the Vhollans and you Earthmen use."

Dilullo thought that that was probably true. The Kharalis had not had space-travel for too long, and they were the kind of insular, tradition-ridden people who were not very good at it. They had no star-shipping at all; the ships of other stars brought them goods to exchange for the rare and valuable gems and metals of Kharal. When he came to think of it, he wouldn't want to try bucking that nebula in a planet-cruiser as they had.

He said gravely, "If I seem to reflect on the courage of the men of Kharal, I apologize."

The Kharali lords looked only a little less angry. "But," added Dilullo, "I must know more of this. Did your captured Vhollan know anything of the nature of the weapon?"

The old Kharali spread his hands. "No. We have questioned him many times under the drug, the last time only a few days ago, but he knows nothing more."

"Can I talk to this Vhollan captive?" asked Dilullo.

Instantly, they became suspicious. "Why would you want to confer with one of our enemies, if you are to work for us? No."

For the first time, Bollard spoke, in the soft lisp that seemed so incongruous from his moon-fat face.

"It's too damn vague, John."

"It's vague," Dilullo admitted. "But it might just be done." He thought for a minute, and then he looked across the table at the Kharalis and said, "Thirty light-stones."

They stared at him puzzledly, and he repeated patiently, "Thirty lightstones. That is what you will pay us if we succeed in doing this thing for you."

They looked first incredulous, then furious. "Thirty lightstones?" said the young Kharali lord. "Do you think we would give little Earthmen the ransom of an emperor?"

"How much is the ransom of a world?" said Dilullo. "Of Kharal? How many of your lightstones will your enemies take if they conquer you?"

Their faces changed, only a little. But, watching them, Bollard murmured, "They'll pay it."

Dilullo gave them no time to reflect on the magnitude of his demand. "That will be the payment if we find and destroy the weapon of your enemies. But first we must learn if we can do that, and the learning will be very risky for us. Three of the lightstones will be paid to us in advance."

They found their voices this time, snarling their anger. "And what if you Earthmen take the three jewels and go your way, laughing at us?"

Dilullo looked at Odenjaa. "You were the one who looked for Mercs to hire. Tell me, did you hear of Mercs ever cheating those who hired them?"

"Yes," said Odenjaa. "Twice it happened."

"And what happened to the Mercs who did that?" pursued Dilullo. "You must have heard that, too. Tell it."

A little reluctantly, Odenjaa replied. "It is said that other Mercs took them, as prisoners, and delivered them over to the worlds which they had swindled."

"It is true," said Dilullo, to those across the table. "We are a guild, we Mercs. Nowhere in the galaxy could we operate if we did not keep faith. Three lightstones in advance."

They still glared at him, all except the oldest man. He said coldly, "Get the jewels for them."

One of the men went away, and after a little time he came back and with an angry gesture sent three tiny gleaming moons rolling across the table toward the Earthmen. Tiny, thought Dilullo, but beautiful, beautiful, seeming to fill a part of the room with dancing, dazzling swirls of light. He heard Bollard suck in his breath, and it made him feel like a god to reach a hand and grasp three moons and put them in his pocket.

There was a sound at a door and Odenjaa went there, and when he came back from the door his eyes glittered at Dilullo.

"There is something that concerns you," he said hissingly. "One of your men has intruded, has tried to kill . . ."

Two tall Kharali men came in, supporting between them a drunkenly staggering figure.

"Surprised?" said Chane, and then fell down on his face.

V

It seemed to Chane before he awoke that Dilullo's voice was speaking to him from a great distance. He knew that this could not be. He perfectly remembered how, numbed by the stun-gun's effect, he had fallen down when his captors released him.

He remembered lying flat on the floor and hearing a Kharali voice say, "This man does not go with you. He must remain here to be punished."

And Dilullo's voice calmly answering, "Keep him and punish him, then," and his captors picking him up and dragging him through many levels to a place of cells, into one of which they had thrown him.

Chane opened his eyes. Yes, he was in the rock cell, which had a barred door opening into a red-lit corridor, and in the wall opposite the door a nine-inch square loophole window looking out at the glowing night sky of Kharal.

He lay on the damp rock floor. He had sore places in his ribs, and now he remembered that they had kicked him for a while after they dragged him into this cell.

Chane felt that some of the numbness had left him, and he hauled himself to sit with his back against the wall. His head cleared. He stared around the cell, and felt a wild feeling of revulsion.

He had never been caged before. No Starwolf was ever imprisoned . . . if one was caught on a raid he was ruthlessly killed at once. Of course these people didn't know he was a Starwolf in everything but appearance. That did not change his fierce claustrophobic resentment.

He was about to get up and try his strength on the thick metal door-bars when it happened again. He heard the tiny voice of Dilullo speaking to him as from a great distance.

"Chane. . .?"

Chane shook his head. A stun-gun could have odd aftereffects on the nervous system.

"Chane?"

Chane stiffened. The tiny whisper was not directionless. It seemed to come from just below his own left shoulder.

He looked down at himself. There was nothing there but the button that secured the flap of the left pocket of his jacket.

He turned his head a little, and brought the pocket and its flap-button up to his ear.

"Chane!"

He heard it quite clearly now; it came out of the button.

Chane brought the button around to the front of his face and whispered into it.

"When you gave me this fine new jacket, why didn't you tell me this button was a little transceiver?"

Dilullo's voice answered dryly. "We Mercs have our little tricks, Chane. But we don't like everyone to know them. I would have told you later, when I was sure you wouldn't desert us."

"Thanks," said Chane. "And thanks for walking off and letting the Kharalis keep me."

"Don't thank me," said the dry voice. "You deserved it."

Chane grinned. "I guess I did, at that."

"It's too bad," said the tiny voice of Dilullo, "that tomorrow morning they'll take you and break both your arms, as retribution. I don't know what you'll do when they turn you out then to die slowly."

Chane brought the button back around to his lips and whispered, "Did you go to the trouble of calling me and letting me know about the transceiver just to express your sorrow?"

"No," answered the voice of Dilullo. "There's more to it than that."

"I thought there was. What?"

"Listen carefully, Chane. The Kharalis hold a Vhollan officer prisoner, presumably in the same prison area you're in. I want that man. We're going to Vhol, and we won't be under suspicion there if we take them one of their own whom we've got free."

Chane understood. "But why didn't you ask the Kharalis for him?"

"They got suspicious when I even asked to talk to the man! If I'd asked them to let me take him away, they'd be convinced I was going to throw in with the Vhollans."

"Won't they be just as suspicious if I break this Vhollan out?" asked Chane.

Dilullo answered sharply. "With luck, we'll be away from Kharal and their suspicions won't matter. Now don't argue, but listen. I don't want this man to know *why* you're helping him escape, so tell him you need him to guide you out, that you were brought in unconscious, and so on."

"Neat," said Chane. "But you forget one thing, and that's getting out of this cell."

"The button of your right-hand jacket pocket is a miniaturized ato-flash. Intensity six, duration forty seconds. The stud is on the back," Dilullo said.

Chane looked down at the button. "And how many more of these little tricks have you got?"

"We have quite a few, Chane. But you don't. I didn't trust you with more than two and didn't even tell you about those."

"Suppose this Vhollan isn't imprisoned here, but somewhere else?" asked Chane.

Dilullo's whisper was untroubled. "Then you'd better find him. If you come out without him, don't bother coming to the ship. We'll take off and leave you."

"You know," said Chane admiringly, "there are times when I think you'd make a Starwolf."

"One more thing, Chane. We have to come back to Kharal, if we succeed, to get our pay. So no killing. Repeat, *no killing*. Out."

Chane got to his feet and silently flexed his arms and legs for minutes until he was sure the last numbness had left them. Then he tiptoed to the barred door, pressing his face against it.

He could see a row of similar doors opposite, and at the far end of the corridor he could just see the feet of a guard who sat sprawled in a chair there. He stepped back, and thought.

After a time he carefully unhooked both of the buttons from his jacket. The transceiver button he put into a shirt pocket. Then he took off the jacket, and got down on the floor by the barred door.

He unobtrusively wrapped the jacket around the base of one of the door-bars, leaving the bar exposed at one point. He carefully brought the tiny aperture of the button ato-flash against the bar, using his free hand to throw a fold of the jacket over the other hand and the button. Then he pressed the stud on the back of the button.

The tiny flash was veiled by the jacket, and its hiss was drowned by the cough Chane let go. He kept the flash on for twenty seconds, and then released the stud.

Little tendrils of smoke came up from scorched parts of the jacket. Chane used his hands as fans to draw the smoke into the cell, so it would go out the loophole window instead of drifting down the corridor.

He unwrapped the scorched jacket. The bar had been burned through.

Chane considered. He could burn through the bar another place and move a section, but he did not want to do that unless he had to; he might need the ato-flash again.

He put the tiny instrument in his pocket, and laid hold of the severed bar and tested it. He felt pretty sure from the feel of it that his Varnan strength was enough to bend it now. But he was also pretty sure that it would make noise.

If you stopped to think too much, you could die before you made up your mind. Chane gripped the severed bar, and let all his revulsion at being caged will his muscles into a wild surge of power.

The bar bent inward, with a metallic sound.

There was just space enough for him to squeeze out, and he went out fast for it had to be quick or not at all.

The Kharali guard jumped up from his chair to see the Earthman bounding at him like a dark panther, with incredible speed.

Chane's hand chopped and the guard fell senseless with his hand reaching vainly toward a button on the wall. Chane eased him to the floor and then searched him, but there was no weapon on the man, and no keys. He turned, his gaze searching along the corridor. He saw nothing that looked like a spy-eye. Apparently the Kharalis, who didn't care much for gadgets, had figured the alarm-button was enough.

Apparently, also, they didn't put many people in jail, for most of the cells were empty. Chane was not surprised. From what he had seen of them, the Kharalis were the type who would get more pleasure out of executing or punishing a man in public than in jailing him.

In one cell, a humanoid lay sprawling and snoring, his hairy arms moving in his sleep. He had some swollen bruises, and from him came an overpowering stench of the acid intoxicant.

Two more cells were empty but in the next a man was sleeping. He was about Chane's size and age and he was a white man. Not swarthy white, not Earthman white, but an albino white with fine white hair. When Chane hissed and awakened him, he saw the man's eyes were not albino but a clear blue.

He jumped to his feet. He wore a short tunic quite unlike the Kharali robes, and a sort of officer's harness over it.

"Do you know the way out of this city?" Chane asked, speaking galacto.

The Vhollan's eyes widened. "The Earthman they dragged in a while ago. How—".

"Listen," Chane interrupted. "I got out of the cell. I want to get out of the whole damned city. But I was unconscious when they brought me in, and don't know where I am. If I get you out of there, can you guide me? Do you know the ways?"

The Vhollan began to babble excitedly. "Yes, yes, I know; they have taken me in and out many times, for questioning. I won't answer them, so they drug me for some reason and bring me back, but I've seen, I know. . . ."

"Stand back, then." Chane bent down and used the remaining power of the ato-flash to cut through the base of a door bar. There was not quite enough power to cut through it completely.

The bar was nine-tenths severed. Chane sat down, braced his feet against the other bars, and then grabbed the nearly-severed one just above the cut. He let it go fast with a muttered curse. It was still hot.

He waited a minute, tried again, and found it had cooled enough. He braced his feet and put his back into it and pulled. The long muscles that Varna had given him slid and swelled and the nearly-severed bar broke free with a *pung*. He didn't relax, he kept pulling, and the bar bent slowly outward. The Vhollan squeezed out fast.

"You've got strength!" he exclaimed, staring.

"It only looked like it," Chane lied. "I'd cut through

the top of the bar before I woke you."

The Vhollan pointed toward the door at the end of the corridor opposite to the one where the guard had sat.

"The only way out," he whispered. "And it's always locked from the other side."

"What's beyond it?" Chane demanded.

"Two more Kharali guards. They are armed. When the one in here wanted out, he simply called through the door to them."

The man, Chane noted, was trying to speak quickly and to the point, but he was shaking with excitement.

Chane pondered. He could only see one way to get that door open, and so they would have to try it and see what happened.

He took the Vhollan by the arm and ran with him, silently, down the corridor to where the guard lay slumped. He had the Vhollan stand with his back against the wall, just beside the alarm button. Then Chane took the unconscious guard and leaned him up face foremost against the Vhollan.

"Hold him up," Chane said.

It did not look too convincing, he thought. The unconscious guard was taller, and his robed figure leaned forward in a drunken, improbable way. But he did hide the Vhollan standing against the wall, and if the deception was only good for a few seconds, that should be enough.

"When I hiss, press the button and stand still," Chane ordered, and then sped back to stand beside the door.

He hissed. A bell rang sharply on the other side of the door. The door swung open a moment later, opening into the corridor with Chane behind it.

There was a moment's pause and then two pairs of feet pounded through the door. The two Kharalis both held stun-guns and they were hurrying but not too much. They had glanced in and seen the inner guard standing with his back to them, and no prisoners out of their cells.

Chane leaped with all his speed behind them and his flat hands struck and flashed and struck again, and the two slumped down. He took the stun-gun from one of them and gave each of them a blast from it to keep them quiet for a while.

He went down the hallway and chuckled as he saw the Vhollan, trying now to get out from under the senseless body, giving the impression of wrestling with his tall Kharali burden. Chane gave that one a blast of the stun-gun, too.

He said sharply to the Vhollan, "Out now. Take the other weapon."

As he passed the cell where the humanoid had been sleeping, he saw that the creature had aroused and was looking out through the bars with red-rimmed, bloodshot eyes, obviously too foggy from drink to make any sense of what was going on, even if he had had the intelligence.

"Sleep, my hairy brother," Chane said to him. "We are neither of us fit for cities."

They went into the room from which the two guards had come. There was no one in it and it had only one other door. That opened out onto one of the broad galleries, and no one was there, either.

The city seemed quieter, almost sleeping. Chane could hear echoes of faint fluting from somewhere beneath, and the bawl of a distant, angry voice.

"This way," urged the Vhollan. "The main moto-walk is this way."

"We'd never make it," said Chane. "There are still too many about, and they could spot us as far as they could see us by our shorter stature."

He went across the gallery and leaned out over its low protective wall, looking out into the night.

The nebula had slid quite a way across the sky as Kharal turned toward the coming day. The silver radiance now came down slantingly, and the grotesque stone gargoyles that jutted out from the steeply-sloping face of the city-mountain threw long, distorted black shadows.

There was a gargoyle at each level, and he estimated that they were about ten levels above the ground. He decided at once.

"We'll go down the outside wall," he said. "It's rough and weathered, and there's the gargoyles to help us."

The Vhollan man looked out and down. He could not get any paler than he was but he could look a little sick, and he did.

"Come along or stay, as you like," said Chane. "It makes no difference to me."

And he thought, *Only the difference between life and death, that's all, if I go back without this man.*

The Vhollan gulped and nodded. They went over the low wall and started down.

It was not as easy as Chane had thought it would be. The rock was not as weathered as the slanting shadows had made it look. He clung on, his fingernails cracking, and lowered himself to the first gargoyle below him.

The Vhollan man followed, flattened with his face against the stone. He was breathing in quick gasps when he reached Chane.

They went down that way, from gargoyle to gargoyle, and each one of the stone monstrosities seemed more blasphemously obscene than the last. At the fifth one, they paused for rest. Chane, observing this one in the silvery nebula-glow, thought how ridiculous he must look, stuck up on the side of the city-mountain, sitting on the stone back of a blobby creature whose face and backside were all together.

He chuckled a little, and the Vhollan turned his white face and looked at him as if in fear.

It became much trickier near the ground, for one of

the great gates was not too far away and there were a
few robed figures bunched there. The two hugged the
shadow like a friend, and went away, avoiding the road
that led to the spaceport but going in that direction.
Nobody stopped them, and the ship took them in and
went away from there.

VI

The man named Yorolin kept talking and talking, filling Dilullo's little cabin with his protestations.

"There's no *reason* why you can't take me back to Vhol," he said.

"Look," said Dilullo. "I've had trouble enough in this system already. We heard there was a war here and we came to sell weapons. But I land on Kharal and get run right off because one of my men is in a fight. It figures that Vhol could be just as hostile. I'm going to the third planet, Jarnath."

"That's a semi-barbarous world," said Yorolin. "The humanoids there are a poor lot."

"Well, they might be glad enough to get some modern weapons, and might have something valuable to trade for them," said Dilullo.

Chane, sitting in a corner and listening, admired the bluff Dilullo was putting up. It was good . . . good enough that Yorolin was now looking desperate.

"I belong to one of the great families of Vhol and I have influence," he said. "Nothing will happen to you. I guarantee it."

Dilullo pretended doubt. "I don't know. I'd like to do some business at Vhol, if I could. I'll think about it." He added, "In the meantime, you'd better get some sleep. You look as though you'd about had it."

Yorolin nodded shakily. "I have."

Dilullo took him out into the narrow corridor. "Use Doud's cabin, over there. He's standing his turn on the bridge."

When Dilullo came back into the cabin and sat down, Chane waited for the blast. But Dilullo reached into a locker and brought out a bottle.

"Do you want a drink?"

Surprised, but not showing it, Chane nodded and accepted the drink. He didn't like it.

"Earth whisky," said Dilullo. "It takes getting used to."

He sat back and looked at Chane with a bleak, steady gaze.

"What's it like on Varna?" he asked, unexpectedly.

Chane considered. "It's a big world. But it's not a very rich world . . . at least, until we got space travel."

Dilullo nodded. "Until the Earthmen came and taught you how to build starships, and turned you loose on the galaxy."

Chane smiled. "That was a long time ago but I've heard about it. The Varnans tricked the Earthmen as though they were children. They said all they wanted to do was to engage in peaceful trade with other worlds, like the Earthmen did."

"And we've had the Starwolves ever since," said Dilullo. "If the independent starworlds could quit quarreling with each other just once, they could join together and go in and clean Varna out."

Chane shook his head. "It wouldn't be that easy. In space, no one is an even match for Varnans for no one can endure the acceleration-pressures they can."

"But if a big enough coalition fleet moved in . . ."

"It would find it tough going. There are many mighty starworlds in that arm of the galaxy. We Varnans have never raided them, instead we trade with them, our loot for their products. They benefit by us, and they'd resist any attempt by outsiders to enter their space."

"A damned immoral arrangement, but that wouldn't

bother Varnans," grumbled Dilullo. "I've heard they have no religion at all."

"Religion?" Chane shook his head. "Not a bit. That's why my parents came to Varna, but they got nowhere in their mission."

"No religion, no ethics," said Dilullo. "But you've got some laws and rules. Especially when you go out on raids."

Chane began to understand now, but he only nodded and said, "Yes, we do."

Dilullo refilled his own glass. "I'll tell you something, Chane. Earth is a poor world too. So a lot of us have to go out in space to make a living. We don't raid, but we do the tough, dirty jobs of the galaxy that people don't want to do themselves.

"We're hired men. But we're independent . . . we don't run in packs. Someone wants Mercs to do a job, he comes to a Merc leader with a reputation . . . like me. The leader signs on the Mercs best fitted for the job, and gets a Merc ship to come in on shares. When the job's over and price of it split up, the Mercs disband. It may be a completely different bunch next time I take on an operation.

"What I'm getting at," he continued, and now his eyes bored into Chane's face, "is that while we're together on a job, our lives may depend on all orders being obeyed."

Chane shrugged. "If you'll remember, I didn't ask for any part of the job."

"You didn't ask for it but you've got it," Dilullo said harshly. "You think a hell of a lot of yourself because you've been a Starwolf. I'll tell you right now that as long as you're with me you're going to be a pretty tame wolf. You'll wait when I tell you to wait, and you'll bite only when I say 'Bite!' Do you understand?"

"I understand what you're saying," answered Chane carefully. After a moment he asked. "Do you think you can tell me what we're after on Vhol?"

"I think I can," said Dilullo, "for if you open your

mouth about it there, you're likely to be dead. Vhol is only a waystop, Chane. What we're after is somewhere in the nebula. The Vhollans have got something in there, some kind of weapon or power that the Kharalis fear and want destroyed. That's the job we're hired for."

He paused, then added, "We could go straight to the nebula, and then fly around in it for years searching, without finding anything. It's better to go to Vhol and let the Vhollans *lead* us to what they've got out there. But it's going to be tricky, and if they guess what we're up to, it'll be our necks."

Chane felt a kindling interest. He saw the face of danger and it was a face he had known all his life, since first he had been old enough to go raiding from Varna. Danger was the antagonist with whom you struggled, and if you bested him you came away with plunder and if you lost you died. But without the struggle you were simply bored, as he had been bored on this ship until now.

"How did the Kharalis find out about this Vhollan weapon?" he asked. "Yorolin?"

Dilullo nodded. "Yorolin told them the Vhollans had something big out there, but he didn't know what it was. But Yorolin doesn't know he told them anything . . . he was drugged, unconscious, when they pumped him."

Chane nodded. "And presently you'll let Yorolin persuade you to go to Vhol?"

"Yes," said Dilullo. "He won't find it too hard to get me to go there. I hope it'll be as easy for us to leave there!"

When Chane went back into the crew-room there were only four men in it, for the Mercs stood duty as crewmen in flight. They were sitting in the bunks and they had been talking, but they stopped talking when he came in.

Bollard turned his moon-fat face toward him and said, in his lisping voice, "Well now, Chane . . . did you have a good time in the city?"

Chane nodded. "I had a good time."

"That's nice," said Bollard. "Don't you think that's nice, boys?"

Rutledge gave Chane a hot-eyed stare and said nothing, but Bixel, without looking up from the small instrument he was dissembling, drawled that that was real nice.

Sekkinen, a tall rawhide man with a look of gloom about him, had no time for subtleties. He said loudly to Chane, "You were supposed to stay with the ship. You heard the order."

"Ah, but Chane's not like us, he's something special," said Bollard. "He'd have to be something special, or John wouldn't take a rock-hopper prospector and make him a full-fledged Merc."

Chane had known from the first that they resented having to accept him, but there would be more than mere resentment if they knew the truth about him.

"The only thing is," Bollard said to him, "that your busting in like that might just have made the Kharalis so mad that they'd have killed us. What if that had happened?"

"I'd have been sorry," said Chane, with a sweet smile.

Bollard beamed at him. "Sure you would. And I'll tell you what, Chane. If it ever happens again like that, to keep you from being broken-hearted about it I'll just kill you so you don't suffer all that sorrow."

Chane said nothing. He was remembering what Dilullo had said about Mercs' lives depending on each other, and he knew that the lisped warning was in earnest.

He was thinking that these Earthmen might not be Varnans but that they could be just as dangerous in a different way, and that Mercs had not got their tough reputation for nothing. It seemed like a good time to keep his mouth shut, and get some sleep.

When he awoke the ship was in its landing-pattern

around Vhol, and he joined a few of the Mercs at the forward port to look at the planet. Through drifting clouds they saw dark blue, almost tideless, oceans and the coasts of green continents.

"It looks a lot like Earth," said Rutledge.

Chane almost asked, "Does it?" but he managed not to ask that betraying question.

As the landing-pattern took them lower, Bixel said, "That city's not like any on Earth. Except maybe old Venice, blown up fifty times."

The ship was approaching a flat coast fringed by a multitude of small islands. The sea rolled between the islands in hundreds of natural waterways and on the islands were crowded the white buildings, none very lofty, of a far-stretching city. Further inland, where the land rose a little, was a medium sized spaceport and beyond it rows of tall white blocks that looked like warehouses or factories.

"A more advanced world than Kharal," said Rutledge. "Look, they've got at least a half-dozen starships of their own on that port, and lots of planetary types."

When they landed and cracked the lock, Yorolin spoke first to the two white-haired young Vhollan port officials in his own language.

The Vhollan officials looked suspicious. One of them spoke in galacto to Dilullo, after Yorolin indicated him as the leader.

"You carry weapons?"

"Samples of weapons," Dilullo corrected.

"Why do you bring them to Vhol?"

Dilullo put on a look of indignation. "I was only doing your friend Yorolin a favor to come here at all! But maybe we can do some business here."

The official remaining courteously unconvinced, Dilullo patiently explained. "Look, we're Mercs and all we want to do is make a living. We heard there was some sort of war in this system so we came with some samples of late-type weapons. I wish now we'd never come! We land on Kharal and before we can even talk business to them, they run us off because one of my men got into trouble. If you people don't want to see what we've got to offer, all right, but no need to make a big thing out of it."

Again Yorolin spoke rapidly to the official in their own tongue, and finally the official nodded.

"Very well; we allow the landing. But a guard will be placed outside your ship. None of these weapons are to be removed from it."

Dilullo nodded. "All right, I understand." He turned to Yorolin. "Now I want to get in touch with somebody in your officialdom who would be interested in buying late-type weapons. Who?"

Yorolin thought. "Thrandirin would be the man . . . I'll let him know at once."

Dilullo said, "I'll be right here, if he wants to get in touch with me." He looked over the Mercs. "While we're here, you can take turns in town liberty. Except you, Chane . . . you get no liberty."

Chane had expected that, and he saw the Mercs grinning their satisfaction. But when Yorolin understood, he made lengthy objection.

"Chane is the man who saved me," said Yorolin. "I want my family and friends to meet him. I insist upon it!"

Chane saw frustration and irritation appear on Dilullo's face, and he felt like grinning back but he did not.

"All right," said Dilullo sourly. "If you make such a point of it."

While they waited for Vhollan guards to come, before which the port officials would not let them off the ship, Dilullo found a chance to speak privately to Chane.

"You know what we're here for. To find out what's going on in the nebula, and where. Keep your ears open but don't seem inquisitive. And, Chane . . ."

"Yes?"

"I'm not convinced that Yorolin is all that grateful. It could be they'll be trying to find out some things about us from you. Watch it."

VII

They had all been drinking and were gay, and a couple of the men were more than that. There were three girls and four men, besides Chane, and they were a merry, crowded cargo for the skimmer as it wended slowly along the crowded waterways under the glowing nebula sky.

Yorolin was singing a lilting song which the girl beside Chane, whose name was Laneeah or something that sounded like it, translated for him. It was about love and flowers and things of that sort and Chane didn't think much of it; on Varna the songs had been of raiding and fighting, of running galactic dangers and coming home with treasure. However, he liked the Vhollans, and their world being the outermost of their red-giant sun's planets, it was pleasantly tropical and not burned dry like Kharal.

The waterways were calm and the wind was only a heavy breeze laden with drifting perfume from the flowering trees that grew on either side. These islands were the pleasure part of the Vhollan city, and in fact were the only part Chane had seen except the surprisingly pretentious villa where he had met Yorolin's parents and friends, and where his party had got started.

He had remembered Dilullo's admonition to keep his ears open, but he didn't think he was going to hear anything from this crowd that would help them any.

"We don't see many Earthmen here," said Laneeah. She spoke galacto well. "Only a few traders now and then."

"How do you like us?" asked Chane, feeling a wry amusement at being classed as an Earthman.

"Ugly," she said. "Colored hair, even black hair like yours. Faces that are red or tan, not white." She made a small sound of disgust, but she was smiling as though she did not find him ugly at all.

It made him think suddenly of Varna and of Graal, most beautiful of the girls he had known there, and how she had contrasted her splendid fine-furred golden body with his hairlessness, and mocked him.

Then the skimmer drew in to a landing and there were many lights and jovial music and they went ashore. There was a sort of bazaar of amusements here, small peaked buildings with colored lights under the tall flowering trees, and a swarming, aimless crowd of people. The Vhollans made a handsome sight, they were proud of their white bodies and white hair and wore their knee-length tunics in brilliant colors.

In an arbor of immense flame-colored flowers they sat and had more of the fruity Vhollan wine, and Yorolin pounded his fist on the table and spoke with passion to Chane.

"Out in deep space, that's where I should be, like you. Not paddling around in a miserable planet-cruiser."

His face was flushed with the wine and Chane felt the drink himself, and reminded himself to be careful.

"Well, why aren't you?" he asked Yorolin. "Vhol has starships; I saw them on the spaceport."

"Not so many," said Yorolin. "And it takes seniority to get a berth in one of them, but someday I'll be on one; someday . . ."

"Oh, stop talking about stars and come on and have some fun," said Laneeah. "Or Chane and I will leave you here."

They went on, passing some places, entering others. A kaleidoscope of impressions: jugglers tossing silver bells, flowers grown from seeds in seconds and drifting down on their heads, more wine, and dancers, and still more wine.

It was in this last drinking-place, a long low room with fire-bowls in braziers for illumination and walls of flaming red, that Yorolin suddenly looked across the room and exclaimed, "A Pyam! I haven't seen one for years! Come on, Chane; this will be something for you to tell about."

He led Chane across the room, the others being too engaged in chatter to follow.

At a table sat a stocky Vhollan man, and on the table was a creature that was secured to the man's wrist by a thin chain. It looked like a little yellow mannikin shaped like a turnip, with two small legs, its body going up to a neckless, pointed head, with two small blinking eyes and a small baby mouth.

"Can it speak galacto?" asked Yorolin, and the man with the chain nodded.

"It can. It brings me many a coin from the offworld people."

"What the devil is it?" asked Chane.

Yorolin grinned. "It's not related to the human, though it vaguely looks that way. It's a rare inhabitant of our forests . . . it's got some intelligence and one remarkable power." He told the Vhollan, "Have your Pyam give my friend a demonstration."

The Vhollan spoke to the creature in his own language. The creature turned and looked at Chane, and somehow the impact of the blinking gaze was disturbing.

"Oh, yes," it said in flat parrot-like words. "Oh, yes, I can see memories. I can see men with golden hair and they run toward little ships on a strange world and they are laughing. Oh, yes, I can see. . . ."

With sudden alarm, Chane realized what the strange

power of the Pyam was. It could read minds and memories and babble them forth in its squeaky tones, and in a moment it would babble a secret that would be his death.

"What kind of nonsense is this?" Chane interrupted loudly. He spoke to the Vhollan man. "Is the thing a telepath? If it is, I challenge it to read what I am thinking at this moment."

And he turned and looked at the Pyam and as he did so he thought with fierce, raging intensity, *If you read more from my mind I will kill you, right now, right this minute.* He put all the will power he had into concentrating on that thought, into packing it with passionate conviction.

The Pyam's eyes blinked. "Oh yes, I can see," it squeaked. "Oh, yes. . . ."

"Yes?" said Yorolin.

The blinking eyes looked into Chane's face. "Oh yes, I can see . . . nothing. Nothing. Oh, yes. . . ."

The Pyam's owner looked astounded. "That's the first time it ever failed."

"Maybe its powers don't work on Earthmen," said Yorolin, laughing. He gave the man a coin and they turned away. "Sorry, Chane, I thought it would be interesting for you. . . ."

Did you? thought Chane. *Or did you arrange for the beast to be here and lead me right to it, so it could probe my mind?*

He was taut with suspicion now. He remembered Dilullo's warning, which he had almost forgotten.

He let none of it show in his face but went back to the table with Yorolin and drank and laughed with the others. He thought, and then, after looking carelessly around the room, he came to a decision. He began to drink more heavily, and he made a show of doing so.

"Not so much," said Laneeah, "or you will not last the evening."

Chane smiled at her. "The space between the stars has no wine in it and a man can get awfully dry."

He kept on drinking and he began to act as though he was pretty drunk. His head rang a little but he was not drunk at all, and he kept an eye on the Vhollan with the Pyam, across the room. A few people had gathered around them, and the Pyam squeaked at them, and finally they gave coins and went away.

The stocky man then picked up the Pyam, carrying it under his arm like an overgrown baby, and went out. He went out the back door, as Chane had hoped he would.

Chane gave it a few seconds and then staggered to his feet. "I'll be back in a moment," he said thickly, and walked a little unsteadily toward the back of the place as though heading for a place of necessity.

He heard Yorolin laugh and say, "Our friend seems to have underestimated the wines of Vhol."

Chane, at the back of the room, shot a glance and saw that they were not looking after him. He slipped quickly out the back door and found himself in a dark alleyway.

He saw the shadowy figure of the stocky Vhollan, going away down the alley. Chane went after him fast, going on the tips of his toes in leaping strides that made no sound. But apparently the Pyam sensed him, for it squeaked, and the man turned around sharply.

Chane's bunched fists hit him on the point of the jaw. He did not use all his strength, which he thought was foolish, but all the same he did not feel like going back to Dilullo and saying he'd killed someone.

The man fell, dragging the Pyam down with him by the chain, and the creature squeaked in horrified alarm.

Be quiet! Be very quiet, and I will not hurt you, thought Chane.

The creature became silent and cringed, as much as its absurd little legs would allow it to cringe.

Chane took the end of the chain away from the unconscious man. He dragged the Vhollan into a lightless space between two outbuildings.

The Pyam made a small whimpering sound. Chane patted its pointed head and thought, *You will not be hurt. Tell me, was your owner hired to bring you to this tavern?*

"Oh, yes," said the Pyam. "Gold pieces. Yes."

Chane considered for a moment, and then asked mentally, *Can you read the thoughts of someone who is a little way off? Like across a room?*

The Pyam's squeak, despite its dogmatic affirmative opening, was doubtful. "Oh yes. Not unless I see his face."

Speak whispers now, thought Chane. *Whispers. No loud sound, no hurting.*

Carrying the Pyam, he slipped back to the door of the drinking-place and opened it a few inches.

The man at the table across the room, he thought, *the man I am looking at.* And he looked at Yorolin.

The Pyam began to squeak in a subdued, conspiratorial chirping.

"Oh yes . . . did Chane suspect the trick? How could he . . . but he looked a bit as if he did . . . it didn't work anyway and I'll have to report to Thrandirin that I couldn't confirm our suspicions . . . we *can't* take chances . . . what's Chane doing back there . . . is he being sick? Maybe I'd better go and see. . . ."

Chane silently slipped back into the darkness of the alley. The Pyam's little blinking eyes looked at him fearfully.

They tell me you're from the forest, thought Chane. *Would you like to return there?*

"Oh, yes. Yes!"

If I turned you loose, could you get there?

"Oh yes, oh yes, oh yes, oh yes. . . ."

That's enough, thought Chane. He removed the thin chain and set the Pyam down on the ground. *All right. Go, little one.*

The Pyam waddled rapidly into the shadows and went away. Chane thought that, with its telepathic sense to warn it of obstacles, it would make it.

He turned around and went back to the door. Yorolin was worried about him, and he must not keep his dear and grateful friend waiting.

VIII

The big starship came down majestically toward the spaceport, shining and magnificent in the nebula-glow, seeming to hang for a moment in the sky.

Then it settled down slowly into the area of the port that was reserved for the military ships of Vhol.

In the navigation room of the little Merc ship, Dilullo and Bixel, the radarman, stared at each other in amazement.

"That's not a warship. Perfectly ordinary cargo carrier. What's it doing in the military reservation?"

"Docking," said Dilullo, and leaned over Bixel's shoulder to study the scanner and the radargraph.

"It came in on a fifty degree course," said Bixel.

Dilullo nodded, his worn face harsh in the hooded glow. "So it didn't come from the nebula. . . ."

"Not unless it came the long way round."

"That's exactly what I mean. They might be going and coming by different ways, setting roundabout courses deliberately to make it difficult to get a fix on them."

"They could be," Bixel said, "and that would put us in kind of a fix . . . not to be funny. Couldn't we just go back to the idea that they're playing it straight? I was much happier that way."

"So was I. Only there must be some special reason why an ordinary cargo ship plunks down in a maximum-security military area. Of course it may be something else entirely . . . but if they had brought something important back from the nebula, that's what they'd do with it." He straightened up. "Keep tracking all arrivals and departures. Maybe some pattern will come clear."

He got out of the cramped little room and went below to Records, an even more cramped little room, where he dug out the stock list, price list, and spec sheets for all the sample weapons he had aboard. Nobody seemed passionately interested in even talking to him about his weapons, and if they really had something tremendous out in the nebula they would hardly need them. Nevertheless, he felt that he should be ready if called upon.

A little later Rutledge summoned him, and Dilullo put the microspools in his pocket and went to the lock. Rutledge pointed. A big skimmer—the things had wheels and were ground-cars as well as watercraft—was coming fast toward them across the spaceport.

A Vhollan officer and a civilian and a bunch of armed soldiers got out of the craft and approached the Merc ship. The civilian was middle-aged, a stocky man with authority in his massive head and face. He came to Dilullo and surveyed him coldly.

"My name is Thrandirin, and I am of the Government," he said. "The spaceport tower reported that you have been using your radar."

Dilullo swore inwardly, but kept his face and voice untroubled. "Of course we have. We always test radar while in dock."

"I'm afraid," said Thrandirin, "that we shall have to ask you and your men to live off-ship while you're here, and visit your ship only under escort."

"Now wait a minute," said Dilullo angrily. "You can't do that . . . just because we tested our radar."

"You could have been tracking our warships," retorted Thrandirin. "We are in a state of war with Kharal, and the movements of our ships are secret."

"Oh, damn your war with Kharal," said Dilullo. "The only thing about it that interests me is money." And that was true enough. He pulled the microspools out of his pocket and shook them in his hand. "I'm here to sell weapons. I don't care who uses them against what, or how. The Kharalis frankly said no and kicked us out. I'd appreciate it if you Vhollans would be as honest. Do you want to buy or don't you?"

"The subject is still under discussion," said Thrandirin.

"Which is Universal Bureaucratic for we'll get around to it sometime. How long are we expected to wait?"

The Vhollan shrugged. "Until the decision is made. In the meantime, you will evacuate your ship within the hour. There are inns over in the port quarter."

"Oh, no," blazed Dilullo. "No, I won't. I'll call my men in and take off, and the view of Vhol going away from it will be the best view we've had yet."

A wintry quality came into Thrandirin's voice. "I regret that we can't give you takeoff clearance at this time . . . perhaps not for a few days."

Dilullo felt the first whispering touch of a net gathering around him. "You've no legal right to detain us if we want to leave your system, war or not."

"It's only for your own protection," said Thrandirin. "We've had word that a squadron of raiding Starwolves is in the Cluster and may be near this area."

Dilullo was genuinely startled. He had forgotten Chane's assertion that his former comrades would not easily give up the hunt for him.

On the other hand, Thrandirin was obviously using this alarm about Starwolves as an official excuse to keep him here. He doubted, looking at the Vhollan's bleak face, that the man would care if all the Mercs in creation were in danger.

He thought rapidly. There was no possibility of their defying the order, and the worst thing he could do now was to make too big a fuss. That would only confirm their suspicions.

"Oh, all right," he said sourly. "It's a ridiculous thing, and our ship will be left unguarded. . . ."

"I assure you," said Thrandirin smoothly, "that your ship will be closely guarded at all times."

It was a veiled warning, Dilullo thought, but he let it go. He went into the ship and called together what Mercs were there, and told them.

"Better pack a few things," he added. "We may be living quite a few days on Star Street."

Star Street was not so much a place as a name. It was the name that starmen invariably gave to whatever street near a spaceport afforded fun and comfort. The Star Street of Vhol was not too much different from many others that Dilullo had walked.

It had lights and music and drink and food and women. It was a gusty, crowded place but it was not sinful, for most of these people had never heard of the Judeo-Christian ethic and did not know they were sinning at all. Dilullo did not have an easy time keeping his men with him as he looked for an inn.

A buxom woman with pale green skin and flashing eyes hailed him from the open front of her establishment, where girls of different hues and at least three different shapes preened themselves.

"The ninety-nine joys dwell here, oh Earthmen! Enter!"

Dilullo shook his head. "Not I, mother. I crave the hundredth joy."

"And what is the hundredth joy?"

Dilullo answered sourly. "The joy of sitting down quietly and reading a good book."

Rutledge broke up laughing, beside him, and the woman started to screech curses in galacto.

"Old!" she cried. "Old withered husk of an Earthman! Totter on your way, ancient one!"

Dilullo shrugged as her maledictions followed them

down the noisy street. "I don't know but what she's right. I'm feeling fairly old, and not very bright."

He found an inn that looked clean enough and bargained for rooms. The big common room was shadowy and empty, the inn's patrons having apparently gone forth to sample the happiness Dilullo had rejected. He sat down with the others and called for a Vhollan brandy, and then turned to Rutledge.

"You go back to the ship. The guards may not let you inside, but wait around near it and as our chaps come in from liberty, tell them where we're staying."

Rutledge nodded and went away, Dilullo and the others drank their brandy for a little while in silence.

Then Bixel asked, "What about it, John? Is this job blown?"

"It isn't yet," said Dilullo.

"Maybe we shouldn't have come to Vhol."

Dilullo felt no anger at the criticism. The Mercs were a pretty democratic lot, they would obey a leader's orders but they didn't mind telling him when they thought he was wrong. And a leader who was wrong too many times, and ended up too many missions with empty hands, would soon have a hard job getting men to follow him.

"It seemed like our best chance," he said. "We wouldn't get far dashing into the nebula and looking for a needle in that size of a haystack. Do you know how many parsecs across the nebula is?"

"It's a problem," Bixel said, making the understatement of the decade, and dropped the subject.

After a while the other Mercs began to come in, most of them fairly sober. Sekkinen brought a message from Rutledge, at the spaceport.

"Rutledge said to tell you they unloaded some stuff from that cargo ship in the military port. He could see them through the fence. There were some crates, and they hustled them into the warehouse."

"They did, did they?" Dilullo said. And added, "That makes it even more interesting."

He was glad when Bollard came. Despite his fat and sloppy look, Bollard was by far the ablest of his men and had been a leader himself more than once.

When Bollard had heard, he thought for a little time and then said, "I think we've had it. I'd say, get off Vhol as soon as we can, take our three lightstones and better luck next time."

That was a good sound point of view. With the Vhollans suspicious of them, it was going to be awfully hard to pull this one off. It made sense to do just as Bollard said.

The trouble was that Dilullo did not like getting licked. The trouble also was that Dilullo could not afford to get licked. If he fell on his face with this job it could mean the beginning of the end for him as a Merc leader. He was getting old for it. Nobody had thought much about that because of his record, but he had thought about it. Plenty. Perhaps too much. And he thought that all it would take was one big walloping failure like this to make them say he was just a bit past his work. They'd say it regretfully. They'd talk about how big he'd been in the old days. But they'd say it.

"Look," he told Bollard. "All is not lost. Not yet, anyway. All right, we can't use our radar to get a line on our destination. But there's another possibility. A ship came in and landed in the military port. A cargo ship, not a warship. It wouldn't land there unless it was particularly important."

Bollard frowned. "A supply ship for whatever they're working on in the nebula. Sure. But what does that do for us?"

"It wouldn't do anything if the ship was just loading up with supplies and going out . . . that is, not unless we could follow it. But it brought something with it. Rutledge saw them unload some crates and rush them into the military port warehouse."

"Go on," said Bollard, eyeing him with a cold and fishy eye.

"If we could get a look at what's in those crates . . . not just a look but an analyzer scan . . . something we could compare with the record-spools for point of origin . . . it might give us an idea of what they're doing out there, and where."

"It might," said Bollard. "Or it might not. But the point is that getting in and out of that warehouse, past all their security arrangements, is going to be just about impossible."

"Just about," said Dilullo. "Not absolutely. Anybody want to volunteer?"

In derisive words or by gloomy shakes of the head, they let him know what the answer was.

"Then the old Merc law applies," said Dilullo. "Nobody wants to volunteer for a mean job, the job goes to the last man who broke the rules."

A beautiful smile came onto the moonlike face of Bollard. "But of course," he said. "Of course. Morgan Chane."

IX

Chane lay on his back and looked up at the nebula sky, and let his hand trail in the water as the skimmer glided silently through the channels.

"Are you going to sleep?" asked Laneeah.

"No."

"You drank an awful lot."

"I'm all right now," he assured her.

He was all right, but he was still very much on guard. Yorolin had not done anything except drink some more and get highly expansive and genial, but that one glimpse the Pyam had given him into Yorolin's mind had been enough.

They had wandered along the pleasure-places and Yorolin had wanted Chane to see something he called the feeding of the Golden Ones. Chane gathered that these were some kind of sea-creatures and that feeding them was a regular event. He didn't think much of feeding fish as fun, and he had managed to separate Laneeah from the others and entice her into a skimmer ride through the islands. Yorolin had made no objection at all and Chane had found that fact suspicious.

"How long are you going to be on Vhol, Chane?"

"It's hard to say."

"But," said Laneeah, "if all you're doing here is trying to sell weapons, it won't take long, will it?"

59

"I'll tell you what," said Chane. "We've got another purpose in coming to Vhol. Maybe I'd better not tell you."

She leaned with quick interest, her clear-cut face outlined against the glowing nebula.

"What's this other thing you're doing here?" she asked. "You can tell me."

"All right," he said. "I'll tell you. We've come here for this . . . to grab beautiful women wherever we can find them."

And he grabbed her and pulled her down.

Laneeah screeched. "You're breaking my *back!*" He loosened his grip a little, laughing, and she pulled away. "Are all Earthmen as strong as you?"

"No," said Chane. "You might say that I'm special."

"Special?" she said scornfully, and slapped his face. "You're like all Earthmen. Repulsive. Horribly repulsive."

"You'll get used to that," he said, not letting go of her.

The skimmer glided past the outermost islands and the open sea was like a wrinkled sheet of silver under the glowing sky. From the lights back on the pleasure island there drifted a scrap of lilting music.

There came a distant *phat!* sound from the shore and a moment later there was a muffled splash somewhere near the skimmer. It was repeated, and suddenly Laneeah jumped up in terror.

"They've started to feed the Golden Ones!" she cried out. "So we'll miss it," said Chane.

"You don't understand . . . we've drifted out onto the feeding grounds! Look . . . !"

Chane heard the *phat!* sound again and then saw that a big dark mass had been catapulted out from the pleasure island. The mass hit the sea not far from their skimmer, and as it floated he saw that it looked like some kind of dark, stringy fodder.

"If one did hit us, it wouldn't hurt us . . . ," he began,

but Laneeah interrupted him by screaming.

The sea was boiling furiously right next to the skimmer. The light craft rocked and tilted, and then there was a roaring, swashing sound of disturbed waters.

A colossal yellow head broke surface. It was all of ten feet across, domed and wet-glistening. It opened an enormous maw and snapped up the mass of stringy food. Then it chewed noisily, at the same time looking toward them with eyes that were huge and round and utterly stupid.

Now Chane saw that other heads were breaking surface eagerly in the whole area. Gigantic golden bodies with oddly arm-like flippers, bodies that would have made a whale look like a sprat, thrashed and broached as the creatures eagerly made for the masses of food-fiber that continued to arrive from shore.

Laneeah was still screaming. Now Chane saw that the creature nearest them, having devoured its food, was moving straight toward the skimmer. It was only too obvious that the great brainless brute took the skimmer to be an unusually large ration and was eager to devour it.

Chane picked up the emergency paddle from the bottom of the skimmer and struck with all his strength the top of the wet, domed head.

"Start the motor and steer out of here," he shouted to Laneeah, without turning.

He raised the paddle to deal another blow. But the Golden One, instead of charging, opened its huge mouth and delivered a thunderous bawl.

Chane broke into laughter. It was obvious that nothing had ever hit the leviathan painfully in its whole life, and it was bawling like a smacked baby.

He turned his head, still laughing, and told Laneeah, "Damn it, stop screaming and start up."

She could not have heard him over that Brobdingnagian bellow, but the sight of Chane laughing seemed to shock her out of her hysteria. She started the little motor and the skimmer glided away.

The light craft rocked, tilted and floundered on the waves that the Golden Ones were making. Twice again one of the creatures mistook them for something edible and bore down on them and each time Chane swung the paddle. It seemed that he had guessed right and that no one or nothing had ever dared to touch these colossi, for although they could not really have felt much pain, the shock and surprise seemed to confuse them.

They reached the pleasure island and Yorolin and the others came running to them, and Laneeah, still tearful, pointed accusingly at Chane.

"He *laughed!*"

Yorolin exclaimed, "You could have been killed! However did you drift out there?"

Chane preferred not to go into that. He said to Laneeah, "I'm sorry. It was just that the thing's stupid surprise was so funny."

Yorolin shook his head. "You're not like any Earthman I ever met. There's something wild about you."

Chane did not want Yorolin thinking along that line, and he said, "Some more drinks seem called for."

They had some more, and a few more than that, and by the time they dropped Chane at the spaceport, they were a noisy party and Laneeah had almost, if not quite, forgiven him.

Rutledge met Chane before he reached the ship. "How nice of you to show up," he said. "I've been hanging around for hours waiting for you, though of course I haven't minded."

"What's happened?" asked Chane.

Rutledge told him as they walked along Star Street, still ablaze with lights and raucous with rowdy sounds. Rutledge dropped off at a drinking-place to alleviate his boredom and Chane went on along to the inn.

He found Dilullo sitting alone in the common room

with a half-filled glass of brandy in front of him.

He said, "Your Starwolf friends are still after you, Chane."

Chane listened, and then nodded. "I'm not surprised. Ssander had two brothers in that squadron. They won't go back to Varna until they've seen my dead body."

Dilullo looked at him thoughtfully. "It doesn't seem to worry you much."

Chane smiled. "Varnans don't worry. If you meet your enemy you try to kill him and hope you succeed, but worrying before then does no good."

"Fine," said Dilullo. "Well, I worry. I worry about meeting up with Varnans. I worry about these Vhollans and what they'll do next. They're definitely suspicious of us."

Chane nodded, and told him about Yorolin and the Pyam. He added with a shrug, "If the mission fails, it fails. Come to that, I like the Vhollans a lot better than the Kharalis."

Dilullo eyed him. "So do I. A lot better. But there's more to it than that."

"What?"

"There's two things. When a Merc takes on a job, he keeps faith. The other thing is that these likable Vhollans are carrying a war of conquest to Kharal."

"So they're going to conquer Kharal . . . is that such a terrible thing?" asked Chane, smiling.

"Maybe not to a Starwolf. But an Earthman sees things differently," said Dilullo. He drank his brandy and continued slowly. "I'll tell you something. You Varnans look on raids and conquest as fun. Other starworlds—lots of them—see conquest as a good and right thing. But there's one world that doesn't like conquest at all, it's so peaceable. And that's Earth."

He set his glass down. "You know why that is, Chane? It's because Earth was a world of war and conquest for thousands of years. Our people have forgotten more about fighting than any of you will ever learn. We were soaked in conquest right up to our ears for a long, long time and that's why we don't have much use for it any more."

Chane was silent. Dilullo said, "Ah, what's the use of talking to you about it. You're young and you've been raised wrong. I'm not young, and I wish to heaven I was back at Brindisi."

"That's a place on Earth?" asked Chane.

Dilullo nodded moodily. "It's on the sea, and in the morning you can see the sun coming up out of the mists of the Adriatic. It's beautiful and it's home. The only trouble is, you can starve to death there."

Chane said, after a moment, "I remember the name of the place my parents came from, on Earth. It was Wales."

"I've been there," said Dilullo. "Dark mountains, dark valleys. People who sing like angels and are golden-hearted friends till you get them mad, and then they're wildcats. Maybe you got something from there as well as Varna."

After a few moments, Chane said, "Well, so far it's a standoff. We haven't found out anything; they haven't found out anything. So what happens next?"

"Tomorrow," said Dilullo, "I will put on a very large and convincing show of trying to sell these people some weapons."

"And what about me?"

"You?" said Dilullo. "You, my friend, are going to figure out how to do the impossible, and do it quickly, cleanly, and without being seen, let alone caught."

"Mmm," said Chane, "that should keep me busy for an hour or two, what do I do after that?"

"Sit and polish your ego." He shoved the brandy bottle over. "Settle down. I've got some talking to do. About the impossible."

When he was finished, Chane looked at him almost

with awe. "That might even take me three hours to figure out. You have a lot of faith in me, Dilullo."

Dilullo showed him the edges of his teeth. "That is the only reason you're alive," he said. "And you'll be as sorry as the rest of us if you let me down."

X

Next night, Chane lay in the grass well outside the military port and studied its lights. In one hand he held a six-foot roll of thin, neutral-colored cloth. His other hand held tightly to a collar that was around the neck of a snokk.

The snokk was both furious and frightened. The animals looked something like a furry wallaby, or small kangaroo. But they had a doglike disposition and ran happily in packs in some parts of the town. This one was not happy, for attached to the collar was a leather hood that completely muffled its head. It kept trying to dig its hind feet into the ground and bound away, but Chane held it.

"Soon," he whispered soothingly. "Very soon."

The snokk responded with a series of growling barks that were effectively muffled by the hood.

Chane had done his homework well. Now he looked at the conical tower that rose from the central building. That was where the ring-projector was, and he had by day seen the searchlights around it, though now they were dark.

He began to crawl forward, dragging the reluctant snokk along. Chane went with every muscle tense. At any moment he would cross the edge of the ringlike aura of force projected to enclose the whole military port. When he crossed that, things would happen very quickly.

He went on, going slowly but making sure that he was set to move fast at any moment. The snokk gave him more and more trouble but he relentlessly dragged it on with him. He could see the lights and the loom of the big starships on the port, warcraft with grim, closed weapon-ports in their sides. He made out the low structure that was the warehouse.

It happened about the moment that Chane expected it to happen. A sharp alarm rang across the port, and the searchlights flashed into life. Their beams swung swiftly in his direction.

Those lights, triggered and aimed by computers linked to the ring-apparatus, could move fast. But his Varna-born reactions gave Chane a slight edge. He acted, when the alarm first sounded, with all the speed he had.

His right hand ripped the hood and collar off the head of the snokk. With the same forward motion he threw himself flat on the ground and pulled the square of neutral-colored cloth over himself and lay still.

The snokk, freed, went off across the port with great hopping leaps, sounding an outraged series of howling barks. Two searchlights instantly locked onto the animal, while the other beams wove an intricate mathematical pattern to cover the whole edge of the port.

Chane lay quite still, trying to look like a bump in the ground.

He heard a fast skimmer come out onto the port and stop some distance from him. He heard the furious barks of the snokk receding.

Someone in the skimmer swore disgustedly, and someone else laughed. Then it went away again, back the way it had come.

The searchlights, after a little more probing, went out.

Chane continued to lie still under his cloth. Three minutes later the searchlights suddenly came on again and swept the whole area once more. Then they went out again.

Chane came out from under the cloth then. He was

grinning as he rolled it up.

"A Starwolf child could get in there," he had told Dilullo when he had finished his reconnaissance. But that had just been a little bragging, and anyway, he had only come this first step: the rest of the job would not be child's work at all.

He worked his way patiently toward the warehouse, keeping to the shadows as much as possible, using his camouflage cloth whenever he stopped to listen. The warehouse, a low flat-roofed metal building, did not seem to be guarded, but if there was anything important in it, there were sure to be cunning devices to expose an intruder.

It was almost an hour before Chane stood in the dark interior of the warehouse. He had entered by the roof, first using small sensors to select an area of the roof free of alarms, then using a hooded ato-flash to cut a neat circle. If he replaced the cutout and fused it into place when he left, it might be a long time before it was noticed.

He took out his pocket-lamp and flashed its thin beam. The first thing he saw was that the crates from the cargo-ship had been unpacked.

Three objects stood upon a long trestle-table beside the crates. Chane stared at them. He walked around the table to inspect them from all sides. Then he stared at them again, shaking his head.

He had handled a lot of exotic loot in his time. He thought he could identify, or at least take a guess at, almost everything in the way of artifacts and the stuff whereof they were made.

These three objects mocked him.

They were all made of the same substance, a metal that vaguely resembled pale, hard gold, but was like nothing he had ever seen before. In form they were all different. One was a shining, fluted ribbon reared like a snake three feet high. One was a congery of nine small spheres, held rigidly together by short, slender rods.

The third was a truncated cone, wide and thick at the base, with no openings and no decoration. They were beautiful enough to be ornaments, but somehow instinctively he knew they weren't. He could not guess at the purpose of any of them.

Still shaking his head, but reminding himself strongly that he didn't have all night, Chane took from a belt-pouch a minicamera and a small but highly sophisticated instrument Dilullo had given him; a portable analyzer that poked and probed with fingering rays among the molecules of a substance and came up with a pretty accurate chart of its essential components. Because of its extreme miniaturization it had a limited usefulness, but within those limitations it was useful indeed. Chane applied its sensor units to the base of the spiraled golden ribbon and clicked it on, and then began snapping quick record shots with the little camera.

The truncated cone occluded a portion of the nine-sphere congery. He reached out and moved it . . . the metal was satin-smooth and chilly and surprisingly light. He leaned past it to aim the camera's tiny flash-pod at the golden spheres. And suddenly he went rigid.

There was a whisper of sound in the dark warehouse.

He swung on his heel, his hand going to the stunner inside his jacket, his little beam probing every corner. There were these enigmatic golden objects, and some piles of regulation ship-stores cases.

Nothing more. And no one.

The sound whispered a little louder. It was like someone, or something, trying to speak in a breathy murmur. Now Chane identified its source. It was coming from the cone.

He stepped back from the thing. It lay in the beam of his light, shining and still. But the breathy whisper from it grew in volume.

Now a light came up from the cone, as though emanating from the solid metal. It was not ordinary light; it was a twisting tendril of soft glowing flame. It twisted higher, endlessly pouring out of the cone, until there was a great wreath of it several feet above his head.

Then, without warning, the wreath of light exploded into a myriad of tiny stars.

The whispering voice swelled louder. The little stars above floated down in showers. They were not mere sparks or points of light: each one was different, each like a real star made inconceivably tiny.

They swirled and floated around Chane, yet he could not feel their touch. Red giants and white dwarfs, smoky orange suns and the evil-glowing quasars, and their perfection was so absolute that for a moment Chane lost perspective. They seemed to him real stars, and he was a giant standing in a cascade of swirling suns.

The murmuring voice was still louder, and now he could hear strange, irregular rhythms in it.

Someone, or something, singing?

Of a sudden, Chane realized his peril. If there was an alarm-device here triggered by sound, it could be activated by this.

He grabbed for the cone, to search for some control on it. But before his hand quite touched it, the swirling stars around him vanished and the whispering singing ceased.

He stood, a little shaken by the experience, but understanding now. This seemingly-solid cone was an instrument that reproduced audio-visual records, and was turned on or off by the mere proximity of a hand.

But who, or what, had made such a record as this?

Chane, after a moment, cautiously examined the other gold-colored objects, the fluted spiral and the congery of spheres. But no wave of the hand produced in them any reaction.

He stood, thinking. It seemed evident that the Vhollans, who had brought these things here, had not made them. Then who had?

A people inside the nebula? One that had mastered unknown technologies? But if so . . .

He heard a slight clicking sound from the door.

Instantly, Chane stiffened. There *had* been a sonic-triggered alarm in here. Guards had come, and were softly unlocking the combination of the door.

Chane thought swiftly. He ran to the golden cone. He passed his hand over it, and the whispering sound began and the tendril of light grew up from it. Chane thrust the analyzer and the camera into his pouch, already moving away.

The door clicked softly again. Chane sprang to one of the corners of the room, and crouched behind cases of stores.

In the darkness, the wreath of light above the cone exploded again into tiny stars, and the whispering swelled.

The door opened.

There were two helmeted Vhollan guards and they had lethal lasers in their hands, and they were ready to fire at once. But for just a second, their eyes were riveted by that amazing cataract of stars.

Chane's stun-gun buzzed and dropped them.

He had, he thought, only a few minutes before the guards were missed. His plans for getting out of the port required much more time than that.

A grin crossed his face and he thought, *The hell with clever plans. Do it the Starwolf way.*

The small skimmer the guards had come in stood outside the warehouse. Chane reached down and took the helmet off one of the unconscious men, and put it on his head. It would conceal the fact that his hair was not the albino white of Vhol, and it would help to hide his face. The guard's jacket concealed his non-Vhollan clothing.

He jumped into the driver's seat of the skimmer, turned it on, and went racing and screaming toward the main gateway of the military port.

The searchlights on the tower came on and locked onto him. He waved his free arm wildly as he drove up to the gateway, and shouted to the guards there. He hardly knew a word of Vhollan so he kept his shout a wordless one, relying on the screaming of the siren to make it unintelligible anyway. He pointed excitedly ahead and goosed the skimmer to its highest speed.

The guards fell away, startled and excited, and Chane drove on into the darkness, laughing. It was the old Varnan way: be as clever and tricky as you can but when cleverness won't work, smash right through before people wake up. He and Ssander had done it many times.

For a fleeting moment, he was sorry that Ssander was dead.

XI

"They didn't see me," Chane said. "Not to recognize me as a non-Vhollan. I can vouch for that. They didn't see me at all."

Dilullo's face was very hard in the lamplight, the lines cut deep like knife-slashes in dark wood.

"What did you do with the skimmer?"

"Found a lonely beach, drove it out onto the water a way, and sank it." Chane looked at Dilullo and was astonished to find himself making excuses. "It was that damned cone, that recorder thing. I had no way of knowing what it was, and it went on all by itself when my hand got near it." He saw Dilullo looking at him very oddly, and he hurried on. "Don't worry about it. I came in over the roofs. Nobody saw me. Why would they suspect us? Obviously some of their own people must be overly prying or they wouldn't have all that tight security. If there are no thieves on Vhol it'll be the rarest planet in the galaxy."

He tossed the belt pouch on Dilullo's lap. "I got what you wanted, anyway. It's all there." He sat down and helped himself to a drink from Dilullo's brandy bottle. The bottle, he noticed, had taken a severe beating, but Dilullo was cold and stony sober as a rock.

"Just the same," Dilullo said, "I think the time has come to say goodbye to Vhol." He set the pouch aside. "Have to wait on these till we have the ship's techlab."

He leaned forward, looking at Chane. "What was so strange about these things?"

"The metal they were made of. The fact that they were unclassifiable as to function. Above all, the fact that they came from an area—the nebula—that doesn't have any inhabited world with a technology above Class Two level."

Dilullo nodded. "I wondered if you remembered that. We studied all the microfile charts on our way here from Kharal."

"Either the microfile charts are wrong, or something else is. Because those things are not only from a very high technology, but a very alien one."

Dilullo grunted. He got up and lifted a corner of the curtain across the window. It was already dawn. Chane turned off the lamp and a pearl-pink light flooded into the little room of the inn on Star Street.

"Could they have been weapons, Chane? Or components of weapons?"

Chane shook his head. "The recorder thing certainly wasn't. I couldn't swear to the other two, of course, but they didn't *feel* like it." He meant an inner feeling, the instinctive recognition by a practiced fighter for any deadly instrument.

"That's interesting," Dilullo said. "Did I tell you, by the way, that Thrandirin wants to inspect our wares tomorrow, with a view to buying? Go get some sleep, Chane. And when I call you, wake up fast."

It was not Dilullo who waked him, though. It was Bollard, looking as though he had just waked up himself, or was perhaps just on the verge of going to sleep.

"If you have any possession here that you can't bear to leave behind you, bring it . . . just so long as it'll fit into your pocket." Bollard scratched his chest and yawned. "Otherwise forget it."

"I travel light." Chane pulled his boots on. They were all he had taken off before he slept. "Where's Dilullo?"

" 'Board ship, with Thrandirin and some top brass. He wants us to join him."

Chane paused in his boot-pulling and met Bollard's

gaze. The small eyes behind those fat pink lids were anything but sleepy.

"I see," said Chane, and stamped his heel down and stood up. He grinned at Bollard. "Let's not keep him waiting."

"You want to go down and explain that to the guards?" He smiled back at Chane, a fat lazy man without a care in the world. "They're posted front and back, ever since last night. Confined to quarters, Thrandirin said, for our own protection during a period of emergency. Something happened last night that upset them. He didn't say what. He only allowed Machris, the weapons expert, and one other man to go with Dilullo to the ship. So we have almost a full crew. But the guards have lasers. So it's going to be a little bit of a problem. . . ." Bollard seemed to ponder a moment. "John said something about you coming in over the roofs. Could that be done by others, say, fat slobs like me?"

"I can't vouch for the construction," Chane said, "but if you don't fall through you shouldn't have any trouble. It'll have to be done quietly, though. These buildings aren't very high, and if they hear us we'll be in worse trouble than if we'd just butted them head on."

"Let's try," said Bollard, and went away, leaving Chane wishing it were night.

But it was not night. It was high noon, and the sun of Vhol shone white and bright overhead, driving a shaft of brilliance down through the trapdoor when Chane pushed it carefully open.

There was no one to be seen. Chane stepped out and waved the others after him. They came quietly up the ladder one at a time, and at intervals they went quietly across the roof, not running, in the direction Chane had pointed out.

Meanwhile, Chane and Bollard kept watch of the streets below in front of and behind the inn. Chane drew the alley because Bollard was in command and therefore got the most important post. Motionless as one of the carved stone gargoyles of Kharal, he peered down into the alley from behind a kitchen chimney. The Vhollan guards were a tough-looking lot, standing patiently in good order, not minding the sun nor the chatter of small urchins gathered to stare at them, nor the invitations of several young ladies who seemed to be telling them they could go and have a cooling drink and be back before they were missed. Chane disliked the Vhollan guards intensely. He preferred men who would loosen their tunics and sit in the shade and chaffer with the ladies.

The Mercs were not as good as Varnans, nobody was, but they were good enough, and they got off without attracting any attention from below. Bollard signaled that all was clear on his side. Chane joined him and they went on their way toward the spaceport.

The roofs of Star Street were utilitarian, ugly, and mercifully flat. The Mercs moved across them in a long irregular line, going as quickly as they could without making any running noises for people to come up and investigate. The line of buildings ended at the spaceport fence, separated from it by a perimeter road that served the warehouse area. The gate was no more than thirty yards away, and the Merc ship sat unconcernedly on its pad a quarter mile beyond.

It looked a long, long way.

Chane took a deep breath and Bollard said quietly to the Mercs, all bunched together on that ultimate roof, "All right; once we start moving, don't stop."

Chane opened the trapdoor and they went down through the building, not worrying now about making noise, not worrying about anything but getting where they wanted to go. There were three floors in the building. The air was stale and heavy in the corridors, sweet with too much perfume. There were a lot of doors, mostly closed. The sound of music came up from below.

They hit the ground floor running, passed through a series of ornate rooms that were chipped and worn and moth-eaten in the daylight that leaked in through the curtained windows. There were people in the rooms, of various sizes, shapes, and colors, some of them quite strange, but Chane did not have time to see exactly what they were doing. He only saw their startled eyes turned on him in the half-gloom. A towering woman in green charged at them, screeching angrily like a gigantic parrot. Then the front door slammed open with a jingling of sinful bells, and they were out in the clean hot street.

They headed for the gate. And Chane was astonished at how rapidly Bollard could make his fat legs go when he really wanted to.

There was a watchman's box beside the gate. The man inside it saw them coming. Chane could see him staring at them for what seemed like minutes as they rushed closer, and he smiled at the man, a contemptuous smile that mocked the slow reactions of the lesser breeds. He himself, or any other Starwolf, would have had the gate closed and half the onrushing Mercs shot down before the watchman's synapses finally clicked and set his hand in motion toward the switch. Actually the time lapse from initial stimulus to reaction was only a matter of seconds. But it was enough to bring Chane in stunner range. The watchman fell down. The Mercs pounded through the gate. Bollard was the last of them and Chane saw Bollard staring at him with a very peculiar expression as he passed, and only then did he realize that in the necessity of the moment he had forgotten all about being careful and had raced ahead of the others, covering the thirty yards at a speed well-nigh impossible for a normal Earthman.

He swore silently. He was going to give himself away for sure if he wasn't more careful, perhaps had already done so.

Somebody shouted, "Here they come!"

The Vhollan guards had finally been alerted. They were coming down Star Street at the double, and in a minute, Chane knew, those needle-like laser beams would begin to flicker. He heard Bollard's almost unconcerned order to spread out. He punched the switch and jumped through as the gate began to swing. Bollard was fishing something out of his belt-pouch, a bit of plastic with a magnetic fuse-and-coupler plate. He slapped it onto the end of the gate as it swung past, just above the lock assembly. Then Chane and Bollard ran on together toward the ship.

Behind them there was a pop and an intense flash of light as the gate clanked shut. Bollard smiled. "That fused the gate and the post together. They can cut through, of course, but it'll take 'em a couple minutes. Where did you learn to run?"

"Rock-jumping in the drift mines," said Chane innocently. "Does wonders for the coordination. You should try it sometime."

Bollard grunted and saved his breath. The Merc ship still seemed a million miles away. Chane fumed at having to rein himself in to the Mercs' pace, but he did it. Finally Bollard panted, "Why don't you go on ahead like you did before?"

"Hell," said Chane, pretending to pant also, "I can only do that in spurts. I blew myself."

He panted harder, looking back over his shoulder. The guards were approaching the gate now. One of them went into the watchman's box. Chane assumed that he tried the switch, but nothing happened. The gate remained closed. Some of the guards fired through the mesh. The whipcrack and flash of the lasers scarred the air behind the Mercs but the range was too long for the small power-packs in the hand weapons. Chane thanked the luck of the Starwolves that the guards had not thought they might need heavier weapons.

There was not as yet any sign of life around the Merc ship. Presumably the Vhollans within would feel perfectly safe, believing that the ship's crew was bottled up at the inn, and Chane was sure that Dilullo would see to it that the demonstration was held where the visitors wouldn't be inconvenienced by noises from outside.

Still and all, there should be a guard. . . .

There was. Two Vhollans in uniform came out of the lock to see what was going on. They saw, but they were already too late. The Mercs knocked them down neatly with their stun-guns. The skimmer in which Dilullo and the Vhollan officials had come was parked beside the boarding steps. Bollard ordered the men aboard and motioned to Chane. Together they tossed the unconscious men into the skimmer and started it, heading it back without a driver toward the fence. The guards from the inn had cut their way through the gate.

Bollard nodded. "That all worked out real nice," he said.

They scrambled up the steps and into the lock. The warning hooter was going, the CLEAR LOCK sign flashing red. Dilullo had not wasted any time. The inner lock door clapped shut and sealed itself almost on Chane's coattails.

Members of the crew with flight duty hurried to their stations. Chane went to the bridge room with Bollard.

There was quite a crowd in it, all Mercs but one, and all but one jubilant. The one was Thrandirin. Dilullo stood with him before the video pickup grid, so that there should not be any mistake when the message went out.

Dilullo was talking into the communicator.

"Hold your fire," he was saying. "We're about to take off, so clear space. And forget about your intercept procedures. Thrandirin and the two officers will be returned to you safely if you do as I say. But if anybody fires off so much as a slingshot at us, they die."

Chane hardly heard the words. He was looking at the expression on Thrandirin's heavy, authoritative face, and it filled him with pure joy.

The drive units throbbed to life, growled, roared, screamed, and took the Merc ship skyward. And nobody fired so much as a slingshot as it went.

XII

The Merc ship hung in the edge of the nebula, lapped in radiance.

Dilullo sat in the wardroom with Bollard, studying for the hundredth time the photographs and the analyzer record on the objects in the warehouse.

"You'll wear them out with eyetracks," Bollard said. "They aren't going to tell you anything different from what they already have."

"Which is nothing," Dilullo said. "Or worse than nothing. The photographs are clear and sharp. I see the things, therefore I know they exist. Then along comes the analyzer record and tells me they don't."

He tossed the little plastic disc onto the table. It was blank and innocent as the day it was made, recording zero.

"Chane didn't handle it right, John. Attached the sensors wrong, or forgot to turn it on."

"Do you believe that?"

"Knowing Chane, no. But I have to believe something, and the fault isn't in the analyzer. That's been checked."

"And rechecked."

"So it has to be Chane."

Dilullo shrugged. "That's the most logical explanation."

"Is there another one?"

"Sure. The things are made out of some substance that the analyzer isn't programmed to identify. I.e., not on our atomic table. But we know that's ridiculous, don't we?"

"Of course we do," said Bollard slowly.

Dilullo got up and got a bottle and sat down again. "We're not doing anything else," he said. "Get Thrandirin and the two generals in here. And Chane."

"Why him?"

"Because he saw the things. Touched them. Set one off. Heard it . . . singing."

Bollard snorted. "Chane's fast and he's good, but I wouldn't trust him any farther than he could throw me."

"I wouldn't either," said Dilullo. "So bring him."

Bollard went out. Dilullo put his chin in his fists and stared at the disc and the photographs. Outside the hull the pale fires of the nebula glowed across infinity . . . endless parsecs of infinity in three dimensions. Up in the navigation room Bixel read micro-books from the ship's library for the third time over and drank innumerable cups of coffee, keeping vigil over the radar which remained as obstinately blank as the analyzer disc.

Bollard came back with Chane and Thrandirin and the two generals, Markolin and Tatichin. The -in suffix was important on Vhol, it seemed, identifying a certain gens which had acquired power a long time back and hung onto it with admirable determination. They figured largely in administrative, military and space-flight areas, and they were accustomed to command. Which made them less than patient prisoners.

Thrandirin opened the game, as he always did, with the How-long-are-you-going-to-persist-in-this-idiocy gambit. Dilullo countered, as he always did, with the As-long-as-it-takes-me-to-get-what-I-want one. Then all three told him that was impossible, and demanded to be taken home.

Dilullo nodded and smiled. "Now that we've got that out of the way, perhaps we can just sit around and have a

drink or two and talk about the weather." He passed
the bottle and the glasses around the scarred table. The
Vhollans accepted the liquor stiffly and sat like three
statues done in marble and draped in bright tunics.
Only their eyes were alive, startlingly blue and bright.

Thrandirin's eyes rested briefly on the photographs
in front of Dilullo and moved away again.

"No," said Dilullo. "Go ahead, look at them." He
passed them down. "Look at this, too." He passed the
disc. "You've seen them before. There's no need to be
bashful about it."

Thrandirin shook his head. "I say what I have said
before. If I knew any more than you do about those
objects I would not tell you. But I don't. I saw them in
the warehouse, and that is all. I am not a scientist, I am
not a technician, and I have no direct part in this operation."

"Yet you are a government official," said Dilullo.
"Pretty top-level, too. Top enough to dicker for
weapons."

Thrandirin made no comment.

"I find it very difficult to believe that you do not
know where those things came from," said Dilullo softly.

Thrandirin shrugged. "I don't see why you find it
difficult. You questioned us with a lie-detector of your
latest type and it should have proved to you that we
know nothing."

Tatichin said brusquely, as though it were an old sore
subject with him, "Only six men know about this thing.
Our ruler, his chief minister, the chief of the War De-
partment, and the navigators who actually take the
ships into the nebula. Even the captains do not know
the course, and the navigators are under constant
guard, virtual prisoners, both in space and on Vhol."

"Then it must be something of tremendous impor-
tance," Dilullo said. The three marble statues stared at
him with hard blue eyes and said nothing. "The

Kharalis questioned Yorolin under an irresistible drug. He told them that Vhol had a weapon out in the nebula, something powerful enough to wipe them off the face of their world."

The hard blue eyes flared brighter on that, but the Vhollans did not seem too surprised.

"We assumed that they had," said Thrandirin, "though Yorolin could not remember anything beyond the fact that the Kharalis had drugged him. A man cannot lie under that drug, it is true. But he can tell only what is in his mind, no more, no less. Yorolin believed what he said. That does not necessarily make it so."

Now Dilullo's eyes grew very hard and his jaw set like a steel trap. "Your own unlying minds have told me that you too have heard this, and that you are indeed planning the conquest of Kharal. Now that being so, isn't it strange that you were interested in buying weapons from us? Ordinary puny conventional little weapons, even though rather better than the ones you have, when there's a super-weapon lying at hand here in this nebula?"

"Surely we answered that question for you," said Thrandirin.

"Oh, yes, you said the weapons were needed to ensure the safety of the nebula. Now that doesn't make a whole lot of sense, does it?"

"I'm afraid I do not follow your line of reasoning, and I definitely do not enjoy your company." Thrandirin rose, and the generals rose with him. "I most bitterly regret that I did not have you imprisoned the moment you landed. I underestimated your—"

"Gall?" said Dilullo. "Nerve? Plain stupid rashness?"

Thrandirin shrugged. "I could not believe that you would come openly to Vhol from Kharal if you had actually taken service with the Kharalis. And of course there was Yorolin . . . we knew the Kharalis would never have given him up willingly, and the fact that you did help him to escape seemed to prove your story. So we hesitated. There was even some discussion"—here he looked rather coldly at Markolin—"about hiring you for our own use against Kharal. You were very adroit, Captain Dilullo. I hope you are enjoying your triumph. But I will remind you again. Even if you should manage to find what you're seeking, they have been warned by sub-spectrum transmission from Vhol. They will be expecting you."

"*They?* Heavy cruisers, Thrandirin? How many? One? Two? Three?"

Markolin said, "He can't tell you, nor can I. Rest assured the force is sufficient to guard our . . . installation." The hesitation before that word was so brief as to be almost unnoticeable. "And I can assure you also that the value of our lives is not great enough to buy your safety there."

"That is so," said Thrandirin. "And now we would prefer to return to our own quarters, if you please."

"Of course," said Dilullo. "No, stay here, Bollard." He spoke briefly over the ship's intercom, and in a moment another man came and took the Vhollans away. Dilullo swung around and looked at Chane and Bollard.

"They wanted to buy our weapons, and they thought of hiring us to use against Kharal."

"I heard that," said Bollard. "I don't see anything too strange about it. It just means that their super-weapon isn't operational yet and won't be for some time, so they're hedging their bets."

Dilullo nodded. "Makes sense. What do you say, Chane?"

"I'd say Bollard was right. Only . . ."

"Only what?"

"Well," said Chane, "that recorder thing in the warehouse. If they're constructing a weapon out here in the nebula, they sure aren't bothering to construct audio-visual recorders, and anyway it wasn't a Vhollan artifact." Chane paused. There was something else itching at his mind, and he waited till it came clear. "Besides, what's all this secrecy about? I can understand tight security, sure. And I can understand them being afraid that the Kharalis might hire somebody to go into the nebula, just as they did, and try to capture or destroy the weapon. But they're so afraid that they don't even trust men like Thrandirin and the generals to know where those came from or what they are." Chane pointed to the photographs of the three golden objects. "One of those things makes very strange music and shoots stars, but is no more than an audio-visual recorder. And what is so thunderingly secret about that? It doesn't make sense to me at all."

Dilullo looked at Bollard, who shook his head. "I didn't see his star-shooting recorder, so I can't say yes or no. Why not just come out and say what's on your mind, John?"

Dilullo picked up the little blank analyzer disc, the plastic zero. "I'm beginning to think," he said, "that this may be more important than what Vhol does to Kharal, or vice versa. I think the Vhollans have got hold of something big, all right . . . something so big that it frightens the wits out of them. Because," he added slowly, "I don't think they understand whatever it is, or know how to use it, any more than we do."

There was a lengthy silence. Finally Bollard said, "Would you care to explain that a little better, John?"

Dilullo shook his head. "No. Because I'm only guessing, and a man's a fool to go galloping off on a wild guess. The only way we'll ever know is to find the thing and see for ourselves. And I'm beginning to think the Vhollans are right when they say we never will."

He punched the intercom to the navigation room. "Start a sweep pattern, Finney. Plot it to cover as much of the nebula coast as possible without leaving any gaps. That supply ship has to come from Vhol sometime, and all we need is a little bit of luck."

The voice of Finney, the navigator, came back in tones of pure acid. "Sure, John. Just a wee little bit of luck."

Presently the Merc ship was on her way, an infinitesimal spider spinning a small frail web across the burning cliffs of the nebula, and everybody aboard knew what her chances were of catching the tiny fly she wanted. Particularly when the fly had ample warning.

Chane had lost all sense of the passage of time, and Dilullo was acutely aware that there had been far too much of it, when Bixel looked up from his radar screen and said, in a tone of utter disbelief:

"I've got a blip."

Dilullo had one moment of triumphant joy. But it did not last long, for Bixel said, "I've got another. And another. Hell, I've got a flock of them."

Dilullo bent over the radar screen with a cold premonition clutching at his heart.

"They've changed course," Bixel said. "Heading straight for us now and coming fast. Awfully damned fast."

Bollard had wedged himself into the little room and was peering over both their shoulders. "Those aren't supply ships. Could be a squadron of Vhollan cruisers . . . if they've decided they don't mind losing their friends."

Dilullo shook his head dismally. "Only one kind of ship is that size, moves in that kind of formation, and has that kind of speed. I guess Thrandirin wasn't lying after all, about the Starwolves."

XIII

The first Chane knew about it was when the *Red Alert* signal came howling over the ship's intercom, followed at once by a burst of acceleration that set the ship's seams creaking and laid Chane up hard against a bulkhead. He had been stretched out in a borrowed bunk half asleep, but only half, and even that much was a major achievement. He hated waiting. He hated this business of dangling in a vacuum, waiting for another man to make the decisions. Wisdom and the instinct for survival told him he had better be patient because he had no other choice at the moment. But his physical being found it difficult to obey. It was not used to being inactive. A lifetime of training had taught it that inactivity was the next thing to being dead, a state fit only for the lesser breeds who were meant to be preyed upon. A Varnan fought hard, and when he was through fighting he enjoyed the fruits of his victory just as hard, until it was time to go fight again. Chane's metabolism revolted against waiting.

The alert and the frantic leaping of the ship were like a sudden release from prison.

He jumped up and went into the main passageway. Men were running in what appeared to be wild confusion, but Chane knew it was not, and in a matter of seconds everyone was at his station and the ship was quiet with a quivering, breathing quietness. The quiet of a very different sort of waiting.

Chane had no assigned station. He went on toward the bridge.

Dilullo's voice came rasping over the intercom, speaking to the whole ship.

"I've got a little bad news for you," it said. "We've got a Starwolf squadron on our tail."

Chane froze in the passageway.

Dilullo's voice seemed to have a personal edge in it, a warning edge, as it went on, "I repeat, we have a Starwolf squadron in pursuit." *Talking to me,* Chane thought. *Well, and here we are. They've caught up with me, Ssander's brothers and the rest.*

Dilullo's voice continued. "I am taking evasive action. We'll fight if we have to, but I'm going to do my damndest to run. So prepare for max stress."

Meaning, I won't have time to warn you of abrupt changes in course or velocity. Just hang on and hope the ship holds together.

Chane stood still in the passageway, his body braced, his mind racing.

He might have been in worse spots in his career but he couldn't remember one off-hand. If the Mercs should have any reason to suspect his origin they would kill him long before Ssander's brothers could possibly reach him. And if they didn't suspect him, he would die anyway when the Starwolf squadron caught them.

Because it would catch them. Nobody got away from the Starwolves. Nobody could go fast enough, for nobody could endure physically the shattering impact of inertial stress that the Starwolves endured, maneuvering their little ships at man-killing velocities. That was what made them unbeatable in space.

The Merc ship wrenched screaming onto a tangential course. It seemed to Chane that he could feel the bulkhead bend under his hand. The blood beat up in him hard and hot. He straightened up as the ship steadied again, and went on forward to the bridge room.

It was dark there except for the hooded lights of the

instrument panels. Dark enough so that the red-gold
fire of the nebula seemed to fill it, pouring in through
the forward viewport. Illusion, of course; the viewport
was now a viewscreen and the nebula it showed was not
the actuality but an FTL stimulus simulcrum. The illusion was good enough. Dilullo's head and shoulders
loomed against the fireglow, and the ship plunged
through rolling, whipping clouds of cold flame. The
suns that set the nebula gas to burning with their light
fled past like flung coals.

Dilullo looked up and saw Chane's face in the glow
and said, "What the hell are you doing here?"

"I get restless just sitting," Chane said in a flat, quiet
voice. "I thought I might be able to help."

The copilot, a small dark rawhide man named
Gomez, said irritably, "Get him out of here, John. I
don't need any rock-hopper pilot breathing down my
neck. Not now."

Dilullo said, "Hang on."

Chane grabbed a support girder. Again the ship
screamed and groaned. The metal bit into Chane's
flesh, and again he thought he could feel it bend. The
image in the viewscreen blurred to a chaotic jumble of
racing sparks. Then it steadied and they were falling
down a vast long chute between walls of flame, and
Gomez said, "One more time, John, and you're going
to crack her bones."

"All right," said Dilullo. "Here's the one more
time."

Chane heard more than the ship cry out. The men
were beginning to crumple under the hammering.
Gomez sagged in his chair. Blood sprang from his nose
and went in dark runnels over his mouth and chin.
Dilullo sighed a great sigh as the breath was squeezed
from his lungs. He seemed to lean over the control
panel and Chane reached forward to take the ship,
drew back as Dilullo forced himself erect again, his
mouth open and biting savagely on air, dragging it into

him by main force and stubbornness. On the other side of the bridge room a man hung sideways against his recoil harness and did not move. Unnoticed, Chane grinned a sardonic grin, and clung to his girder, and breathed evenly against the pressure of the inertial hand that tried to crush him and could not.

Then he wondered what he was grinning about. This toughness he was so proud of was about to be his doom. The Mercs could not match it, and so the Starwolves would win.

He wondered if they knew that he was aboard the Merc ship. He didn't see how they could, for sure. But they must have tracked him to Corvus, and that would be enough. They would shake out the whole cluster until they found him or made sure he was dead.

Chane grinned again, thinking how Dilullo must be regretting his own cleverness in keeping his tame Starwolf alive. Chane felt no responsibility for the results. That had been all Dilullo's idea, and Chane could even take a certain cruel pleasure in the way he was being paid out for it.

He knew that Dilullo must be thinking the same thing. Just once Dilullo turned and met his eye, and Chane thought, *He'd give me to them now if he could, if it would save his men. But he knows it wouldn't. The Varnans couldn't let these men live, not knowing what I might have told them. Wouldn't let them live, in any case, for helping me.*

The ship lurched and staggered, slowing down. The viewscreen flickered, blanked out, became again a window onto normal space. They drifted underneath the belly of a great orange sun, veiled and misty in the cloudy fire.

After a minute Dilullo said, "Bixel?" And again, "Bixel!"

Bixel's voice came faintly from the navigation room. He sounded as though he was snuffing blood out of his own nose. "I don't see anything," he said. "I think—"

He choked and gasped and went on again, "I think you shook 'em."

"Just as well," muttered Gomez, mopping himself. "One more time and you'd have cracked *my* bones to a jelly."

Chane said, "They'll be along." He saw Gomez and some of the others turn and glare at him, and he pretended weakness, sliding down along the girder to sit on the floor beside Dilullo. "They know we can't take it like they can. They know we have to stop."

"How did you get to be such an expert on Starwolves?" asked Gomez. Not suspiciously. Just slapping down a bigmouth. Chane slumped against his girder and shut his eyes.

"You don't have to be an expert," he said, "to know that."

And how many times I've done this, he thought. *Watched a ship run and dodge and twist, half killing the men inside, and we watched and followed and waited until the strength was beaten out of them. And now I'm on the receiving end. . . .*

Bixel said over the intercom, "They're here."

The Starwolf ships dropped into normal space, showing their bright little blips like sudden sparks on the radar screen. Distant yet. Too far off to be seen. But zeroing in.

Chane's hands ached to take the controls from Dilullo, but he kept them still. It was useless anyway. The Merc ship was no stronger than the men who built it.

"Coordinates!" said Dilullo, and Bixel's tired voice answered, "Coming."

The computer beside the copilot's chair began to chatter. Gomez read the tapes it fed out. Chane knew what he was going to say and waited till he said it.

"They're globing us."

Yes. Break formation and dart like flying slivers of light all around the exhausted prey. Englobe it, disable it, close and pounce.

"What the devil do they want of us?" roared Bollard's voice from the engine-room.

There was a little silence before Dilullo said, "Maybe just to kill us. It's the nature of the beast."

"I don't think so," Chane said, and he thought, *I know damn well.* "I think they'd have knocked us apart back there on first contact. I think this is a boarding action. Maybe they . . . got wind of something in the nebula. Maybe they think we know."

"Up shields," said Dilullo.

Bollard's voice answered, "Shields up, John. But they can batter them down. There's too many."

"I know." Dilullo turned to Gomez. "Is there any gap in that globe?"

"Nothing they couldn't close long before we got there."

Bixel's voice, high and tight, said, "John, they're coming fast."

Dilullo said quietly, "Does anyone have any suggestions?"

Chane answered, "Take them by surprise."

"The expert again," said Gomez. "Go ahead, John. Take them by surprise."

Dilullo said, "I'm listening, Chane."

"They think we're beat. I don't have to be an expert to know that, either. They're stronger than ordinary people, they count on that, and they count on people feeling helpless and giving up. If you suddenly bulled at them head on, I think you might break out, and you better do it fast before they blow your tail off."

Dilullo considered, his hands poised over the controls. "The shields won't hold for long, you know. We aren't a heavy."

"They won't have to hold long if you go fast enough."

"I may kill some men doing it."

"You're the skipper," Chane said. "You asked, I'm only answering. But they'll die anyway if the Starwolves get hold of you. And maybe not so cleanly."

"Yes," said Dilullo. "I guess you don't have to be an expert to know that, either. Full power, Bollard. And good luck all."

He brought his hands down onto the keys.

Braced against the girder, Chane felt the acceleration slam against him, driving his spine back into the steel. The fabric of the ship moaned around him, quivered, shuddered, swayed. He thought, *She's breaking up!* and tensed himself for the whistle of air through riven plates and a sight of the nebula above his head before he died. Through the viewplate he could see the fiery veils curling past, whipped like sea-mist over their onrushing bow. Something struck them. The ship jarred and rolled. Brush lightning burned blue inside the bridge room and there was a smell of ozone. But the shield held. The ship rushed on, gaining speed. There were brutal sounds of men in agony. Chane watched Dilullo. A second blow struck. Bollard's voice, thick and choking, said, "I don't know, John. Maybe once more."

"Hope for twice," said Dilullo.

Now there was something ahead of them, dark and solid in the glow. A Starwolf cruiser, diving in to block them.

"Their reactions are faster than ours," Dilullo said in a strange half-laughing voice, and drove straight toward it.

Chane was standing now, bent forward, his belly tight and his blood pounding gloriously. He wanted to shout, *Go ahead; do it the Starwolf way! Drive, because they won't believe you have the strength or the guts to do it! Make him step aside; make him give way!*

The next two blows hit them head on. Chane could see them coming, buds of destruction loosed by the Starwolf ship to burst into full bloom against their shield. He could picture the man guiding that ship . . . man, yes, human, yes, but different, shaped by the savage

world of Varna to a sleek-furred magnificence of
strength and speed . . . the face high-boned, flat-
cheeked, smiling, the long slanted eyes, cat-bright with
the excitement of the chase. He would be thinking,
"They're only men, not Varnans. They'll turn back.
They'll turn back."

Somebody was shouting to Dilullo, "Sheer off; you'll
crash him!" Several people were shouting. The small
cruiser seemed to leap toward them, heading straight
for the eyebrow bridge and the viewport. In a couple of
seconds they would have it in their laps. The cries
reached a peak of hysteria and lapsed into hypnotized
silence. Dilullo held course and velocity, so rigidly that
Chane wondered if he was dead at his post. The Starwolf cruiser was so close now that he thought he could
almost make out the shape of the pilot behind the
curved port, and he tasted something in his mouth,
something coppery, and knew that it was fear.

He thought he saw the face of the Starwolf pilot sof-
ten into disbelief, into belated understanding. . . .

In a sudden swerve that would have killed any other
living thing, the cruiser went aside past their starboard
bow. Chane waited for the grinding crunch of a side-
swipe, but there was none.

They were out of the globe, and clear.

The viewport blanked as they passed over into jump
velocity, became again a viewscreen. Dilullo leaned
back in his chair and looked at Chane, his hard face
looking broken in the fireglow, mottled dark in the
hollows and squeezed white over the bones.

"Respite," he said. "They'll come again." His voice
was harsh and reedy, his lungs laboring for breath.

"But you're alive," said Chane. "It's only when
you're dead that there isn't any chance at all." He
stared at Dilullo and shook his head. "I've never seen
anything better done."

"And you never will," Dilullo said, "until I kill you." He half fell out of the chair, looked at Gomez, shook him, then jerked a thumb at the controls. "Take over while I check the damage."

Chane sat down in the pilot's chair. The ship was slow and heavy under his hands, but it was good to feel any kind of a ship again. He sent it plunging deeper into the nebula, threading the denser clouds where it might be a little harder to follow.

Dilullo came back and took the controls again until Gomez could relieve him. One man was dead, and there were four sickbay cases, including General Markolin. No one but Morgan Chane was in good shape.

They dropped back into normal space in the heart of a parsec-long serpent of flame that coiled across a dozen suns.

Bixel, who had had some rest and stopped his nosebleed, sat watching his radar screen. The men slept. Even Dilullo slept, stretched out on a bench in the bridge room. Chane dozed, while time crept by with a kind of dazed sluggishness . . . so much time that Chane began to hope that the hunters had given up.

But it was only a hope, and it vanished when Bixel pushed the alarm button and cried out over the intercom, "Here they come again."

Well, thought Chane, *it was a good try, anyway. A damned good try.*

XIV

The bright relentless little sparks flew swiftly across the radar screen. Dilullo looked at them, a cold dull sickness at the pit of his stomach. Damn them. Damn Morgan Chane and his own smartness in keeping him alive. If he hadn't kept him . . .

He would be in just as much trouble, Dilullo told himself. The wolfpack was never known to let any promising prey slip through its jaws, and a Merc ship could be carrying anything . . . like, say, a fortune in lightstones for the payroll.

And yet . . .

He looked at Chane through the doorway, sitting quiet in the bridge room, and considered what would happen if he dropped him out of a hatchway, suited and attached to a signal flare.

He looked at the spark again, racing towards him, and he was suddenly angry. He was so angry he shook with it, and the cold sickness in him was burned away. Damn these arrogant whelps of Starwolves. He wasn't going to give up anything. Not because he knew it wouldn't stop them anyway, but because he wasn't going to be pushed and knocked around like a little boy unable to defend himself against the big boys. It was too humiliating.

He strode back to the pilot's chair and strapped in, his body protesting in every fiber as he did so. He told it to shut up.

Gomez protested, and he told him to shut up, too.

"But, John, the men can't take any more. Neither can the ship."

"Okay," said Dilullo. "Then let's see to it that there's not one shred of bone or meat left for those wolves to snap their teeth on." He shouted over the intercom to Bollard: "Full power and never mind the shields."

He could see the ships now. Over his shoulder he said to Chane, "Come on up here, where you can get a good view."

Chane stood behind him, against the girder. "What are you going to do?"

"I'm going to make them destroy us," Dilullo said, and pressed the keys.

The Merc ship leaped forward, toward the oncoming squadron.

Bixel's voice blasted over the intercom. "John, I've got another one, a heavy. A heavy! Coming up on our tail!"

It was a moment before that registered. Dilullo was committed now to angry death, his whole attention fixed on the Starwolf ships. He heard Bixel all right, and he heard others shouting at him, but they were somewhere beyond a wall.

Then Morgan Chane's fingers closed on his shoulder in a grip so painful that he couldn't ignore it, and Chane was saying, "Heavy cruiser! It must be Vhollan . . . the guard force Thrandirin talked about. They must have been looking out for us . . . picked us up when we came within range of their probes."

Dilullo's mind broke out of frozen rage and began to work at full speed. "Get a fix!" he snapped to Bixel. "Estimated course and velocity." He looked at the Starwolf ships again, this time with a kind of fiendish pleasure. "Shields up, Bollard! Shields up! We're going to give our Starwolf friends something big to play with. Gomez . . . hit that aft monitor screen."

He could see the formation of little Starwolf ships ahead of him very clearly. It was shaping into a flying U, the wings stretching out almost fondly to enfold him.

Below the viewport a screen flickered to life bringing him a picture of what was behind him. A big starcruiser loomed out of the nebula drift, closing fast. He wondered what the skipper was thinking as he saw and recognized the Starwolf squadron. He thought it must be something of a shock to him, having come after one small Merc ship only to find that the Vhollans' private preserves had been invaded by a much more numerous and deadly enemy.

It must be something of a shock to the Starwolves, too . . . seeing a heavy cruiser where they had expected only an exhausted prey.

The ship-to-ship band sprang to life. A man's voice shouted in sputtering galacto, "Mercs! This is the Vhollàn cruiser. Cut power immediately or we'll disable you."

Dilullo opened his transmitter and said, "Dilullo talking. What about the Starwolves?"

"We'll take care of them."

"That's nice," Dilullo said. "Thanks. But may I remind you that I have Thrandirin and two generals aboard. I wouldn't want to take any chances with their safety."

"Neither would I," said the Vhollan voice grimly, "but my orders are to stop you first and worry about your hostages second. Is that clear?"

"Perfectly," said Dilullo, and notched his power up two steps. The ship jumped forward and he began to yaw it back and forth so that it ran toward the Starwolves the way a fox runs, never giving a clean target for a shot. It was hard on the ship, hard on the men, but not nearly so hard as the licking force-beam of the cruiser that missed them because of it.

The Starwolf formation was breaking up and scattering, so as not to provide a bunched-up target for the cruiser. It was almost in the nature of an after-thought that they fired at the Merc ship. It bucked and rolled twice as the missiles impacted on its screen, and then it was through the squadron, going away and going fast, and the monitor screen showed behind him the big Vhollan cruiser and the Starwolf ships locked in battle, the swift wicked little ships darting and snapping at the huge heavy like dogs around a bear.

Dilullo glanced up and saw Chane's black eyes fixed upon the monitor, his expression both relieved and re-gretful.

Dilullo said, "I'm sorry we can't stay around to see who wins."

The battle faded, left behind in the glowing mists, and then even the mists were left behind as the Merc ship climbed into overdrive.

Chane said, with a ring of pride he could not quite conceal, "They'll keep that heavy busy, all right. It has the weight, but they have the speed. They won't try to crush it . . . but if nobody else interrupts, they'll just sting it to death."

"I hope they all have fun," said Dilullo edgedly, and spoke into the intercom. "Bixel, did you get an ECV?"

"I'm feeding it into the computer now. I'll have the backtrack in a minute."

They waited. Dilullo saw that Chane was studying him with a new expression . . . what would you call it? Respect? Admiration?

"You were really going to do it," Chane said. "Make them destroy us so they couldn't get anything."

"These Starwolves," said Dilullo, "are too sure of themselves. Somebody, someday, is going to stand up and surprise the life out of them."

Chane said, "I wouldn't have believed that once, but now I'm not so sure."

"Here it is," said Gomez, the computer tape chatter-ing out under his hand.

Gomez studied the tape and set up a pattern on the sky-board. "Extrapolating from estimated course and velocity, the cruiser probably came from this area." He punched the identifying coordinates and a microchart slid over the magnification lens and filled the area bounded by the pattern. Dilullo leaned over to study it.

The area was part of the coiled fire-snake, that part that might be likened to the head. At about the place where a parsecs-long fire-snake might have an eye, there was a star. A green star, with five planetary bodies, only one of which was large enough to be rightfully called a planet.

Dilullo became aware of somebody looking over his shoulder. It was Bollard, his round face still placid in spite of some ugly blotches that might be bruises or burst veins.

"Everything okay in engineering?" Dilullo asked.

"All okay. Though we don't deserve it."

"Then I suppose we'd better have a look at that."

Bollard frowned at the green star, the baleful eye of the fire-snake.

"Might or might not be the place, John."

"We'll never know till we look, will we?"

"I won't even answer that. Do you think you can sneak in behind that cruiser while it's busy with our Starwolf friends?"

"I can try."

"Sure you can try. But don't get too biggity just because you bulled down a Starwolf. One cruiser found us, but if one cruiser was all they had on guard they'd never have sent it away to look. There must be another one waiting planetside, watching to see if we slip by. And they'll know by now that we have."

"Thanks, Bollard," said Dilullo. "Now go back down and encourage your drive-units."

He set the course for the green sun.

They dropped back into normal space dangerously near to a band of drift between the two little outer worlds of the system of the green star, and they hid there, pretending to be an asteroid circling lazily with all the others in the misty, curdled light, the thick nebula gases glowing icy green here instead of the warm gold around the yellow stars. It made Dilullo feel cold and oddly claustrophobic. He found himself gasping for breath and wondered what was the matter with him, and then he remembered how once when he was a child he had lain drowning at the bottom of a pool of still green water.

He shook the nightmare away, reminding himself that his father had come in time to save him, but that Daddy wasn't here now and it was up to him.

He went into the navigation room to check with Bixel. There was a lot of clutter on the long-range probe scanner screen. It took a while to sort things out, but there was no doubt about the result.

"Another heavy cruiser," Bixel said. "On station by the planet, flying an intercept patrol pattern. We haven't got a chance of getting past him."

"Well," said Dilullo, "at least we know we're in the right place."

He went back into the bridge room, shoving past Bollard in the doorway. Bollard said, "What now?"

"Give me five minutes to think up a brilliant plan," Dilullo said.

Chane beckoned to him. He was standing beside Rutledge at the radio control center. Rutledge had opened the ship-to-ship channel, and Dilullo could hear voices crackling back and forth in Vhollan.

"That's the two cruisers—the one fighting the Starwolves and the one at the planet ahead," Chane said. "They're doing an awful lot of talking." He smiled, and again there was that touch of pride only half hidden. "They sound pretty upset."

"They have a right to be," said Dilullo. "Not only us invading their privacy, but a flock of Starwolves. Go get Thrandirin up here. He can translate."

Chane went out. Dilullo listened to the voices. They did sound upset, and increasingly so. Because he had made the relatively short jump in overdrive, the actual lapse of time since they left the battle was not great, and it sounded as though it was still going on . . . the two cruiser captains were shouting back and forth at each other now, and Dilullo grinned.

"Sounds like one of 'em is yelling for help and the other one is telling him he can't come."

He fell silent as Chane came in with Thrandirin. He watched the Vhollan's face, saw his expression change as he heard the heated voices on the radio.

"The Starwolves are giving your cruiser a hard time, aren't they?" he asked.

Thrandirin nodded.

"Will the one at the planet go to help him?"

"No. The orders are quite clear. One cruiser is to remain on station at all times, regardless of what happens."

The voices on the radio stopped yelling and one of them said something in a cold, hard matter-of-fact tone. After that there was a silence. Dilullo watched Thrandirin's face, not unaware of Chane standing behind the Vhollan with a half-smile on his mouth and his ears pricked forward.

The second voice answered in what sounded like a brief affirmative. He could almost see the face of the man making it, a man heavily burdened with decision. And Thrandirin said angrily, "No!"

"What did they say?" asked Dilullo.

Thrandirin shook his head. Dilullo said, "Well, if you won't tell us we'll wait and see."

They waited. There was no more talk from the radio. The bridge room was quite silent. Everybody stood or sat like statues, not sure what it was they waited for. Then Bixel's voice came sharply over the intercom.

"John! The one at the planet is breaking out of pattern."

"Is he coming this way?"

"No. Heading off at an angle of fourteen degrees, with twice that much azimuth. Going fast." And then Bixel cried, "He's jumped into overdrive. I've lost him."

"Now," Dilullo said to Thrandirin. "What did they say?"

Thrandirin looked at him with weary hatred. "He has gone to help the other cruiser against the Starwolves. He had to make a choice . . . and he decided that they were a far greater threat than you."

"Not very complimentary to us," said Dilullo. "But I won't quarrel, since it leaves the planet clear."

"Yes, it does," said Thrandirin. "Go ahead and land. There's no one to stop you now. And when our cruisers have finished with the Starwolves, they'll come back and catch you on the ground and stamp you flat."

Bollard said, "For once I agree with him, John."

"Yes," said Dilullo, "so do I. You want to turn back now?"

"What?" said Bollard. "And waste all the trouble that we've been through?"

He hurried off to his drive-units. Chane, full of private laughter, took Thrandirin away.

Dilullo took the Merc ship out of the drift and full speed in toward the planet.

XV

It would have been easier, Dilullo thought, if they knew what they were looking for. But they didn't, and they didn't even know how long they had to look for it, except that it might not be long enough. Dilullo had found a chance to speak to Chane alone.

"What's your guess? You know them; you've been in actions like that before. How will it go?"

Chane had said, "The Starwolves are fearless, but not brainless. One heavy cruiser they would gamble with, and as you heard, they had it in so much trouble its captain was screaming for help. But two heavy cruisers . . . no. Even without the losses they must have had, that's too much weight for them. They'll pull out."

"Out of the fight? Or out entirely?"

Chane shrugged. "If Ssander were still calling the turns, it would be entirely. The squadron's been away from Varna for a long time, much longer than it planned to be. It's run into trouble it wasn't expecting and can't handle . . . two heavies. Ssander would have balanced the knife . . . the killing end against the head . . . and reckoned that it was wiser to live and let vengeance wait until tomorrow. I think they'll go." He smiled. "And when they do, those two cruisers will be back here in a hurry to clean up their less important problem."

"Don't forget that you're part of that problem," Dilullo reminded him.

Now the Merc ship scudded low across the curve of the planet . . . lower than Dilullo liked. But the atmosphere was oddly thick, muffling the little world in an almost impenetrable curtain. After he got down through it far enough he understood what made it that way. The world seemed to consist of one vast dust storm, whipped and driven by tremendous winds. Where he could see it, the surface was all rolling dunes and rock. In some places the dunes had flowed over the ridges and the stiff reaching pinnacles; in others the rocks were high and strong enough to hold back the dunes, and in the lees of these grotesquely eroded walls were long smooth plains, showing a darker color than the piled dunes. Dilullo was not exactly sure what that color was. The sand, or dust, might have been anything from light tan to red, back on Earth, but under the green sun the colors were distorted and strange, as though a child had been perversely puddling them together to see what ugly muddiness he could invent.

"Not exactly a place you'd pick for looks," said Dilullo.

Gomez uttered something uncomplimentary in Spanish, and Chane, who was haunting the bridge room again and peering over their shoulders, laughed and said, "If someone wanted to hide something where nobody would be likely to look for it, this would be the place."

Bollard's voice came over the intercom from engineering. "See anything yet?" When Dilullo told him no, he said, "We'd better get lucky pretty soon, John. Those cruisers will be back."

"I'm praying," Dilullo said. "That's the best I can do right now."

They swept over the night side, peering for lights; seeing none, they headed into a dawn that flushed chartreuse and copper sulphate instead of rose. Beyond the dawn, where the sun was high, a range of black peaks rose out of the dunes, their buttressed shoulders fighting back the waves of sand. On the other side of the range—the lee side protected from the prevailing wind, on a fan-shaped plain as smooth as a girl's cheek—was the thing they were looking for.

At the moment he saw it Dilullo knew it could not have been anything else; that, in fact, subconsciously, he had known what it would be, ever since Chane came back from the Vhollan warehouse with the pictures and the analyzer disc that registered nothing.

It was a ship. His brain told him it couldn't be a ship, it was too colossal, but his eyes saw it and it was.

A ship like nothing he had ever seen before or even dreamed of. A ship so huge it could never have been launched from any planet; it must have been built in space, taking shape in some nameless void under the hands and eyes of Lord knew what creators, a floating world alone and free, without binding sun or sister planets. A world, long and dark and self-enclosed, and not designed to stay forever in one fixed orbit, but intended to voyage freely in the vastness of all creation. This far it had voyaged. And here it lay, beached at last on this wretched world, its massive frame broken, lost, dead and lonely, half buried in the alien sand.

Chane said softly, "So that's what they were hiding."

"Where did it come from?" Gomez said. "Not from any world I know."

"A ship that size was never built just to run between the worlds we know," said Dilullo. "There isn't any technology in our galaxy that could have built it. It came from outside somewhere. Andromeda, perhaps . . . or even further."

"I don't think that that thing was ever supposed to land on any planet . . . and if that is so, the pull of gravity would be enough stress to break it," Chane said.

"Look!" interrupted Dilullo. "They've sighted us."

There was a small huddle of metal-and-plastic domes at the foot of the cliffs. Men started running out of

them as the Merc ship came down lower. Other men
appeared out of the broken side of the monster ship,
ants crawling from the carcass of a giant that had over-
leaped the dark gulf between the island universes and
had killed itself in the leaping.

Dilullo spoke sharply over the intercom to the whole
company. "We move as soon as we land. I think these
men are specialists, civilians, but some of them may put
up a fight, and there may be a guard force. Use stunners and don't kill unless you have to. Bollard . . ."

"Yes, John!"

"Man the assault chamber and cover us. After we
have secured the position, we'll establish a defense
perimeter around both ships as fast as we can. I'm
going to land as close as I can to the big one. The
cruisers won't be able to clobber us with their heavy
weapons without damaging the big one, and I don't
think they want to do that. Pick what men you need,
Bollard. Okay, we're going in."

Then the Merc ship was down on the green-umber
plain, with the massive ragged flank of the alien craft
looming up beside them like a mountain range of metal. Dilullo cracked the lock and went out through it at
the head of the Mercs, with Chane running easily at his
shoulder like a good dog. The Vhollan specialists,
much alarmed, were running about and doing a lot of
shouting but not much else. They were not going to be
a problem, Dilullo thought, and then he saw the other
men.

There were about twenty of them, white-haired
Vhollans in uniform tunics, looking ghastly in the green
glow. They seemed to have come out of the great ship.
Perhaps they lived in it, guarding it even from their own
people so that no unsupervised act could occur, no un-
authorized fragment of material be removed unseen.
These men had lasers, and they moved with a nasty
professional precision, heading straight for the Mercs.

Bollard let go with a round of gas shells from the

ship. The Merc ships did not carry much heavy arma-
ment, since they were primarily transports designed to
get the men to where the action was. But they did often
have to land or take off in areas of intense hostility, and
so they carried some weaponry, chiefly defensive. The
non-lethal gas shells were very effective at breaking up
offensive group action.

The Vhollan soldiers coughed and reeled around
with their hands over their eyes. Most of them dropped
their lasers on the first round because they could not
see to shoot and were therefore likely only to kill each
other. The second round took care of the laggards.
Mercs with breathing masks completed the disarming
and rounding up. Others had the civilians in hand and
were looking into the domes for a place to put them.

"Well," said Chane, "that was easy enough."

Dilullo grunted.

"You don't look very happy about it."

"In this business things don't come easy," Dilullo
said. "If they do you generally wind up paying for it
later on." He looked up at the sky. "I'd give a lot to
know how soon those cruisers will be back."

Chane did not answer that, and neither did the sky.
Dilullo got busy with Bollard, driving the Mercs to set
up the defense perimeter, hauling out every weapon
they had, including the samples, and setting men with
power tools to make emplacements for them, blasting
pits in the sand. Other men brought out the siege-
fences of lightweight hard-alloy sections that had been
useful to the Mercs on many hostile worlds, and set
them up. They worked fast, sweating, and all the time
Dilullo kept watching the sky.

It was an ugly sky, murky and dull. The sun looked
like a drowned man's face . . . there was that drowning
symbol again . . . glowing with sickly phosphorescence
through the dust and the nebula gas. It stayed empty.
The wind blew. They were screened from the full force

of it here by the cliff wall, but it made screaming noises overhead, ripping past the pinnacles of dark rock with furious determination. A fine spray of sand drifted down, into the eyes and ears and mouth, down the collar, sticking and grating on the sweaty skin.

Dilullo was versed in strange worlds, in the taste and feel of the air, the sensation of the ground under his feet. This one was cold and gritty, sharp-edged, unwelcoming, and, though the air was breathable, it had a bitter smell. Dilullo did not like this world. It had turned away from the task of spawning life, preferring to spend its eons in selfish barrenness.

Nothing had ever lived here. But something, someone, for some reason, had come here to die.

Bollard reported to him at last that the perimeter was established and fully manned. Dilullo turned and looked up at the mountainous riven hulk looming above them. Even in the heat of preparation he had been conscious of it, not only as a physical thing but as a spiritual one, an alienness, a mystery, a coldness at the heart and a deep excitement hot and flaring in the nerves.

"Is Bixel manning the radar?"

"Yes. So far, nothing."

"Keep in close touch and don't let him get sleepy. Chane . . ."

"Yes?"

"Find out which one of those specialists is in charge of the project and bring him to me."

"Where'll you be?"

Dilullo took a deep breath and said, "In there."

The Vhollans had jury-rigged a hatchway in one of the broken places in the great ship's side. Other rents in the metal fabric had been covered with sheets of tough plastic to keep out the wind and the sifting dust.

Dilullo climbed the gritty steps to the hatchway and went through it, into another world.

XVI

Chane walked under the loom of the great ship, toward the dome where the Vhollans were being held. He was not thinking of either one at the moment. He was thinking of two heavy cruisers and a squadron of Starwolves, somewhere out beyond that curdled sky . . . wondering how the battle went, and who had died.

He did not like this feeling of being all torn up inside. He hated the Starwolves, he wanted them dead, he knew they would kill him without mercy, and yet . . .

Those hours on the Merc ship had been some of the hardest of his life. It was all wrong to have to fight your own kind and cheer on the man that was beating them because you told him how. Chane could never remember a time when things had not been simple and uncomplicated for him; he was a Starwolf, he was proud and strong, full member of a brotherhood, and the galaxy was a glorious place full of plunder and excitement, all theirs to do with as they wished.

Now, because his brothers had turned against him, he was forced to herd with the sheep, and that was bad enough, but the worst of it was he was beginning to like one of them. Dilullo was only human but he did have guts. No Starwolf could have done better. It hurt Chane to say it, even to himself, but it was true.

Damn. And what were they doing out there, those swift little ships biting and tearing at the cruiser? They had it in bad trouble, that was certain, or the second cruiser would never have gone. Chane smiled with unregenerate pride. The Vhollans had handed this world to the Mercs on a silver platter, rather than run the risk of the Starwolves breaking through.

One heavy cruiser the Starwolves could handle. But not two. *I should be out there,* he thought, *helping you, instead of being glad the cruiser held you and hoping the second one will blast you to atoms.*

As they would probably blast him and Dilullo and the rest of the Mercs when they came back.

Well, that would take care of his problems, anyway. He despised all this prying about inside himself, trying to sort out emotions he had never been forced to feel before. So the devil with it.

The dome was before him and he went in. The Vhollans were penned together in what seemed to be a lounge or common room, under the watchful eyes and ready stun-guns of four of the Mercs, headed by Sekkinen. It took a few minutes to cut through the half-hysterical gabble after Chane explained to Sekkinen what Dilullo wanted, and began questioning the civilians in galacto. Eventually they came out with a lean, studious-looking Vhollan in a rumpled blue tunic who stared at the Mercs with a superciliousness mixed with the fright of the scholar confronted suddenly by large and violent men. He admitted that his name was Labdibdin, and that he was chief of the research project.

"But," he added, "I wish to make clear that I will not cooperate with you in any way whatever."

Chane shrugged. "You can talk to Dilullo about that."

"Don't lose him," said Sekkinen.

"I won't lose him." Chane took Labdibdin's arm, and he put his strength into the grip so that the Vhollan winced in pain and then looked at Chane, startled by such strength in a human grasp. Chane smiled at him and said, "We won't have any trouble. Come along with me."

The Vhollan came. He walked stiffly ahead of Chane, out of the dome and back over the cold sand, under the tremendous sagging belly of the ship. The thing must be a mile long, Chane thought, and a quarter that high . . . it was quite obvious now that it had never been intended to land.

He began to be excited, wondering about the ship, where it had come from, and why, and what was in it. The keen Starwolf nose scented loot.

Then he remembered that Dilullo was running this show, and his ardor cooled, for Dilullo had all those odd ideas about ethics and property.

He pushed the Vhollan with unnecessary force up the steps and through the hatchway.

A gangway bridged a twenty-foot gap of empty darkness that went down deep below the level of the sand, into the bowels of the ship. At the end of the gangway was a transverse corridor running fore and aft, as far as Chane could see in both directions. Worklights had been rigged by the Vhollan technicians. They shed a cold and meager glare, unfitting to the place, like matches in the belly of Jonah's whale. They showed the sheathing plates of the corridor to be the same pale-gold metal he had seen in the warehouse back on Vhol. It must have had great tensile strength, because it was relatively undamaged, buckled here and there but not broken. The whole corridor tilted slightly, the floor running unevenly uphill and down. Even so, the floor-plates were not shattered.

The inward wall was pierced by doorways set at intervals of fifty feet or so. Chane went through the nearest one.

And found himself perched like a bird in the high midst of what looked like a cosmic museum.

He had no way of estimating the space it occupied. It

went high overhead and far below, deep down beyond the level of the sand outside, and on either hand it stretched away into dimness, lit here and there by the inadequate worklights.

He stood on a narrow gallery. Above and below there were further galleries, and from them sprang a webwork of walks that spanned the vast area spider-fashion, all interconnected vertically by a system of caged lifts. The lifts and the walks were designed to give access to all levels of the enormous stacks that filled the place, marching in orderly rows almost like the buildings of some fantastic city. The pale-gold metal from which they and the walkways had been constructed had again proved its toughness; the original perfect symmetry had gone with the inevitable buckling and twisting, walks were skewed and stacks leaned out of true, and probably there was damage he couldn't see, farther down, but on the whole it had survived.

And there was enough rich plunder here to keep four generations of Starwolves happy.

Chane said to Labdibdin, in a voice hushed with awe, "These must have been the greatest looters in the universe."

Labdibdin looked at him with utter scorn. "Not looters. Scientists. Collectors of knowledge."

"Oh," said Chane. "I see. It all depends on who does it."

He moved forward along the canted walk, clinging to the rail and urging Labdibdin ahead of him. The transparent windows of the nearest stack showed only an imperfect view of what was inside. The tough plastic had cracked and starred in places. But there was a way in from the walk. He scrambled through it and stood in a large room crammed with cushioned cases.

Cases of stones: Diamonds, emeralds, rubies, precious and semi-precious stones from all over the galaxy. And mixed with them were other stones, chunks of granite and basalt and sandstone and marble and many more he couldn't name. All stones. All together.

Cases of artifacts: Curved blades of silversteel from the Hercules markets, with fine-wrought hilts, and crude axes from some backward world; needles and pins and pots and buckets and chased gold helmets with jeweled crests, belt-buckles and rings, hammers and saws . . . bewilderment.

"This is only a tiny sample," said Labdibdin. "Apparently they meant to classify later on, when they would have plenty of time . . . probably on the homeward voyage."

"Homeward where?" asked Chane.

With a look of strange uneasiness, Labdibdin said, "We're not sure."

Chane reached out and touched one of the cases that held the jewels. The plastic cover was cold under his fingers but he could feel the heat of the red and green and many-colored stones like a physical burning.

Labdibdin permitted himself a bitter smile.

"The cases were power-operated. You passed a hand, so, over this small lens, and the lid opened. There is no power now. You'd have to blow it open."

"Impractical, right now," said Chane, and sighed. "We might as well find Dilullo."

They found him without trouble, a little farther along, looking at a collection of boxes of dirt. Just plain dirt, as far as Chane could see.

"Soil samples," said Labdibdin. "There are many such, and collections of plants, and samples of water, and minerals, and gases . . . atmospheres, we suppose, from all the worlds they touched. Endless artifacts of all sorts. . . ."

"What about weapons?" Dilullo asked.

"There were some weapons among the artifacts they collected, but the sophisticated ones were permanently disarmed. . . ."

Dilullo said, "Don't play vague with me. I don't care what they collected. I'm only interested in their own weapons, the weapons of this ship."

Labdibdin set his jaw and answered, biting his words off one at a time as though he hated them: "We have not found any weapons in this ship, except the useless articles in the specimen cases."

"I can't blame you for lying," said Dilullo. "You wouldn't want to give us a weapon to use against your own people. But half the Cluster is talking about what you have here . . . the super-weapon that's going to conquer Kharal. . . ."

A faint pinkness crept into Labdibdin's cheeks, the nearest thing to a flush that Chane had seen in these marble-skinned people. His fists clenched and he pounded them up and down on the railing in a kind of desperation.

"Weapons," he said. "Weapons." His voice choked. "My own people keep pushing and pushing and pushing, wanting me to find weapons for them, and there aren't any! There is not a sign of a weapon in this ship. There is no record of a weapon of any kind. *The Krii did not use weapons!* I keep telling them that and they will not believe . . ."

"The Krii?"

"The . . . people who built this ship." He shook his hand in a wild gesture intended to take in all the collection stacks. "In all these, in *all* of them, there is not one single specimen of a living thing, not a bird, not an animal, not a fish nor an insect. They didn't take life. I'll show you something."

He went away from them, half running. Dilullo looked at Chane. They both shrugged, puzzled by the man's violence, not at all believing what he said.

"Keep a close eye on him," Dilullo muttered, and they ran after the Vhollan, Dilullo a bit slowly on the canted metal walk—it was a long way down—Chane skipping lightly on Labdibdin's heels.

He led them to a service lift, rigged by the Vhollans
and run by a portable generator. They got into it and it
dropped them rattling down and down, past level after
level of the stacks with the bits and pieces of a galaxy
hoarded in them. Then it stopped and Labdibdin led
them forward into a great oblong chamber that had
obviously been a coordinating center for the ship and
was now serving the same purpose for the Vhollan
technicians.

Some of the original furniture was still there, though
the Vhollans had moved in a few sketchy conveniences.
It gave Chane a start when he looked at it. The height
of a table made him feel like a child in grown-up land,
but the contoured chairs that went with it were too
narrow to accommodate even his lean bottom. No
wonder the Vhollans had brought their own.

He saw the smooth-worn places on the chairs and
table, the many subtle marks of use. Here someone or
something had sat and worked, manipulating a built-in
mechanism of some sort with banks of keys that were
not intended for human fingers, had worn the keys
smooth and bright, and worn a deep hollow in the
unidentifiable padding of the chair.

"How long?" asked Chane. "I mean, how long
would they have been on the ship?"

"That's a silly question," Labdibdin answered tartly.
"How long is long? By their reckoning or ours? Years
or decades, or perhaps only months. And I wish I
knew. I wish I knew! Look here."

He stood in front of a pedestal, quite high, made
from the pale-gold metal. It had a console in front with
an intricate arrangement of keys. "It has its own
power-unit, independent of the ship," he said, and
stretched his hand out to it.

Chane laid his own hand on the back of Labdibdin's
neck and said softly, "I can snap it between my fingers.
So be careful."

"Oh, don't be a fool," snarled Labdibdin.

"Weapons, weapons! You're the same as they are at Vhol; it's all you think of."

A shimmering appeared in the air above the pedestal. Labdibdin turned to Dilullo and demanded, "Will you allow me to proceed?"

Dilullo was watching everything, the Vhollan, the room, Chane, the array of unfamiliar and unguessable articles ranged here and there for study. He seemed to be watching outside the ship as well, picturing the ugly green sky in his mind and wondering when the cruisers would appear in it. He seemed to be listening for something, beyond the great engulfing silence of the ship.

He nodded to Chane, who stepped back. Labdibdin, muttering, picked up a pair of very odd gloves with long slender rods curving out from some of the fingers. He pulled them on and began pecking delicately at the console keys.

A three-dimensional image took shape in the shimmer on top of the pedestal. Chane stared at it and asked, "What is the thing?"

"You're an Earthman and you don't know?" Labdibdin said. "It's keyed from there."

Dilullo said, "It's a species of bird on Earth. But what's the purpose of this demonstration?"

Labdibdin snarled, "To prove what I was saying. The Krii did not take life, not of anything. They collected images only."

He pecked with the rods at the console. In quick succession images appeared and vanished . . . insects, fish, worms, spiders. Labdibdin shut the instrument off and turned, flinging his gloves away. He looked at Chane and Dilullo, a haggard, harried man beneath his scholarly arrogance.

"I wish to heaven somebody would believe me. There seems to have been some kind of a defensive system, a powerful screen that they could use to protect the ship. We couldn't get it to work."

Dilullo shook his head. "It wouldn't work here, even if you had the power for it. A screen works in space but not when a ship has landed . . . the force is instantly grounded and dissipated."

Labdibdin said, "That's what our technicians said. But anyway, one thing is sure . . . the Krii did not use offensive weapons!"

Chane shook his head. "That just isn't possible."

"I'm beginning to believe him," said Dilullo. "The Krii, you called them? You've deciphered their records, obviously."

"Some of them," Labdibdin admitted. "I have the best philologists on Vhol here, working themselves into breakdowns. I tell you, they've pushed us and pushed us until we're all ready to drop, insisting that we come up with what they want, something to knock a world apart with. They don't seem to care half as much about the ship itself . . . or the real knowledge we might gain from it." He ran his hand lovingly over the table edge. "Stuff from another galaxy, another universe. A different atomic table . . . totally alien life-forms . . . what we could learn! But we have to waste time with all research oriented toward finding the weapons that don't exist. We're going to lose so much. . . ."

"Another galaxy," said Dilullo. "Different atomic table . . . I made a pretty good guess. How much do you know about these . . . Krii?"

"They were devoted to learning. Apparently they had embarked on a project to study all of creation . . . one guesses at other ships in yet other galaxies, performing the same task of collecting samples. Their technological level must be unbelievably high."

"Still, they crashed."

"Not quite. A crash landing, rather . . . and of course this ship was never meant to land. Something happened. The relevant parts of the ship are pretty well demolished, and the records relating to the crash naturally very brief and sketchy, but it seems obvious there was an explosion in one of their power-cells, which damaged their life-support system so extensively they could not hope to make the voyage home. Of course nothing in this galaxy would do them any good in the way of substitute or repair. They seem to have chosen this world deliberately, because it is isolated and uninhabited, well hidden in the nebula . . . and it was only by the merest accident that a Vhollan prospector looking for rare metals happened to find it."

"Suitable place for a graveyard," said Dilullo. "Did you find any bodies of the Krii in the wreck?"

"Oh, yes," said Labdibdin. "Yes, indeed, we found a number of them." He looked at Dilullo with haunted eyes and added, "The only thing is . . . they don't seem to be dead."

XVII

They were deep in the very heart of the ship, walking down a long corridor with their footsteps ringing hollow from the metal vault, echoing away behind them to be lost in silence. The lights were sparse here, with long dim intervals between.

"We don't come here very often," said Labdibdin. He spoke very softly, as though he were anxious not to be heard by anyone or anything but the two Earthmen. From his first bristling hostility, the Vhollan had softened to an astonishing degree.

He's a driven man, Dilullo thought. *It's a relief to him to talk to anyone, even us . . . to break that stifling bond of secrecy. He's been imprisoned here for too long a time, practically entombed in this ship with . . . with whatever I am about to see, which is enough to make his shoulders droop and his knees give way a little with every step. He's ready to crack, and small wonder.*

The footsteps sounded indecently loud in Dilullo's ears, and somehow dangerous. He was acutely conscious of the silence around him, the vast dark bulk of the ship that enclosed him. He saw his own smallness: an insect creeping in the bowels of an alien mountain. What was worse, he felt like an intruding insect, impertinently making free with someone, or something, else's property.

Dilullo wondered what Chane was thinking. He didn't give much away. Those bright black eyes seemed always to be the same, alert to every sensation, interested in everything, but never introspective. Perhaps that was a better way to go through life, just taking everything as it came, day to day, minute to minute, never worrying and never trying to get beneath the simple outward surface of things. It was when you got to thinking that things became complicated.

Or was Chane really as matter-of-fact as he always seemed? Dilullo suddenly doubted it.

Labdibdin held up his hand. "We're almost there," he whispered. "Please go carefully."

The smooth floor and sheathing of the corridor became a series of overlapping collars. "To take up the shock," Labdibdin said, making a telescoping motion with his hands. "The chamber is mounted in a web of flexible supports, so that almost nothing short of complete annihilation of the ship could harm it."

Dilullo went carefully, lifting his feet high so as not to stumble.

There was a doorway, open, and more of the dim Vhollan lights beyond. The doorway was exceedingly tall and narrow. Dilullo stepped through it, his shoulders rubbing on both sides.

He had some idea of what he was going to see. And yet he was not prepared at all for what he saw.

Beside him Chane uttered a Varnan oath, and his hand strayed automatically to his stunner.

If he were truly a wolf, Dilullo thought, he would be snarling with his ears flat and his hackles up and his tail tucked under his belly. And I feel like that right now, myself . . . or perhaps, more accurately, I feel like a shivering ape-ling huddled in the night while Fear stalks past.

Because these things were Fear. Not rational fear, which is a survival mechanism. No. This was the blind and mindless fear that cringes in the flesh, the xenophobic shrinking of the protoplasm from what is utterly alien and strange.

He could see why the Vhollans did not come here often to visit the Krii.

There were perhaps a hundred of them. They sat in orderly rows, each one upright in a high and narrow chair, in something of the attitude of the old Pharaohs: the nether limbs close together, the upper ones, with the long delicate appendages that served them for fingers, resting on the arms of the chairs. They wore only a simple drapery, and their bodies had the appearance of dark amber, not only in color but in substance, and in form they might have been either animal or vegetable, or a combination of the two, or a third something that defied analysis in the terms of this galaxy. They were very tall, very slender, and they seemed to have neither joints nor muscles but to flow all together like the ribboned weed that sways in tidewater pools.

Their faces consisted mostly of two big opalescent eyes set in a tall narrow head. There were breathing slits at the sides of the head, and a small puckered mouth that seemed pursed in eternal contemplation.

The eyes were wide open and they seemed to stare, all one hundred pairs of them, straight into Dilullo's heart.

He turned to Labdibdin, to get away from that staring, and he said, "What makes you think they're not dead? They look petrified."

But in his bones he knew that Labdibdin was right.

"Because," answered Labdibdin, "one of the records we deciphered was a message sent by them *after* they crash-landed here. It gave the coordinates of this system, and it said"—he ran his tongue nervously over his lips, looking sidelong at the rows of eyes—"it said they would wait."

"You mean they . . . sent for help?"

"It would seem so."

"And they said they'd wait?" asked Chane. "Looks to me as though help never came and they waited too long." He had gotten over his first shock and decided the things were harmless. He went to examine one more closely. "Didn't you ever dissect one, or do any tests, to make sure?"

"Try touching it," Labdibdin said. "Go ahead. Try."

Chane put his hand out tentatively. It stopped in midair some eighteen inches from the body of the Krii, and Chane caught it away, shaking it. "Cold!" he said. "No, not really cold . . . icy and tingling. What is it?"

"Stasis," Labdibdin said. "Each chair is a self-contained unit with its own power supply. Each occupant is enclosed in a force-field that freezes it in space and time . . . a little warp-bubble wrapped around it like a cocoon, impenetrable. . . ."

"Isn't there any way to shut it off?"

"No. The mechanism is self-encapsulating. This was a survival system, very carefully constructed and thought out. In a stasis field they require no air, and no sustenance, because time is slowed to a stop and their metabolic processes along with it. They can wait forever if they have to, and be safe. Nothing can get at them, or harm them in any way. Not that we wanted to harm them." Labdibdin looked at the Krii, hungering. "To talk to them, to study them, to know how they think and function. I've been hoping . . ."

He stopped, and Dilullo asked him, "Hoping what?"

"Our best mathematicians and astronomers have been trying to work out some kind of a time-factor. That is, to translate *their* time of transmission of the call for help and *their* estimate of how long it would take the rescue ship to reach them. It isn't at all easy, and our people have come up with four possible dates for the arrival of the rescue ship. One of them is . . . approximately now."

Dilullo shook his head. "This is all going a little too fast for me. I have an intergalactic ship, then I have its whole crew sitting here staring at me, and now I have another intergalactic ship on the way. And it might be coming, like now?"

"We don't *know*," said Labdibdin despairingly. "It's only one of four estimates, and a 'now' might mean yesterday or tomorrow or next year. But that's the reason Vhol has been pushing us so hard here, just in case. . . . For myself, I've been hoping it would come while we're here, hoping I'd have a chance to talk to them."

Chane smiled. "Don't you think they'll be angry when they find you've been meddling with their belongings?"

"Probably," Labdibdin said. "But their scientists. I think they'd understand . . . not the weapons part, but the rest of it, the wanting to know. I think they'd understand that we *had* to meddle."

Again he was silent, and very sad. "This whole thing has been a terrible waste," he said. "Rushed and hurried and all for the wrong objectives. The only chance we'll ever have in my lifetime, certainly, to learn even a little about another galaxy, and the stupid bureaucrats back on Vhol can't think of anything except their piddling little war with Kharal."

Chane shrugged. "Everybody has his own idea of what's important. The Kharalis would be more interested in knowing that there isn't a super-weapon out here than they would be in learning about fifty galaxies."

"The Kharalis," said Labdibdin, "are a narrow and ignorant lot."

"They are that," Chane said, and turned to Dilullo. "The Krii aren't being much help either. Don't you think we'd better get back up?"

Dilullo nodded. He took one more look at the ranks of the not-dead but not-alive creatures, sitting so patiently in hope of their resurrection, and he thought that their alienness went deeper than the matter of form or even substance. He couldn't quite analyze what he meant by that, and then he thought, *It's their faces. Not the features. The expression. The look of utter calm. Those faces have never known passion of any kind.*

"Do you see it too?" Labdibdin said. "I think the specie must have evolved in a gentle environment, where it had no enemies and no need to fight for survival. They haven't *conquered* anything . . . I mean in themselves. They haven't suffered and learned and turned away from violence to seek a better path. It just was never in them. Love isn't in them either, by the way, judging from their records. They seem to be completely without visceral emotions of any kind, so they can be good with absolutely no trouble at all. It makes me wonder if their whole galaxy is different from ours, without all the natural violences that obtain on our planets . . . climatic changes, drought, flood, famine, all the things that made us fighters in the beginning and gave us survival as the victor's crown . . . or whether the world of the Krii was an isolated case."

"As a human I have to stick with my visceral emotions. They may make us a lot of trouble but they're also all what makes life worth living. I don't think I envy the Krii too much," Dilullo said.

Chane laughed and said, "I don't want to be irreverent, but our dead look more alive than they do. Let's go. I'm tired of being stared at."

They went, back along the hollow-ringing corridor, and this time Dilullo had a queer cold prickling at his back, as though the hundred pairs of eyes still watched, piercing through metal and dim light to follow him.

How they must have wondered, studying the strange wild natives of this star-jungle, the lovers, the killers, the saints, the sufferers, the triumphant damned.

"I don't think it means very much," he said suddenly, "to *not* do something, unless you've wanted very much to do it."

"That's because you're human," said Labdibdin. "And to a human perfect peace is as good as death. The organism decays."

"Yes," said Chane, with such vehemence that Dilullo was startled into smiling.

"He doesn't mean just war, you know. There are other kinds of fighting."

"Right. But to a flower, say, or a tree—"

The tiny transceiver in Dilullo's pocket-flap spoke
with Bollard's voice. "John," it said. "Bixel's got those
two blips on his radar."

"Coming," said Dilullo, and sighed. "What price perfect peace?"

XVIII

Labdibdin had been sent back to the domes with another Merc, and Chane sat in the bridge room waiting to know why Dilullo had wanted him here instead of on what was presently going to be the firing line. Through the door of the navigation room he could see Bixel hunched over his radar screen, following the approach of the cruisers. Rutledge was handling the ship-to-ship radio. Dilullo and the captain of one of the Vhollan cruisers were talking on it.

The Vhollan's voice came in loud and clear. *Senior captain,* Chane thought, *with spit, polish, and efficiency crackling in every word of his bad galacto.*

"I will offer you this one chance to surrender. Your only other alternative, as you must realize, is death. I surely don't have to point out to you the hopelessness of fighting two heavy cruisers."

"Then why do it?" said Dilullo dryly. "Supposing I did surrender? What would the terms be?"

"You would be returned to Vhol for trial."

"Uh huh," said Dilullo. "It would be so much simpler for you just to turn out the firing-squad right here . . . simpler and *quieter*. But assuming you really did take us back to Vhol, then we could plan on either A: execution for penetrating military secrets; or B: rotting in a Vhollan prison for the rest of our lives."

He looked over at Chane with lifted eyebrows. Chane

shook his head. So did Rutledge. Bixel, who was listening over the intercom, said, "Tell him to go—"

"You would at least have a chance to live," said the Vhollan. "This way you have none."

"My men seem to have a different opinion," Dilullo answered. "They say no."

The cruiser captain sounded impatient. "Then they're fools. Our heavy beams can blast your ship."

"Sure," said Dilullo. "Only you won't use them because if you do you will also blast this big prize package you're supposed to be guarding. Why do you think I cuddled up so close to it . . . because I loved it? Sorry, Captain. It was a good try."

There was a pause. The cruiser captain muttered something in low exasperated Vhollan.

"I think he's calling you names," said Rutledge.

"Very likely." Dilullo leaned to the mike. "By the way, Captain, how did you do with the Starwolves?"

"We drove them off," said the Vhollan curtly. "Of course."

"Of course," said Dilullo, "but not without some damage. How is the other boy feeling, the one that was screaming so loud for help?"

"I don't think he's feeling too good, John," said Bixel. "He's yawing around a lot, as though some of his drivetubes weren't functioning just right."

Chane thought, *The Starwolves would have had him if the second cruiser hadn't come up. It must have been a great fight.*

He wondered if Ssander's brothers had survived it. If they had, he was still going to have to face them some day. They wouldn't give up, and sooner or later . . .

But he was proud of them.

The Vhollan captain was giving Dilullo one last chance to surrender, and Dilullo was saying no.

"You may get us, friend, but you'll have to fight for it."

"Very well," said the captain, and his voice was cold

and flat and hard now as a steel blade. "We'll fight. And no quarter, Dilullo. No quarter."

He broke off transmission. Chane stood up, impatient, his belly tight with anticipation. Rutledge looked up at Dilullo.

"That's telling them, John. By the way, do you have any plan at all for getting us out of here?"

"Something will come to me," said Dilullo. "Are you tracking them, Bixel?"

"Tracking. They're coming in now. . . ."

"What's the heading?"

Bixel told him, and Dilullo went to the viewport. Chane joined him. At first he could see nothing in the dirty green murk. Then two dark shapes appeared, very distant, and small. They grew with enormous swiftness. The constant screaming of the wind outside was drowned in rolling, booming thunder. The Merc ship trembled once, and twice. The cruisers swept past, high over the crest of the ridge, went into landing position, dropped their landing gear, and disappeared behind the ridge.

Dilullo sighed, much as though he had been holding his breath. "I hoped they'd do that."

Chane stared at him, surprised. "They just about had to, if they were smart. They can't use their heavy beams against us . . . as you told him . . . but we're not hampered. We could have peppered them with our portable missile launchers. I was hoping they'd be foolish enough to land within our range."

"Maybe they did just that," Dilullo said. He pointed to the wall of cliffs, the jagged fingers holding back the sand. "Do you think you could climb up there?"

He knows I can, thought Chane . . . and said, "It would depend on how much I had to carry with me."

"If you had two men to help you, could you muscle one of those portable launchers up to the top?"

"Ah," said Chane. "Now I see. The ridge screens us from their heavy beams, so if we took off on a low trajectory they couldn't stop us. But they could come right hot on our heels and catch us in space, unless . . ."

"Exactly," said Dilullo. "Unless they couldn't."

Chane said, "I'll get in there."

Dilullo nodded and lifted the tansceiver button. "Bollard?"

Bollard's voice came back thready and small. "Yes, John."

"Pick me the two strongest men you can think of, break out some coils of heavy duty line, detach one missile-launcher from your perimeter, and get them all assembled. Don't forget the ammo, about ten rounds."

Chane said, "Make it twenty."

"You won't have time," said Dilullo. "They'll uncork their lasers and blow you off the ridge before you could fire that many." Then he paused, looking at Chane. He said into the transceiver, "Make it twenty."

"You don't want men," said Bollard's voice. "You don't even want mules. You want . . . yes, John. On the double."

Dilullo went to the door of the navigation room. "Stay with it, Bixel."

Bixel looked at him, round-eyed. "But why? The cruisers are down now, and he said the Starwolves had gone, so . . ."

"Just stay with it."

Bixel leaned back in his chair. "If you say so, John. This is easier than getting shot at."

"Would you like me to stay with the radio?" asked Rutledge.

"No."

Rutledge shrugged. "No harm in asking. But I might have known. You're a hard man, John."

Dilullo grinned bleakly. "Let's go see how hard."

He beckoned to Chane. They went down from the bridge room to the open lock, and out into the cold gritty air and the shifting sand.

The Mercs were deployed along the defense perimeter, dug in behind the assault-fence or manning the emplacements. They were waiting quietly, Chane saw. Good hard tough pros. They would be fighting for their lives in a short while . . . just as long as it took the men off the cruisers to get organized and make the long march around the end of the cliff wall. But nothing was happening now and so they were taking it easy, tightening their collars to keep the sand out, checking their weapons, talking back and forth unconcernedly. Another day, another dollar, Chane thought, and not a bad way at all to make a living. It wasn't like the Starwolf way, of course. It was a job and not a game; it lacked the dash and pride. These were hired men, as against the free-booting lords of the starways who had no masters. But since for a while at least he was denied the one, the other wasn't too bad a substitute.

"Still think you can do it?" Dilullo asked. They were walking down the line toward where Bollard was hauling one of the portable launchers out of its emplacement and shouting orders about regrouping and closing the gap. Chane looked up at the cliffs, his eyes narrowed against the dust.

"I can do it," he said. "But I'd hate to get caught halfway up."

"What are you hanging around for, then?" asked Dilullo. "Concentrate on their drive-tubes. Try to disable both cruisers, but take the undamaged one first. Watch out for return fire, and when it comes, run like hell. We'll wait for you . . . but not too long."

"You just worry about holding them off here," said Chane. "If they crack the perimeter we won't have any place to run to."

The coils of heavy-duty line had arrived, thin hard stuff with little weight to it. Chane draped one over his shoulder and took up one end of the launcher cradle. Bollard had provided him, as ordered, with the two strongest men in the outfit, Sekkinen and a giant named O'Shannaig. Sekkinen took the other end of the cradle.

O'Shannaig loaded himself with the missile belts . . .
nasty little things with warheads of a non-nuclear but
sufficiently violent nature. They couldn't kill a heavy
cruiser. Applied in exactly the right places, they could
make it hurt.

Chane said, "Go." And they went, running in the soft
sand, under the belly of the monster ship, and then out
from under its ruined bow, past the huddled domes
where the Vhollan technicians were locked up. Chane
suddenly remembered Thrandirin and the two generals
and wondered what Dilullo would do with them.

Sekkinen began to blow and flounder, and Chane
slowed down impatiently. He was going to have to pace
himself or wear out his team too early. O'Shannaig was
doing better because he had his arms free. Even so, he
was sweating and his steps had lost their spring. It was
hard going in the sand. The weight of their burdens
pressed them down so that they waded in it, and it
slipped and rolled and clutched their ankles. They found
themselves on solid rock at last, right under the loom of
the cliffs.

"Okay," Chane said. "Sit a minute while I have a
look." He pretended to be panting hard, to match their
panting, and moved away slowly, craning upward at the
black cliffs.

They looked sheer enough, standing straight up in
a monolithic wall until they broke at the top into those
eroded pinnacles that tore the passing wind and made it
shriek.

O'Shannaig said in his quiet burring voice, "John
must be daft. T'is not possible to climb yon, not with all
this around our necks."

"With or without it," said Sekkinen. He looked at
Chane without love. "Unless you can pass some kind of
a miracle."

XIX

Chane didn't know about miracles, but he knew about strength and obstacles and what a man could do if he had to. No, not a man, a Starwolf. A Varnan.

He walked along the foot of the cliff, taking his time. He knew the men from the cruisers would be moving by now and that if he did not reach the top of the cliff before they came around and spotted him, he was going to be caught with either the launcher or the ammunition or one of the other men dangling helplessly midway and it was going to be bad. Even so, he did not hurry.

The wind was going to be a problem up there. In the dead calm under the cliff, he could look up and see the wind, made physical by the sand it carried in smoking clouds from the dune. Wind like that could carry away a man, or a missile launcher, with equal ease, even though it might drop them sooner.

He wished the drowned sun would burn a little brighter. That was one reason the cliff looked so smooth. The flat dim light did not show up the faults and roughness. Green on black . . . that didn't help any either. Chane began to hate this world. It didn't like him. It didn't like life of any kind. All it liked was sand and rock and wind.

He spat the taste of dust and bitter air out of his mouth and went on a little farther, and found what he was looking for.

When he was sure he had found it, he lifted the

transceiver button and said, "I'm about to see what I can do about that miracle. Bring the stuff along."

He rearranged the coil of rope and his other gear so that nothing stuck out to catch, and he began to climb up the chimney he had found in the rock.

The first part of it wasn't so hard. The trouble came when the chimney washed out and left him on a nearly sheer, nearly vertical face, halfway to the top. He had thought the face was roughened enough to give him a chance, and he had gambled on it. It turned out to be very poor odds.

He remembered that other climb he had made, down the outside of the city-mountain on Kharal. He wished with all his heart he had those gargoyles here.

Inch by inch he worked his way up, mostly by the sheer strength of his fingers. After a while he found himself in a kind of hypnotic daze, concerned only with the cracks and bulges of the rock. His hands hurt abominably; his muscles were stretched like ropes to the breaking point. He heard a voice saying over and over in his head, *Starwolf, Starwolf,* and he knew it was telling him that a man would quit now, and fall, and die, but that he was a Starwolf, a Varnan, too proud to die like an ordinary man.

The shrieking wind deafened him. The hair of his head was plucked and tweaked with such sudden violence that it almost blew him off the rock. A shock of panic went through him. Blown sand bit into his flesh like a shot. He cowered tight against the cliff-face, looked up, and saw that he had reached the top.

He was still not home free. He had to worm his way a little farther, laterally now, below the crest of the ridge until he was in the lee of a pinnacle. He clambered up into a kind of nest in the eroded rock and sat there, gasping and trembling, feeling the rock quiver under him with the violence of the wind, and he cursed Dilullo, laughing. *I'm going to have to stop this,* he thought. *I let him sucker me into one thing after another because I have to show off how good I am. He knows that, and he uses me. Can you do it, he asks, and I say yes. . . .*

And I did it.

A tiny voice sounded under the noise of the wind. "Chane! Chane!"

He realized now that it had been calling for several minutes. He lifted the transceiver.

"Sekkinen, I'm sending down the line. You can toss a coin, but one of you is going to have to come up here with another line. Third man to stay down and make fast. We'll have to haul the stuff up."

He found a solid, sturdy tooth of rock to anchor the line on. Apparently O'Shannaig had won the toss, or lost it; it was his long body that came gangling up the cliff, his red-gold hair and craggy face that appeared over the lip of the hollow. Chane laughed, panting now in all honesty. "Next time I'll ask them to send me a small weakling. You weigh, my friend."

"Aye," said O'Shannaig. "I do that." He flexed his arms. "I was pulling, too."

They sent the second line down. Sekkinen made both of them fast on the launcher and they hauled it up and wrestled it into the hollow, and then brought up the belts.

"Okay, Sekkinen," said Chane into the transceiver. "It's your turn now."

They hauled him up in double-quick time, a big and tough and very unhappy man, who crawled into the hollow muttering that he was never built to be a monkey on a string. The hollow was getting overcrowded. Chane knotted a line around his waist, and a second one over his shoulders. The second one was hitched at the other end to the launcher.

"This is the tricky part," he said. "If I blow off, catch me."

With Sekkinen paying out and O'Shannaig snubbing around the rock tooth, Chane slid out of the hollow and over the crest, into the full fury of the wind.

He didn't think he was going to make it. The wind was determined to fly him into space like a whirling kite. It hammered and kicked him, tore his breath away, blinded him and choked him with sand. He hugged the pinnacle, finding plenty of handholds now where the full force of erosion had been at work, working himself around to the windward side. He was at the crest of the great dune now, and it was like riding one of the giant waves on Varna's lava beaches, high and dizzy, breathless with the spume. Only this spume was hard and dry, flaying the skin from his face and hands. He cowered and crawled in it, and presently the wind was pinning him flat against the rock and he could see the cruisers resting down at the foot of the dune.

He could also see the tail end of a line of armed men marching out of sight around the end of the cliff.

There were hollows on this side of the pinnacle as well, where the softer parts of the rock had been gnawed away. The wind fairly blew him into one and he decided not to argue with it; this would do as well as another. He spoke into the transceiver.

"All right," he said. "Up and over, and watch yourselves."

He braced himself in the hollow, right at the front, with his back against one wall and his feet against another. He laid hold of the second line and began to haul it in, hand over hand.

Praying as he did that the launcher wouldn't get away from his friends and fall down the cliff—because if it did, he would go with it.

It felt as though he were hauling on the rock itself. Nothing moved and he wondered if Sekkinen and O'Shannaig were not able between them to manhandle the launcher up and over those vital few feet of the crest to where he could get a purchase on it. Then all of a sudden, the tension eased and the launcher came leaping at him in a flurry of sand and he shouted to them to snub it. It skidded and slowed to a stop, the belts trailing after it on the snubline.

Chane heaved a sigh of relief. "Thanks," he said. "Now get on back to the ship, quick. The Vhollans are coming."

He wrestled the launcher into position in front of the hollow, a two-man job. While he was doing it, O'Shannaig's voice, maddeningly slow, replied that, "It wouldna be richt to go without you."

In desperation, Chane shouted into his transceiver.

"Bollard!"

"Yes?"

"I'm in position. Will you tell these two noble jackasses to clear out? I can run faster than they can; I'll have a better chance without them. When these lasers cut loose, I don't want to have to wait for anybody."

Bollard said, "He's right, boys. Come on down." From the noises he heard then, Chane gathered that since it was an order, Sekkinen and O'Shannaig were going down the ropes a lot faster than they had come up. He finished laying out the belts and slapped the first one into place in the launcher.

"Chane," said Bollard, "the column has just come in sight."

"Yeah. If I don't see you again, tell Dilullo . . ."

Dilullo's voice cut in. "I'm listening."

"I guess not right now," said Chane. "I'm too busy. The cruisers are practically underneath me. The wind is murder, but these missiles don't much care about wind. . . . One of these cruisers has taken a beating, all right. I can see that."

He laughed. *Good for the Starwolves!* He centered the guidance hairs until they met exactly on the clustered drive-tube assembly of the undamaged cruiser.

Dilullo's voice said, "I'll bet you a half-unit that you don't get off more than ten."

Dilullo lost. Chane got off ten in such quick succession that the first laser didn't crack until he had turned from the bent and smoking tubes of the first cruiser to the already slightly battered ones of the second. The heavy laser beam began chewing its way along the crest . . . they didn't have him zeroed yet, but they would in a minute. Rock and sand erupted in smoke and thunder. Chane got off four more and the second laser unlimbered and blew the dune not thirty feet below him into an inferno. Then, all of a sudden, the lasers stopped and the launcher stopped and there wasn't any more sound of battle.

And a great shadow passed overhead and blotted out the sun.

XX

Eerie quiet; eerie twilight. Chane crouched in the hollow, his neck hairs prickling. He tried the launcher mechanism and it was dead under his fingers, as though the power-pack operating the trigger assembly had gone out.

The laser-pods on the cruisers remained dark and silent.

"Bollard!" he said into the transceiver. "Dilullo! Anybody!"

There was no answer.

He tried his stunner and that was dead too.

He looked skyward and he could not see anything, except that somewhere up there in the murk and dust and nebula-mist something hung between the planet and the sun.

He fought his way out of the hollow and back over the crest to the other side, taking up his life-line as he went, swinging free for dreadful seconds as the wind took him around the corner and dropped him back into the place he had started from. He could see the Merc ship, the defense perimeter, and off to his left the men from the Vhollan cruisers fanned out into an attack formation with anti-personnel weapons. A couple of the Merc gas-shells had apparently burst among them a little before, because some of them were reeling around in the characteristic fashion and wisps of vapor were still shredding away on the wind. Other than that, everybody was just standing and staring at the sky or fiddling with weapons that had inexplicably stopped working.

Chane went down the line hand-over-hand to the bottom of the cliff, and started running.

Out on the plain, in the dusk of that great shadow, the Vhollans seemed to be smitten with a sudden panic desire for togetherness. Their outflung line receded, coiling in upon itself. It became a mob of frightened men, expecting attack from they knew not what and demoralized by the realization that they had been deprived of any means of defending themselves, beyond their bare hands and pocket knives. Chane could hear their voices clamoring, thin and far away under the wind.

He knew how they felt. Stripped and naked, and worse than that . . . at the mercy of something or someone too powerful to fight, like tiny children with paper swords against a charge of militia. He didn't like it either. It made him scared, an emotion he was not accustomed to.

He heard orders being shouted up and down the Merc line. They were beginning to fall back on the ship, hauling their useless weapons with them. But as he passed the domes, Chane met Dilullo and a couple of men.

"The Krii rescue ship?" asked Chane.

"It has to be," Dilullo answered. "Nothing else . . ." He looked skyward, his face a bad color in the unnatural twilight. "The radar isn't working. Nothing's working. Not even the hand torches. I want to talk to Labdibdin."

Chane went with them to the dunes. It was dark inside and sounds of near-panic could be heard. Rutledge had replaced Sekkinen as door-guard, and as soon as he saw Dilullo he ran toward him, demanding to know what was happening.

"My stunner doesn't work and the transceiver . . . I've been calling. . . ."

"I know," Dilullo said, and pointed to the door. "Let them out."

Rutledge stared at him. "What about the Vhollans? What about the attack?"

"I don't think there's going to be an attack now," said Dilullo, and added under his breath, "At least, I hope not."

Rutledge went back and unlocked the door. The Vhollans poured out in an untidy mass, and then paused. They too began looking up at the sky, and babbling. Their voices had become oddly hushed.

Dilullo shouted for Labdibdin, and presently he came jostling through the crowd, with several more of the scientists on his heels.

"It's the ship," said Labdibdin. "It must be. This force that has inhibited all power equipment . . . and all weapons, too, hasn't it . . ."

"It has."

". . .is a purely defensive device, and the Krii were masters of non-violent means of defense. We were using weapons here, you see. I could hear the lasers up on the ridge. So they stopped us."

"Yes," said Dilullo. "You're the expert on the Krii. What do you suggest we ought to do?"

Labdibdin looked upward at the hovering shadow, and then at the great dark derelict that bulked so large on the sandy plain.

"They don't take life," he said.

"Are you sure of that, or just hoping?"

"All the evidence . . ." said Labdibdin, and stopped. He was awestricken before the might and the imminent nearness of the Krii ship.

Chane said, "What difference does it make? We don't have anything left but our claws and teeth. It's up to them whether they kill us or not."

"That being the case," said Dilullo, "what do you think, Labdibdin?"

"I'm *sure* they don't take life," said Labdibdin. "I'm staking my own life on it. I think if we don't oppose or provoke them in any way, if we go back into our ships and . . ." He made a helpless gesture, and Dilullo nodded.

"And see what happens. All right. Will you take that message to your cruiser captains? Tell them that's what we're going to do, and urge upon them as strongly as you can the wisdom of doing likewise. It seems pretty obvious that this whole thing is out of our hands now, anyway."

"Yes," said Labdibdin. "Only . . ."

"Only what?"

"A few of us may come back . . . to watch." He looked again at the mighty derelict, in whose dark belly the hundred Krii sat waiting. "Only to watch. And at a distance."

The Vhollans streamed out over the plain toward the milling mob from the cruisers. Chane and Dilullo and the other Mercs hurried back to the Merc ship.

"How did it go on the ridge?" Dilullo asked as they went.

"Good," said Chane. "It'll take them a while to make repairs on those cruisers . . . neither one's in shape to get off the ground." He smiled wryly. "Your plan worked just fine. We can take off any time now."

"That's nice," said Dilullo. "Except we don't have any power."

They both looked skyward.

"I feel like a mouse," said Dilullo.

Rutledge shivered. "Me, too. I hope your Vhollan friend is right and the cat isn't carnivorous."

Dilullo turned to Chane. "Are you worried now?"

Chane knew what he meant. *Starwolves don't worry.* He showed the edges of his teeth and said, "I'm worried."

Starwolves are strong, and that's why they don't worry. The weak worry, and today I am weak, and I know it. For the first time in my life. I would like to claw their big ship out of the sky and break it, and I feel sick because they made me helpless. And it was no trouble to them to do it. They just pushed a button somewhere, a flick of one of those long stringy digits, and the animals were suppressed.

He remembered the passionless faces of the Krii, and hated them.

Dilullo said mildly, "I'm glad to know there's something that can get you down. Are you tired, Chane?"

"No."

"You're fast on your feet. Run ahead and get Thrandirin and the generals out of the ship. Tell 'em to go to blazes with the rest of the Vhollans. If the Krii decide to let us have our power back sometime, I want to go, and I don't want to bother dropping our guests off at their home planet. I don't think it would be very healthy."

"I doubt it," said Chane, and took off running.

And as he ran, he thought, *Here I go again. Why didn't I just tell him I was tired? Pride, boy. And when you were a very little boy your father used to tell you how it went before a fall.*

I guess he was right. It was pride in what I had done in that raid that made me fight with Ssander when he tried to cut in on my share of the loot.

And here I am. Not a Starwolf any more, not really a Merc, either . . . . just living on their sufferance . . . and at this moment I'm not even a man. Just an annoyance to the Krii. And if that isn't a fall . . .

He reached the ship, fighting his way through the Mercs who were loading in the weapons and equipment, on the chance that it all might work some day again. It was pitch dark inside, the only light coming in through the open hatchways, which of course would not close now. He groped his way to the cabin where the three Vhollans were locked up, let them out and guided them down, and when they stood outside he watched their faces and smiled.

"I don't understand," said Thrandirin. "What is it? I see our men going away without fighting, and the light is strange. . . ."

"That's right," said Chane, and pointed at the vast

loom of the wrecked Krii ship. "Someone else has come looking for that. Someone bigger than us. I think you can kiss it goodbye." He gestured skyward. "For there's another just like it up there now."

The Vhollans stared at him like three night-goggling birds in the weird dusk. "If I were you," said Chane, "I'd get going. You can talk the whole thing over with Labdibdin . . . while we all wait."

They went. Chane turned to help with the loading, which had all to be done by hand.

They were concentrating on the most valuable items and they were working awfully fast, so they had a good part of the job done when there began to be a new sound in the sky, and Chane looked up and saw a big pale-gold egg sinking toward them out of the shadowy clouds.

In a quiet voice Dilullo said, "Into the ship. Just put everything down and go."

Only about a third of the men were working outside, passing the things through the cargo hatch along a kind of human belt that extended to the storage hold. They did what Dilullo told them, and Chane thought he had never seen an area cleared so quickly. He followed Dilullo and Bollard up the steps to the lock, moving in a more dignified fashion, perhaps, but not much more. Chane's heart was pounding in a way it had not done since he was a child waking from a nightmare, and there was a cold, unpleasant knot in his middle.

The open and unshuttable lock chamber seemed dreadfully exposed.

"Whole damn ship's open," Bollard muttered. There was sweat on his round moon face, and it looked cold. "They could just walk in. . . ."

"Can you think of anything we can do about it?" asked Dilullo.

"Okay," said Bollard. "Okay."

They stood and watched while the big gold egg came and settled gently onto the sand.

It sat there for a time and did nothing, and they continued to watch it, and now Chane had a feeling it was watching them. They were in plain sight if anybody wanted to look real hard, though they were taking pains not to be conspicuous. It was probably dangerous, and they should go farther in. But that was no protection either since they couldn't close the hatches, and they might as well see what was going on. The Krii would know perfectly well they were here anyway.

The Krii, when finally they did appear, seemed not to be interested one way or the other.

There were six of them. They emerged one after another through a hatchway that opened low down in the side of the egg, extruding a narrow stairway. The last two carried between them a long thin object of unguessable purpose, shrouded in dark cloth.

Very tall and slender, their seemingly jointless bodies swaying gracefully, they moved in single file toward the great ship. Their skins, Chane noted, were not quite so dark an amber as those of the Krii he had seen frozen in stasis. Their limbs were extremely supple, the long-digited hands looking almost like fronds stirring in the wind.

They walk so tall, he thought, *because they're not afraid of us. And if they're not afraid, it must be because they know we can't hurt them. Not* won't *hurt them. Can't* hurt them.

They did not even look at the Merc ship. They never turned those narrow high-domed heads to left or right to look at anything. They marched quietly to the entrance and went up the steps and disappeared inside the enormous wreck.

They were in there a long time. The men got tired of standing in the lock and clawed their way in the darkness up to the bridge room, where they could be more comfortable and still watch.

Bollard said, "So far, they're peaceful."

"Yes," said Dilullo. "So far."

The golden egg sat on the sand and waited, its long rows of ports gleaming dully in the dim light. It did not have the conventional drive-tube assembly, Chane noted, and there were no external signs at all of what kind of power was used. Whatever it was, it functioned in the inhibiting force-field where nothing else did. Naturally. A defensive device wasn't much good if it immobilized you along with your enemy.

He saw movement in the entrance to the great wreck, and he said, "They're coming back."

The six came out, and after them the hundred.

In single file, forming a long swaying line, they marched out of the dark tomb where they had waited . . . how long? Their garments fluttering, their large eyes wide in the dimness, they marched across the blowing sand and into the golden shuttle-craft that would take them to the rescue ship, which would take them home. Chane looked at their faces.

"They're not human, all right," he said. "Not one of them is laughing, or crying, or dancing, or hugging someone. They all look as peaceful and harmonious as they did when they were . . . I was going to say 'dead,' but you know what I mean."

"No visceral emotions," said Dilullo. "And yet that other ship has made a tremendous long voyage to find them. That argues emotions of some sort."

"Maybe they were more interested in saving the experience these Krii have had, than in saving the Krii themselves," said Chane.

"I'm not interested either way," said Bollard. "I only want to know what they're going to do to us."

They watched, and Chane knew that from the open lock and the cargo hatch the other Mercs were watching, waiting, and tasting the bitter taste of fear, just like he was.

It wasn't that you minded dying so much, though you didn't look forward to it. It was that you minded the way you were going to die, Chane thought. *If these long limber honey-skinned vegetables decided to finish you,*

*they would do it coolly and efficiently, and so remotely
that you wouldn't even know what hit you. Like gassing
vermin in a burrow.*

The last of the hundred entered the shuttle-craft and
its hatchway closed upon them. The golden egg
hummed and rose up into the whirling dust and cloud
and was gone.

"Now maybe they'll let us go?" said Bollard.

"I don't think so," said Dilullo. "Not just yet."

Chane swore a short fierce oath in Varnan, the first
slip of that kind he had made, but Bollard didn't notice
it.

He was too busy looking at the fleet of golden eggs
that had appeared, dropping one after the other until
there were nine neatly lined up on the sand.

Dilullo said, "We might as well make ourselves comfortable. I believe we're going to have a long wait."

And long it was. Just about the longest wait that
Chane could ever remember, penned up in the little
iron prison of the ship. They ate cold rations, lived in
the dark, and looked hungrily at the open hatchways
that mocked them. Toward the end Dilullo had to use
all his powers of persuasion, including his fists, to keep
the men inside.

Presumably the officers of the Vhollan cruisers were
having the same trouble, and presumably they succeeded, because the Vhollans kept clear. Once or twice
Chane thought he saw figures moving the dust-whirls
underneath the cliff. It might have been Labdibdin and
some of the other technicians; probably was. If so, they
did their watching from a discreet distance.

There was one comfort. The Vhollans couldn't use
this interval to repair their tubes. Not unless they did it
with little hammers and their bare hands.

Chane paced and prowled, and finally sat moping,
sullen as a caged tiger.

Outside the Krii worked steadily, neither slow nor
fast, keeping a methodical rhythm that rasped the

nerves just to watch it. They never once came near the Merc ship. As far as they were concerned, it seemed, the Merc ship did not exist.

"Not very complimentary," said Dilullo, "but let's keep it that way. Maybe Labdibdin is perfectly right and they don't take life. That wouldn't stop them from having some highly effective method of suppressing people, the way they suppress machines, and their idea of the seriousness of resultant damage to the organism might not agree with ours. Lord knows what their metabolism is like, or their nervous systems. You can wreck a man pretty thoroughly and still leave him living. They simply might not understand what they were doing."

Chane agreed with him. Still, it was hard to have to look at the irritatingly remote and lofty creatures day after day and not want to try rushing out and killing a few just to vary the monotony.

The shuttle-craft came and went, disgorging various equipment, taking the Krii technicians back and forth. A considerable amount of work was being done inside the wreck, but of course there was no way of knowing what that was. Outside, the Krii were setting up a complex of transparent rods that gradually took the form of a tunnel. They built that out from the entrance of the ship to a distance of about thirty feet, and then at the end they erected a kind of lock-chamber. At the ship end, the tunnel-like structure was sealed to the opening by a collar; they left only a narrow aperture for the technicians to go and come.

One day, light appeared suddenly through the rents in the ship's hull.

"They've got the power on again," said Dilullo. "Or jury-rigged a replacement for it."

"How do they run their generators when we can't?" Chane demanded. "They're in this inhibiting field too."

"They developed the inhibiting field, and would know how to shield their own equipment against it. Or their power system may be so different from ours . . . I mean, they don't even have the same atomic table."

Chane said, "However they do it, they're doing it. And if they've got the power on, all those cases will open up. . . ."

All those cases of jewels and precious metals. The loot of a galaxy, the way he saw it. It made his mouth water. Even the Starwolves had never aspired to such splendid heights.

A golden egg attached itself to the lock chamber at the end of the tunnel.

Chane pressed close to the viewport, with Dilullo and Bollard beside him. Nobody said anything. They waited, feeling that something decisive was about to happen.

The tunnel-like structure of crystal rods began to glow with a shimmering radiance that made its outline blur and shift. The radiance intensified, flared, then settled to a steady pulsing.

Things began to appear in it, gliding smoothly and swiftly from the great ship to the golden egg.

"Some kind of a carrier field," said Dilullo. "It makes the stuff weightless and kicks it along. . . ."

Chane groaned. "Don't give me any scientific lectures. Just look at that. *Look* at it!"

The loot of a galaxy went by, just out of reach, streaming steadily from the hold of the Krii ship into the golden egg; into a series of golden eggs that operated in an endless belt-shuttle, loading and rising and returning in a circular pattern.

The loot of a galaxy.

"And they're not even going to spend it," Chane said. "They're going to all of this trouble just to *study* it."

"Blasphemy, according to your ideas," said Dilullo, and grinned at Chane. "Don't cry."

"What are you talking about?" asked Bollard.

"Nothing. Except our friend here seems to have a frustrated case of sticky fingers."

Bollard shook his head. "The devil with our friend.

Look; they're loading all the specimens the expedition gathered. When they're finished, what then?"

It was not a question that was intended to be answered, and nobody tried.

But eventually the answer came.

The last items went down the carrier field and the glow died. Methodically the Krii dismantled their equipment and returned it into the clouds. The great hulk became dark again and now it was empty, drained of all use and meaning.

Finally, and at last, one of the Krii walked toward the Merc ship. It stood for a moment, very tall, swaying slightly with the wind, its great passionless eyes fixed on them.

Then it flung up one long thin arm in an unmistakable gesture, pointing to the sky.

It turned then and went back to the single golden egg that remained. The hatch closed, and in a moment the trampled sand was empty.

All of a sudden the lights were on in the Merc ship and the generators were jarring the bulkhead as they jolted into life again.

"He told us to go, and I think I know why," said Dilullo. He began to bellow urgently into the intercom. "Secure hatches! Flight stations on the double! We're taking off!"

And they took off, going like a scalded rocket in a flat trajectory that took them away from the cliff wall at an angle too low for the Vhollan laser beams to bear on them until they were out of range.

Dilullo ordered the ship into a stationary orbit and told Rutledge, "Get that camera working. I've a pretty good idea what's going to happen and I want to record it."

Rutledge opened the pod that held the camera and turned the monitor screen to *ON*.

Chane stared with the others into the screen that showed them what the camera was seeing.

"Too much dust," said Rutledge, and manipulated

the controls, and the picture cleared as the camera saw with different eyes, exchanging a light-reflectant image for one composed by sensor-beams.

It showed the great wrecked ship, lying monstrous on the plain. It showed the ridge and the two Vhollan cruisers beyond; the cruisers seemed like tiny, little miniatures for children to hang on strings and whirl around their heads.

After a while Rutledge looked at Dilullo, and Dilullo said, "Keep filming. Unless you want to go home broke."

"You think the Krii are going to destroy the ship?" asked Chane.

"Wouldn't you? When you know people have been meddling and prying with it, people with much less technological skill than yours but with much more war-like natures . . . would you leave it there for them to study? The Krii couldn't remove everything. The drive system, the generators, all that would be left, and the defensive mechanisms. Given time, the Vhollans might learn how to duplicate them in terms of our atomic table. Besides, why else would the Krii have told us to get clear? They wouldn't care about our fight with the Vhollans, and whether we got away or not. I think they didn't want us to get killed by any action of theirs."

The image remained static on the screen, the vast dark broken outline of the ship quite clear against the sand.

Suddenly a little spark flashed down and touched the hulk. It spread with incredible swiftness into a blinding flame that covered all that huge fabric of metal from stem to stern and ate it up, devoured it, crumbled it to ashes and then to atoms, until there was nothing left but a mile-long scar on the sand. And presently even that would vanish.

The Vhollan cruisers, shielded by the ridge, were unharmed.

Dilullo said, "Shut off the camera. I guess that shows we did our duty."

"We?" said Rutledge.

"The Kharalis hired us to find out what was in the nebula that threatened them, and destroy it. We found it, and it has been destroyed. Period." He looked down at the Vhollan cruisers. "They'll be getting busy on repairs now. I don't see any more reason to hang around."

There wasn't a man aboard who wanted to quarrel with him.

They climbed up out of the atmosphere, and out from under the shadow that had oppressed them for so many days, where the giant ship had hung between them and the sun.

Whether by accident or design, Dilullo chose a course that took them, not close but close enough to see . . .

Close enough to see a vast dark shape breaking out of orbit, beginning the long voyage home across the black and empty ocean that laps the shores of the island universes.

"No visceral emotions," said Dilullo softly, "but, by God, they've got something."

Even Chane had to agree.

The Mercs had expansive ideas about doing some celebrating and Dilullo just let them go ahead and try. As he had foreseen, they were too tired, and those off duty were glad enough to crawl into their bunks for the first decent sleep they had had in so long they couldn't remember.

Chane, not all that exhausted, remained in the wardroom for another drink with Dilullo. They were all alone now, and Dilullo said, "When we get to Kharal, you'll stay in the ship and make as though you never existed."

Chane grinned. "You don't have to talk me into that. Tell me, do you think they'll pay over the lightstones?"

Dilullo nodded. "They'll pay. In the first place, nasty

as they are in some ways, they keep their word. In the second place, the films of that monster ship will so impress them that the sight of it being destroyed will make them glad to pay."

"You don't plan to tell them that it wasn't really us who destroyed it?" Chane asked.

"Look," said Dilullo; "I'm reasonably fair and honest but I'm not foolish. They hired us to do a job, and the job is done, and we're pretty well battered up from it. That's enough." He added, "What will you do with your share when we sell the lightstones?"

Chane shrugged. "I hadn't thought about it. I'm used to taking things, not buying them."

"That's a little habit you'll have to get over if you want to stay a Merc. Do you?"

Chane paused before answering. "I do, for the time being, anyway. As you said before, I haven't got any place else to go. . . . I don't think you're as good as the Varnans, but you're pretty good."

Dilullo said dryly, "I don't think you'll ever make the best Merc that ever was, but you've got capabilities."

"Where do we go from Kharal?" Chane asked. "Earth?"

Dilullo nodded.

"You know," said Chane, "I've got kind of interested in Earth."

Dilullo shook his head and said dourly, "I'm not too happy about taking you there. When I think of the people there walking up and down, and looking at you and not knowing you're a tiger impersonating an Earthman, I wonder what I'm getting into. But I guess we can clip your claws."

Chane smiled. "We'll see."

THE
CLOSED
WORLDS

I

He walked the streets of New York, and tried to behave as though he were an Earthman.

If they find out what I really am, I'm dead, thought Morgan Chane.

He looked like an Earthman. Not too tall, with wide shoulders and black hair and a face of dark, hard planes. And he could speak the language well enough. These things were not strange, since his dead parents had been natives of this world. This Earth, which he had never seen until a few days ago.

Don't even think of the fact that you're a Starwolf!

Nobody knew that, except Dilullo. And Dilullo was not going to tell anyone, at least as long as they stayed partners. Which in effect gave Dilullo the power of life and death over him, for death was the swift and certain sentence meted out to a captured Starwolf on nearly every world in the galaxy.

Chane smiled, and thought, *The hell with it.* Danger was living, and if you avoided danger, you were only existing. Anyway, there was small risk of being suspected for what he was, here on a world where he looked just like everyone else. Nobody would even notice him in the crowd.

But they did. People looked at Chane, and looked back at him again. There was a springiness in his step that he could not quite hide. He had been born and reared on Varna, the world of the hated Starwolves, and that was a big and heavy planet. He could adjust his muscles to the lesser gravitation of smaller planets like this Earth, but he could not completely hide the latent strength and speed of his body. And there was something in his dark face, a touch of just faintly inhuman ruthlessness, that made him stand out.

The men looked at him with something of the expression with which they looked at the not-men one occasionally met in this starport quarter. The women looked at him as though they were both scared and attracted. These side-glances began to make Chane a little uncomfortable. He was not afraid of any of these people—a Varnan could break one of them in half—but he didn't want to start anything.

"You've got a genius for finding trouble," Dilullo had told him. "If you get into any here, you're all through as a Merc."

Chane had only shrugged. But the truth was that he didn't want to stop being a Merc. The Mercs . . . the name was short for mercenaries . . . were the second toughest people in space, the hardbitten men, most of them Earthmen, who went out and did all the dirty, dangerous jobs in the galaxy for pay. They were not as tough as the Starwolves, but the Starwolves had thrown him out, and being a Merc was better than anything else open to him.

Chane left the crowded street and went into a tavern. It was pretty crowded too, but most of the customers were men off the starport and their girls, and most of them were too exhilarated to pay attention to Chane. He ordered whisky and drank it, and thought that no matter what Dilullo said it was poor stuff, and then he ordered some more. The din was loud around him but he dropped away from it as he brooded.

He remembered Varna, the place that had always been home to him. The great, harsh, unfriendly, over-sized planet which gave its children nothing except the unmatchable strength and speed which its cruelly heavy gravitation bred into their bodies. Even to Chane it had given that, when he had survived being born there. It was as though Varna was a stern mother who told her sons, "I have given you strength and that is all I have to give . . . go forth and take whatever else you want."

And they had gone forth, the sons of Varna! As soon as they learned the way to make starships, from foolish Earthmen who were trying to encourage trade, the Varnans swarmed out to loot the lesser worlds. They were unbeatable in space; no other people could stand the acceleration pressures they could stand. Across the galaxy went the fear of the quick and ruthless ones—the Starwolves!

A smile crossed Chane's brooding face like a ripple upon a dark pool. He could see in memory of the times when their little squadrons would come home, dropping down out of the starry sky toward their grim mother world, the lights, the loot spread out and the laughter, nobody caring much that some had died in the foray: the Varnans striding like conquerors into their cities, their tall bodies splendid in their fine golden-down hair, their high-boned faces proud and their cat-slanted eyes bright.

And he had been one of them. He walked proud with them; he raided the starworlds with them; he lived in the tingle of danger.

It was all gone now; they had driven him out. He would never see Varna again, and here he was, sitting in a stinking room in a dull city on a dull planet.

"Having fun, Chane?"

A hand fell on his shoulder and he looked up into the long, horselike face of Dilullo.

"I'm having fun," said Chane. "I can hardly remember a time when I've had more fun than now."

"That's fine," said the older man, and sat down. "That's just fine. I was afraid you might be pining for

some of the fighting and killing and robbing that
Varnans call fun. I was so worried about it that I
thought I'd keep an eye on you."

Dilullo's bleak, no-colored eyes had an ironic twinkle
in them. He turned and ordered a drink.

Chane looked at him, thinking that there were times
when he hated Dilullo and that this was one of the
times.

Dilullo turned back and then he said, "You know,
Chane, you look like a bored tiger sitting there. But the
tiger is going to stay bored, and on a short leash. This
isn't one of the outworlds, it's Earth; and we're kind of
strict here."

"It does seem a bit dull, now that you mention it,"
said Chane.

Dilullo's drink came and he drank half of it. Then he
said, "I thought you might feel that way. So you may be
glad to hear that we might just have another job coming
up."

Chane looked up quickly. "What job? Where?"

"Don't know yet," said Dilullo. He finished his
drink. "But a very big shot in interstellar trade named
Ashton wants to see me in the morning. I assume he
doesn't want to see a Merc leader without some
reason."

"Do you want to take on something so soon?" said
Chane. "I mean, we did pretty well on that job for
Kharal. I'd suppose you'd want to take a rest."

Dilullo's hard mouth tightened. He looked down at
his empty glass, his stubby, strong fingers twirling it
around.

"I get my hair cut real short, Chane," he said. "But I
can't get it cut short enough to keep the gray from
showing around the edges. I'm getting a little old to
lead Mercs. If I turned down a good offer, I might just
not get another."

Just then a man came hurrying into the place. He was
a tall, hardbitten man who wore the same kind of

belted Merc coverall that they wore. He looked around and then hastened over to them.

"You're John Dilullo, aren't you?" he said. "I've seen you down at Merc Hall, though I never met you." He babbled, in his excitement. "We just found Bollard. Someone said you were in here, and I came—"

Dilullo had got to his feet and his face was suddenly twice as craggy and harsh. Bollard had been his second in the job they had last worked, and he was an old friend.

"You found him? What does that mean?"

"In an alley only a block or two from here," said the other. "Looks like he was stunned and robbed. We put in a call for the police and then someone said they'd seen you—"

Dilullo interrupted again, taking the babbling man by the arm and propelling him toward the door.

"Show me," he said.

He and Chane rapidly followed the man down the street. Darkness had fallen a little while ago, and the lights were on; the sidewalk was not yet too crowded.

The man kept babbling. "Don't think he's bad hurt, only stunned. I knew him right away, he was leader on a job I went on a year ago."

Dilullo muttered an oath. "I thought he was too old to be this sort of fool."

Their leader ducked into a narrow alley between looming warehouses. "This way . . . around the next corner. I don't know if the police are here yet. We called them first thing . . ."

They were halfway to the corner when from the darkness behind them came the whisper of a stunner, notched way down.

Dilullo dropped unconscious. Chane completed only a quarter of a turn before it dropped him too.

Chane was not unconscious. The stunner, to avoid being too noisy, had been notched down to just the exact power sufficient to knock a man out.

An ordinary man, that is. But Chane was not an ordinary Earthman; Varna had bred tougher muscles and a tougher nervous system, and he did not go all the way out.

He fell and hit the pavement and lay there, face up, his eyes open, his limbs almost paralyzed. Almost. He could still move his muscles a bit, though they felt vague and remote.

He made no movement. The Starwolf cunning that a lifetime had fostered told him not to move yet, not until he had conquered at least some of the numbness.

As through a mist, he saw the man who had guided them here looking down at them, and then another man came running from whatever dark doorway he had hidden in for his ambush. Both men were wavering, unreal figures to Chane's eyes.

"This one," said the pseudo-Merc. He bent over Dilullo's unconscious figure and began to search him.

"I still don't think he'd have them on him," said the other man.

"Look," said the other, searching frantically. "He got six Kharali light-stones for his share of the last job and he hasn't been to any place to deposit them. I told you, I've been watching him . . . *ah!*"

He had drawn out from Dilullo's inner clothing a little pouch, and he shook its contents into his hand. Even in the darkness, the light-stones shone with that inner radiance that made the gem desired by all the galaxy.

Six jewels, Chane thought dully, and all Dilullo had gone through to get them, all that hell and danger in Corvus Cluster. The wise Dilullo, who kept his share in stones instead of selling them as Chane and the others had done.

Chane still made no movement. He could feel more life coming back into his nerves and muscles, but not enough yet. The other man bent over him and took his money from his pocket, but he still did not move. He wasn't ready . . .

Next moment he decided that he had to be ready. The pseudo-Merc stood back and began to take off his coverall, and as he did so he spoke quickly to the other man.

"Cut their throats. They could both identify me. I'll get this thing off and we'll get out of here."

The dark figure of the second man bent over Chane; there was a gleam of steel in his hand.

Kill, Starwolf! thought Chane, and willed all his strength into his half-numbed muscles.

He surged up and his hand moved and cracked across the jaw of the man with the knife. He was half-numbed and he didn't have all of his Varnan strength, but there was enough to send the man with the knife reeling and falling. And then the man was lying still.

Chane was already on his feet, staggering, unsure, but going into his charge. The psuedo-Merc had his legs tangled in the coverall he had been removing. He scrabbled in his clothes for a hidden weapon, but Chane reached him before he got it out.

The flat of Chane's hand struck across the pseudo-Merc's throat. The man made a gulping sound, staggered, and fell over. Chane fell too. He was too numb to stay erect, and he lay for a few minutes before he could start to get up again.

He had to rub his legs for minutes, with hands that felt like mittens, before he could trust himself to stand. Then he went over to one man and then the other, and looked at them. They were hurt and unconscious, but they were not dead.

Chane thought that if his strength hadn't been halved by the stunner, they would have been killed. But maybe it was just as well. Dilullo had this foolish prejudice against unnecessary killing . . .

He went over to Dilullo and knelt and massaged the nerve-centers. Presently Dilullo came around.

The other Merc looked up dazedly. Chane said softly, "I thought that he was too old to be this sort of fool. Wasn't that what you said, John?"

Dilullo was taking it in by now. "You killed them?"

"I did not," Chane said. "I was a good little Merc. I have to admit it was because I wasn't strong enough, after taking the shock that knocked you cold."

"They were after my light-stones, of course," Dilullo said thickly. "I was a bloody fool to keep them on me, but I didn't think this could happen to me."

Chane retrieved the jewels and his own money.

"All right, let's move," said Dilullo. "We ought to drag them to the police, but law means delays and I don't think we want to hang around Earth courtrooms, with a job maybe coming up."

They went on through the alley and so into the bright streets again.

"John," said Chane.

"Yes?"

"I forgot to thank you for coming down to keep an eye on me."

Dilullo said nothing.

II

The enormous cream-colored building that housed Ashton Trading was not too near the starport. It stood by itself in a wide space, in impressive aloofness. There was a big park for cars and fliers behind it, and a landscaped approach in front. Dilullo put coins in his auto-taxi and went inside, to an equally impressive interior of golden marble from a far starworld.

Officials, clerks, secretaries, bright of face and neatly dressed, came and went in quiet efficiency. They made Dilullo feel that his drab, belted coverall was distinctly out of place. But when a lift took him to the topmost level of offices, his reception was courtesy itself.

A rather exquisite young man offered a chair which Dilullo declined, and went into the inner offices. Looking around, Dilullo saw heads of girls and men looking at him from their desks. He heard the word "Merc".

Glamor, that's what I've got, thought Dilullo sourly. *I'm a Merc, an adventurer, somebody to look at.*

The hell of it was that he had once felt that way about it, when he was a very young man. He could have gone into interstellar trade and made money like the men who worked for the Ashtons, but that was too tame. He would be a Merc and people would look up to him.

And now here he was, middle-aged and worn around the edges, standing figuratively if not literally with hat

in hand hoping for a good job from the traders he had
once despised.

"Mr. Dilullo? This way, please."

He was ushered deferentially into a very big office
whose wide windows looked out far across the starport
quarter to the towers and docks and ships of the port
itself.

Dilullo had his mental hackles up. He had had business with tycoons before and he did not like the type.
He took James Ashton's proffered hand without enthu-
siasm.

"Thank you for coming, Mr. Dilullo," said Ashton.
"I feel lucky that you are available."

Ashton, he conceded, did not look like a tycoon. He
looked like a graying scholar of middle age, with a good
face and friendly eyes and a certain awkwardness of
manner.

Dilullo said bluntly, "Mr. Ashton, your secretary
who contacted me said you had a job you'd like me to
undertake. What job?"

And he thought, *Whatever it is, it's something real
mean. Ashton Trading doesn't need Mercs for anything
that isn't.*

Ashton took from a drawer a photograph which he
handed over, a picture of a man some years younger
than himself but with a strong resemblance.

"That's Randall Ashton, my brother. I want you to
find him."

Dilullo looked up at him. "Find him? You mean you
have no idea where he is?"

"I know where he is, in a general way," said Ashton.
"He's in the Closed Worlds."

"The Closed Worlds?" Dilullo frowned. "I don't
think I . . . wait a minute. Isn't there a star out beyond
Perseus Arm with a triplet of planets . . . ?"

Ashton nodded. "The star Allubane. It has three
planets—the Closed Worlds."

Dilullo's frown deepened. "Now I remember. A

queer, isolated little system where they don't like visitors and kick out any who come. If you don't mind my asking, what the devil took your brother there?"

Ashton leaned back. "That takes a little explanation, Mr. Dilullo. But first let me say that while I know Randall is in the Closed Worlds, I don't know where he is in them, and I don't know whether he's alive or dead. It would be your job to find him and bring him back if he's living."

"Why do you need Mercs for that?" Dilullo asked skeptically. "Your firm has got hundreds of starships, thousands of good men working for you."

"Traders," said Ashton. "Not fighters. To get in and out of the Closed Worlds is going to be dangerous."

"But Government . . ."

"The Terran Government can't do a thing," Ashton answered. "It would be interfering with an independent starworld if it did. And the messages it sent to Allubane have just not been answered."

He spread out his hands. "You see now why I thought of the Mercs. They—and you in particular, Mr. Dilullo—have successfully performed some highly dangerous tasks. I've heard a great deal about you chaps."

"The Closed Worlds," muttered Dilullo. "I've heard something more about that system. It was a long time ago."

Yes, it was a long time ago. It was on my third Merc job, when I was young and proud as the devil of being a Merc. On Arcturus Two, and we'd just finished a job and made money. We felt good, and I sat there with the rest of them in the hot, steamy night, drinking the liquor that was far too strong for me, looking as casual as though I'd done this for a lifetime, listening to old Donahue talk.

Old Donahue? My God, I'm older now than Donahue was then, and where's it all gone—the youth and the careless money—and the friends? The little white night-bats they called iggin *kept darting in and out under the smoky lights, and I drank and looked as though it was all nothing to me—not the strange smells nor the sounds nor the slithery women who brought us drink, and all the time I was bursting with pride, I, the poor boy from Brindisi who had grabbed himself a handful of stars.*

What was it Donahue said about Allubane? "They've got something big there. Something so big they won't let anyone in lest it be taken away from them. They booted our behinds out of there as soon as we landed. Something damned big, there in the Closed Worlds."

"This business," Ashton was saying, "has been in our family for four generations. My father wanted to make sure it stayed that way. When Randall and I were youngsters, he sent us out—as ordinary crewmen, mind you—on a whole lot of star-trading voyages. It was supposed to teach us the business from the ground up."

Ashton shook his head. "With me, it worked. I learned, and I liked the business. I've been with it ever since. But with Randall, it turned out differently. He got fascinated by all the exotic, alien peoples he met on far starworlds. So fascinated that, despite my father's objections, he went back to university and took up extra-terrestrial anthropology. He's a first class expert in the field now."

"Is that what he's doing out at Allubane?" asked Dilullo.

Ashton nodded. "Randall had already made several field trips. Of course, having all the money he needs, he could afford to fit up his small outfits in the finest style. And on one of those trips he heard of some big scientific mystery in the Closed Worlds."

"Exactly what?"

"I don't know," Ashton said. "He wouldn't tell me, or anyone else. He said it was so fantastic that nobody would believe him until he brought back proof. For all I know, he may have been on a wild-goose chase.

"Anyway, he went. He got four specialists together, took a small cruiser and crew from the firm—you understand, he's a full partner—and out he went to Allubane. He hasn't come back."

Ashton paused. "Well, that's it. Not a word from him for five months. I don't know what he's doing there, but I want to know, and I'm willing to pay a Merc party to go out and find him. There may be big trouble or no trouble at all. Just find him."

"What if we find him dead?" asked Dilullo.

"In that case, I'll want you to bring back legal proof of his death."

"I see."

Ashton said, "You don't see. Get that look off your face. I love my brother and I want him safe. But if he is dead, I've got to know it—I can't run a big business when nobody knows whether the co-owner of the business is alive or dead."

Dilullo said soberly, "Mr. Ashton, I would like to apologize for what I just implied."

Ashton nodded. "It's understandable. Business men, if they're successful, are supposed to be a combination of wolf and shark. But Randall's a fine man, and I'm worried about him."

He reached into his desk and brought out a folder which he handed to Dilullo. "I've had prepared all that's known about Allubane's worlds. Our company's pretty well briefed on most starworlds, but even so, it's scanty. I assume you'd like to study this before making a decision about taking the job."

Dilullo nodded, and took the folder. He started to rise, saying, "I'll take this and read it."

"Read it now," said Ashton. "That is, you have the time. Nothing is more important to me right now than Randall."

Dilullo was surprised. He picked up the folder and

began to read the pages in it, while Ashton worked quietly with his papers.

Dilullo's long face got longer, as he read. *This is a sour one,* he thought. *It's no good, no good at all. Turn it down.*

And have them say that John Dilullo's getting too old for the tough jobs?

He read the material through, then went back and read some parts of it again, and then slowly closed the folder.

Ashton looked up, and Dilullo said slowly, "Mr. Ashton, this would be a nasty job. I hope you'll believe that I'm not saying that so I can run the price up on you."

Ashton nodded. "I believe you. I couldn't hold this chair if I couldn't size up men. Go ahead."

"I'll give you my honest opinion," said Dilullo. "I think your brother's dead."

He tapped the folder. "Look at what you have here. There's the fact that these people of Arkuu, the main one of the three planets of Allubane, won't have strangers on their worlds. Anybody lands there, they run them right out. It's been that way since starships first landed there.

"All right," Dilullo continued. "Your brother went there months ago. If the Arkuuns had run him out, you'd have heard from him long ago. But you didn't. Yet this record shows they've never let a living stranger stay there. The obvious conclusion is that he's dead."

Ashton had a sadness in his face as he said, "I'm afraid you have logic on your side. But I can't just accept logic, with my brother out there, perhaps needing help badly. I've got to find out."

He went on. "I read all that material. I realize the danger involved. All I can do is say that I'll pay well for the risk. All your expenses, and five hundred thousand Earth dollars fee if you bring back Randall or definite information as to his fate."

And, Dilullo thought, *a Merc leader's share is one-fifth, and the ship-owner's share a fifth, and the rest share alike. That's a hundred thousand and that's the big, beautiful house above Brindisi that I've wanted all my life.*

He said, "That's an awful lot of money."

"It's Ashton Trading money," said Ashton. "Which means it's Randall's as much as mine. Maybe it can help him. What about it, Dilullo?"

Dilullo thought, but not for very long. He could see the house, the white walls and the portico, the flaming flowers spilling down the slope in front of it.

"I'll take on the job," he said. "But I'm not the only one, remember. I have to get a bunch of Mercs to go with me, and I've got to show them this material. I never led men into danger without warning them. I don't know if I can convince them, even for that money."

Ashton stood up. "Fair enough. I'll have the contracts drawn up, in the hopes that you can."

Dilullo hesitated a split second, not knowing whether or not he should offer to shake hands with as important a man as this one, but Ashton simply stuck out his hand.

All the way back to the hotel Dilullo kept thinking about a hundred thousand dollars. He clung to the thought because he had a growing feeling in his bones that he had taken on a job that was just too big and tough for Mercs.

Chane was waiting in the hotel room.

"What about the job?" he asked.

"It's a sweet one," said Dilullo. "It's big, and the money's real big. All I have to do is convince a dozen Mercs to lose all their good sense and go with me."

He told Chane. Chane stiffened, and an odd look came into his dark face.

"Allubane?"

"Yes. It's a star in the Perseus Arm and it has three planets."

"I know where it is," said Chane. He began to laugh a little. "So much for Varna law. I'm going to Allubane."

Dilullo stared. "What's this? Do you know anything about the Closed Worlds?"

"Not much," said Chane. "But years ago they heard on Varna that there was something big, something terrific, guarded by the people of that planet Arkuu, so a raiding Varnan squadron went there."

"What did they find?"

Chane shook his head. "They didn't say, not to anybody except the Council. They came back with nothing at all. But then the Council decreed that no Varnans were ever to go back to Allubane—that it was too dangerous a place."

Dilullo simply stared at him in silence until the impact of Chane's words really hit him.

If the Starwolves, who feared neither man nor God nor devil, were afraid of something at Allubane, that something had to be big and dangerous.

"Ah, you would come up with something like this," he said. "If this gets around, I'll never be able to sign a Merc for this mission. Do me a favor, will you, Chane? Go away somewhere, for a little while."

"Where?"

"You said once you'd like to see where your parents come from on Earth. It's a place in Wales, you said. You can get there quick."

Chane considered. "I think I will. I don't much like this place."

"And Chane," said Dilullo. "Don't come back till I call you. You almost Jonahed the last job; I'm damned if I'll have you Jonah this one."

III

Chane walked the streets of the old town, narrow ways, with low buildings, that slanted down toward the sea. The day was dark with great clouds and a mist and spume blew in from the ocean; the worn stones under his feet were wet and glistening. The wind was raw and boisterous, muttering of coming gales.

He liked this place. It was almost as grim and harsh as Varna. And he liked the people, though they had looked at him with neither any particular friendship nor hostility. He suddenly realized that it was their voices he liked. They talked in a queer, lilting way, just the way his father had talked, and he remembered that his father had called it the "singsong."

There did not seem to be very much in this small place of Carnarvon, except a big hulking wreck of a castle down by the sea, so he went that way. The place was ancient and battered but had a sort of grandeur under the stormy sky. There was an old man in a uniform coat at the gate who sold tickets. Chane bought a ticket and started in.

Then he thought of something, and went back and asked, "I wonder if you could tell me something. You've lived here a long time, I take it?"

"All my life," said the old man. He had short, snow-white hair and a bony red face, and surprisingly bright blue eyes which he fixed on Chane.

"Some of my family came from here," Chane said. "I wondered if you knew anything about them. A Reverend Thomas Chane, who grew up here in Carnarvon."

"Caernarfon, we Welsh call it," said the old man. "It means 'fortress in Arfon.' And well I remember the Reverend Thomas. He was a fine young man, devoted to the Lord, and he went away to the stars to convert some wicked heathen and died there. Are you his son?"

Caution stirred in Chane. It was the fact that he had been born on Varna that had made him a Starwolf, and he didn't want talk about that going around.

"Just a nephew," he said.

"Ah, then you'll be David Chane's son, that went away to America," nodded the old man. "I am William Williams, and I am glad indeed to meet one from the old families who had come back."

He ceremoniously shook hands with Chane. "Yes, yes, the Reverend Thomas was a fine man and a strong preacher. I do not doubt that he converted many out on that distant world before the Lord took him."

Chane only nodded, but as he passed on into the castle he was remembering his father on Varna. The little chapel where there was never any congregation except some Varnan children who came in to listen to the Earthman who spoke their language so poorly. His father's small figure valiantly erect and his face aglow as he preached, and his mother playing the small electronic organ, both of them dying slowly as Varna's heavy gravitation slowly dragged the life out of them, but neither of them admitting it, neither of them willing to quit and go back to Earth.

He walked around and found that the looming castle was really only a hollow shell, a great open space inside it. He climbed the towers and the battlements of the walls, and wondered what it would have been like to fight in the way that they did, back in the far past, with swords and spears and primitive weapons. He supposed that some of his own ancestors had been fighters like that.

He mused, liking the lowering sky and the harsh old stones and the silence, until William Williams came to him, wearing now a worn wool jacket instead of the uniform coat.

"We close now," said the old man. "I'll walk up through town with you and show you a few of our sights . . . it's on my way."

As they walked, with the sky dusking into twilight, it seemed that the old chap was more interested in asking questions than in answering them.

"And you came from America? Of course, that was where David went, long ago. Is it a good job you have there?"

"I'm not there very much," Chane said. "I've worked in starships for a long time."

He thought how Dilullo would react to that discreet description of a Starwolf's profession, and smiled a little.

"Ah, it's a wonderful thing that men can go to the stars but it's not for me, not for me," said William Williams. He stopped, and steered Chane toward the door of a low stone building. "We'll have a pint together, if you'll so honor me."

The room inside was low and poorly lit, and there was no one but a barman and three young men farther along the bar.

Williams paid for the pint with the utmost dignity, insisting, "It is my pleasure, to buy an ale for one of the Chanes."

Chane thought the stuff was mild as water but he did not want to say so. He suggested having another, and the old man dug an elbow into his ribs in a roguish sort of way, saying, "Well, since you've twisted my arm, I must break my usual rule."

When that was finished he took Chane along the bar to the three young men and told them, "This is the son

of David Chane of Caernarfon, and you've all heard of
that family. And these are Hayden Jones and Griff
Lewis and Lewis Evans.''

They mumbled acknowledgment to Chane. Two of
them were small and nondescript young men but Hayden Jones was a very big, dark young man with very
bright, black eyes.

"And now I must say good night and be getting
along,'' the old man told Chane. "I leave you in good
company and hope you come home again.''

Chane said goodbye, then turned to the three young
men and suggested that he buy them a drink.

There was a furtive hostility about them, and they
did not answer him. He repeated the offer.

"We do not need damned Americans coming here to
buy our ale for us,'' said Hayden Jones without looking
at him.

"Ah,'' said Chane. "That may be true. But you need
better manners, don't you?''

The big young man whirled and his hand cracked and
Chane found himself, amazed, sitting on the floor of
the room. The old Starwolf anger flared up in him
bright as fire, and he gathered himself.

Then he saw Hayden Jones turn to his two companions, not saying anything but on his face the pleased
smile of a child who had just made everyone notice
him. There was something so naive in that smile that
the bright anger faded away as fast as it had come.

Chane relaxed his muscles and got to his feet. He
rubbed his chin and said, "You have a hard hand on
you, Hayden Jones.''

He stuck out his hand and grasped Jones' shoulder in
a bruising grip, putting his Varna strength into it. "I
have a hard hand too. If it's a fight you must have I'll
oblige you. But what I would really like to do is buy a
few drinks.''

Hayden Jones looked startled, and then he grinned
sheepishly and looked at his two companions. "Well,

now," he said. "We can always fight later, can't we, after we've had those drinks?"

They had the drinks, and then they had some more, and when the barman finally shoved them out the door it was late night and the gale had broken. The wind threw rain at them like smallshot as they went down the slanting streets, singing the songs that Chane's three companions had been trying to teach him.

An upstairs window opened and an elderly female's voice screeched at them. Hayden Jones turned and shouted, with great stateliness.

"Be quiet, is it? And when, Mrs. Griffith, have you been so unpatriotic that you cannot hear the national anthem of Wales?"

The window slammed down and they went on. Outside the hotel, Hayden Jones said, "Now, about the fight . . ."

"Let us save it until next time," said Chane. "Late at night, I have no stomach for it."

"Until next time!"

They grinned at each other and shook hands. Chane went inside and up to his room. When he got there the little communic he had placed on the old-fashioned wooden bureau was buzzing. He switched it on, and John Dilullo's voice came through.

"Chane? You can come back now. I've got a crew."

Chane acknowledged, feeling a strong sense of regret. Ancestral memories or not, he had taken a liking to this place and these people. He would have wished to stay longer. But he was obedient, and booked his passage on the first New York rocket. All the way across the Atlantic he was thinking, *I will come back to that place some day and have that fight. I think it would be a good one.*

Back in New York, Chane went into the building on a side street in the starport quarter that was formally the Headquarters of the Guild of Mercenaries, but which was always called Merc Hall.

In the big main room he looked up at the wall where the crews were posted. There were neat directories of white letters on black backgrounds. He read the first one.

Leader: Martin Bender
Second: J. Bioc
Ship-captain: Paul Vristow

There followed under that a dozen other names, some of which were not Earthman names at all. Then, below that;

Destination: Procyon Three.

He went along the wall, reading the other directories, and he thought, Achernar, Vanoon, Spica, Morr, the Mercs really got around. Until he saw

Leader: John Dilullo
Second: J. Bollard

And on with the other names. "Morgan Chane" was at the bottom of the list.

Dilullo's voice rasped in his ear. "Well, did you expect to be first? Remember, you're a pretty new Merc. You have no seniority."

"I'm surprised," said Chane, "that Bollard would go out again this soon."

Dilullo smiled bleakly. "Bollard's one of the few Mercs who's a family man. He's got a raft of children he adores. He's also got an ugly, nagging wife. He stays home just long enough to turn over his takings and then gets out to space again."

Dilullo added, "We're made up. I'm going to call Mr. Ashton; if he's free, I'll go over and sign the contract. Wait here."

Chane waited, and presently Dilullo came back with a surprised look on his face.

"You know what? Ashton's coming over here. He said he wants to meet the whole crew."

Dilullo, impressed, hurried out to get the crew to-

gether in one of the smaller rooms of the Hall. Bollard
came in and saw Chane, and his fat, round face creased
in an affectionate smile.

"Ah, the rock-hopper," he said. "I saw your name
on the list, Chane. I haven't decided yet whether I'm
happy about it."

"Be happy," said Chane.

Bollard shook his head, laughing as though he'd
heard the best joke in the world. "No, I'm not sure.
You nearly jammed us into big trouble the last time,
though I have to admit you did noble helping to get us
out of it."

"Mr. James Ashton," said Dilullo's voice, speaking
gruffly as though he refused to be impressed by a very
important person.

Ashton smiled and nodded and went through the
introductions. The Mercs were all as polite as Sunday-
school scholars. They eyed the man of money with
unliking eyes.

Then Ashton surprised them. He began to talk to
them, looking a little bit upset and embarrassed, but
very earnest and determined, like a fussy schoolteacher
trying to explain something.

"I've been worrying about you men," he said. "I
offered a big lot of money for men to go to the Closed
Worlds and look for my brother, and I know the money
is why you're going. But I feel worried . . ."

He broke off, and then resolutely started again. "I've
been thinking: I may be endangering a lot of men's
lives, to save the one life of my brother. So I thought I
should tell you . . . this job will be dangerous, as I'm
sure Mr. Dilullo has explained. But if it's too dangerous, I want no man's death on my conscience. If the
risks are too great, draw back. If you come back and
tell me that it was not within reason to go on, I'll still
pay two thirds of what I offered."

The Mercs said nothing but there was a sudden thaw
in their attitude. Finally Dilullo said, "Thanks, Mr.

Ashton. Mercs don't quit very easily. But thanks, just the same."

When Ashton and the other Mercs had gone, Dilullo told Chane, "You know, Ashton's a good sort. The fact that he made an offer like that, that he's worried about us, will make us knock ourselves out for him at Allubane."

Chane said, with an ironical smile, "Sure it will. And maybe that's just why he said that."

Dilullo looked at him disgustedly. "I wouldn't have a Starwolf's mind for anything you can name. No wonder that you don't really have a friend in the universe."

"But I have," said Chane. "I made some, in the place called Wales. Fine fellows, full of fight and fun, and they taught me some great songs. Listen to this one—it's an old war-song about the Men of Harlech."

He threw back his head and sang, and Dilullo winced.

"There's never been anybody Welsh who didn't fancy he could sing," he said. "Not even a Starwolf."

"It's a grand tune," said Chane. "It's worthy of being a Varnan battle-song."

"Then get ready to sing it in the Closed Worlds," Dilullo said. "I've got a feeling that my greed for money and a fine house is taking us to big trouble there."

IV

The little Merc ship, a Class Twenty, plodded out through the system of Sol and then jumped into overdrive and went on its way.

The vast, sweeping spirals of the galaxy, the irregularly curved arms of denser star-concentrations, dwarfed the ship to a mere infinitesimal mote. Far behind it, Cygnus Arm was a gigantic rampart of gleaming suns. It stretched in a rimward direction to a galactic latitude of twenty degrees, then split off into two almost equally awesome continents of stars, the Vela Spur and Orion Spur.

The ship moved on and on, putting the great mass of Orion Spur behind it, swinging past an elongated tangle of "hot hydrogen" clouds, heading toward the glittering sprawl of Perseus Arm, nearly at the rim. It did not move in a completely straight course, even in overdrive. The wheel of stars that was the galaxy was a rotating wheel, and relative positions altered constantly, and then the computers would clack and talk among themselves and change the course a little.

In the bridge, Kimmel, the captain and co-owner of the craft, looked at the rep-chart's gleaming lights.

"Everything seems all right," he said to Dilullo.

The slight emphasis on "seems" was characteristic. Kimmel was a small, bald, nervous man who worried about things nearly all the time. He worried mostly about the ship taking any damage.

Lots of Merc leaders had got so bored with Kimmel's worrying that they wouldn't sign with him. But Dilullo had known him a long while, and preferred a worrying captain to a carefree one. He knew that Kimmel, if anything threatened his precious ship, would fight like a lion.

"Sure it's all right," he said. "Nothing to it. Just take us out to Perseus Arm and break out within normal-drive distance of Allubane."

"And what then?" said Kimmel. "Have you looked at the S-Chart of that Allubane system? Rotten with drift, and the radar will likely be all fouled up by radio emissions from the hydrogen clouds there."

"Cool hydrogen," Dilullo interrupted.

"I know, I know; it's supposed to emit only on the twenty-first centimeter band, but if there's gas debris colliding with it, cool hydrogen can blow the radar faster than hot. And suppose it does just that?"

"Suppose nothing of the sort," said Dilullo soothingly. "Just remember, Kimmel, I'm not going to do anything reckless—my skin is as dear to me as this old tub is to you."

"Old tub?" cried Kimmel. He began an angry statement. Dilullo went away, a slight smile on his hard face. He had been steering Kimmel away from his worries by that approach for a long time, and the captain had not caught on yet.

In his small cabin, Dilullo got out the papers that James Ashton had given him and studied them.

He thought about four people.

Dr. Martin Garcia, of the Cuernavaca School of Extra-Terrestrial Anthropology; S. Sattargh, exchange instructor from the University of Arcturus Three; Jewett McGoun, formerly a free-lance interstellar trader; and Dr. Jonas Caird of the Foundation of Extra-Terrestrial Sciences in New York.

He looked the names over again. There was one of them that did not seem to fit.

Jewett McGoun, free star-trader. What was he doing with four scientists?

Dilullo read further in the notes that James Ashton had made for him. And after a while he muttered, "Ah-huh."

It was Jewett McGoun who had first told Randall Ashton about something big and wonderful in the Closed Worlds. He had, so Randall had averred, brought solid evidence of his story. But Randall would not show this evidence to his brother and he would not tell the exact nature of what he was going after.

"You wouldn't believe me," Randall Ashton had said. "But I'll tell you how big it is—it could absolutely revolutionize the exploration of the universe."

More than that he would not say. And so they had gone eagerly off to Allubane . . . four questing scientists and Mr. Jewett McGoun.

It smelled, Dilullo thought. It smelled at him right off the pages of these notes.

There had long been a story, told by many another like old Donahue, of a great secret in the Closed Worlds. It probably had been dreamed up just because the Closed Worlds *were* closed.

But take that story and build on it, contrive phony evidence, then present the whole thing to an enthusiastic student of the extra-terrestrial who also happened to be a millionaire, and you could toll him off to Allubane. And once you had him there, there were a good many different ways by which you might enrich yourself from him.

But if McGoun had only been selling a phony story about something big in the Closed Worlds, why did the Starwolves fear to go there?

"Ah, curse that Chane," muttered Dilullo. "He can spoil anything, even a good theory."

The ship went on and on, for one ship-day after another, and it seemed that it was going to rush through overdrive for an eternity, until finally there came a time when the siren hooted.

Dilullo thought, *It's about time,* and went up from his cabin, heading for the bridge. He passed the small cubby where Chane was doing substitute duty for the radar man.

He stuck his head in and said, "You haven't been bored, have you, Chane?"

Chane gave him a bright smile. "Now why would I be bored? Here I am, in a ship going almost half as fast as a Varnan ship would go, crawling along, at a pretty good clip. Why in the world would I be bored?"

Dilullo grinned a little. "That's good to hear. But just in case you *have* been bored, I rather imagine there'll be some action soon. And, Chane . . ."

"Yes?"

"You'll be happy to know that if there is any action, anything really dangerous, I'll see to it that you're right in the forefront. Are you grateful?"

Chane said between his teeth, "I'm grateful, you old so-and-so."

Dilullo was laughing a little when he reached the bridge. He had no sooner reached it than the siren hooted the second warning. He grabbed a stanchion as the ship went out of overdrive.

The lights went dim and the whole fabric of the vessel seemed to shudder and dissolve. So did Dilullo's personal being. No matter how often he went through this, he never lost the moment of panic fear, the conviction that his shredded atoms were dispersed for all time and could never be gathered again. It was like the old ancestral falling-dream, only infinitely worse. Then, as always, they hit bottom, the transition was over, and they were in normal space again.

They were just outside the edge of the Perseus Arm. It was one thing to call it that, to mark it on the map as one of the outer spirals of the galaxy. It was another thing to be there, to look out the viewport at the titanic coast of stars, high as heaven and flaring as hell.

"Now, David," said Kimmel. "Now let us go on."

Dave Mattock, the pilot, shoved the control levers and the ship started moving toward the nearest star in the Arm, a topaz-colored sun.

Mattock was renowned among Mercs for two reasons. One was that he chewed tobacco. Hardly anyone had used tobacco in any form for a long time; there were mild drugs that were much safer and just as sedative. Almost no one had actually chewed the stuff for decades, but as a boy, Mattock had been taught the habit by a rapscallion old grandfather in the Kentucky hills, and he had never given it up.

The other reason Mattock was famous was that he had never lost his temper with Kimmel. It had been said often in Merc Hall that when Mattock quit piloting, Kimmel would have to retire, for no other pilot would be able to take the worrying captain.

"Easy, easy!" cried Kimmel. "We've got to take this system carefully. Remember what I told you about those cool hydrogen clouds. And that drift . . . that terrific drift . . ."

Mattock, a large powerful man with a large, rock-jawed face, paid not the slightest attention. He chewed, and he moved the controls.

"Godalmighty, David, are you trying to pile us up?" cried Kimmel. He was almost dancing up and down now, leaning over Mattock's shoulder, reading the dials, not quite wringing his hands but almost doing that. "We've lots of time, lots of time . . ."

Mattock spat, with ringing accuracy, at the plastic pail in the corner that was a fixture when he was on the bridge. He said nothing.

"Ah, that's it . . . that's it . . . careful does it," squeaked Kimmel. "After all, David, we want to be careful, don't we? That's a good careful boy . . ."

Mattock read the computer figures flaring across the screen and calmly punched down on the power.

There came from Kimmel a squeal like that of a stricken rabbit; he clutched his hands over his bald head like an old woman awaiting doomsday.

Dilullo grinned. He had had a good many landings with Kimmel and Mattock and they had never changed much.

He looked out ahead. They were running down fast toward Allubane, and the topaz sun glared bright and wicked in his blue eyes.

The computer began to stutter now and then. The emissions from the cool hydrogen clouds one couldn't even see were interfering with radar information, and without information the computers were just metal and wire and crystals. Useless.

Dust whispered along the hull. They were getting into the edges of the drift and it was bad—not the worst, but bad enough. It always made Dilullo wish that the suns and planets were as clean and tidy as they looked on the star-charts, with nothing between them but nice, clean open space. But it wasn't that way at all; their making had left many of them a bit messy around the edges. In time the debris would be all swept up by their gravitational fields, but human beings didn't have that kind of time.

The whispering became a crackling, outside the hull. Kimmel went and buried his face against the wall of the bridge-room. Dilullo watched him admiringly. This was the next-to-last phase for him, the "I can't look" phase.

The crackling outside the hull eased, then came back again, a little stronger. The computers went off for a whole minute, a silence that was dread-inspiring.

Kimmel came away from the wall. He came and sat down in the co-pilot chair. He sat quite still, his head stuck forward, his eyes stony, a little glazed, his shoulders hunched.

Dilullo nodded to himself. This was the final phase, the "All is lost, sunk in despair" phase.

Mattock calmly turned his head and spat regally into the bucket.

The computers came back on again and the crackle

of drift faded; before them there came into view three planets, two on this side of the star and the third halfway around it.

Dilullo thought, it was like that which Berlioz had written about the second movement of Beethoven's Fourth Symphony: ". . . the great chords come up like newly-created worlds swimming up, fresh and beautiful from the hand of God."

He felt proud of himself for a moment; no other Merc captain would know things like that. And then he thought forlornly, *But I only know them because I was alone and lonely for so long, and so much time to read.*

He looked at the Closed Worlds as one looks at the eyes of an enemy. And they went on down toward the smoky yellow flare of Allubane.

V

Chane smelled danger in the silence.

He stood with a half-dozen other Mercs on the battered spaceport in front of their ship. The hot lemon-colored sunlight poured down and the warm wind whispered around them; there was no other sound.

The massive white marble city beyond the spaceport climbed a slope in tier after tier of ancient-looking buildings. It was too far away to be heard, and the silence did not bother Chane. But here on the spaceport it was too quiet. There was no movement at the warehouses and other buildings. The eight or nine small planetary cruisers near them, four of which had missile-launcher ports in their sides, had no activity around them.

"Just take it easy," said Dilullo. "Be casual. It's safer to wait and let them make the first move."

Milner, beside Chane, muttered, "It would be safer still by a damn sight to be wearing our stunners."

Milner was a foul-mouthed, fighty little man whom none of the other Mercs liked much, and who got berths only because of his superlative skill in using and servicing weapons. Yet Chane had to agree with him.

But Dilullo had been dogmatic about it. They had to come in to Allubane One—its planet-name was Arkuu—and take its people by surprise, but they mustn't seem to be looking for a fight.

They had managed the surprise all right. They had

homed in on the other side of Arkuu, and then had whipped half around the planet toward this capital city of Yarr without sending any notice of arrival or requesting landing-permission.

Chane had looked down on Arkuu as it rolled rapidly away beneath them, and thought it was not much of a world.

Crimson jungle covered a lot of it. Here and there, where the land rose into dark mountains, the jungle gave way to forests of deeper red. Once there was an ocher-colored sea, with tawny rivers snaking into it.

And cities. Cities of white marble that had been great and gracious once, but now were whelmed by the red tide of the jungle. Cities with no life stirring in their broken stones, the wrecks of the past, brooding under the topaz sun like old, dead kings whose glory is long forgotten.

Chane felt a sharply heightened sense of the mystery of this far world. Once its people must have been great indeed, to build such cities and to have gone out and colonized the second planet. What was it that had made them throw it all away? What was it that made them set their faces against interstellar travel, so that they made their system into the Closed Worlds?

Then their ship had come over the ridge of a valley and below them was another white city but this one still living, with people and a few ground-cars moving in its streets and some light fixed-wing fliers buzzing in the sky. With no warning at all, they had landed at the little planetary spaceport.

And now they waited, with Bollard and Kimmel and four others inside the ship just in case, and the sun was hot and nothing was happening.

Dilullo spoke without turning. "I'll do the talking."

A ground-car had emerged from the city and was coming across the spaceport toward them. It stopped a little way from them and two men got out of it and approached.

Chane, looking at the men, felt a sharp surprise.

He had expected the people of this decayed civilization to be limp, effete, weak. But these two were as impressive as he had ever seen.

They were tall, wide-shouldered, powerful-looking men, with pale golden skins and deep yellow hair and eyes of an icy blue-green. They wore short belted jerkins that left arms and legs bare, exposing superb muscles. They were about the least effete-looking men Chane had ever encountered.

One of the two, the younger and taller one, spoke to Dilullo in galacto, the lingua-franca of the galaxy. He spoke it a bit rustily.

"You are not welcome here," he said flatly. "Did you not know that the Closed Worlds are . . . closed?"

Dilullo gave him a straight answer. "We knew it."

"Then why did you come here?"

"I would like to give my reasons to those in your government with authority."

The younger man said, "We come from government and speak for it. I am Helmer and this is Bros. Now speak—why did you land here?"

Dilullo squared his shoulders as though he knew that he was heading into it now, but there was no way out of it.

"We came to look for a man," he said. "An Earthman, Randall Ashton by name, and his companions."

The two Arkuuns were silent for a moment. Chane saw them glance at each other, and then the one named Helmer answered.

"The man you look for is not here."

"Then where is he?"

Helmer shrugged. "Who knows? He was here, and then he went away."

"To one of the other two planets?"

Helmer merely shrugged his broad shoulders again. "Who knows?"

Chane thought, *I'd like to try knocking the answer out of him. The muscles he's got he'd give even a Varnan a tussle.*

As though he caught the thought, or detected it from Chane's expression, the tall young Arkuun suddenly looked directly at him. It was as though, towering and great-limbed as he was, he recognized a potential powerful antagonist in the compact figure and dark, faintly mocking face of Chane.

Then he turned back to Dilullo. "You are to go," he said. "We cannot service starships here, but we can give you food and water. Take them and go."

"Now wait a minute," said Dilullo. "You may be hermits here, but there are certain rules in the civilized starworlds about the right of repatriation of nationals. If you knew more about the galaxy as it is, you'd realize . . ."

He was interrupted by Bros, the older man, who laughed suddenly. His laughter was loud and nervous, oddly mirthless.

"Did you hear that, Helmer?" he said. "If we Arkuuns only knew more about the universe. But he is right. Our people have never been anywhere, have they?"

He laughed again, and a sardonic smile came onto Helmer's strong face.

To Chane, there was something ominous, hidden, in this sudden mirth. But it stung Dilullo.

"Let me tell you something," he said in an edged voice. "This man Randall Ashton is an important man, and comes from people with power. If I go back and report that you won't even tell what's happened to him, you'll sooner or later have a force come here that'll knock the Closed Worlds wide open."

Helmer's face became instantly stone cold. "Ah," he said. "Is it so?"

Chane groaned inwardly and thought, *Your foot slipped that time, John—a Starwolf child would have known better.*

He felt like shaking Dilullo. He looked away, toward the city, and his eye was caught by a point of light that came and went in one of the taller buildings, where a window that seemed to be swinging in the wind caught and reflected the lemon sunlight.

"Since you make threats," Helmer was saying icily, "I too will threaten. Go now, or you do not go at all."

He turned his back on Dilullo, and he and Bros went to their car and sped away.

Dilullo turned around and looked sourly at the Mercs. "Right up against a blank wall," he said. "Well, your peerless leader isn't doing so good. Anybody got any ideas?"

"I've got one," Chane said. "I'd get back in the ship and go out of here as though the devil was riding our tail."

Dilullo stared at him, as though a Chane counseling flight was a new and upsetting phenomenon.

Chane explained, with insulting carefulness. "You told him that if you got back and made your report, it would bring big trouble on them. *If* you got back."

It sank in. The Mercs looked from Chane to Dilullo, and Dilullo's face became longer.

"You're right," he said. "I tried a bluff and it didn't work, and we've bought it if we stay here. Emergency take-off."

They ran into the ship. The locks slammed shut, and within a minute the hooter blared its warning. Mattock took them skyward with a slamming rush. The friction-alarms started screeching like hysterical women, but Mattock ignored them. Presently they were out of atmosphere.

Chane had gone to his post at radar; he scanned the planet falling away behind them. Presently he saw what he expected to see.

"Two Arkuun ships coming out fast after us," he said, and added, "I think we can expect some missiles."

"Up shields," Dilullo ordered, and then swore. "We

may have made it easier for them. They wouldn't have dared use those missiles on the spaceport, so close to the city."

"Shields up," came Bollard's voice.

The ship rocked to a *blam-blam* impact, and Bollard added, "And about time."

It did not look too good to Chane. The Merc ship had no launchers; its shields were light ones and would not take a prolonged hammering.

Kimmel was hanging over Mattock's chair and now he began talking to him. Chane expected more worried wailing, but he did not know Kimmel the way Dilullo did, and was surprised.

"Now, David," Kimmel was saying, "we have to shake those cruisers off fast. If a screen fails, we can take damage. Costly damage." He quivered a little like a nervous terrier as he said that. "So you head for that stream of drift zenithward from Allubane Two."

Mattock looked up at him. "Hit the drift?"

"Yes, David, it's our best chance. I saw those ships at the spaceport; they're old types and can't have radar as good as ours. We can throw them off in the drift; they won't chance it for long. But with our good radar you can take us on through, David."

Mattock spat mightily and said, "Hit the drift. Okay."

The ship veered sharply. Chane watched the radar screen. They were hauling away from the Arkuun cruisers, but not fast enough to get clear out of missile range. He told that to Dilullo.

"Ah, I played the devil with my smart bluff," Dilullo muttered. "And we didn't even find out if Ashton's party are alive or dead."

"Some of them are alive," Chane said.

"How do you know?"

Chane did not turn from the screen as he said, "A window up in one of those bigger buildings in the city kept swinging and reflecting sunlight. It was blinking 'ASHTON' in ship code."

"You didn't tell me that," Dilullo accused.

Chane smiled. "I didn't want to tell you anything that might distract you from pulling tail fast."

A salvo hit the screens and the ship rocked wildly. The thunderous noise drowned Dilullo's answer to that.

Chane was just as glad.

VI

They were in the drift now, and it was bad. It was so bad that Kimmel kept his mouth completely shut, which was always a sign of danger. The computers clacked and worried as they ran on down toward Allubane Two.

They passed zenithward of that spinning planet. It looked to Chane not unlike Arkuu, except that the jungles were forest on this second planet, and rather thin forest at that. There were none of the ancient white marble cities, but more modest towns of stone. Lights shone here and there from the dark side of the planet.

Chane scanned the screen. "They've broken off pursuit."

Kimmel looked at Dilullo. "Now what? Do we head back to Sol? Remember, John, we get two-thirds of the money just for trying. We certainly tried."

Dilullo looked at him bleakly. "We didn't do anything. I tried a stupid bluff and we had to hightail it out of there. You think I want to take a story like that back to Merc Hall?"

"But what, then. . . . ?"

"We're going back to Arkuu," Dilullo said decisively. "But in a different way. Head out of this system, get Allubane Three between us and the primary, and then swing back and land on that planet."

"Allubane Three? But it's supposed to be uninhabited, nothing much there at all."

"Exactly the kind of place we need, so set down there," said Dilullo.

The ship went on, edging out of the drift. It went beyond the third planet, which was a tawny, barren-looking ball, and then swung back again, running up the planet-shadow.

They came down upon a world that was almost desert, a world with bitter-looking seas and sad, barren lands with scant vegetation and no sign of people at all. Mattock brought them down near a seashore and cut the power.

"*Very* well done, David," said Kimmel.

"Get the launchers out and set them up," said Dilullo on the intercom, and rattled off names.

Chane's was one of them and he went down into the hold. They squeezed and tugged, hauling the portable missile-launchers past the stored skitter-flier and ground-car, manhandling them out of the cargo port.

The air was cold. This was the outermost of the Closed Worlds, and the sun had little warmth in it. They set up the launchers, and then stood by them, keeping an eye on the sky.

Chane and the Merc named Van Fossan manned one of the launchers. Van Fossan was a lean, blond, thirtyish young Hollander, with an eager eye and a face like a young hound's.

"What do you think John will do now?" he asked Chane.

Chane shrugged. What he wanted to say was that Dilullo should get his brains back into his head from where he had been carrying them, but an odd feeling of loyalty forbade him voicing the thought.

"No people, but some life here," said Van Fossan a little later. "Look at that."

The smoky yellow flare of Allubane was setting out over the ocean. Van Fossan pointed to two black, big, snaky-looking winged things flying out there. He added,

"*. . . when sunset, like a crimson throat to Hell,*
Is cavernous, she marks the seaward flight

Of homing dragons dark upon the west."

Chane looked at him. "What do you mean? That sky isn't crimson; it's dark yellow."

"It's a poem," Van Fossan said, and added disgustedly, "English is your mother tongue. Don't you know your own poetry?"

"I don't know many poems," said Chane. "I know some songs . . ." He broke off, and his lips twitched.

No, he thought. *I will not sing those songs for Nico. They were the songs we sang on Varna when the raiding squadrons were in, and they would not be good for Earthman ears.*

He dreamed again of Varna. Would he ever go there again? He felt somehow that he would, though it might be going to his death. The brothers of Ssander, whom he had killed in the fair fight that had got him chased out of the Starwolves, would never forgive him.

The yellow sky darkened to a dusky saffron, but no ships appeared in it.

"Chane," said Van Fossan in a low voice. "Look."

Chane turned his attention from the sky to the barren landscape around them.

Then he saw. A furry, dark animal about the size and look of a bear but with six limbs, was industriously digging out a bush only a few hundred feet from them. There were three more of the animals, but they were much farther away.

The creature dug out the bush and started chewing on its root. It looked with mild, stupid eyes as it did so, and then it seemed for the first time to become aware of the ship and the men. It stopped chewing and looked at them. Then it made a low growling sound.

It seemed to be saying, *"Errrrr!"*

Chane looked it back in the eye.

Again it said, *"Errrrr!"*

Chane suddenly uttered a tremendous roar and ran forward toward the creature, flailing his arms wildly.

The animal dropped the root and scuttled frantically

away, and Chane stopped running, and laughed and laughed.

"Chane, you damn crazy fool! It could have been dangerous!" stormed Van Fossan.

"What the devil is going on out here?" demanded Dilullo's voice in the dusk. He had come out of the ship.

Van Fossan explained. Dilullo grunted. "If standing watch is that much fun we'll cut short your turn, Chane. Come on in and sweat with us."

Chane followed him in. In the main bunkroom, under the lights, Bollard and Kimmel and Milner sat around the table.

"Sit down," Dilullo said. "We're trying to decide how to tackle this thing."

"And so of course we need the advice of our newest Merc," said Bollard.

Dilullo told him, "Chane was the one who spotted that code-signal and the only one who knows which building it is. He ought to hear this."

Bollard shrugged, but shut up.

Dilullo told Chane, "We figure that Randall Ashton, or at least some of his party, are prisoners in that building. They saw an Earth-type ship land—you can't mistake our ships with their eyebrow bridges—and they tried to tell us they were there. If Ashton's in there, we've got to get him out. If he's not there, someone is there who should know where Ashton is."

Chane nodded.

Kimmel broke in, saying quickly, "And of course we can't risk landing the ship there again. They'll be expecting that; they'll be all set for us and they'll hit our ship with everything they've got."

He closed his eyes, as though the wrecking of his beloved vessel was too horrible to contemplate.

"So," Dilullo patiently continued, "we're not going to land the ship on Arkuu. We'll swing over and drop the skitter-flier well outside the city, by night. In the flier

will be a small party of us. We'll try to get the Ashton
people in that building out of there. If we do, we'll call
the ship to come back and pick us up outside the city."

Chane nodded again but said nothing. He was not being
asked his opinion of the plan, and did not venture to give it.

"I'll lead the landing party," Dilullo told him. "I think
Bollard and Milner and Janssen too . . . and you, Chane."

"Of course," said Bollard. "How could we leave out
the heroic Chane—the man who nearly got us scragged
on Kharali by his playfulness, the man who on Vhol
was off boating with a pretty girl while we sat and
sweated it out under the gun . . ."

". . . and also," Dilullo added, "the man who can
identify the building we have to reach."

"Oh, all right," said Bollard. "But don't you think our
party will be a mite small? Five men, to invade a planet?"

"Fifty would be no better, if they caught us," Dilullo
said. "The flier won't carry too many, remember, and
we may be bringing back four people with us."

He stood up. "Milner, I want you to help check out
the weapons we'll take with us."

Twenty-four Earth hours later, the Merc ship came
back to Arkuu. Dilullo had picked a time when the capital city was on the dark side of the planet. But the ship
went downward a hundred miles away from the city.

Dilullo went over their maps with Kimmel, marking
down a spot for emergency rendezvous in case they could
not get a call through. Then he went down to the hold,
where the others were ready in their places in the flier.

Janssen, the sandy-haired, stocky Merc who was the
best man with a flier, sat at the controls, and Dilullo,
Bollard, Chane, and Milner in the sketchy bucket-seats.

They could see nothing, here in the dark hold. It was
up to Mattock, in the bridge of the ship, to pick the
place and the altitude for the drop. They could hear the
hold bulkheads closing.

Then the big ejection-port in the side of the hold slid
open. They got just a glimpse, over Janssen's broad

shoulders, of a vista of jungle below, lighted by one of the two moons of Arkuu.

"Now," said Mattock's voice from the intercom.

Janssen's hand slammed down on the ejection button. The flier shot out through the port like a bullet.

Its wings and rotors unfolded automatically as it went out. They bit into the atmosphere, finding it roiled and bumpy from the wake of the ship. Janssen steadied the flier gently and swung it around, only a few thousand feet above the jungle.

"Luck, John," said Kimmel's voice from the communicator.

Janssen set a course and the skitter-flier leaped fast. It went high over the jungle like a humming shadow. It had been especially designed for jobs like this one; it had VTO and a motor so near noiseless as to make no difference.

In less than an hour they glimpsed the lights of the city. There were not many; it was late at night here, the way Dilullo had planned it.

"Get over the east side of that spaceport and then take her down," he told Janssen. And to Chane, "Take the scope. Talk Janssen in to the roof of that building you caught the signal from."

Chane watched through the scope as the flier dropped vertically downward. He finally identified the building, which had a few lighted windows.

He gave Janssen direction. After a moment he added, "There's something else. A man seems to be standing guard on the roof."

"Ah, the bastards," said Bollard. "They must have got suspicious we'd come back."

"Could be the guard is a regular thing," Dilullo said curtly. "Anyway, we have to get him before we go down farther. Hold it, Janssen. Milner, use the heavy duty stunner hooked to the scope. Non-lethal."

Milner gave him a wizened grin and came forward, hauling the weapon that looked like an old-fashioned bazooka. He set it into place on the mount atop the scope in the firing-port, and with quick efficiency clicked the synchronizing links into place. Then he opened the port.

Janssen had slowed their descent. Milner peered through the scope, the white of his one eye visible. He made adjustment of its positioning-wheels, squinted again, then pressed the trigger.

The stunner droned. Milner cut it, then raised his head and gave them another pleased, toothy grin.

"He's out."

"All right, Janssen," said Dilullo. "Go on down."

The flier landed on the roof, quiet as an over-sized dragonfly. Dilullo cracked the cabin door and all of them but Janssen went out of it fast, Milner toting along the heavy-duty stunner.

Dilullo's voice, low but forceful, drove them. The building had several stories, and he split them up, each to search through one of its levels.

They ran down stone stairways, feebly illuminated by occasional glowing bulbs in the walls. Chane had the second highest level; he left the stairway and went down a long, poorly-lit corridor, his stunner in his hand.

The marble blocks of the walls had been beautiful once, but they were cracked and grimed with age. This whole world had an antique, battered look, Chane thought. He wondered again what there could be about it that had made the Varnans, who were afraid of nothing, forbid their raiders coming here.

He opened doors along corridors. Nothing. Dark, musty rooms with nothing in them.

Then he found a door that was locked. As he tried it, he thought that he heard movement inside.

Chane drew a pocket atoflash out, with his left hand. Keeping the stunner ready in his right, he used the flash to cut out the lock.

The door swung open and a girl looked at him from the lighted room beyond.

VII

This girl was no little slip of a thing. She was nearly as tall as Helmer had been, and had the same kind of pale-gold skin and yellow hair. She too wore a belted jerkin, of silken white material, and she had magnificent arms and legs that the garment showed to full advantage.

Her gray-green eyes stared into Chane's, in complete astonishment. She opened her mouth, and he thought that she was going to shout. He was too close to her to use the stunner without getting a backlash from it. He dropped the atoflash and grabbed her, putting his hand over her mouth.

And he got the surprise of his life. This young woman, for all her delectable curves, was stronger than anything feminine he had met since he left Varna. She nearly threw him headlong before he managed to clamp down a tighter grip on her.

Bollard came loping into the corridor from the stair. In danger, he was quite unlike the fat, sloppy Bollard of relaxed moments. His face was drawn tight and the stunner in his hand was ready.

He saw Chane grappling with the tall Arkuun girl; he lowered his weapon a little and stood staring, in wonder and admiration.

"By God, Chane, I have to hand it to you," he said.

"You do find fun wherever you go. I hear something up here and come running to save you, and I find you wrestling with a big beautiful blonde."

"Get John," said Chane. "She was locked up here; there may be others."

He relaxed his grip a little as he spoke. Next moment he was sorry. The Arkuun girl got her teeth around one of his fingers and bit it to the bone.

Chane did not take his hand off her mouth. He swung her around a little, looking into her blazing eyes, and smiled at her.

"I do like a girl with spirit," he said. Then he drew his hand back and cracked her across the point of the chin.

He only used the flat of his hand but he put some of his Starwolf strength into it. The girl's head jerked back and she went out cold.

Chane lowered her to the floor, where she sat with her back against the wall, looking like a discarded doll. As an afterthought, Chane bent down and crossed the long, beautiful legs at the ankles, and put her hands together in her lap. He looked down at her admiringly, as he sucked his bitten finger.

"Isn't she something?" he said.

Dilullo came hurrying into the corridor, with Milner behind him.

"Two guards down at the entrance . . . we stunned them," he said. "Nothing else. What have you got here?"

Chane told him. Dilullo went along the further doors. There was one other door that was locked.

When Dilullo tried it, they heard an excited voice inside, and then a hammering of hands on the door.

"Stand back," said Dilullo.

With the atoflash, he cut the door open.

A young Earthman with stiffly-upstanding black hair and a high-cheekboned Spanish-Indian face came out. His eyes were wild with excitement.

"You're the Earthmen from that ship?" he cried. "I saw it . . . ! I tried to signal . . ."

"Hold on," said Dilullo. "You're one of Ashton's party?"

"Martin Garcia. It's been weeks . . . months . . ."

Dilullo interrupted. "Where are the others?"

"Caird's dead," said Garcia, making an effort to calm down. "Died here more than a week ago. Killed? No, he wasn't killed. He caught a bug, seemed to get weaker and weaker. I stayed with him when Ashton and McGoun and the others left."

"Where's Randall Ashton now?" demanded Dilullo.

Garcia spread his hands. "My God, I don't know. He and McGoun got away with the ship and crew, weeks ago. They thought they could find the Free-Faring. The Arkuuns here had forbidden us to look for it, but they went anyway. The Open-Worlders helped them get their ship away. I stayed because Caird looked so bad."

"John, there's no time now for life stories," said Bollard. "If Ashton isn't here, let's go, and get the facts out of this chap later on."

Garcia had caught sight of the girl sitting with her hands in her lap further along the corridor.

"Vreya . . . did you kill her?" he exclaimed.

"She's only unconscious," said Bollard. "Who is she, anyway?"

"She was one of the Open-Worlders who helped Ashton get away," said Garcia. "She can talk galacto, and they used her as a secret contact. But Helmer's men caught her and locked her up here like me."

"Would she know where Randall Ashton and the others have gone?" demanded Dilullo.

"I don't know," said Garcia. "I think so."

"We'll take her along with us," Dilullo said decisively. "Now out of here on the double!"

Chane picked up the unconscious girl effortlessly, and they hurried back to the roof. When Janssen, in the flier, saw the long golden legs dangling from Chane's arms, he uttered a low whistle of appreciation.

"Well, you found something, anyway."

"Save the humor," said Dilullo. "Get us out of here—back the way we came. And move!"

The flier went up and away from there, and started arrowing back out across the moonlit jungle. Garcia, in a bucketseat beside Dilullo, talked rapidly but not incoherently. He had got over his first excitement.

"We were there for nearly two months, the four of us," he said. "In Yarr, the city back there. Randall kept trying to find out from the Arkuuns about the Free-Faring, but their officials wouldn't tell us a thing and kept demanding that we leave. Then the Open-Worlders made secret contact with Randall."

Garcia went on. "The Open-Worlders are Arkuuns who dissent from the rule of keeping the Closed Worlds closed. They want to open the system to interstellar trade. She's one of them."

He nodded toward the girl Vreya. Chane had dropped her into a seat and buckled its strap across her, but she was still unconscious.

"Why would these dissidents want to help Ashton get away to find this—what did you call it?—the Free-Faring? I take it that's the mysterious thing he was after."

"Yes." Garcia shrugged. "They said it was because they wanted him to bring them weapons later on, for a coup. They'd help him find the Free-Faring if he'd promise the weapons."

Bollard grunted, but made no comment. Garcia added, "Anyway, they helped Ashton and Sattargh and McGoun and the crew make a break for the ship and get away. One of them went along, but Vreya, was caught. Caird was sick, dying, so I wouldn't go."

Dilullo made a sound of disgust. "So Randall Ashton not only had to come to the Closed Worlds to chase his interstellar wild goose, he had to get mixed up in local politics and intrigues as well."

He looked sourly at the girl. "Wake her up, Chane."

"With pleasure," said Chane.

He kneaded the nerve centers in the back of the girl's neck until her eyes fluttered open. She looked around the plane, and then looked back at him with a flaming stare.

"You're really too big a girl to bite," he said.

Garcia spoke to her earnestly in galacto. "Vreya, these are friends. They come from Earth looking for Randall Ashton."

Vreya's cool gray-green eyes measured them. Then she asked, "Did you bring a big force of ships?"

Dilullo shook his head. "One small ship. A couple of dozen men."

The Arkuun girl looked disappointed. "What can you expect to accomplish with no more force than that?"

"We didn't come here to interfere in Arkuun politics," said Dilullo pointedly. "We just came to get a few men and take them back to Earth."

Chane, watching the girl's profile, guessed that she was thinking rapidly, trying to evaluate this new factor in the situation. She was, he thought, no fool. With that magnificent body and all that strength she didn't really need a keen mind, but he thought she had one.

Dilullo interrupted her thinking. "Where's Randall Ashton?"

She shook her bright head. "I don't know."

"Why don't you know? You were one of the Arkuun party who got Ashton and the others out of Yarr. Your party helped him to escape so he could find this thing, this . . ."

"Free-Faring," said Garcia.

"You must know where he was going, to find this thing," said Dilullo.

"But I don't," said Vreya. "The Free-Faring has been lost, hidden, for a long time. One of the men with Ashton, the man named McGoun, thought he knew where it could be found. We helped him escape, but I was caught."

Dilullo stared at her. "What is this thing he's looking for, anyway—this Free-Faring?"

Vreya remained silent, but a light came briefly into her eyes and then was gone. Dilullo turned to Garcia. "You must know—you came all the way out here to the Closed Worlds to look for it."

Garcia looked uncomfortable. "Ashton didn't tell us all that McGoun told him. Of course, it's been a legend for a long time but the stories are contradictory."

"Come off it," said Dilullo. "You must know *something* of what the thing is supposed to be."

Garcia got a dogged look on his face. "It's supposed to be something by which a man can go anywhere in the universe in a minute."

They stared, and then Chane uttered a low laugh. "Just like that?" he said. "Convenient."

"For God's sake!" cried Dilullo. "You mean you followed Ashton all the way to Allubane for a myth as crazy as that?"

Vreya spoke, her face flushed, her eyes bright. "It is no myth." This time she did not try to conceal the intensity of her interest. "It existed. It may still exist."

Dilullo could only shake his head. Janssen spoke from the control-chair of the flier, turning his head toward them.

"I'd just like to remind you, John, that it'll soon be daylight and that the Arkuuns have fliers and will be looking for us."

Dilullo frowned. Then he said, "No use calling the ship back till we find Ashton or some clear lead to him. We'll set down for a while."

"Set down?" exclaimed Janssen. He motioned toward the dense jungle underneath them, brightly illumined now that the second moon had climbed into the sky. "There isn't an opening in that stuff big enough for a fly to set down!"

"We passed over some ruined cities," Dilullo said. "Set down in one of those."

Janssen grunted, and changed the course of the flier. Vreya had not understood their English, but when she saw the white gleam of ruins far ahead, she understood.

"I have to warn you," she said in galacto, "that there are highly dangerous life-forms in the jungles."

"I haven't a doubt of it," said Dilullo, looking down distastefully at the moonlit expanse. "Nevertheless, we have to hole up somewhere and camouflage the flier and wait till the search for us dies down."

"And then what?" asked Bollard.

Dilullo shrugged. "Why, then we go ahead and do the job we were hired for . . . we look for Randall Ashton."

"You always make it sound so simple, John," said Bollard.

"That's because it is," said Dilullo sourly. "Danger and sudden death are always simple things. Take her down, Janssen."

VIII

Chane walked amid shifting, ever-changing shadows as he went through the towering ruins. The two moons were both up, and they struck down a glow of tarnished silver light that made the white walls and buttresses and statues as unreal as a dream. The soft light was kind to the ruins, and it was not too apparent where a roof had fallen in or a wall had collapsed.

The breeze was warm and sluggish, and heavy with the dry-rot smell of the jungle. There were little sounds of small animals and birds that lived in the ruins, but nothing else. Under his feet the stone blocks were here and there thrust askew by roots, but the old builders had worked well and the streets were still streets.

"Now what does this place remind me of?" Chane asked himself.

Then he remembered. It had been two years ago, when the Starwolves had raided the Pleiades. Chane had been one of them, and Nimurun had been the leader; he had always been reckless, even for a Varnan. He had got their squadron boxed and it had looked like a fight at long odds.

But they had found a hidey-hole, an uninhabited, lifeless little planet that had been blasted by some past war. Its metal buildings that remained were twisted and misshapen like the tortured ghosts of buildings. For three days and nights they had lain hidden and listened to the wind moan through those wrecked buildings, but they had not been found. Eventually they had got safely out of the Pleiades.

Chane did not like ruined cities. He liked cities that were bustling with life and full of costly and desirable things that could be looted.

He grinned. *That's Starwolf thinking,* he told himself. *You must keep remembering that you're a good honest Merc now.*

They had landed here less than an hour ago. A camouflage net had been drawn quickly over the flier, and none too soon, for presently other fliers from the direction of Yarr had swung over the ruins, circling and circling and then gone on again. That the hunt for them was on, was quite obvious.

Then Janssen got the jitters. He swore that he glimpsed men flitting around in the jungle beyond the ruins, spying on them. Dilullo had patiently pointed out that it was quite impossible that any Arkuuns could have got here this soon. Janssen persisted in his assertion.

"I'll go out and have a look around," Chane had volunteered. He was already bored with sitting on his hunkers under the net.

"No," said Dilullo. "If there are any of them out there, we'll know it soon enough."

"Ah, let him go, John," said Bollard. "He's young blood, he's restless; can't you see that? He's not like us poor old crocks."

Dilullo shrugged. "Okay, Chane, take a look and see what Janssen's spooks are."

Chane nodded, and told Bollard, "I'll do my best to come back safely. For your sake."

Bollard guffawed and said that Chane was going to be the death of him one of these days as Chane had left them.

In the ruins, there was apparently nobody at all. But there was life of some kind out in the jungle. He paused once, hearing a sound, and caught the echoes of a faraway cry, long, falling inflections that were wordless yet sounded as though they might have come from a human throat.

There was no sharp line of demarcation between city and jungle. Chane gradually passed into a zone where there was more vegetation than ruins, and then it came to be thick jungle with only an occasional bulk of carved stones here and there amid the foliage.

He had been in many forests on many worlds. It was a favorite Starwolf tactic to land by night in such places and then make their spring from that cover, upon their target. Chane knew how to move silently, to slip always from one shadow to another, to bring his foot down softly. He stopped from time to time to listen, but there were only the small cheepings and rustlings normal to any jungle.

He listened for a repetition of that weird far away call but he did not hear it again.

No one, he thought. *Janssen was just seeing things.*

Then an odd thing happened. The skin between his shoulders seemed to tighten, and the short hairs on the back of his neck seemed to rise.

Danger. And near . . .

The Starwolves had no sixth sense, but they had trained the five they had to an utter keenness. Something—some smell, or almost inaudible sound—had reached and warned him.

Chane silently whirled around. He thought that he just glimpsed a white something vanish behind one of the giant trees.

He went there, his stunner in his hand.

Nothing.

There was the faintest of rustles and he spun around fast again, and thought he glimpsed another vague white shape flit from sight.

With appalling suddenness, the voice he had heard from far away sounded loudly from close by. It was not a human voice, and it spoke no words. It laughed, a kind of sobbing, shivery laughter.

Then the unhuman sound cut off sharply, and there was silence again.

Chane waited, his face dark and dangerous in a bar of the shifting moonlight. They were around him and they thought they had him, and so they were laughing.

He faced back toward the ruined city. He was not afraid, but he had all a Varnan's cunning caution. This world and what it might contain were new to him; he must go carefully.

He took a half dozen steps and then something came out of the brush ahead of him.

He thought at first that it was a man, and then as the moonlight shifted slightly he saw that it was manlike but not human. It had arms and legs and a body and a head. It wore no clothing, and was apparently sexless. It came slowly toward him and he saw a face that had softly glowing big eyes, no nose at all—just a blank space where the nose should be—and a nauseatingly pretty little mouth.

Chane triggered the stunner, aiming directly at the thing. Nothing happened at all, except that the thing uttered that sobbing laugh again.

He notched the stunner to lethal and fired again.

Again, nothing happened.

He knew then that the stunner, designed to paralyze the nervous system of a mammalian or near-mammalian creature, was useless.

A sudden thought occurred to him. The thing had been a little too obvious about coming out and holding his attention. There could be another one behind him . . .

Chane started to turn but did not complete the movement. A living weight landed on his back, and smooth cold arms went around his throat. The grip tightened, swiftly choking him.

All right, thought Chane. *But you haven't caught a man: You've caught a Starwolf.*

He put all his Varnan strength into a great surge of arms and shoulders to break the grip.

It did not break. He realized, even as he began to gasp for air, that he had finally met something as strong as he was. Perhaps stronger.

That appalling knowledge triggered a wild revulsion in Chane's mind. He stopped trying to break the choking grip. He flexed his knees and sprang, hurling himself and the thing upon his back with him, away from there.

He turned in mid-air and when they hit the ground the white shape on his back hit underneath him. The impact jarred its hold, not much, but enough to weaken it. Chane burst free.

The white man-thing was up quicker than a cat, coming at him and making a hideous little mewing sound. Chane's hand flashed and hit its neck. The neck should have broken but it did not. It was like hitting pure gristle and muscle without a bone.

He pretended he was going to strike again, but it was his foot that flashed this time and his boot caught the thing in the stomach. It was knocked back into the brush.

Chane whirled around just in time. The one that had been laughing was only a few feet from him, the delicately-fingered white hands reaching for him.

He struck and struck. He was sweating and scared now, the more so because he thought he could hear the light running steps of a third thing coming.

Chane suddenly sprang and ran. He could not face two of these creatures—it was doubtful if he could even match one. Three, if there were three, would certainly kill him.

He went through the brush with all the furious speed of which his body was capable. And he could not lose the things. They flitted almost beside him, lithe and swift as white panthers, seeking to draw ahead of him and cut off his escape.

He was among the marble ruins and they were about to block his way, when he heard yelling voices, and then the hiss and flash and searing crack of a portable laser letting go.

The white ones went away into the brush so fast that he hardly saw them go, and then he saw Dilullo coming through the ruins with Janssen and with Milner, the latter holding one of the portable lasers in his hands.

"We heard you threshing around out there," said Dilullo. "Who the devil were they?"

"Not who—what," said Chane. He was more shaken than he had been for a long time. "They aren't people. I don't know what they are, but it's something pretty nasty." He added, for Dilullo's especial benefit, "They almost got me." His voice had a note of dismayed incredulity. Dilullo got the warning.

They went back to where the flier hid under its camouflage net. The others were there, Bollard and Garcia and the girl Vreya.

Chane described what he had met out in the jungle. When he had finished, Vreya said, "The Nanes."

"The what?"

"The word *Nane*, in our language, means 'not a man'. They're not too bright, but they're deadly."

"You didn't mention them, that I recall," Dilullo said to her, in an edged voice.

Vreya turned toward him. "I told you there was dangerous life in the jungles. What do you expect me to do—mother you?"

Bollard exploded into laughter, and Chane grinned. Dilullo looked angrily at them. "What kind of evolution could produce things like that?"

Vreya looked around at the tall ruins that towered into the silver light. "There were great scientists in these cities in the old days. It was they who created the Free-Faring. And it is said that they also created the Nanes. The creatures don't breed. But on the other hand they were made to be practically immortal, and there are still some of them in the jungles."

Milner said in a whining voice, "A real ugly world we've come to, I think. I don't like it."

"Nobody," said Dilullo, "has ever paid Mercs big money to go somewhere and have a good time. Go to sleep. Chane, you've kept us all up with your prowling. You can stand first watch."

Chane nodded, and took the portable laser from Milner. The others went and got into their sleeping bags and stretched out.

The two moons wheeled across the starry sky, the distance between them getting bigger all the time and the forked shadows more bizarre. From far out in the jungle came a sobbing cry.

Chane smiled. "No, my friend," he muttered. "Not again."

After a while he heard movement, and turned. Vreya had got out of the sleeping bag they had given her. She walked out to where Chane stood guard amid a tumbled mass of giant blocks, and sat down on one of the blocks.

Chane watched her, admiring her beautiful arms and legs. They were all silver now in the tarnished light.

"This place depresses me," she told him.

He shrugged. "I'll admit I've seen more amusing places myself."

She looked at him somberly. "It doesn't mean anything to you. You've just come here; it's only another strange world to you, and you'll soon go away again. But to us . . ."

She was silent for a time, and then said, "This was a great trading city, once. There was a big starport north of here. Ships went out and traded with star-worlds far up what you call the Perseus Arm. And others went farther. The people of Arkuu were starfarers for generations. Now we live in dust and memories on two little planets, and there are no more stars for us at all."

Her voice took on a note of passion. "Because of old, superstitious fears, we have become the Closed

Worlds. No one must come to Allubane, and we must not go away from it. But some of us work to lift that senseless ban, and because of it we are called plotters and traitors by men like Helmer, who follow blind dogmas."

Chane felt a strong sympathy. He had lived too long as a Starwolf not to sympathize with anyone barred from roving the starways.

"Perhaps the time has come when the Closed Worlds will be open again," he said.

She said nothing to that, but looked away at the ruined towers that had been strong and joyous once.

Chane felt a surge of warmth toward her. He went to where she sat and bent over her.

Her shapely knee came up and cracked his chin. He saw stars as he staggered back.

He shook his head to clear it. She was looking at him with contemptuous self-assurance. Chane suddenly leaped and grabbed her. His hand went over her mouth as it had done the other time.

She struggled with the strength of a tigress. But Chane used all his iron force and held her.

"Now," he whispered in her ear, "I can do just what I want to do."

Again she tried to break free, but the Starwolf strength held her. "And what I want to do," Chane whispered, "is . . . tell you that I like you."

He gave her a great smacking kiss on the cheek and then let her go and stepped back. And at the mingled rage and astonishment on her face, he began to laugh.

Vreya looked at him, her hands clenched into fists, and then her face softened and she laughed also.

She said in a low voice, "Raul will be very angry with me for this."

And, still laughing, she came up close to Chane and kissed him on the mouth.

IX

Dilullo woke up in the morning with pains in his shoulders and his rump. He had slept in the aisle of the flier instead of out in the open like the others. He had met and faced many strange forms of life on many worlds, but one thing he could never get used to was insects. The thought of them crawling over his face had made him prefer the hard floor to a sleeping bag outside.

He felt rusty and mean. He got a drink of water and brushed his teeth, and then went outside. The topaz sun was well up over the horizon, throwing a flood of yellow light over everything. He went out from under the camouflage net, toward the brushy ruins a little distance away.

As he went he passed the girl Vreya, lying in her sleeping bag, her yellow hair rumpled and her face in the repose of slumber looking childish and cherubic. He gazed down at her with an oddly fatherly feeling.

Probably a no-good wench, he thought, *and doubtless trying to use us all for her own purposes. But a nice-looking girl.*

He went on and met Janssen, who had taken over the second watch. Janssen yawned and said that nothing had happened.

When Dilullo returned he went into the flier and came back out with one of the documents that James

Ashton had given him. It was a map of Arkuu—not a very good map, since the Closed Worlds had forcefully discouraged topographical surveys—but the only one he had.

He sat down on the shady side of the flier with his back against a wheel and frowned at the map. After a minute, he looked around. Nobody was stirring. Dilullo reached into the pocket of his coverall and brought out a small case. He took from it a pair of spectacles and put them on and then re-examined the map.

A few minutes later, a shadow fell across him. He looked up quickly. It was Chane, regarding him with interest.

Dilullo gave him a hard, challenging stare. He meant it to say, "Yes, I wear spectacles to read when no one's around, and you had better keep your mouth shut about it."

But the stare was wasted. Chane was pure brass. He looked down at Dilullo and said,

"I never saw those before. Eyes getting a little weak, eh?"

Dilullo snarled. "Is that any of your business?"

Chane started laughing. He said, "John, let me tell you something. You're the smartest among us, and you could probably beat up any one of us, except me, of course."

"Of course," said Dilullo, between his teeth.

"Stop worrying about getting old," Chane continued. "All around, you're the best man—except me, of course . . ."

"Of course," said Dilullo, but he had a bleak grin on his face now.

He took the spectacles off and put them away. "All right, break out some rations for breakfast. And wake up your girl friend. I want a serious talk with her."

Chane looked puzzled. "My girl friend?"

Dilullo said, "Look, my eyes may be a little weak at

reading, but I generally know what's going on around me. Get her."

When Vreya came, Dilullo motioned to her to sit down, and then spoke to her in galacto.

"We brought you along because we thought you might be able to tell us where Ashton went. But you're not a prisoner. If you want to go back, you can stay here and signal the next flier that comes over looking for us."

"Go back to being locked up?" said Vreya. "No, I don't want to go back."

"I take it, then," said Dilullo, "you want to join your friend who went with Ashton—what was his name?"

"Raul," she said. "He's the leader of our party. The Open-Worlders, they call us, because we want the freedom of the stars again." She added bitterly, "Helmer calls us other things, like conspirators and traitors."

"All right, stay with us and guide us to where Ashton and Raul and the others went," said Dilullo.

Vreya shook her head. "It's not that easy. All I know is the general area they were going to. It's where the legends have always said the Free-Faring was hidden, but it's a big area."

"How big? Show me, on the map."

Vreya's fine eyes studied the map intently. Dilullo handed her a pencil, and with it she drew a large irregular circle in the north.

"Somewhere in there," she said.

Dilullo looked, and his face grew long. "That's the devil and all of a big area. And mountains, too."

"The highest on Arkuu," she said. "There are valleys of jungle between them."

"Oh, fine," he muttered. "We can't search an area like that from the air." He frowned, thinking. Then he said, "You told me that this area is where legends put the Free-Faring. I take it Helmer and his bunch would know the legends, too?"

She nodded. "Yes; he went with fliers to look for Raul and Ashton and the rest, but it's as you said: you can't comb an area like that from the air."

"Then," said Dilullo, "Helmer would know that we're heading there, too, since he knows we're out to find Ashton." He shook his head. "That spells trouble."

The others were awake. Janssen came in from guard duty and they sat around in a circle under the net, eating their breakfast rations.

When they had finished them, Dilullo began an informal council of war. He had found long ago that Mercs would do almost anything you asked them, if they knew beforehand what they were into, and what the reasons were. You could not order them around high-handledly; you had to lay it out to them.

He laid it out to them. Nobody said anything for a little while. Then Bollard, who was always pessimistic when he was separated from the supply of beer in the ship, shook his head.

"So we go up to this mountain area," he said. "What do we do there? I mean, if Helmer and the other Arkuuns couldn't find Ashton and his bunch when it's their world, how can we?"

"We've got a few gadgets the Arkuuns don't seem to have," Dilullo pointed out. "Like metal-locators of considerable accuracy. If Ashton's ship set down somewhere up there, we should be able to find it and pick up the trail from there."

They thought about that and did not seem very enthusiastic, but nobody objected. They knew it was risky, but being a Merc was a risky business.

"Janssen," said Dilullo.

"Yes?"

"You got a look at the Arkuun fliers that first time we landed at the spaceport. What do you think of them, compared to ours?"

Janssen was a nut about fliers. He considered

starships a way of making a living, but dull. Flying a winged craft in atmosphere really excited him.

He said, "They really looked pretty good, John. But a little old-fashioned. They don't have VTO, I don't think they have the speed we have, and I doubt if they have the range."

Vreya, who had been getting increasingly bored with a conversation she did not understand, demanded to know what all this was about. Chane told her, in galacto.

"Of course our fliers are old-fashioned," she said bitterly. "We do not go out to the stars any more; we do not know what progress is being made on other worlds. We do not know what goes on in the galaxy. My clothes are the same that Arkuun women have worn for generations."

They looked at her, at the short jerkin and her golden arms and legs, and all of them except Dilullo and Garcia uttered a unanimous wolf-whistle.

"Knock it off," said Dilullo. He added, poker-faced, "Chane, I appoint you to chaperone this friendless girl and protect her from these Casanovas."

Chane goggled and said, "Huh?" and Dilullo felt pleased with himself, thinking, *That's the first time I ever took Chane by surprise.*

He turned to the others. "As I've told you, I've got an idea that Helmer, or some of Helmer's men, will be up in that area waiting for us. What I want to know first is, could we slip up by night and land in the center of that area. Janssen?"

Janssen frowned, but after a moment he reluctantly shook his head. "I'd love to try it, for the heck of it. But landing by moonlight in the midst of high mountains, with no beacons and God knows what downdrafts—I have to tell you, John, it'd be suicide."

Dilullo nodded. "Okay, I'll take your word for it. So we go by daylight and run our chances. Milner?"

"Yes?"

"You fit one of the heavy lasers to the firing port of the plane. I've an idea we may want it."

Milner's weazened face cracked in a grin. "Figure to blast them out of the sky if they get in our way, eh?"

Dilullo said levelly, "You are a bloody-minded so-and-so. We are not going to kill anyone unless we have to, to save our own necks. Remember, this is the Arkuuns' world, and not ours. I don't want any big sweat with them; I just want to get Randall Ashton and go. If we meet fliers you'll try to disable them, nothing more."

Milner went sulkily off to mount the laser.

An hour later they had the camouflage net rolled up and stored inside the flier, and Janssen took them up out of the ruins into the lemon-colored glare of Allubane.

Dilullo, looking down from his seat, saw something flash out of the jungle and then, for a moment, he saw a face looking up at him, a noseless white face with glowing eyes and a horrible little mouth. It flashed out of sight as Janssen threw in the horizontal drive.

Dilullo thought, *No wonder Chane was shaken up last night, if that's what he met. Not only hideous, but dangerous as well. Strong . . . too strong even for a Varnan.*

He looked at Chane, sitting beside Vreya and talking to her in a low voice, and thought, *I wish I were young and carefree like that again.* And then he thought, *But I never was as carefree as Chane; nobody ever was, except a Starwolf.*

Their flier went north and north for hours. Endless red jungle, starred here and there by old white ruins. A yellow river seemed to run north-south and was a big, tawny flood.

It seemed as though the crimson jungle would go on forever. But finally, as Allubane was declining toward the horizon, Janssen spoke from where he handled the controls.

"John."

Dilullo went up and looked over his shoulder. Far ahead, dark mountains shouldered the yellow sky.

"They're plenty high," he said.

"Not the mountains," Janssen said. "This side of them, at about twelve o'clock."

Dilullo peered. His far sight was pretty good, and presently he saw the small black specks against the lemon sky, getting rapidly bigger.

"Fliers," he said dismally. "I was afraid of that." He turned around and yelled, "Milner!"

Milner, who had been looking singularly unlovely as he slept with his mouth open, came bounding out of his seat.

"Man that laser," said Dilullo. "Remember what I told you—no killing if we can help it. Aim at their tail sections."

Milner shrugged. "You show me a nice safe way to shoot people out of the sky without hurting them, I'll do it."

Dilullo gave him the special smile that he reserved for people who were being difficult. "Try to, Milner," he said.

Milner had seen that smile before; he muttered, "Oh, all right," and went to the firing-port.

"Buckle in," Dilullo told Chane and the others. "I think we're in for a little rough flying."

The three Arkuun fliers came rushing at them. Janssen, moving swiftly, flipped the controls and their own flier stood on its tail. Something flashed by and there was an explosion well behind them.

"Missiles," said Janssen. "Pretty close, too."

"Close with them," said Dilullo. "Be ready with that laser, Milner."

Janssen did a swift loop and sent the flier rushing forward again. The three Arkuun craft, fast but not so maneuverable, tried to take evasive action, but Janssen brought the flier down on them from a higher altitude.

"Look, I'm one of those old pilots back in the Twentieth Century's World War One that I read about!" said Janssen happily. "Dogfights in a Spad, yet! *Eh-eh-eh-eh-eh!*" And he made a sound like a machine-gun going off.

"For God's sake, why did I have to go to the stars with a comedian!" said Dilullo.

Then the three Arkuun fliers rushed up at them.

X

The laser flashed and cracked. Milner was aiming for the leading flier.

He missed. Janssen threw the skitter-flier around in a fast curve and then came back toward the other fliers again.

"How many chances do you need to hit something?" he said, without turning his head.

Milner, who was an expert with the laser and rarely missed, said something so unprintable that it made Dilullo glad that Vreya couldn't understand it.

Missiles zipped past them, but far wide. The Arkuuns veered their course, but a shade too late. Milner let go with the laser again, slicing through the tail of the leading flier.

Chane sat and watched the flier go fluttering down. He felt an enormous interest in this kind of fighting, which was new to him. The Starwolves rarely used air-fliers in fighting; they usually didn't have the time to haul them out and get going with them, when they raided a world.

He saw that the damaged flier was heading toward the only possible landing place in the thick jungle—the wide, tawny river that ran away southward. The pilot made it; he saw the flier smack the water and its two occupants scrambling out of it. Chane grinned. Dilullo, with his prejudice against killing, would be pleased.

Vreya, beside him, was not looking out now. She was looking at Chane in surprise and wonder.

She started to say something but at that moment Janssen threw the skitter-flier around in a roll-over and turn that threw them hard against their belts.

The Arkuuns seemed momentarily bewildered by the unexpected maneuver. Milner triggered the laser, aiming at the nearest of the two fliers. He missed again, just grazing and cutting a few inches off the wing-tip of the Arkuun craft.

Milner's profanity this time was unspeakable. He swung the laser around.

"Hold it," said Dilullo. "They're sheering off."

The Arkuun fliers, their occupants apparently losing nerve, were now racing away toward the east.

"Let them go," said Dilullo.

He unfolded the map on his knees and squinted at it. "There's a city named Anavan marked, not too far to the east," he said. "They'll soon be back with more fliers, so we don't have unlimited time. Janssen, you set up a sweep pattern. Bollard can run the locator."

Chane found Vreya still studying him with a wondering look. "You were amused when we were in danger," she said. "You were smiling."

Chane shook his head. "Just covering up my nervousness, that's all."

"I don't think so," said Vreya. "You're different from these others. Last night while you were out in the jungle, that man"—she nodded her head toward Milner—"caught me away from the others. I broke his hold easily and hit him in the face. He had nothing like your strength."

Chane shrugged. "My strength just comes from regular exercises and leading a moral life."

Vreya's gray-green eyes became mocking. "When did you start leading it—early this morning?"

Bollard had taken the co-pilot seat. In front of it were the instruments of the metal-locator, along with the radioactive-matter detector, the atmosphere analyzer, and all the other complex instruments you needed if you meant to use a flier on alien worlds. The locator was designed to throw a broad fan of force, analogous to radar but responsive only to metal.

"Garcia says that Ashton's ship is a Class Four, crew of eight," Dilullo said. "Set it so it won't get echo from anything much smaller than that."

Bollard grunted, and bent to adjust the controls on the face of the instrument. Finally he said, "Okay."

Dilullo nodded to Janssen, who started the skitter-flier on an east-west course.

Chane said, "Vreya."

"Yes?"

"You don't want us to find Randall Ashton, do you?"

Her eyes went cold. "Why wouldn't I?"

"Because," Chane said, "I think it was you and your Open-Worlders who wanted him lost in the first place. Why should you people come and get Ashton free, so he could go off into the wilderness searching for the Free-Faring?"

"I told you," she said. "We offered that in exchange for weapons he would bring us later . . ."

"That's a thin explanation," said Chane. "I think you wanted Ashton lost—good and lost—because you'd found out he was a very rich and very important man back on Earth. You people figured there'd be an expedition of some kind come cracking into the Closed Worlds to find him, and that's what you wanted."

Her face became stormy and he thought for a moment that she was going to hit him.

"Now I want to tell you something about John," said Chane. "He never gives up. He won't give up now. He'll keep searching with the locator for Ashton's ship until he finds it. Or until Helmer gets a report from those two fliers, and comes here with a bigger squadron to shoot us out of the sky. Helmer will do that, won't he?"

"Yes," she said bitterly. "He and his fanatics who

follow old superstitions and dogmas will kill, if necessary, to keep the Closed Worlds closed."

"Janssen and Milner are pretty good," said Chane. "But I don't think they can stand off a squadron."

"You're trying to frighten me," she accused.

Chane grinned. "I don't think you frighten very easily, lovely. But I believe you've miscalculated. You think John will give up searching before Helmer comes. I'm telling you he won't."

Doubt replaced the anger in her eyes. Chane added, "If you know anything that'll get us down from this sitting-duck position, now is the time to tell it."

She looked again at Dilullo, standing behind Bollard, and the bleak, grim look in his harsh-boned face seemed finally to convince her.

"All right," she said.

Chane said to Dilullo, "Vreya has remembered something that might help us find the ship."

"Ah-huh," said Dilullo. "I kind of thought she might."

Chane decided that while Dilullo might not have the cunning of a Starwolf, he was pretty good at running a bluff.

Vreya studied the map again and then made a pencil-mark on it. "There is the place where they were going to land the ship. Then they would use a small flier to begin searching for the Free-Faring."

Chane thought, *And Ashton would be off on a wild-goose chase that would keep him lost till it made big trouble for the Closed Worlds. Yes.*

Dilullo took the map to Janssen and presently the skitter-flier started going almost due north, at its highest speed.

Vreya turned her face pointedly away from Chane. He shrugged, closed his eyes, and went to sleep.

He woke up to find the skitter-flier was still humming quietly along. Most of the others were sleeping. Chane knew that it was hours later, for the yellow flare of Allubane was much farther down the sky.

He went forward and looked over Janssen's shoulders.

"Rugged," said Janssen. "Real rugged."

Ahead of them, a stupendous range of dark mountains shouldered up against the sky. Beyond it, they could see isolated peaks of still other ranges, like great fangs.

"It's a mess," said Janssen. "And a valley in that mess is where we're heading. Wish me luck, Chane."

"Luck," said Chane, and went back to his chair.

Vreya was sleeping like the others, and he thought it wisest to let her sleep.

A little later, Dilullo woke up, yawning and stretching. "How long now?" he asked Janssen.

"Half an hour . . . maybe a little more," said Janssen.

Dilullo came fully awake. He went forward and bent over the pilot's shoulder.

"All right," he said. "It's time we started getting clever. We have to assume the Arkuuns have pretty good radar. The way they smacked our ship out in space would indicate that."

"So?"

"So change course. Don't go toward the spot behind the range we're actually heading for. Cross the range a long way west of that spot, come down behind the range and then fly back east under cover so they can't radar us."

Janssen turned around and looked at him. "Did you ever fly one of these things much, John?"

"I can handle one if I have to," said Dilullo. "I never made a profession out of it."

"Be glad of that," said Janssen. "You won't be worrying so much when I carry out that order of yours."

The skitter-flier went over the range, heading obliquely in a northwest direction now. Chane looked down at the dark, bare humps of the mountains.

Already the forested valleys between them were starting to fill with dusk.

Janssen swung them down behind the range, then started eastward. It was dizzying flying, for the mountains towered up all around them, stark against the lemonish glare of the setting sun. The change of direction woke the other Mercs. Bollard lamented audibly that he had no beer. The others looked yawny and stupid. A lot of the time, Chane thought, a Merc looked and felt that way.

"Just up ahead," said Janssen finally. "That valley."

They were approaching a place where a forested valley angled off northeastward into the mountains.

"All right," said Dilullo to Bollard, and Bollard turned the locator on again.

The skitter-flier went up the angling valley at no more than a thousand feet above the treetops.

"Take her up a bit," said Bollard. "I can't sweep the whole valley this low."

Janssen took the flier up. In no more than ten minutes, Bollard exclaimed, "Got it." He added, "I think."

They peered down. Chane could see nothing but a forest of incredibly huge and lofty trees. But at one point in the crimson sea of foliage, there was a break. It was a clearing where there appeared to have been a fire in recent years, but there was nothing much in the clearing.

"It could be it," said Dilullo. "They could have landed in that clearing and then used the ship's power to kick it back under the trees. Those trees are far enough apart, and a Class Four is a small enough ship, to make it possible."

He made a quick decision. "Take us down there, Janssen."

Janssen circled around and came back and then dropped them down on VTO drive. The skitter-flier came to rest in the clearing.

They went out of the flier and looked around in the twilight. From the air, the clearing had looked untouched. But once on the ground, Chane saw instantly where a small ship had landed, and had then been kicked beneath the gigantic trees. The scars in the ground had been camouflaged with brush and litter, but you could see them clearly enough when you stood on the ground.

Dilullo started following the camouflaged scars in the ground. They passed under the shade of the trees. Only on one or two worlds had Chane ever seen trees so huge. They went hundreds of feet into the air, and they were a thousand feet or more apart, as befitted their mightiness. The twilight under them was deepened almost into darkness.

They had not far to go. A bare few hundred feet ahead, a bulk of metal glinted dully.

"As easy as that," said Chane.

"A little too easy," said Bollard. "Mercs don't get anything this easy."

A few minutes later, Chane decided that Bollard was right. They were nearing the ship when Dilullo stopped and looked down and to one side.

Chane looked that way and saw something white. Bones. Human bones, polished clear by the scavengers or insects of the forest.

"You're an anthropologist, Garcia," said Dilullo. "Take a look."

Garcia went and bent over the bones, and they all waited until he took a look.

"Definitely terrestrial," said Garcia. He looked troubled. "Three Earthmen. But what bothers me is that the skulls of two of them and the arms of one have been torn clean loose from the main skeleton."

"Animals?"

"I don't think so," said Garcia. He added, "None of them is Ashton or McGoun. I know the shape of their skulls."

"A pity," muttered Bollard. "If we could find Ashton's indubitable remains, we could take them and go peacefully home and make a lot of money without any more trouble."

Dilullo said nothing, but led on toward the ship. Outside it, he stopped again. There were more bones. They seemed to be of two men, but they were so mixed up that it was hard to be sure. Not only skulls but three arms and one leg were torn loose and lying at a little distance.

Chane looked without any emotion as Garcia examined these. He had seen too many men die to be much affected by their remains. Vreya looked tensely on, beside him.

Again, Garcia shook his head. "Two more terrestrial types, but not Ashton or McGoun."

The lock door of the ship yawned wide. It looked dark inside the craft but Dilullo led the way unhesitatingly in.

There was light enough to see the mess. It was a real mess, not just the fact that there were more broken bones in here. The whole interior of the ship was broken up.

Every instrument, every control, seemed to have been shattered or twisted. It was as though a tornado of destruction had raged through the ship, smashing all but its heaviest components.

Chane looked down at the floor where he stood. There was a brown smear there where blood had dried. And there was a print in the smear . . . the print of a toeless foot. He remembered very clearly where he had seen such a toeless foot, only the night before.

Vreya looked down too, and shivered.

"So that was it," she said. "The Nanes."

XI

"Go back and get two lasers," Dilullo said sharply to Chane. "And tell Janssen to taxi the skitter-flier here."

He did not need to tell Chane to hurry. Chane went at a fast lope back through the deepening dusk. He glanced this way and that as he ran, half expecting to see a white shape slip from behind one of the mighty trunks, but there was nothing. Chane had had a good many fights on more starworlds than he could remember, but he had never fought anything so frightful and repulsive as the white man-things he had met the night before.

He got two of the smaller portable lasers and gave Janssen Dilullo's message. Then Chane ran back, keeping just as wary an eye as before.

Dilullo took one of the lasers and gave Milner the other. "Stand guard outside the lock," he told Milner. "I want the flier covered at all times when Janssen brings it up."

He swung around. "The rest of you get the bones and wreckage out of the ship, so we can spend the night there. You can use hand-lamps inside, but no lights outside the ship."

They got the lamps and went inside. Dilullo angled his light around and then started picking his way over the debris in the corridor that led forward.

"I'm going to look for the ship's log," he said. "Garcia, you come with me."

233

Chane and Bollard, and Janssen, after he had brought the flier up, started clearing up the mess. Vreya found and cleared a gimballed chair that had escaped damage, and sat gloomily watching them.

They got the bones and wreckage out of this main compartment and worked back through a couple of the tiny cabins. In one of them, Janssen uttered an exclamation.

"Hey, look at this."

He picked up a bottle of brandy that had miraculously escaped breaking when the contents of a cabinet had been pulled out. He happily opened it, but Bollard interrupted.

"What? Drinking on the job? Hand over that bottle."

Janssen handed it over. "Aw . . ." he began.

"Could be anything in this liquor," said Bollard. "As subleader, it's my responsibility to test it."

He up-ended the bottle and took a mighty drink. "It's okay," he said, wiping his lips. "Have one."

Janssen and Chane each had one, and then they finished clearing the cabin. When Chane went back into the main compartment it was dark, but he could see Vreya sitting with her back to him, looking tensely at the open lock-door.

He slipped noiselessly up behind her and suddenly grabbed her from behind the chair.

Vreya let out a screech and jumped up, and then turned around and spoke with rapidity and fury. In her passion she forgot, and used her own language.

Chane listened in admiration, and when she paused for breath, he said in galacto, "All wasted. I can't speak Arkuun, remember."

"I can give you a translation," she began, but he shook his head. "Don't bother. My sensitive feelings might be hurt."

She told him what he could do about his sensitive feelings, and he went laughing out through the lock to where Milner stood guard in the darkness.

Milner said there was nothing stirring, and Chane went back in to find Dilullo and Garcia coming back from the bridge, their hand-lamps cutting through the gloom.

"What's going on back here?" said Dilullo. "I heard a yell."

"Vreya's a little nervous," said Chane. "You can hardly blame the girl."

Vreya told Chane angrily, "Talk galacto when you're talking about me."

"Might as well," said Dilullo, switching to the lingua-franca. "It'll save repeating to her later. What's that you've got there?"

The latter words were addressed to Janssen, who with Bollard had come from aft.

"Bottle of brandy I salvaged," said Janssen. "I was bringing it to you."

"I'll bet," grunted Dilullo. He took the bottle and offered it to Garcia, who refused, then took a drink from it and set it down on the floor beside him.

"I found the log," he said, and Chane saw that he held a thick book whose plastic cover had been ripped apart and whose leaves were falling out. "It doesn't help us much. This ship got here the first night, they butted it back under the trees for concealment, and next day, Ashton, Raul, Sattargh and McGoun started out in the small skitter-flier they had stored in the hold. Captain and crew were to wait here for them."

"What I figured," said Bollard. "And the Nanes took the crew by surprise and tore them apart."

"Raul would have warned them about the Nanes," Vreya said sharply.

Dilullo nodded. "Probably he did. But if so, they took the warning too lightly. How many of these nasty creatures are there, anyway?"

"Nobody knows, really," said Vreya. "But there are more here in the north than anywhere else on Arkuu. There's a dead city west of here that was one of the great science centers in the ancient days, and more of the Nanes were created there than anywhere else. They were supposed to be programmed for absolute obedience, but as time went on, slow chemical changes in their bodies apparently destroyed their programming. They broke out."

"And your people just let them go?" said Bollard incredulously. "They didn't even try to hunt down those creepy horrors?"

"Efforts to do so were made," said Vreya. "But the Nanes are utterly elusive in the forest. And by then the city was dying, and few people were left; Arkuu was in decay." She added bitterly, "As it has continued to decay, ever since our worlds were closed."

"Which brings us to the main point," said Dilullo. "You and this chap Raul belong to the Open-World party. You two were chosen to contact Ashton's group because you could speak galacto?"

"That is so," said Vreya.

"Did you and Raul tell Ashton you could lead him to this Free-Faring?"

"No!" said Vreya. "We helped him escape, so he could search for it. We only knew the general area where the legends said it was. It was the man McGoun who said he had a way of finding its exact location."

Dilullo looked at Garcia. "How could McGoun find this thing when even the Arkuuns don't know where it is?"

Garcia explained. "McGoun came to Arkuu a year ago, to trade. Actually, he was trying to find out the secret of the Closed Worlds. He pretended his ship was disabled, and hung around. Finally he contacted an Arkuun who had an old record about the Free-Faring. It didn't tell where the thing was, but it told a good bit about its principle. The Free-Faring was described as a force that could detach the electro-encephalographic pattern of the mind from the body, and then send the mind—still conscious and observant—anywhere it wished to go, with incredible speed."

"Oh, for God's sake," snorted Bollard, and reached for the brandy bottle.

Garcia said stubbornly, "I know it sounds wild. But McGoun bought that record secretly for a big price, and then brought it to Randall Ashton. Ashton consulted physicists and psychologists. They said the principle, as described in scientific terms, was sound enough."

"That still doesn't explain how McGoun was going to find the thing," Dilullo pointed out.

Garcia said, "Raul and Vreya had told us the general area where legend put the thing. Ashton intended to find it by a sort of radio-compass. One sensitive to radiation within the wavelengths described by the old Arkuun record."

Dilullo frowned. "A pretty long chance, to bring Ashton all the way here."

"You know what?" said Bollard. "I don't think much of this Ashton. He tolls four people along with him on a harebrained trip to the Closed Worlds, he leaves one of them dying in Yarr while he goes off to chase a legend, and he leaves a crew of eight men here to get slaughtered while he follows his will-of-the-wisp further."

"We're not being paid to like Ashton, but to find him," Dilullo reminded him.

"And how do we do that?" asked Bollard.

"By doing what he did—detecting the radiation of the Free-Faring and going in that direction. You've got a radiation-detector."

Bollard asked Garcia, "What was the wave-length of this radiation?"

Garcia looked guilty. "I don't know. I'm sorry, but that stuff is out of my field. Sattargh set up the instrument. I remember he said this described radiation was a little shorter in wavelength than even gamma rays."

Bollard grunted. "That's a fine precise scientific datum to work on."

"Can't you broaden the sensitivity-band of our detector downward?" demanded Dilullo.

"I can try. But I sure can't do it right now. I'm blown."

Dilullo stood up, stretching wearily. "We all are. This has been a day. Janssen, you relieve Milner for the second watch."

Chane awoke in the middle of the night, where he slept on the floor of the main compartment. It was quite dark, but he could hear breathing and a careful movement.

Then he smiled. They had given Vreya one of the small cabins, but she had come out and was lying down beside him. He couldn't blame her for being scared in there alone.

Next morning, Bollard tinkered for hours with the detector in the control-panel. There was nothing for the others to do but wait. Milner said loudly that this was the devil of a place and he would be glad to get away from it. The others did not bother answering. They sat, with the lasers across their knees, and watched the trees.

Finally Bollard said, "It's hooked up again."

Dilullo went to sit in the pilot's seat beside him, and the others peered over his shoulders. Chane saw the smooth bright lines flowing steadily across the graduated detector-grid.

They waited while Bollard used the sensor-control to rotate the little sensor outside the flier hull, for a full circle around the landscape.

The bright lines remained level and untroubled.

"Nothing," said Bollard.

"If the radiation source is beyond those mountains, we couldn't get it down here. We'll have to go up high."

Bollard nodded. "I was afraid you'd say that. Still, I'd as lief take a chance with Helmer's fliers as with the creepy critters in this forest."

Janssen took the pilot-chair. There was no way they could first scan the sky, for the towering trees all around the clearing barred off the view except directly overhead. They would just have to run their chances.

Janssen taxied the flier out into the clearing. Then he took them up out of the forest on the VTO drive. With strained eyes and with the questing radar they scanned the sky, but saw no fliers.

They went higher, until they were well above the altitude of even the highest mountains. Then, as they circled, Bollard tried his detector again. It showed no response.

"Ah, I told you this was too vague," he muttered, as he started rotating the sensor. "Probably Ashton himself found that out, and . . ."

He was suddenly silent. Chane, looking over his shoulder, saw that the flowing level lines of light were level no longer. They had flung themselves upward in a sharp loop, quivering wildly, as though they strained toward a mighty heartbeat far away.

"By Heaven. I think we've got it!" said Dilullo.

"We've got something else," said Milner. "We've got company. Lots of company."

And he pointed back through the window, at the fliers coming after them fast.

XII

Chane looked back at the light Arkuun fliers coming after them. There were five of them.

"Helmer's radar may not be as good as ours, but it seems to work," he said.

"Crack on speed, Janssen," said Dilullo. "The direction the sensor was pointing—ten o'clock."

The flier leaped forward. They began to draw away from the pursuers.

Chane looked at Dilullo. "You know, if this is the way to Ashton and the others, that means we're leading Helmer right to them."

"What else are we going to do?" demanded Dilullo. "We can make deceptive maneuvers all over the sky but their radar will find us. Landing and hiding again will get us nowhere. We might as well go on and see if this is the way to Ashton, and worry about the rest later."

Dilullo spoke for the benefit of all of them, and there were no dissenters. Chane laughed, and almost said, *You're beginning to think like a Starwolf!* but he didn't say it.

The mountains came toward them rapidly. High as the flier was, it was not too high above the summits. There was no vegetation at all on the higher slopes, just stone and scree. Under the topaz sun the ranges looked infinitely inhospitable, and the deep valleys between them that were filled with forest were not much more inviting.

The flier bucked and kicked as Janssen fought tremendous drafts. He went higher and things quieted down a bit as they rushed on over the rumpled, tumbled landscape.

The fliers pursuing them were falling behind; the skitter-flier had more speed, though not too much more. That Helmer would follow them as long as he had them on his radar, Chane had not the slightest doubt.

The mountains got worse instead of better as they went on. Chane thought that they made the harsh ranges of Varna look small. Varna was a heavy planet and its gravity held down the effects of diastrophism. But here, long ago, the processes of mountain-building had functioned on a gigantic scale.

What was worse, these ranges did not run in nice parallel lines, but were jumbled helter-skelter, criss-cross, every which way. It looked as though this part of Arkuu had been the playground of colossal children and that they had left the place pretty messed up.

"I can see why something could be hidden up here for a long time," said Chane.

Vreya nodded. "Even the Nanes do not come into these mountains."

The pursuers had dropped back out of sight and they were over what seemed the worst of the mountain-jumble, when Bollard spoke sharply.

"John, take a look at this grid. I don't like it."

Chane could see that the loops on the radiation-detector were now practically throwing themselves off the grid, twitching wildly.

"We don't know what's ahead but whatever it is we're getting bloody close to it—and it's almighty strong."

Dilullo nodded. "Sheer off a bit, Janssen. Thirty degrees."

The flier banked off in a curve. Bollard kept
watching the detector. Presently the loops began to
diminish in size. He rotated the sensor unit. When it
pointed off northwestward instead of north, the loops
came on strong again.

"Ah-huh," said Dilullo. "We'll make a wide curve
around till we get a closer fix on this thing."

Janssen kept the flier swinging in a wide curve. Bollard kept changing the angle of the detector-sensor.
Finally, when they had made a circle of a score of miles
across, Bollard pointed.

"Somewhere over that region," he said, pointing
toward a lofty, dark mountain shaped like a flattened
cone. "I can't pinpoint it more than that."

"All right, we'll edge over in that direction and see
what the scope tells us," Dilullo said.

"I don't think," said Chane, "that we're going to
have much time for fancy reconnoitering."

He pointed southward, where five gleaming fliers
were coming over the mountains toward them.

Dilullo muttered an oath. But Chane admired the
way he then went cold and calculating. Dilullo looked
again at the fliers, estimating distance, and then he
went to the scope and swung it, peering toward the
conical mountain.

Janssen glanced uneasily back at him. "I can't maneuver out of this one, John—not against five fliers."

"Head fast for the base of that mountain," said
Dilullo. "The whole area around there is covered with
rocks and talus. Helmer's fliers can't land near there
but you can put us down with the VTO."

"Your faith in my ability is touching, but it's going to
kill us all one of these days," said Janssen. "All right."

He sent the flier into a long oblique rush. The
Arkuun fliers were coming up fast now. Apparently the
range was too long for their missiles as yet, but Chane
felt that they were going to be in range awfully
soon.

Janssen slowed their rush and then went into the vertical descent. The conical mountain now loomed up over them like a thundercloud and the drafts around it made the flier kick and shudder as it went down. Below, Chane saw a mass of detritus studded with huge boulders, with only a few possible landing-places. He hoped that Janssen was as good as Dilullo thought he was.

He was that good. He touched them down beside a towering boulder, on a flat area of bare rock no bigger than a house.

"Outside fast, and take the lasers and the emergency packs," said Dilullo. "They'll be over us in a minute!"

They grabbed the weapons and the packs and tumbled out of the flier. There was a screaming in the sky as the Mercs ran like the devil. Dilullo was leading them toward an even bigger boulder a hundred yards away.

"We could have stayed behind the first boulder and had as much cover!" panted Bollard, who hated running.

"I want to draw their fire away from the flier," Dilullo answered shortly. "We're going to need it."

Chane, running easily, took Vreya's arm to help her along. She shook herself loose, angrily.

"I don't need help!"

"No more you do," said Chane, admiring her flashing golden legs.

Then they dived behind the bigger boulder, just as the missiles began going off around them. "Rock-dust and chips of stone blew into their faces, and the explosions seemed deafening.

The fliers screamed by high overhead, heading toward the mountains. But they were already starting to curve around.

"We'll have them back in a moment," said Dilullo. "Shift to the other side of the boulder." He added angrily, "Damn it, Chane—*move!*"

Chane was staring wonderingly at the five fliers. Two of them, the two at one end of their formation, had passed right over the top of the conical mountain.

The other three were coming around and beginning a swoop that would take them lower over the Mercs. But those two were behaving oddly. They drifted away as though out of control, turned their noses downward, and went into a rambling, suicidal dive that crashed them on the rocks not far away.

"What the devil?" began Dilullo, and then cried, "Jump!"

They got around to the other side of the boulder just before the missiles came. This time the boulder took a direct hit on its other side, and heaved up as though about to explode to fragments.

But it settled back, leaving them shaken. They picked themselves up as the fliers screamed on past.

"What brought those two down?" demanded Milner. "We sure didn't."

"I got a good look at the one that crashed nearest to us, just before it hit," said Chane. "The men in it seemed to be dead, their heads hanging, before they even hit the ground."

"They were the only two that went right over the mountain," said Dilullo, staring up at the vast, dark conical mass. He frowned in thought. Then he said, "Chane, you can operate that detector in the flier?"

Chane nodded. "Then get back there fast and get a fix on the radiation again," said Dilullo. "I want to know whether it seems to come from that mountain."

"What's the matter with me going?" demanded Bollard. "I'm the best instrument man here."

"You're also a famous beer-drinker, and fat, and Chane can run twice as fast as you," said Dilullo. "Does that answer your question?"

Chane grinned, and took off. When he was around the boulder and out of sight of the rest of them, he put his Starwolf speed into it, bounding over the broken rock like a panther.

He thought, as he had thought many times before, that Dilullo gave him a lot of the dirty jobs because he knew Chane had that Varnan strength and speed. The devil of it was that he couldn't use it openly without making others suspect his Starwolf origin, and that had got him into some pretty tight pinches.

As he ran he looked away to the east, expecting the Arkuun fliers to come screaming back at them. But the three fliers were circling, not moving back to another attack on the Mercs.

Chane could understand that. Helmer—if Helmer had not been in one of the two crashed fliers—would certainly be cautious now about flying near the mountain.

Chane dived into the flier, and to the cockpit. He turned the detector on, then started rotating the sensor.

When the sensor pointed toward the conical mountain, the detector seemed to go crazy. The strength-indicator loops of light became wild squiggles, as though there wasn't a big enough grid to show what was happening to them.

Chane tried two complete rotations of the sensor and both times it happened. He shut off the instrument, and jumped out of the flier.

Looking eastward, he was surprised to see the three Arkuun fliers going away. When he reached the boulder, the Mercs had come out from behind it. They too were watching the departing fliers.

Chane pretended to pant as he asked, "You think they're scared off?"

"I wish they were," said Dilullo. "But as we were coming down I noticed a flat area miles east of here, big enough for them to land their fliers on. I think they'll be back, on foot. We've not got all the time in the world."

Chane told him of what the detector had revealed. Dilullo's horse-like face got longer as he looked up at the huge bulk of the conical mountain.

"Then whatever makes the radiation is on the mountain," he said. "Has to be. If the source was further away, the mountain itself would block the detector."

"Then that's where Ashton went?" said Bollard. "Where this Free-Faring is supposed to be?"

"We'll hope so."

Bollard shook his head. "It gets crazier. A multi-millionaire nutty enough to come to a hole like this chasing a myth about the Free-Faring. And then those Arkuuns in the two fliers tumbling dead out of the sky, just like that."

"Maybe they weren't dead," said Vreya.

Chane looked at her. "I saw them, Vreya. I saw them as they fell."

"Maybe their minds had been released from their bodies," she said. "That's what the Free-Faring was supposed to do. Maybe that's why they fell."

XIII

From high up in the windy darkness, on a ledge a third of the way up the mountain, Chane stared down with Dilullo and Bollard.

"Nothing yet," he said. "Maybe they won't try it till daylight."

"They'll try it," said Dilullo. "I've seen a lot of men, and these Arkuuns are some of the toughest. Besides, there'll be one of the moons up in a few minutes."

They continued to watch and listen, looking down the narrow, twisting path by which they had ascended. Presently there was an elfin shimmer of light from the horizon and the nearer of the two silver-pink moons floated up into the sky.

They had got up here just as night was falling. There had been a short, frenzied time of activity down below, before they left. As Allubane set, they had worked feverishly to get out of the flier all their gear that they might need.

Milner and Janssen had come back from scouting, just as it was getting dark. Milner had found what they were looking for, a nest of tall rocks not too far away, in which the flier could be hidden with the hope that it would not be too easily found.

In the twilight, Janssen had done a marvellous job of piloting, taking the flier up only a few yards and hedge-hopping with it and putting it down amid the concealing rocks of that nest. Then he had come running back and they had shouldered their packs and started for the mountain.

They found the path almost at once. It looked as though it had been worn by the feet of ages, twisting here and there amid the beetling rocks and crags, going steadily up the steep slope. They reached this ledge just as complete darkness fell, and here they stopped. The others were chewing rations farther along the ledge, while Chane and Bollard and Dilullo, their lasers in their hands, had gone down and watched the path.

"You hear anything?" Bollard asked Chane. "I notice you've got keen ears."

"Not a thing," said Chane.

The second moon came up, perpetually chasing the first one, and the tarnished silver light became stronger.

Chane saw Dilullo peering intently downward, his harsh face made harsher by the light.

"They're down there," said Dilullo. "And they'll try it sooner or later. I wish I had a guarantee we'll live the night out."

Chane grinned. "What do you care? You've got no wife and children to worry about."

Dilullo said in a flat voice, "That's right, I haven't. All right, I'll watch from a little higher up. I'll have Milner and Janssen relieve you in three hours."

Dilullo turned and went back up the path. Bollard looked after him, watching him go in the silver light.

When Dilullo was out of sight, Bollard did a thing that utterly amazed Chane. He turned and struck Chane with all his force, with a flat hand across the face.

Bollard was flat and sloppy but he was strong. Chane staggered back against an outcropping boulder beside the path. Bollard came in and grabbed him by the collar.

It was not the moon-faced, cheery Bollard now.

Bollard had been a Merc for many years and you did not live years like that without some iron in you, and all the iron showed in his moonlit face as he glared at Chane.

"You ever say a thing like that again and I'll kill you, Chane," he said, his fist raised.

Chane was too astonished even to lift his hands. "What . . ." he began.

Bollard lowered his fist. "You mean you don't know? John never told you?"

"Told me what?" demanded Chane.

"You made that crack about John having no wife and children," said Bollard. "He had them once, years ago. A beautiful wife and a little boy and a girl. He came back with me from a mission to Spica, to find there'd been a fire in his house and all three of them dead."

Bollard looked down the moonlit, rocky slope. "I remember that after the funeral, I went with John where his house had been, and we looked at the ashes. He kept saying to me, 'It doesn't make sense, that a man can fly to the stars and yet lose his whole family in a stinking, lousy fire. It just doesn't make sense.' "

Chane was silent. Then he said, "I'll be back in a moment," and went up the path.

Dilullo was standing where the path joined the ledge, looking and listening, his laser gleaming in the moonlight.

"John," said Chane. "I didn't know. I'm sorry . . ."

"For Godalmighty's sake," said Dilullo. "Now I've heard everything. A Starwolf making an apology. In the whole galaxy, nobody would believe it."

Then he changed his tone and growled, "Get back down there where you're supposed to be, Chane. And forget it. You couldn't know."

Chane said nothing, but turned and went back down the path.

They had watched for more than two hours when they heard sounds. Sounds of feet on rock and grit, trying to be quiet but still audible.

"They're coming," muttered Bollard. "But we won't be able to see them to use the lasers till they're right on us. This is going to be murder. Literally."

"You watch," said Chane. "Maybe I can discourage them a little."

He put down his laser and went to the boulder beside the path and leaned against it. It held firm. He put into his arms and legs all the strength that Varna had given him, and pushed.

The boulder heaved, a very little. He pushed further, and then all of a sudden the boulder came out of the soil and toppled and rolled. It went down the moonlit slope with a mighty noise, clashing against other rocks, bounding and bumping and raising the devil altogether.

They heard a muffled exclamation from down the slope, and a sound of feet moving fast, and then nothing but the receding bump and clash of the big rock going faster and faster down to the valley.

Chane picked up his laser. "I don't think it got any of them—it rolled wide of the path. But it may make them decide to wait till daylight."

Bollard stared open-mouthed. "How in the world could you push a rock that size?"

"It was just barely balanced on the slope," Chane lied. "I felt it sway a little when you banged me back against it."

Dilullo came down and listened with them. There were no more stealthy sounds from below.

"They'll wait for daylight," Dilullo said. "Which means we'd better be on our way well before the sun rises."

Janssen came down presently to relieve Chane.

"What's that lump inside your coverall?" demanded Dilullo.

Unwillingly, Janssen fished out the half-full bottle of brandy. "Thought I'd bring this along, for emergencies."

"Good thinking, Janssen," said Dilullo. "For that, you can have a drink of it."

Janssen's face brightened in the moonlight.

"When you've finished your watch," said Dilullo, and took the bottle from his hand and went up the path.

Chane followed him up to the ledge. Milner was sleeping. Garcia was not in sight. Vreya was sitting and looking up at the sky in which the two moons now rode royally amid the glittering stars of the Perseus Arm. Chane went over and sat down beside her.

"So many stars," she said, in a low voice, and then added passionately, "and we cannot go to them, we must stay forever on our little worlds."

She lowered her gaze and looked at Chane. "You have been to many of them?"

"Not in this Arm," Chane said. "But to many stars . . . yes."

She gripped his hand. "I believe now that the Free-Faring is here, Chane. Very near to us. The gateway to the stars."

He stared at her incredulously. "You can't really think that a man's mind could leave his body and go starfaring?"

"I do think it," she said. Her clear-cut face was rapt. "What I have always dreamed of—the freedom of the universe. And perhaps close . . . very close."

She looked up again at the glistening vault above. Of a sudden, Chane got a strange, chilling feeling that not only did she believe it, but that it might be true.

There was a sound of running feet, and Chane grabbed his laser and sprang up. But it was Garcia who came running from farther along the ledge.

"I've found something," he said. "Not a hundred yards farther along here. Some kind of a passage . . ."

Dilullo got up and he and Chane followed Garcia. They came to a place where there was a cliff of rock right above the ledge. There was enough moonlight to show them the dark opening of a tunnel leading into the rock.

"No hand-lamps till we get well inside," said Dilullo.

They went in, moving cautiously, for the darkness in the tunnel was intense. The floor under their feet seemed perfectly level and smooth. When they had gone a score of steps, Dilullo flashed on his hand-lamp.

Chane looked around wonderingly. They stood in a big man-made tunnel of softly gleaming metal. It was like a square with an arch on top, in cross-section, and it was at least twenty feet across.

It ran straight into the heart of the mountain as far as they could see.

"Some kind of old aqueduct?" said Garcia puzzledly.

"No," said Dilullo. "I think this is a road to something."

Yes, thought Chane. *A road to something. To the Free-Faring?*

He shook off the thought. Vreya's talk was starting to make him think old impossible myths could be true.

"Maybe it's just a blind alley?"

Chane shook his head. "You can feel a strong draft of air coming through from ahead. It opens out somewhere."

Dilullo made his decision. "We're going in. It may be the way Ashton went. At the worst, this tunnel could be far more easily defended than that ledge on the mountainside. Chane, get all the others and bring them here. With all our gear."

When Chane had brought them, Dilullo gave them no time to stare around. He started down the straight tunnel, with Bollard beside him and both their hand-lamps beamed ahead.

There was nothing at all to see. Their boots made echoes in the big metal tube and the echoes were now ahead of them and now behind them, so that the ears were confused. Chane stopped twice and beamed his lamp behind them, under the impression of following footsteps.

The thing went on and on. They were going, straight as an arrow, deep into the heart of the mountain. And still that cool breeze from ahead hit their faces.

The breeze got stronger. The echoes from ahead sounded different.

"Hold it," said Dilullo.

Ahead, the tunnel seemed to debouch into a vast, vaguely lit space.

"Now we'll take this easy," said Dilullo. "Remember what happened to the men in those two fliers. I'll have a look."

Dilullo went forward slowly, until he seemed to stand on the very brink. They saw his head turn this way and that, gazing.

He stood there for what seemed to Chane a long time before he turned around and motioned them forward. They went, with slow steps.

Chane's first impression when he stood at the end of the tunnel was that it opened into the side, not the bottom, of a vast well.

There was no doubt at all that this colossal shaft was man-made, for it was lined with the same gleaming metal as the tunnel. It was at least a thousand feet in diameter, and high above them it was open to the sky. Oblique moonlight struck down and was reflected from the gleaming walls.

There was a wide ledge all around the well, level with the tunnel in whose mouth they stood. They stepped out onto the ledge and peered down. Far, far below them lay the floor of the gigantic shaft. They could see it because it had light down there from another source than the moonlight above.

The light came from an area a hundred feet in diameter, exactly centered in the floor of the gigantic shaft. This area was not smooth but consisted of countless facets, and the facets glowed with a cold blue light, not at all intense but with a strange quality in it that Chane had never seen before.

"Look there!" said Bollard, pointing.

Chane saw now what he had missed in the first stunning impression of the place.

At four points equally spaced around the ledge, wide walks of massive metal ran out into the well. They ran to a circular platform of what looked like glass, exactly the same size as the blue-glowing area on the floor below, and situated exactly above the latter.

Three men lay unmoving on the glass plate out there. One wore the costume of Arkuu, and the other two were dressed in coveralls.

Dilullo twisted the focus of his lamp and sent a long narrow beam at one of the latter two, who lay face upward.

"Ashton!" cried Garica. "And he's dead!"

From far around the well, from the shadowy ledge hundreds of feet away, a voice spoke dully.

"Not dead," it said. "Not dead, but gone. Gone on the Free-Faring."

XIV

"McGoun!" exclaimed Garcia, and a figure advanced out of the shadows.

"Garcia," it said. "And who are these?"

Garcia babbled explanations. As he did so, Dilullo sized up Jewett McGoun.

A stocky middle-aged man who at the moment looked older than he was. His flat, seamy face quivered with self-pity, and his dark eyes were rimmed with red and seemed about to burst into tears at any moment.

"You don't know what I've been through, Garcia," he said. "None of you . . ."

Dilullo's voice cracked like a whip. "Chane! You and Milner watch that tunnel."

Chane nodded and went with Milner to the place where the tunnel debouched onto the ledge. But from there he could see and hear McGoun.

McGoun was practically crying. "A billion dollars. Maybe many billions. Right here, for the taking away. And Ashton . . ."

"What about Ashton?" asked Garcia. "You said he had gone on the Free-Faring? And what about Sattargh?"

McGoun pointed to the glass platform suspended out there over the pit.

"There they are. And Raul, too. They had to try the Free-Faring. They wouldn't be content just to find its secret and then sell it. Billions! But they had to try it . . ."

Dilullo's voice did the whip-crack again. "Let's not have so much weeping. Exactly what happened?"

McGoun knuckled his moist eyes. "Don't push me around. I've been pushed around too much. All alone here, for weeks and weeks. They would come back to their bodies and I'd plead with them, and they wouldn't even listen to me. They'd just eat, and drink, and stare at me, and then go back out there."

"Come back to their bodies?" cried Bollard. "What are you trying to give us?"

McGoun looked dully at him. "You don't believe it? You walk out onto that grid and see. I tried it—it was terrifying. I came right back to my body and I wouldn't try it again. But Ashton and the others kept going and going . . ."

"Oh, nuts," said Bollard. He told Dilullo, "John, if that's Ashton's body out there, we'll need it, to take back to Earth for identification. I'll go out and get it."

"Now wait," said Dilullo. "Let's wait a minute before we do anything foolish."

"Let him go," said McGoun, his face sodden with resentment. "He's so damned ready to call me a liar. Let him try it."

"Where's the flier you came in?" Dilullo asked.

McGoun made a gesture. "Down below that side of the mountain. But it's no good without Ashton. You know—when I threatened to take the flier and go if they didn't quit the Free-Faring, Ashton took and hid some of the small parts. Without them the flier can't operate."

Chane, sitting with his laser across his knees just clear of the tunnel-mouth, glanced toward Vreya. She had not spoken. But she stood there, her eyes brilliant with emotion, gazing toward the glassy disk out there on which the three men lay.

She looked, he thought, like someone who after long hope and despair sees the gateway of a prison stand open and inviting. He began to wonder. Could what

McGoun said be true? Could the men out there be, not dead, but with their minds set free to range all the universe at will?

The hackles came up on Chane's neck at the thought. He did not like such an idea at all. He had been a Starwolf and a free ranger and raider, but physically. Everything in his Varnan training made him recoil from a concept such as this one of using your mind to rove without your body.

A sudden thought came to Chane. Was this Free-Faring what the Varnans had found when they came to raid the Closed Worlds, long ago? Had the thing seemed as repulsive to them as it did to him, a thing from which they would recoil? Was that why Star-wolves had been forbidden ever to go to Allubane?

"I tell you, it's true," McGoun was saying, in a high, sobbing voice. "Look, you don't have to take my word. Just walk out there on the grid and see what happens to you."

Chane noticed that Bollard still looked skeptical, but that Dilullo had a look on his face as though he was not too sure.

"You tell me that this thing can take a man's mind and release it from his body . . ." he began.

"It *can!*" cried McGoun. He pointed down to the floor of the giant shaft, where the central circle glowed with cold blue light. "That down there. It emits a force, straight upward. A column of quite invisible force. The glass-looking grid out there is transparent to it."

And if that is so, Chane thought, the force would strike right on up into the sky, and would hit the two Arkuun fliers and cause the thing that had happened to them.

"You tell them, Garcia," appealed McGoun. "I'm not a scientist; I'm a trader, trying to make an honest profit. I wish to God now I'd never heard of this thing."

Garcia said, hesitatingly, "All I know of the theory of it is what Ashton told me. The glowing area down there is matter so treated as to emit a subtle force perpetually. The force is one that *amplifies* the power of that electric pattern in the brain which we call the mind. It gives the mind-pattern such great power that it can break loose from the synaptic structure in the brain. It can go where it wills, short-cutting the three dimensions by driving across dimensions of which we know nothing. It can return, and affix itself to the brain again, and reactivate the body."

"Oh, for God's sake. . . ." Bollard began.

Chane whirled and triggered his laser back into the long tunnel. The flash and crack were tremendous in that closed space.

They ran to the tunnel, keeping clear of its mouth. Dilullo looked enquiringly at Chane.

Chane shook his head. "Nobody coming. Just a stone or something someone threw into the tunnel, to see if anybody was on guard. I thought I'd better let them know we're here."

"This is a nice spot," Dilullo muttered. He turned and asked McGoun, "Is there another way out of here?"

McGoun shook his head. "No way but the tunnel."

"Then they've got us nicely boxed," said Dilullo. "We've got rations and some water in our packs, but we can't hold out here forever."

"Look," said Bollard. "There's no need to hold out forever. We'll get Ashton's body off that grid—if it's dangerous to go near it, we can snake it off with a rope. We'll come out of the tunnel with all lasers going and cut right through them."

"Ashton will die if you do that," warned McGoun. "His mind can't regain his body unless it's out there on the grid, in the force of the Free-Faring."

Bollard looked as though he was about to make a highly profane reply, but Dilullo held up a hand and silenced him.

"What's that?"

A voice came booming down the tunnel, a man's strong voice speaking as through a long tube.

"I am Helmer. Can I come in truce?"

Dilullo said admiringly, "That man's got guts. He must know that one laser blast down the tunnel would cut him down."

"Well, do we cut him down?" asked Milner hopefully.

"No, we don't," said Dilullo. "Bollard, you've got the loudest mouth here when you want to use it. Call to him that he can come in truce."

Bollard obeyed. They waited. Then they began to hear a man's steps echoing down to them through the long metal tube. They were firm steps, strongly planted, and they got louder and louder, and then Helmer stepped out of the tunnel and stood looking at them.

In the vague light, Helmer seemed twice as impressive as he had in sunlight, his blond head erect, his mighty arms and legs all sculptured muscle, his bleak, icy eyes surveying them one by one.

Then Helmer turned his gaze out into the vastness of the shaft. He looked at the grid and the three motionless bodies on it, and then down at the glowing circle below.

A kind of agony came upon his face as he looked. He seemed to speak rather to himself, than to them.

"So it is true, and there is one of the evil things still left. And after all this time, it has been found."

His lips compressed. He seemed to stand and think for a moment, before he turned and spoke to them.

"Listen to me, strangers. This thing you have searched for and found has great and luring powers. That is true. But also it is a greatly evil thing."

"What evil would come from a thing that is supposed merely to free the mind from the body?" asked Dilullo.

Helmer's eyes flashed cold flame. "You saw the dead cities in the jungle? Go ask them! They were great and living cities once. But each of them had a thing like this, the instrument of the Free-Faring. And the sterile life of the mind was more alluring than the real life of the body, and hundreds by hundreds, century after century, the people of those cities went into the Free-Faring and clung to it until they died."

He looked around their faces again. "The people of the cities withered away, the life dwindled. Until finally a group arose, determined to destroy the Free-Faring and save our people from its insidious corruption. In one city after another, the gateways—like this one—were destroyed. But those who were addicted to the Free-Faring tried to save it, and we have always known that at least one of the gateways remained hidden and intact. Because of that, we determined to close our worlds to strangers, so that not all the galaxy would flock here searching for it. As you have searched—and found."

Dilullo shook his head. "The thing is only an instrument of science. If it does what they tell me it can do, it could be a very noble instrument for all men."

Helmer flung out his hand and pointed toward the three unmoving bodies out on the central grid.

"Look at those who have tasted the Free-Faring! Do they look ennobled? Or do they look drunken, sodden—like dying men?"

"I agree," said Chane.

Helmer turned and looked at him. "Stranger, when I saw you before, I thought that you were more of a man than any outworlder I had met. Now I see that you think like a man."

"I do *not* agree!" cried Vreya. Her face was passionate as she looked stormily at Helmer. "It was fanatics like you who took away from us the freedom of the stars." She turned and pointed at the glass grid, where the three men lay unmoving. "That is the road to infinite freedom, to go anywhere in the universe, to find out anything we wish to know—and you would destroy it."

"I *will* destroy it," said Helmer. "It almost destroyed us, long ago. I will not have this hateful vice corrupt our people again—or any other people."

He turned to Dilullo. "This is what you can do. You can gather your people and go, and we will strike no blow at you."

"But," said Dilullo, "they tell me that if Ashton and the other two are taken off that grid, their minds cannot rejoin their bodies."

"That is the truth," said Helmer. "And it is well. They will be living logs until they die, and that is their punishment."

"No," said Dilullo decisively. "It is the safety of Ashton that is our job, and we cannot do that to him."

"Then," said Helmer slowly, "you will all perish when we destroy the Free-Faring. The choice is yours."

He turned his back on them and strode toward the tunnel. Milner, his teeth showing in a soundless snarl, started to raise his laser but Dilullo knocked it down. Helmer went on into the tunnel.

Chane saw Dilullo turn and give him a cold stare. "Why did you say you agree with him?"

Chane shrugged. "Because I do. I think a thing like this is better destroyed."

"You're a fool and a coward," Vreya said to him. "You're afraid of something you can't understand, afraid of the Free-Faring."

"Frankly, I am," said Chane. He pointed with his laser to the unmoving men out on the grid. "If that's what this fine achievement does to a man, I want no part of it."

He looked back to Dilullo. "Now what?"

"That," said Dilullo, "is the kind of a question that makes a Merc leader wish he wasn't a leader."

"Accept Helmer's terms!" McGoun broke in. His soiled cheeks quivered. "Ashton didn't care about me, all alone here. Why risk getting killed for him?"

"Because," said Dilullo between his teeth, "we signed a contract, and Mercs who break one are thrown out of the guild. It was you, McGoun, with your nosing around in other world's secrets and your hankering for money, who brought us all here. Now shut up."

"But what *do* we do?" asked Bollard.

"We wait," said Dilullo. "We wait till Ashton and the other two come back to their bodies—if what McGoun has said is true—and we grab them, and then we fight our way out."

The great shaft was darkening as the moons of Arkuu slid further down the sky, so that little of their light now penetrated.

Dilullo told Janssen and Bollard to take the second watch at the tunnel, and that they had all better get some sleep. They curled up silently, along the back of the ledge, and presently were asleep. All but Vreya.

Chane watched her. She was sitting and staring almost fixedly at the grid out there, and the three motionless figures on it. She watched it for a long time, before she too stretched out to sleep.

Milner looked around the vast, darkening place. "That ruined city was bad enough," he muttered. "This is worse."

"Don't talk," said Chane. "If any of them try coming through the tunnel, our hearing will be our best warning."

But, looking around, he had to agree that Milner was right. He had never been in a place so curiously oppressive. It was not so much the place itself as the knowledge of what it could do to a man, drive the mind out of his body, make him like one dead. The strong repulsion to that idea stirred in Chane again.

The hours seemed long before their watch ended. Janssen and Bollard, when roused, grunted and took their places at the tunnel, Bollard yawning prodigiously.

Chane took his boots off and stretched out, but he

found that sleep came slowly. He still felt the oppression. It seemed to stifle him. He kept thinking of the three shadowy forms out on that dim grid, wondering where their minds were and what they were doing; wondering what it was like to be a disembodied mind; wondering if they would ever come back. After a time he did sleep, and he had something almost unheard of for him; nightmares.

He woke out of one with a start. There had been a sound, not the occasional stirrings of Bollard and Janssen as they sat staring down the tunnel, but a new, small sound.

He looked around sharply. Vreya was gone.

Chane got to his feet. His gaze swept the vast, darkened space. Then he saw her.

She was walking silently out onto one of the metal walks that led to the central grid. The two guards, their backs to her, had not seen her.

She was going to the Free-Faring . . .

Chane moved with the swiftness and silence of a hunting cat. His unshod feet made no sound. He went in great noiseless bounds after the tall golden girl who walked out toward the grid, over the abyss, as though she went to a lover.

He would reach her in time to pull her back, if she did not turn . . .

At that moment, warned by instinct or the sound of his breathing, Vreya turned.

She flashed him a fierce, wild look and then started to run forward.

Four great strides and a spring and he could catch her before she stepped onto the grid. Chane strode and sprang, and he did catch her right at the edge.

But he had forgotten how strong Vreya was. Even as he caught hold of her, she threw herself forward onto the smooth grid. Chane, holding her, was dragged by her wild surge onto the grid with her.

Next instant, Chane felt his brain explode, and he fell into eternity.

XV

It was not quite a fall. Rather it was as though a great hand, gently but very strong, had grasped, lifted, and flung him outward, and he scudded, stunned and helpless, across a silent nothingness.

He was nothing, alone in nothingness.

He was dead, a soul, a spirit, a palmful of electric impulses tossed out naked among the stars. Now he knew what it was like to be that way.

He was afraid.

And he was angry. Raging, that this violation should have been done to him.

He screamed, a fierce eagle scream that defied the whole cosmos. He could not hear the scream, but he could sense it as a red flash in the nothingness. And it was answered.

"Don't be afraid, Chane. Don't be angry. Look. Look around you . . ."

Vreya. Of course, Vreya. He was not alone. Vreya . . .

"Look, Chane. Look at the stars. Look at the universe." She was not talking. There was no voice in that tremendous silence. Yet he sensed her meaning as he had sensed his own outcry. Her words crashed against his consciousness like a sunburst, all golden and glorious. *"We're free, Chane! Free!"*

He tried to orient himself toward her, tried to see her, and in doing that he saw instead the universe.

The black, black beautiful deeps that ran to the rim of creation, the dark All-Mother with a billion galaxies spangling her breast and the stars like fireflies at her fingertips, and he could see it all, clear and clean. The stars burned with a pure radiance. The coiling nebula glowed, silver clouds against the primal black. All down the long, long darkness the scattered galaxies wheeled and flashed, and he could hear them, and he realized that the nothingness was not silent. It moved and sang with the movements of the suns, the worlds, the moons, the comets, the gaseous clouds, the banks of drift, the cosmic dust and the free atoms, the star-swarms and the galaxies. Nothing was still, and he understood that this was because stillness was death, and therefore forbidden. The universe lived, moved, beat with a vital pulse. . . .

And he was part of it. He too throbbed and moved, caught up in the great cosmic dancing, the Brownian Movement of the universe. Movement of the universe. This evoked a memory, of his body floating in a great sea, becoming one with the life, the pulse, the movement of the sea.

"Vreya!" He called to her, without thinking how he did it. *"Vreya, come back with me!"* The panic that went with the impulse was black, an ugly black that blotted out the radiance. The memory of his body had done that, reminding him that he was not an atom but a man with a face and a name, Morgan Chane, the Starwolf. He looked somehow down, although there was neither up nor down, and saw his body sprawled on the grid beside Ashton and Sattargh and Raul. It was sprawled together with Vreya's body, and they looked like the newly dead, mouths slack, eyes glazed, arms and legs flung wide in limp abandonment. He yearned toward his body.

"Vreya, come!"

She was close beside him now. He could sense her there, a tiny patch of sparkling motes.

"You are afraid," she said, contemptuously. *"Go back, then. Get your feet on the nice safe ground."*

"Vreya. . . !"

"A lifetime . . . waited . . . dreaming . . . now I have it, I am free, free of the stars, free of the universe. Good bye, Chane."

"Vreya!" He flung himself toward the sparkling motes, and he felt her laugh.

"No, you can't hold me now. Do what you will, you can't hold me."

She danced away. The Perseus Arm swung like a burning scythe through the dark behind her, a million stars piled high and shouting as they swung; their voices struck Chane's being and made each separate impulse flare with their splendor. Vreya's tiny gleaming brightened. Once more he felt her laughter, and then she was gone, lost in the blaze of the Perseus suns.

Chane hesitated. He could go back now, revive that disgustingly lax shell that awaited him, make it a man again. Or he could go after Vreya, try again to bring her back . . .

If he let her go she might never come back. She was drunken with the Free-Faring, enough to forget the needs of her body until it was too late, until the beautiful shell perished from lack of food and water. And that would be a waste, a terrible waste. He would never forgive himself if that happened . . .

Really? asked one little mote of him, of the rest of him. *Has the Starwolf truly become noble . . . or is he lying to himself? Does he want secretly to taste a little more of this Free-Faring that so revolts him?*

Chane hung shivering while the toppling blaze of the Perseus Arm swept toward him . . . or was he sweeping toward it? How did you move in this Free-Faring, how did you direct yourself?

Vreya's laughter came to him, faint and distant. *"This way, Chane. It's easy, if you would only stop fighting it. Can't you feel the currents? Like great winds . . . This way . . . This way . . ."*

He felt the currents. They ran between the suns, between the galaxies, lacing the whole together. You caught one and rode it, in the wild twinkling of a second, across distances that would take even a swift Starwolf ship months to span. You fetched up, dazed and shaken, to dance in the whipping corona of a green star, and then go sliding down the little currents that held the green star's worlds around it, calling for Vreya, looking for her, finding her and chasing her through an atmosphere that was the color of a smoky emerald, above strange seas and stranger continents, and there was life there, and her voice made running streaks of silver across his consciousness, crying, *"Oh . . . oh . . . oh!"* in wonder.

And you went on again, pleading with her. You shot a nebula, wrapped in cold fire, and you peered at the drowned suns and the worlds that never saw any other star but their own and no sky but the perpetual icy burning of the cloud. Some of the worlds were barren and some were not, and once Vreya made such a darkness of fear against his mind that he thought she would listen to him and return. But she only darted away, riding the currents like a fleeting spark, toward a cluster of orange suns all mellow as grandfathers, with pretty little planets around their knees. After a while you forgot to plead. You did not really care any more whether Vreya came back to her beautiful body or left it to rot in the crater on Arkuu. You did not even care whether you went back to your own body or not. Because you realized that Vreya was right, and you were wrong.

You realized that the Free-Faring was worth everything. What was the death of a body, a mortal body that would die anyway? What was the death of a city, or a culture, or even a planet—though the planet wouldn't really die, of course, just because men were gone from it. What even was the joy of being a Starwolf, compared to this?

For a Starwolf was planet-bound and ship-bound.

Everywhere he went he must take with him air and water and food and atmospheric pressure, or he would perish just like the lesser breeds. He could only go so fast, and so far. Compared to this Free-Faring, it seemed to Chane that he and his fellows had been no more than weak and clumsy children on those Starwolf raids. Now he was free of all those limitations, the frail and dragging flesh and the heavy shell of iron in which it must huddle, ignominiously. Free, Vreya had said, of the stars and the whole universe, and it was true. He could possess it all, comprehend it all. He could go anywhere he wanted to, fleet, disembodied, safe, timeless.

Anywhere.

Even to Varna.

And he went, forgetting Vreya.

He rode the currents swift as a dream, and the remembered sun blazed before him, tawny gold. He had seen it countless times before but always through a screening viewport or from the planet itself; never like this, undimmed, naked and true. He watched the great storms sweep across it, flaming whirlwinds as big as continents. He watched the bright corona, the whipped banners and the darting, arcing falls of fire. The voice of the sun spoke to him, and even though he knew now that the stars spoke to the whole universe and not to tiny bits of it, he took it for a welcome.

Varna came rolling from behind the sun, a blue and copper ball. He sped to meet it, and on the way he met a Starwolf squadron coming in.

How many times, he thought. *How many times!*

He went in with them, pacing them down, though he could have left them far behind. There were five ships. They must have run into trouble, because two of them showed fresh scars. But he knew how it would be inside the ships, and he was pleased, remembering.

They went with a rush, the five ships and the little patch of glowing motes, down through the atmosphere, screaming, ripping the clouds asunder, sending a long roll of thunder crashing down the sky. And then the city was below them, Krak, the chief city of the Starwolves, a vast loose-jointed sprawl of stone buildings scattered broadcast over a craggy countryside. Each wolf must have his own den, each Varnan his castle, with breathing room around it and a stout wall against predators, in case of a falling-out.

The starport was east of the city, where the rough land fell away to a great plain, burned golden-brown with summer. Chane hung aside and watched the ships go in for a landing, and there was a sadness in his attenuated being. This was home.

The flags broke out from the buildings of the city, bright spots of color against the dull red stone. Traffic began to move down along the road to the starport; ground-cars, people on foot, long vans for the loot.

The ships' ports opened, and Chane slipped lower, weightless, soundless, riding the air.

The Starwolves came out of the ships.

My people. My brothers. My fighting mates. I know them. Berkt . . . Ssarn . . . Vengant . . . Chroll . . .

My brothers.

But they drove me out!

He watched them, the tall powerful men who walked like tigers, muscles gliding under the fine gold-furred skin. He saw the bright-skinned women come from the city, strong women fit for men like these; they laughed and hung the men with garlands of late flowers and brought them the Varnan wine to drink. Chane remembered the pungent dusty sweetness of the garlands and the lovely violence of the wine. No Earthman could drink that wine and stand. None but he, who was Varnan born.

But they drove me out!

He flitted over them, proud and contemptuous. *I am here. You cannot keep me out, you cannot hold me, you cannot kill. For I am greater now than all of you. I see the weakness of your iron bodies, the dullness of your iron ships. I am a Free-Farer, and already I have done things that your feebleness could not endure.*

It was too bad that they could not see him, could not hear his words. They went on drinking and laughing and kissing the women, tossing their heads and squinting their bright cat eyes against the sun. Men and boys from the city brought the loot from the ships and piled it on the long vans. The raiders climbed onto big open ground-cars and rode with their women back into the city, singing as they went.

You have seen them, Chane thought. *Their weakness and their worthlessness. It is time to go now, back to the stars.*

But he did not go, and he wondered if it was possible for a Free-Farer to weep. And that was a strange thought, for he had not once thought of weeping since he was a tiny child in that house, there by the market-place, the one with the snarling masks carved on the rainspouts. Starwolves did not cry.

He moved closer to the house. The little church beside it had long ago fallen into ruin. He hovered outside a tall window, remembering how his mother had tried to furnish the great barren room exactly like the parlor in Carnarvon, and how dwarfed and pallid the furniture had looked compared to the untidy splendors he saw in the rooms of his Varnan playmates. The Reverend Thomas would not have one scrap of the sinful loot beneath his roof.

There was plenty of it there now. A Varnan family had lived there many years, since the outworlders died. Chane himself had lived in the bachelor's quarters, a long sprawling sort of barracks on the other side of the market-place, since he was old enough to go out with the raiding ships.

And they drove me out. Because I killed, in a fair fight, one of them—and they could remember only that I was not of their blood.

He felt not like a Free-Farer but like a ghost.

Time to go . . .

It was night, and the great market-square was a blaze of light. Varnans from the ships and from all parts of the city thronged it, making the stone walls ring. They looked at the heaped loot in the center of the square, and they talked to the raiders and gave them wine and listened to the story of the raid. Berkt had been the leader this time, and he was a great story-teller. Chane listened, rocking on the night wind. How they had struck three different systems, and fought, and come away. Berkt's deep voice rang as he talked. His eyes were yellow and bright, and the other raiders shouted with him, and drank, and held their women. The loot sparkled. Chane rocked like thistledown on the wind, a misty nothing lost in the blaze of light, ignored in the hot vitality of life.

Physical life. They had *done*. They had *felt;* the hammering of the blood, the exquisite visceral pain of mingled fear and excitement, the shock of battle, the joy of physical mastery over body and mind and ship when those elements became a single organism dedicated to survival. Now they were here, breathing the night wind, enjoying their triumph. They could drink, and hold their golden women in their arms; they could laugh and sing, the Varnan songs that made him remember another place and another song, far away. . . . Even in Carnarvon, those men were better off than he. They were not Starwolves, but they too could drink and laugh and fight, and take another man's hand in friendship.

And he . . . he was nothing. A wisp, a sterility, to wander forever looking at wonders he could neither touch nor experience; a useless ghost gathering futile knowledge with which he could accomplish nothing.

He remembered Helmer. He remembered his own body, not as beautiful as these gold-furred brothers of his, but a good strong able active body, tossed away like a discarded glove on an ash heap. He remembered Vreya. And he was sick, in every fleck of this that was now his being.

Sick, and in a panic. What might have happened to his body, while he was busy playing among the stars?

Now indeed it was time to go.

He went, with the roaring voices of the Starwolves echoing in his memory, drowning out the vast impersonal singing of the stars.

Riding the currents, driven by fear, whipped by a wild necessity to be clothed again in flesh, he rushed toward the Perseus Arm. And as he rushed, he called.

"Vreya! Vreya!"

For what seemed an eternity she did not answer, and then he heard her, far away and petulant.

"What is it, Chane? I thought you'd left me."

"Vreya, listen. You must come back . . ."

"No. Too much to see . . . No end, Chane, never an end, isn't it wonderful? Never . . ."

Now he knew what he had to say.

"But there will be an end, Vreya. Very Soon."

"How? What?"

"Helmer. He will destroy the Free-Faring if we don't go back and stop him. It will be gone forever, and we with it. Hurry, Vreya!"

She said crossly, *"What about your friends?"*

"There aren't enough of them. They need us, all of us . . . Raul, and Sattargh, and Ashton too. Call them, Vreya. Search for them. Tell them to come back, tell them to hurry, before Helmer destroys them."

Some of his panic had communicated itself to her. He could feel it. *"Yes, he would do that. He said he would. Destroy the Free-Faring, destroy our bodies . . . and we would die. He mustn't do that. . . ."*

"Then hurry!"

"Where are you going, Chane?"

"Back," he said. *"Back to help them fight."*

And he fled, a bodiless terror, back across the singing stars to Arkuu and a hollow mountain, where a man named Morgan Chane lay dead, or sleeping. . . .

XVI

Chane woke to a sound of thunder. It echoed away and then came again. It did not sound exactly like thunder, though. He tried to open his eyes to see what it was.

His eyes?

Yes. He had eyes, human eyes that flinched from the glare of the sun. He had human flesh again, and bones that ached from being too long in one position, sprawled heavily on the unyielding grid.

He was back.

He lay still for a moment, listening to his own breathing, the sound of the blood moving in his veins. Just to be sure, he clenched his hands, gripping his humanness, so thankful that he could feel it as a kind of joyous pain. Then he got his eyelids open and stared dazedly upward.

He saw the circle of yellow daylight at the top of the shaft, the sun-blaze that made him blink and squint. Daylight? Then time had passed . . .

A small, flying object came slanting down into the shaft from above. He raised himself a little to see, and as he did so, the object hit the upper wall of the shaft and exploded. The sound of the explosion reverberated horribly in the great well. This was the thunder he had heard, and now that he was awake it threatened to crack his eardrums. Small bits of metal whizzed close by him.

"Chane!"

It was the voice of John Dilullo. It sounded frantic, and a long way off.

"Chane—get up!"

Chane turned his head drunkenly and saw Dilullo. He was not a long way off at all. He was standing right at the edge of the grid, on the metal walkway over the abyss.

Chane said, quite sensibly he thought, "You shouldn't stand there, John. You'll get hit."

Dilullo leaned toward him, dangerously close. "Get off that grid! You hear me, Chane? *Get off the grid.*" He shook his head impatiently and swore, and shouted louder. "McGoun says if you stay there much longer the Free-Faring force will start the cycle all over again. Get up. Come here to me."

Chane looked around. Vreya still lay there unmoving. So did Ashton and Raul and Sattargh. She had not yet been able to find them, then, to coax them back . . .

"You want to go out there again, Chane? Has it got you, too—like these others you were so busy sneering at?"

"No," said Chane. "Oh, hell, no! Not again."

He got onto his hands and knees and began moving. Presently he was on his feet, and then he was on the walkway with Dilullo's arm holding him as he staggered.

Another crash of thunder went off overhead.

"What. . . ?" mumbled Chane.

"Helmer's three planes," said Dilullo. "They can't go right over the shaft but they're firing missiles into it from a little distance. Trying to destroy the Free-Faring—and us."

Chane looked all around, and then up. He could not see even a mark on the shining metal walls up there.

"No damage yet," said Dilullo, still supporting and guiding him as they went along the walkway. "We've taken shelter in the tunnel. But sooner or later, the missile fragments will hit those people on the grid."

"She's bringing them," Chane said. "Vreya. At least, I think she is."

They reached the mouth of the tunnel. Inside, McGoun and Garcia and the three other Mercs were sitting. Chane sat down and leaned his back against the wall, and they looked at him in a strange way, almost in awe.

"What was it like?" asked Bollard.

"Oh," said Chane. "You believe it now."

"I guess I have to. What did it feel like."

Chane shook his head. He didn't answer for a moment. Then he said, "When I was a little boy, my father used to tell me about heaven. I didn't like the sound of it. The beauty and the glory part of it were all right, but the rest of it, the not having any physical being and the sitting around doing nothing except to feel holy—that seemed awfully useless. It wouldn't be *you*. Not really."

He paused, then said, "Out there, it was something like that kind of heaven."

He looked back at the distant grid, shimmering in the sunlight. None of the four figures on it had stirred.

There was another burst of thunder high in the well, and a second one followed it almost instantly.

"From the way those bursts come," said Bollard, "Helmer must be using all three of his planes."

McGoun caught at that. "Then why don't we get out through the tunnel and get away while they're busy up there?"

"Because," said Dilullo, "we haven't got what we came for. We haven't got Ashton."

"But don't you realize," pleaded McGoun, "that Helmer will never let any of us get away from here alive?"

"I realize it," said Dilullo. "But we don't go yet."

"Then I'll go by myself," raged McGoun. "The hell with Ashton. I'm going!"

"Go right ahead," said Dilullo. "I'd be glad to be rid of

your babblings. But I have to warn you that Helmer has undoubtedly left a couple of men to blast anybody who comes out of the tunnel."

McGoun sat down again, and was silent.

"I *think* somebody out on that thing stirred a little," said Bollard, staring out at the grid.

"Come on, then," said Dilullo. "Not you, Chane— stay here and get your strength back. I think you'll be needing it pretty soon."

Dilullo, Bollard, and Garcia ran out along the walkway. Chane looked after them. He did not feel particularly weak. But his brain seemed a little numb, and would not quite clear.

Dilullo and the other two stood just outside the grid now, making beckoning motions. They blocked vision. It was not until they turned around, supporting two people, that Chane could see who had awakened.

Raul and Ashton.

Both men seemed so weak and nerveless that Dilullo and the others had to half carry them along the walkway and the ledge and into the tunnel. There they set them down, exhausted by even that small effort.

Ashton stared around him in a dazed, unseeing fashion. He seemed perplexed by the unfamiliar faces.

"Who. . . ?" he started to say, and stopped and shook his head, and began again. "Someone told me . . . if I didn't come back, the Free-Faring would be destroyed. Who. . . ?"

He ran out of breath again. Chane looked at him and thought that Bollard had been right, and this Randall Ashton they had come so far to find was not worth the effort. He looked a bit like his brother, only darker, younger, more handsome. But the good looks were spoiled by a petulant weakness in his expression.

Just now the weakness was physical as well. He was thin and wasted as though by a long illness. Chane thought that if this was what the delights of the Free-Faring made of a man, the thing was no damned good.

Raul spoke now, for the first time. "Vreya?" He too was looking at these strangers, puzzled, confused. Once, Chane could see, he had been as fine a physical specimen as Helmer, but now his tall frame had fallen away to bone and ropy muscle, and his great blond head drooped as though his neck no longer had the strength to support it. "Vreya," he said again. "Vreya!"

"So she found you," Chane said. "But she hasn't come back herself."

Ashton said, "Who are you? And where is . . ." He was making an effort to collect his wits. Underneath the confusion was a growing anger. "Helmer, Vreya said. Helmer would destroy the Free-Faring. So I came back. That girl made me come back!" He started to get up. "Is it true, or was that just a lie, to get me . . ."

He lost his balance and Dilullo caught him, eased him down again.

"It's no lie, Mr. Ashton. Just sit quiet there, and I'll . . ."

But Ashton's eyes had cleared suddenly. He was looking at Dilullo, and the anger was now full grown and ugly.

"You're Mercs," he said. "Who hired you to come here?"

"Your brother, Mr. Ashton."

"My brother. My goddamned meddling brother. Wants me back, I suppose, for my own good." The anger in his face grew hotter. He began to tremble. "I will not leave this place. Not for my brother, not for anybody. Do you understand?"

Raul whispered Vreya's name again, and Chane followed his gaze to the grid. He thought—

Before Dilullo could prevent him, he ran out and across the walkway to the grid.

Vreya still lay motionless, her splendid golden body sprawled near the edge of the grid. Beyond her lay the Arcturian scientist, Sattargh. He had the faint red skin and aquiline face of his kind, and he made not the slightest movement either.

Two missiles *blam-blammed* almost together against the wall of the shaft high above, and fragments rattled off the walkway.

Chane squatted down on the walkway, only two feet away from Vreya, staring at her still form.

Another missile went off above, and this time a fragment ricocheted off the grid only inches away from Sattargh. The glasslike grid and the metal walkways seemed as impervious as the walls.

"Chane, come back here!"

That was Dilullo, with his commander's voice, but Chane paid no attention to the call. He waited, while the missiles went off above. He watched Vreya.

He thought he saw a slight movement of her fingers. She might be back, but still unconscious, numbed, as he had been.

Chane leaned forward, as far as he dared. "Vreya!" he said loudly. "Wake up. Get up."

There was no sign that she heard, no more movements. Chane made his voice harsher, louder.

"Vreya! Wake up or I'll whip you!"

It seemed to take a little time for that to penetrate, but presently she opened her eyes. They were bemused, dazed, but also they had a spark of anger in them.

"Up, I say, or I'll give you the best whipping you ever had in your life!"

He glared at her, and she glared back, her eyes focusing more steadily, the color rising in her cheeks. He lifted his hand, and she made a furious small sound and got to her feet and lurched toward him, her own hand raised to strike.

The moment she came off the grid Chane grabbed her. He held her, easily now because her strength had not returned yet, and he laughed and said in her ear, "Forgive me, Vreya, but you're such a damn strong-willed wench that I thought only a threat like that would get you up."

He picked her up in his arms and carried her back across the walkway and to the tunnel. He set her down carefully, and she sat limply and gave him a stormy look.

It was nothing to the look Ashton was giving Dilullo. He appeared like a man on the verge of losing his mind. But he was not saying anything. Not for the moment. And Dilullo's mouth was set like a steel trap.

Presently Sattargh stirred feebly on the grid, and Bollard and Dilullo ran out and got him and brought him back.

"Thanks, Vreya," said Chane. "Thanks for getting them back here."

"Now that they are back," said Dilullo, "we can try getting the hell out of here. We'll never have a better chance than now, when most of them are up in those fliers."

Vreya said, "I thought you were going to fight Helmer, to save the Free-Faring. Did you lie to me, Chane?"

"Of course he lied," said Ashton. "They don't give a damn about the Free-Faring. All they care about is taking me away from it."

Chane noticed that Dilullo and Bollard were standing between Ashton and the mouth of the tunnel, as though they thought he might try to break back to the grid, missiles and all. Chane took the hint and kept a close eye on Vreya. She was sitting beside Raul now, her hand on his.

Chane said, "We can't fight very effectively from this tunnel, can we?"

She watched him, unconvinced. Raul sat with his head leaned back against the wall, and he watched Vreya, except for the times when he would lift his free hand and look at it, and touch his face, and then his body, feeling the gaunt bones. Chane thought, *He loves her. Perhaps he's thinking now what he almost lost in the Free-Faring.*

He wondered if she loved him. And was astonished at the twinge of jealousy he felt.

The Mercs were collecting their gear while Dilullo brooded.

McGoun said nastily, "You told me the entrance to the tunnel would be guarded."

Dilullo looked at him. "It will be, for sure. Which means we'll have to fight our way out. But if we can do it, and get to the skitter-flier, we have a chance."

He turned to Milner. "You're the best with a laser. Chane, you're the fastest. You two, I think."

Neither made any objection. Milner said, "A light-bomb would help us."

Dilullo nodded. "I thought of that." He took from a pocket a little plastic sphere no bigger than a marble and handed it to Milner. Then he said, "I don't like killing, everybody knows that. But these fanatics intend to kill every one of us, so—take no chances."

Chane still had no boots on. While Milner removed his, Vreya said,

"You did lie."

"About the need to come back, no. About saving the Free-Faring . . ." Chane shrugged. "So far Helmer hasn't done it much damage."

Raul spoke suddenly, with startling violence. "He must. He must destroy it."

Vreya stared at him, shocked. "You can say that, Raul? After you've done it?"

"Because I have done it," he said. "Yes. Look at me, look at Ashton and Sattargh. The Free-Faring is sweet poison, but that is what it is. It is death."

Milner said, "Be sure to bring our boots." Bollard nodded. Milner turned to Chane. They took their lasers and started down the tunnel.

They went quite noiselessly; it was perfectly silent except for the echo from the great shaft behind them when missiles went off. It was dark here in the tunnel, but they could not lose their way.

After a while there was glimmer from up ahead. They went more softly until they were near the bright daylight of the tunnel end.

Milner held up his hand, signalling Chane to stop. Then he drew the little sphere from his pocket, touched a stud on it, and hurled it out through the tunnel opening.

Instantly, Milner and Chane shut their eyes and clapped their free hands over their eyelids.

They knew when the light-bomb went off, not only by the sharp snapping sound that was intended to signal its detonation, but also by the fact that the blaze of light it created was so terrifically intense that even through hand and eyelid it registered.

Next moment, they opened their eyes and plunged out of the tunnel. Chane was first, going low and going fast, not caring if Milner saw his Starwolf speed, in this moment of utter danger.

His speed saved him. For an instant later, the laser mounted in a fixed stand on the ledge to cover the tunnel-mouth was triggered off by an Arkuun man whose eyes were still utterly dazzled.

The laser cut Milner almost in half. Chane bounded to one side as Milner fell.

There were two of the Arkuuns left here to guard the tunnelmouth, and their eyes were beginning to recover and they could see well enough now to kill. They swung their lasers toward Chane.

Chane shot one down, leaping aside with all his blurring Varnan speed just after the weapon's flash and crack.

The remaining Arkuun shot and missed, and then tried to swing his weapon to follow Chane. But already Chane, his teeth showing in a mirthless grin, was firing. The second Arkuun went down.

Chane bent over Milner. There was no doubt at all that he was dead.

Chane ran into the tunnel and put all the power of his lungs into a shout that echoed and re-echoed down the long tube.

"Come on!"

Presently he heard them coming. When they got to him, Dilullo looked down at Milner and said nothing. He just dropped the boots that Milner would no longer need.

As Chane put on his own boots, the others arrived. Bollard and Janssen were dragging Ashton between them.

"I won't go," Ashton was saying, over and over. "I will not leave the Free-Faring!"

Dilullo turned on him and said, "We took a contract to bring you home, Mr. Ashton, and we'll keep it. There's nothing in the contract that says I can't encourage you to come quietly, so here's some encouragement."

And he gave Ashton a violent crack across the mouth with the back of his hard hand.

"Bring him," he said. "And bring Milner's body."

XVII

They went out of the tunnel and along the ledge. Dilullo kept them hugging the inward side.

"Those fliers are still circling around up there over the summit," he said. "If we're spotted going down the mountain, it'll be bad."

When they had followed the ancient path down off the ledge and onto the rock-strewn slope, Dilullo halted them in the concealment of a big boulder. He nodded to Janssen and Bollard, who had carried Milner's body with them.

"This is far enough," he said. "We'll build a cairn over him. But don't show yourselves."

"This is insane," said McGoun, looking upward at the sky, a badly frightened man. "The man's dead, and—"

Dilullo interrupted. "Yes, the man's dead, and he wasn't the man I liked best in the world. But he was a good Merc and he followed me here to die. He's going to have a proper burial."

In the shadow of the big boulder, they built the cairn over Milner's body.

"All right," said Dilullo. "We're starting down now, but not all together. We'll move one or two at a time, from one bit of cover to the next. I'll lead, and you follow the way I go. Bollard, you can help Ashton. Chane, bring up the rear."

They moved out, Dilullo scuttering fast to another big boulder a little way down the slope, then Bollard following with Ashton. Chane thought that Ashton did actually need a helping hand, but that the real reason Dilullo had Bollard stick with him was to make sure he didn't desert them and go back up to the tunnel. Ashton was talking in a moaning whimper now about the Free-Faring, and how he could not leave it.

Chane, waiting to go last, glanced up at the three fliers circling the summit. Then he looked down at his own party, running by ones and twos from boulder to boulder, a deadly game of follow-the-leader.

Chane did not think they could long remain undiscovered. The Mercs were pretty good at this sort of thing, but Ashton and Sattargh and Garcia were not, and neither was Raul, nor Vreya.

They did not even get as far as Chane expected. They were barely a third of the way down the rocky slope when Chane, glancing upward again, saw one of the three fliers break off its circling of the summit and come rushing down toward them.

Chane yelled a warning and skipped behind a rock. He raised his laser, but the Arkuuns seemed to know the range of a portable and the flier kept well above it as the pilot let his missiles go.

The explosion filled the air with rock fragments. Chane peered, but his comrades were all hidden and he didn't know if any of them had been hit.

"Pinned!" he muttered to himself. "That about does it."

The flier went on out away from the mountain so it could circle and come back over them again.

Now the Arkuuns in the other two fliers up there had waked up to what was happening, and they came hurrying to join the attack.

Chane, watching, thought that one of the two, in its haste, went almost over the summit of the mountain. He hoped that the shaft of the Free-Faring had caught it.

His hope died when both fliers came straight on down toward them. The missiles from the lead flier began to bang around him.

Chane hugged his rock. At the same time he glanced away from the mountain. The first of their attackers would be circling back and catch them on the wrong side of their shelters.

The last of the fliers came down over him. To his surprise, it fired no missiles at all. It just went majestically downward in a straight, declining line until it hit the slope and ploughed up the rocks and vanished in flaming wreckage.

"So the Free-Faring *did* catch that one!" thought Chane. "Good."

It did not much help his party, though. Pinned on the mountainside as they were, two fliers were quite enough to finish them off as long as the pilots stayed out of laser range.

The first flier had circled and now was coming back. Chane skipped to the other side of the boulder; as he did so, he saw Dilullo and the others down there below doing the same thing. He thought a few of them were missing, but could not be sure.

The missiles exploded in a line up the slope. One went off close to the boulder behind which Chane crouched.

Chane jumped up and staggered out into the open. He clutched his middle with his free hand. Then he collapsed onto the ground, lying on his back with his eyes open, the laser still clutched in his hand.

To his amazement, as he lay there, he heard feet pounding up the path. Dilullo, sweating and with his chin bleeding from a small gash, looked down at him.

"Chane?"

Chane did not move a muscle. He said, "Get the devil out of here, John, and leave me alone. And try to work your way farther down the slope."

"Ah. I might have known it was some Starwolf

trick," Dilullo muttered, but all the same he looked relieved.

He pounded back down the slope. Then Chane heard one of the two fliers coming back toward the mountain, and heard its missiles banging again.

The flier circled around without loosing any missiles in Chane's vicinity. He began to hope.

It went on and on as he lay there, the fliers relentlessly coming toward the mountainside and firing, and then circling to swing out again. But the uproar seemed to be moving gradually down the slope. Dilullo would be trying to work them lower between attacks, Chane thought.

Lying still, with his arms outflung, he watched each time as the flier that had just attacked came circling over him. The fliers were getting closer to him, for though they stayed out of range of Dilullo and his party, the movement of the party down the slope was lowering the altitude of the attackers. And they had obviously ceased to worry about Chane.

Another banging of missiles and the flier came on and curved around over Chane, lower than before.

Not yet, he thought. *I've got to be sure . . .*

He waited and heard the attack still receding down the slope. He wondered how many of Dilullo's party still survived.

Then, when the sound was even more distant, Chane sensed that the moment had come, and gathered himself. He waited until the flier curved about him; this time it was low enough.

With all the speed that Varna had given him, he jumped, aimed the laser and let go with it.

The bolt went right through the cockpit. The flier did not complete the curve it had begun. It rammed straight into the side of the mountain.

The remaining Arkuun flier, which had been circling around to come in for another attack-run, changed course. The pilot seemed to have become crazed with rage, for he dived the flier straight at Chane, letting missiles go in a steady stream.

Chane had leaped to cover, but the rocks seemed to lift up around him and the air was full of dust. The explosions almost stunned him.

He staggered out when the explosions stopped, but the flier had already swung around and was winging out to turn and make another run at him.

Chane saw Dilullo, over a way from him on the slope, climbing higher than Chane's position, running like mad.

Then Chane ducked and once more the explosions were all around him and he thought when they stopped that he was stretching his luck pretty thin, that he would not get through another of these salvos.

But as the explosions stopped, he heard another sound—the crack of a laser. He jumped up, but he could see nothing for a moment, through the dust.

It cleared a little, and he saw the last Arkuun flier fluttering over and over. It hit the ground and rolled a little way down the slope.

Dilullo came limping down toward him, carrying his laser. "I am not," said Dilullo, "as cunning as a Starwolf at these tricks, but I can imitate them when I see them. I figured that pilot was so mad at you he wouldn't be looking for me higher up."

They went to the wrecked fliers and examined them. No one was alive in them. In one of them Helmer sat with his head lolled back. On his gold-skinned face was nothing now, just a dead-expression.

"Damn all fanatics," said Dilullo bitterly. "They get themselves and a lot of other people killed because they won't argue for their ideas—they have to enforce them."

Chane shrugged. "Well," he said carelessly, "he didn't destroy the Free-Faring, and he didn't destroy us. At least not all of us. How many are left?"

"Raul took a missile fragment right through the

heart. McGoun got another fragment in the stomach, and I think he's bought it. Janssen has a shoulder wound, but not bad."

It was very quiet now on that upper slope. The wind blew through the broken cockpit of the flier and stirred Helmer's bright hair. Dilullo turned and walked wearily away, down toward where the others were. Chane followed him, feeling a little sorry for him and not envying him his conscience.

When they reached the others, Bollard was giving first aid to McGoun, who seemed to be unconscious. Vreya sat crying beside the body of Raul. The others seemed a little stupefied.

"They're all done for," Dilullo told them. "You're safe now. Stay here till you get McGoun tended to and then make a sling litter for him. Chane and I are going down to the skitter-flier."

They started away. When they had gone perhaps fifty yards there was a sudden outcry behind them. They turned, and saw Randall Ashton running away from the group, back up the mountain toward the tunnel-mouth.

Chane said, "I'll get him." He shouted to Bollard to stay where he was and take care of McGoun. Then he trotted after Ashton. There was no hurry about it. He watched Ashton pant and strain and stagger up the steep path, watched him stumble and fall and get up again. *Go on, you bastard,* he thought, *cry for it. Enough men have died because of you that you damn well ought to cry.*

And he was crying when Chane caught up to him, sitting in the dust with the tears running on his cheeks and the sobs choking him. Chane picked him up and laid him across his shoulders, then took him down and dumped him onto the ground, where he lay exhausted.

Dilullo said, "Bollard, if he tries that again, knock him over with a stunner."

"I'd rather use a laser, but okay," said Bollard, not looking up from his work. He was almost as bloody as

McGoun, working feverishly to stop a welling tide that would not be stopped. Chane was tempted to tell him that he was wasting his time, and then decided not to. It was Bollard's time, and anyway he would not welcome the Starwolf type of realism. These men always had to try. He went off again with Dilullo, and this time nothing stopped them.

All the way down the mountain Dilullo said not a word, but Chane knew what the other was thinking. He was thinking the same thing himself.

Highly unwelcome thoughts, but they turned out to be true. When they got into the nest of tall rocks where Janssen had hidden the skitter-flier, they found a fused and shattered wreck. Missiles had been fired carefully into it from close range.

"Helmer was a thorough man," said Dilullo. "Damn him."

"There's still Ashton's plane."

"Do you think he would have overlooked it?"

Chane shrugged.

"Well, we'll check it out. We'll get Ashton and . . ."

"Take a breather, John," said Chane. "I'll go and fetch him."

Dilullo looked at him bleakly. "I'm so old you want to spare me an extra trip up that slope, is that it?"

"You know," said Chane, "you ought to do something about that age-obsession of yours."

"Aren't Starwolves worried about getting old?" demanded Dilullo.

Chane grinned. "The kind of a life a Starwolf leads, he doesn't have too many worries on that score."

"Ah, get out of here and go," said Dilullo. "After all, why should I wear myself out when I've got a big dumb ox like you to run errands."

Chane went, fast, only slowing down when he came within sight of the others up on the slope.

"McGoun's gone," said Bollard. "Died before I could even get the bleeding all stopped."

Chane nodded. He looked at Vreya, who was not crying now but was sitting with her head drooping beside Raul's body.

"John would want you to build up some rocks over McGoun and Raul too, wouldn't he?" said Chane.

"I suppose he would," said Bollard.

Chane went to where Ashton was sitting. "Come along—we want you to show us where your flier's hidden."

"I will not," said Ashton. "I don't want to leave here. Why should I show you?"

A dark smile came onto Chane's face. "If you don't, I will do some things to you that will give me great pleasure."

Sattargh stood up. He said wearily, "I'll show you. I can't take any more of this."

The thin Arcturian went down the slope to where Dilullo was waiting. Then he led them for more than a mile along the base of the mountain.

"We couldn't hide it completely," he said, panting. "But we put sand and rock-dust over it wherever we could, to camouflage it."

When they reached the place to which Sattargh led them, a bay that indented the side of the mountain, they found what they expected to find. Ashton's flier was a fused and shapeless mess.

"Now what?" Chane asked Dilullo.

Dilullo said, "Give me a little time to think up a brilliant inspiration. While I'm doing it, you can tell the others to come on down here."

A few hours later, as Allubane was setting, they sat in a circle and ate their rations and looked dismally at each other. When they had finished eating, Dilullo spoke.

"Now I'll tell you how we stand," he said. "We have no flier to get us out of here. We have no long-range communicator, so we can't call Kimmel on Allubane Two and have him bring the ship here."

He got out the map and spread it out, and had Bollard shine his hand-lamp on it as the dusk gathered.

"Now, a Merc likes to have two strings to his bow," said Dilullo. "I plotted out a rendezvous with Kimmel. If he didn't hear from us at all, he was to come to that rendezvous every ten days."

He put his finger on the spot where the great river that flowed north-south ran into one of Arkuu's seas.

"That's where the rendezvous is," he said.

"And where are we?" asked Garcia.

Dilullo put his finger down on another spot on the map. "Here."

"That's an awful long way," said Garcia. "Hundreds of miles . . ."

"It is," said Dilullo. "But I've thought up a way we can get to that rendezvous."

"So you've thought up a brilliant inspiration after all?" said Chane.

"Yes, I have," answered Dilullo.

"What is it?" Chane asked. "How do we get there?"

Dilullo looked around at them and said,

"We walk."

XVIII

How long had they been walking? Chane tried to reckon it up in his mind. Fourteen days crossing the mountain ranges—no, sixteen, counting the two days they had lost in following a blind lead and returning from it. But how many days in the great forest? How many following the slope of the land downward until it grew hot and humid, and the great trees were replaced by this crimson jungle?

When they had first come over the mountains, Chane had objected to the course Dilullo set.

"This isn't a direct course to the rendezvous. You're angling away northward."

Dilullo had nodded. "But this is the shortest route to that big river."

"The river?"

"Chane, look at these people, the shape some of them are in. They'll never last out the distance to the rendezvous on foot. But if I can get them to the river, we can raft down it to the meeting place."

Chane, looking ahead along the line of his companions as they went through the red jungle, thought to himself that they may have looked poor then, but that that wasn't a patch on the way they looked now.

Sattargh was in the worst shape, but Ashton was not much better. The long periods they had spent in the Free-Faring, returning at only infrequent intervals for food, had sapped their stamina. Garcia was doing better, but he was a scholar, not an adventurer, and he tired fast.

Both Chane and Dilullo had worried about Vreya, but Chane thought now that they needn't have. The tall Arkuun girl was magnificent. Her fine golden legs strode along firmly, and she made no complaints about anything.

The yellow sunlight shafted down in broken bars through the dark red foliage of the taller trees. The smaller growth was a bright scarlet. They plodded along after Dilullo, whose turn it was to lead the way, and they had to stop now and then while Dilullo slashed away some impending brush.

Stopping thus now, Chane noticed that Sattargh and Ashton sat wearily down on the ground, even for this short halt. It was a bad sign. Sattargh was trying, but Ashton was sullen and resentful, and neither of them really had the strength for this trek.

It seemed very silent in the red jungle. Chane had noticed many birds, some of them surprisingly big and exotic looking, but he had seen very few animals.

He said so to Vreya, standing beside him and brushing her yellow hair back from her damp face, and she nodded.

"The Nanes have almost exterminated many species, except a few kinds of big carnivores in the far south."

Chane thought of the pretty little mouth of the thing he had struggled with. "I wouldn't have thought those things could be flesh-eaters. I saw no teeth."

"They were designed to take liquid artificial food," said Vreya. "But they learned to beat animal flesh into a pulp and ingest it that way."

"Nice," said Chane, and at that moment Dilullo finished cutting and they started forward again.

Chane looked narrowly at Sattargh and Ashton. Sattargh struggled to his feet, but Ashton looked as though he was just going to sit there. Then he looked up and saw Chane's eye upon him, and got up.

Chane thought, *At least two days yet, maybe more, and we'll have trouble with him long before that.*

That night they made camp under tall trees, where there was no brush. They made no fire—there was no reason to ask for trouble. They chewed their super-nutritious food tablets and drank the water they had got from streams along the way sterilized with steritablets. As on each night so far, Dilullo insisted that Sattargh and Ashton eat more of the food than they wanted.

Chane sat on the edge of the little clearing, with his back against a big tree and his laser across his knees. Both moons were up and throwing beams of tarnished silver through the foliage. Presently Vreya came through the slanting silver bars of light, and sat down beside him. She uttered a sigh of weariness.

"You've been wonderful, Vreya," he told her. "I didn't think any woman could do it."

"I tire," she said. "But I have something to take back to my people, and I am going to do it."

"The Free-Faring? You'll tell them about it?"

"I will," she said. "I'll take them to it, as many as I can. I'll have them go out in the Free-Faring and see how glorious the outer stars and worlds can be. And we'll open the Closed Worlds, for all time to come."

"You'll only get caught by that insidious thing, the way Ashton and Sattargh and Raul were caught," he said. "You'll end up as they would have ended if we hadn't come."

She shook her head. "No. I will not be caught. *You* were not caught, because you have some wild strength in you that I cannot understand. I too have strength."

"What about those who don't have it?"

"I've thought of that. We'll find some way to protect them, make sure they don't go too far. It can be done, Chane. It's a risk, yes. But what is ever gained without risk?"

He couldn't answer that. Least of all, he.

On the following morning, two hours after they started, Sattargh collapsed. His legs simply crumpled under him.

"Just a little rest," he panted. "I'll be all right then . . ."

Chane had come to have an admiration for the thin, aging Arcturian scholar. He said, "All right, get a rest. I'll tell John."

Dilullo came back, his long face getting longer as he looked at Sattargh.

"Ten minutes rest," said Sattargh. "Then I can go on."

But when the ten minutes had passed and he tried to get up, he fell back.

"Ah-huh," said Dilullo. "I thought so. Get out the sling litter."

The litter, a compact net of thin, strong strings, was affixed to two poles cut from the brush. Garcia took the front end of it and Chane the rear, and they went on.

By the time they camped that night, they were an exhausted lot, except for Chane. They sprawled on the ground in the darkness, unable even to eat until they had some rest. Chane sat, chewing his food-tablets.

Something lithe and white and swift flashed out of the darkness and snatched up Ashton's limp form from the edge of the group and darted away with it.

In a split-second Chane was on his feet and hurling himself in pursuit. He used all his Starwolf speed, not caring whether the others saw or not.

He was only a few yards behind the Nane. The creature could probably have distanced him if it had been unburdened, but it would not let go of Ashton. Crashing through brush, leaping fallen logs, Chane put on a terrific burst of speed. They had come a long way for Ashton, and gone through a lot, and Ashton himself might not be worth it, but the work and wounds and death were not going to be for nothing.

The Nane dropped Ashton and tore with unbelievable strength at Chane's arms. Chane locked his hands together like iron and yelled.

"John! Here!"

The Nane made mewing, sobbing sounds, and struggled to break Chane's grip. Chane did not think he could hold it many moments longer.

There was a crashing in the brush and Dilullo and Bollard came running through the broken moonlight. They had their jungle knives, and they stabbed them into the Nane's body.

The Nane stopped trying to break Chane's grip, and struck with its hands, and Dilullo went flying backward.

Bollard stabbed again and again. Chane could hear the knifeblade driving home with a strange dull sound, as though it was sticking into some sort of sponge.

"Can't *kill* the thing," Bollard panted.

Chane suddenly let go of the Nane's neck. Still riding the creature's back, he shifted his grip downward to pinion the thing's arms.

The strength of those arms was so great that Chane knew he could not hold the grip more than a few seconds. Bollard hacked and stabbed furiously, and all at once the Nane fell down and lay still.

"My God, what a thing," said Bollard, gasping. He was utterly shaken. "Didn't seem to have any vital organs at all . . ."

Chane ran to where Dilullo was getting up from the tangle of brush into which the Nane had hurled him.

"No bones broken," said Dilullo, "but I'll have some bruises. When the critter grabbed me to throw me, I thought its hands would break me in half."

Bollard was bending over Ashton's limp form.

"Choked unconscious," he said. "Probably to keep him from crying out when the thing grabbed him. He should come round."

They carried Ashton back into camp. "Three men on guard at all times," said Dilullo. "Each with one of the lasers."

Vreya was looking at Chane in wonder. "You pursued a Nane?" she said. "I didn't think anyone . . ."

"Looks like we're getting back into their territory," said Dilullo.

Vreya nodded. "Yes, the dead city M'lann where

most of the Nanes were created long ago is not too far southeast of here."

Dilullo got out his map and a hand-lamp, and squatted on the ground studying. "Yes," he said. "M'lann's about a hundred and fifty miles southeast. The river runs through it."

He snapped off the light. "All right, those not on guard might as well get some sleep. We need rest bad enough."

Next morning, they found that the nightmare attack had had one beneficient result. Randall Ashton had recovered consciousness in a state of absolute horror. He made none of his usual sullen objections when they started. He kept looking nervously around the jungle and then back at his companions, as though he was afraid they might leave him alone here. Sattargh said that this day he was able to walk.

In mid-afternoon, as they went along the bank of a small stream. Chane saw a white shape flitting in the brush and let go with his laser at it.

Ten minutes later, two Nanes flashed from behind big trees just ahead of them. Dilullo fired and missed, but Bollard, who had the third laser, cut one down and the other flashed away.

"The woods seem to be full of them," said Bollard. "Have they got some way of letting each other know we're here?"

Chane wondered about that too. The very fact of the existence of the Nanes was nightmarish. They were a by-product of that same science that had produced the Free-Faring, and Chane thought that that science had been a curse to this world, creating a horde of almost immortal horrors to prey upon all life.

That night, Dilullo was sitting rubbing his bruises when Chane gave up his guard post to Janssen. Dilullo said nothing for a time, but his face had deep lines of pain and fatigue etched into it.

"I was just thinking," he said finally. "I was thinking

of a beautiful white house, with a fountain and flowers and everything in it the finest. I was wondering if it's worth it."

Chane grinned. "You'll have your fine house some-day, John. And you'll sit in front of it and admire your flowers for two weeks, and then you'll get up and go back to Merc Hall."

Dilullo looked at him. "That's what I like about you, Chane—you're always so cheery and encouraging. Will you please get away from me?"

Twice in the night they were awakened by laser blasts, as their guards fired at lurking Nanes. In the morning they learned that one of the lasers was dead, its charge exhausted.

Dilullo nodded. "I'm not surprised; we used them pretty freely on Helmer's fliers. Save the other two as much as you can."

That day's march was as nightmarish as the one before, with only one actual attempted attack by Nanes, but with frequent sight of one or two of the creatures slipping along parallel with them.

They had to carry Sattargh most of that day. And by night, Chane saw that Randall Ashton was giving out. He was trying hard; he had been so frightened that he dreaded the possibility of being left behind. But he was just not going to make it much further.

Vreya lay that night as in a stupor when Chane went to her, her eyes closed, her breath gasping. Yet she still had not made one complaint.

He stroked her hair. Weakly, she took his hand to her mouth and made to bite his finger.

Chane laughed and hugged her. "Vreya, I've never seen a girl like you."

"Go away and let me sleep," she mumbled.

Ashton began to give out before they had gone an hour on the next day's march. He started to fall over small obstacles. When Chane was not helping to carry the litter, he took Ashton's shoulder and steadied him.

"Thanks," said Ashton. "I . . . I don't want to fall behind . . ."

Dilullo suddenly called a halt. Ahead of them the tall trees thinned out and they glimpsed a wide tawny flood, turned to brilliance by the yellow light of Allubane.

The river.

They sat down on its bank and for a while they were too stupid and exhausted to do anything but just look at it, the vast heaving flood, rolling between jungled banks, coming out of mystery above, going into mystery below.

"All right," said Dilullo finally. "A raft won't build itself. We haven't got tools to cut trees so we'll have to use one of the lasers. Bollard, see to it. I'll stand guard with the other laser."

The scorching lash of the laser felled and trimmed the trees they needed. But by the time they finished, that laser was exhausted also.

Chane rolled the logs down to the river. Bollard brought from one of the packs a coil of steel twine, thin as cord and strong as cable.

As he showed Chane how to bind the logs together, Bollard said, "I used to read stories where they would bind logs together with vines and make rafts. Did you ever see a vine that would tie anything together so it'd stay tied?"

"I've been on a lot of worlds, and I never did," said Chane.

They used the jungle knives to carve a steering-sweep and a yoke to set it in. Oddly, in all this time there was not a sign of the Nanes.

The raft floated readily. "All right, get our invalids aboard," said Dilullo.

The exhausted members of the party stumbled onto the rough raft and promptly lay down. Chane pushed out into the current of the river with the long steering oar.

They floated. They went down and down the great

river of Arkuu, and the sun set and the stars and moons came up, and then the yellow flare of Allubane rose into the sky again. Most of them just lay flat and rested. But on the first day on the raft, Vreya dived off it and swam around and around, and then got back on board and lay down to dry herself and her short jerkin in the sun.

Chane gave her a leering wink as she lay there. She stuck out her tongue at him and he broke up laughing.

They went down the river and there seemed nothing at all to see but the jungle-covered banks. On the third night, Chane sat with Dilullo at the steering sweep while the others slept. Both moons were in the zenith, and the river had become a running sea of silver.

"Faster than light across the stars," said Dilullo. "And then ten miles an hour on a raft. I feel like an aging Huckleberry Finn."

"Who is Huckleberry Finn?" asked Chane.

"You know, Chane, I'm sorry for you," said Dilullo. "You're an Earthman by descent, but you've got no frame of reference. You don't know the legends, the myths, the stories . . ."

"We have some good legends on Varna," said Chane.

"I'll just bet," said Dilullo. "How Harold Hardhand the Starwolf went raiding and broke a lot of skulls and stole a lot of other people's goods and came home triumphant."

"Something like that," Chane admitted, and then he suddenly got to his feet, staring intently ahead.

The moonlit river was sweeping around in a great curve, and ahead of them on both sides of the river there loomed great, dark ruined towers against the moonlit sky.

"That," said Dilullo, "would be the dead city M'lann."

Chane nodded. "Yes. And look what's waiting for us there."

XIX

At first glance, it looked as though the moonlit ruined city was crowded with hordes of Nanes. Then Chane realized that actually the creatures could be counted only in the dozens, but as he had never seen so many together before, they looked like a crowd. Their bodies gleaming white in the moonlight; they looked almost beautiful from this distance as they ran along the stone quays of the dead city, toward two massive half-ruined bridges.

"Wake up the others," said Dilullo. "We've got trouble."

Chane woke them, and they stared in fear and repulsion at the lithe white shapes. The raft was bearing them steadily down toward the first of the two bridges.

"We've got one laser still operative," said Dilullo. "We've got the ato-flashes—they won't last long, but get them out. There's also the jungle knives."

He added, "Chane, you take the sweep and steer. If we run aground, we're done for. Ashton, you and Sattargh don't have strength enough to do anything; I want you to lie down and hang on."

Chane went to the steering-sweep, and as he went he grabbed Vreya's arm and hustled her along, sitting her down behind the place where he stood at the sweep.

She opened her mouth to protest angrily, and then shut it. They were nearing the first bridge.

There were now at least fifteen Nanes on the bridge, looking in the moonlight like white ghost-men as they waited for the raft. From far across the towering ruins there came long, falling, wordless cries, an unhuman ululation that grew louder as other Nanes answered the calls.

"They're going to jump down on us, John," said Bollard.

"Close your eyes, everybody," said Dilullo, and hurled up three of the tiny light-bombs in quick succession.

Through closed eyelids, it was as though brilliant lightning flashed three times.

There were sounds of splashes nearby, and thumps of things hitting the raft. Chane opened his eyes to see that, even though momentarily blinded, the Nanes had jumped. There were two of them on the raft.

The laser cracked as Dilullo fired, and one of the two creatures on the raft fell overboard, scorched and lifeless. But the other one that had struck the raft had hit Garcia, and had now grabbed him; he was screaming.

Bollard and Janssen sprang upon the back of that Nane, plunging the jungle knives into its body, trying to do it to death and not succeeding. The creature dropped Garcia and whirled around, and at that moment Dilullo triggered the laser and killed it.

"They are coming from behind us," rang Vreya's voice from behind Chane.

The Nanes swam like white man-fishes, and from behind and on either side they were starting to leap up out of the water onto the raft.

Dilullo triggered, but the laser had gone dead. "Lie flat!" yelled Chane, and pulled the big steering-sweep out of its yoke and used all his strength to use it as a flail.

The old battle-cry that he and his comrades had used on so many worlds sprang from his lips. "*Kill, Starwolf!*" he yelled in the Varnan tongue, and swung his oar.

He knocked Nanes back into the water in two tremendous sweeps of the oar. Another of the things came up mewing onto the logs behind him, and Chane used the butt of the oar as a punch and drove the creature's face in.

"Steer!" yelled Dilullo. "Or we'll have more of them on us!"

Chane's battle-fury faded enough for him to see what Dilullo meant. They were drifting down toward the second bridge now. This one had a big section gone out of its central span, but on the projecting parts of it still intact, other Nanes were waiting. And they were going to drift under one of those ends.

Chane put the sweep back in its yoke and strained mightily. The raft swung lumberingly toward the center of the river.

Garcia was lying and moaning but nobody was paying any attention to him. White hands with nailless fingers came up out of the water and gripped the edge of the raft. Bollard spurted the little flare of his ato-flash at the hands, and they let go.

And amazingly, of a sudden, the fight was over. The raft went past the bridge and the creatures on its projecting broken ends seemed to realize they were too far away to reach the raft by swimming. They mewled and sobbed their wordless cries, but that was all.

"Well," said Dilullo. In the moonlight, his face was sweat-streaked and a little wild. "Let's see how we stand."

Garcia's both arms and some of his ribs had been broken by the grip of the Nane. Bollard's left wrist had been fractured by a blow. The others had only bruises.

"When I think how strong those things are, I wonder we're still alive," panted Dilullo. "You did damned good work with that sweep, Chane."

"You take it and steer," said Chane. "I'll help fix up Garcia and Bollard."

"I'll keep well away from shore," said Dilullo. "The last thing we need, if we're ever to get to that rendezvous, is more fighting."

XX

"You look," said Kimmel, "as though you've been having quite a time. Where's Milner?"

"He got it," said Dilullo.

They had waited five days at the rendezvous, where the great river ran into the heaving ocher-colored ocean, before the ship came and saw their smoke signal, and landed at the place which Dilullo had selected.

"You found the man?" asked Kimmel.

Dilullo waved his hand toward Ashton. "Mr. Randall Ashton."

"Found me? They kidnapped me," said Ashton. "I was all right, till they came . . ."

"You were lying there, slowly dying," said Dilullo. "You're going back with me, and I'll take you by the hand right into your brother's office and collect our wages for bringing you. But after that, if you want to come back here and do it all over again and kill yourself, that's perfectly all right with me."

Vreya looked at Chane, where they stood on the edge of the group.

"What about you, Chane? Will you come back some day and go Free-Faring with me again?"

"No," he said. "The Free-Faring is not for me. But maybe I'll come back, at that."

She shrugged her golden shoulders. "By then, I may have another man."

"That's all right," said Chane. "I'll just knock him out of the way."

Vreya smiled. "It sounds interesting."

Dilullo was giving Kimmel some instructions, and Kimmel looked as though he didn't like them.

"It's simple," said Dilullo. "Take the ship up to medium altitude and then come back down and land out on the clear land around that city Yarr. Vreya can get out and we can be on our way before they spot us."

"Now wait a moment," said Kimmel. "I don't like to run a chance going as close to the city as that. The ship . . ."

Dilullo surprised them all. An angry color came into his cheeks and his voice snapped.

"This girl is worth twenty ships," he said. "She has some cockeyed notions, but she acted like a soldier all the way. We'll do it the way I say, and set her down safe."

Vreya went and kissed him. Dilullo gave her an embarrassed smile, and patted her awkwardly on the shoulder.

They did it that way, at dusk, and the last Chane saw of Vreya was as she walked with her swinging stride toward the lights of Yarr.

They went back up fast into the glare of Allubane, and while Kimmel cautioned and pleaded with the imperturbable Mattock, Chane looked back at the Closed Worlds.

He did not think they would be closed much longer. He thought that Vreya had the strength to be a leader. And he thought now that she had been right when she said she was strong enough to resist the deadly lure of addiction to the Free-Faring.

Later, when they had gone into overdrive, Dilullo called him into his little cabin. He pushed the bottle toward him.

"Everybody who does good work likes to have it noticed," said Dilullo. "So I'll say now, you did good work, Chane. There were a couple of times when, without your strength and quickness, we wouldn't have pulled through."

"I thought so, too," said Chane.

Dilullo made a disgusted sound. "Ah, you just can't be nice to some people."

He poured himself another drink. Then he said,

"You know, Chane, you never did tell us much about what you did in the Free-Faring."

"No, I didn't," said Chane.

"Did you go to Varna?"

Chane nodded.

"I thought so," said Dilullo. "There was a kind of a homesick look on your face afterwards. Well, I'll tell you . . . there's different kinds of homesickness, and I've got a special kind of my own. So I think I know a little how you feel."

Chane said, "I'm going to go back to Varna, sometime."

Dilullo looked at him, and then nodded his head.

"Chane, I think you will."

WORLD
OF THE
STARWOLVES

I

He was a long way now from the stars, and that was all right with him.

Damn the stars, thought Dilullo. *I've had enough of them.*

He sat on the browned, sun-warmed grass on the side of the low hill, hunched with his knees drawn up, looking in his gray coverall like an old rock set in the slope. And Dilullo's face had something rock-like in it too, a roughly carved face of harsh planes, his hair graying at the edges.

He looked down at the streets and buildings of Brindisi, at the cape and the mole and the little islands, with beyond them the blue Adriatic shimmering in the hot Italian sun. He knew the old city very well, but it had changed since he had hurried through it as a boy on his way to school.

Working and studying, to get to be a starman, he thought. *And what did the stars give me when I got to them? Danger and worry and sweat, and when I went out to them once too often I came back to find that everybody and everything I had was gone.*

The sun wheeled lower, and still Dilullo sat and stared and remembered. Then he was drawn back to the present by the sight of a man walking up the slope toward him.

He was a young man, compact of figure, his dark

head bare. He wore a coverall and there was something about the easy springiness with which he came up the slope that made Dilullo peer more closely. He had never seen but one man who walked quite that way.

"I'll be damned," he said aloud. "Morgan Chane."

Chane came up to him and nodded. "Hello, John."

"What the devil are you doing here?" demanded Dilullo. "I thought you'd have been long gone from Earth on some Merc job by now."

Chane shrugged. "I would have been, only it seems nobody wants to hire Mercs right now."

Dilullo nodded understandingly. The Mercs . . . the Mercenaries . . . would do tough, dangerous jobs anywhere in the galaxy if the pay was right. But sometimes there just weren't any jobs.

"Well, you got enough money for our job at Arkuu to keep you for a while," he said.

Chane smiled. He smiled easily, and his dark, lean face was that of a very nice young Earthman . . . only Dilullo knew that he was not a nice young Earthman at all but a human tiger.

"I thought," Chane said, "that I'd see how your new house is coming along. Where is it?"

"I haven't started building it yet," said Dilullo.

"Not started?" exclaimed Chane. "Why, it's been weeks and weeks since you quit the Mercs and left us. You didn't talk about anything but this grand new house, and how anxious you were to get it started."

"Listen," said Dilullo testily, "if you're going to spend a lot of money on a house to live the rest of your life in, you don't hurry it too much. You've got to be sure of the right site, the right design . . ."

He broke off and then said, "Ah, what's the use of trying to explain it to you. . . . what does a home mean to a damned Starwolf!"

Chane said, "I'd just as lief you didn't call me that, John. They still hang Starwolves most places if they catch them."

"Don't worry," Dilullo said sourly. "I've never breathed it to a soul. I can well imagine you don't want it told around."

The Starwolves were the natives of a distant heavy planet named Varna, and there was a reason why they were hated and feared all over the galaxy. They were the most competent robbers of all time. Their heavy world had given them unmatchable strength and speed and ability to endure acceleration, and nobody could beat them in space. They had used that advantage to take loot from all over the universe.

Nobody but Dilullo knew that Chane had been a Starwolf. He looked like any other Earthman, and his parents had been Earth folk, but Chane himself was born on Varna and had grown to Varnan strength. He had robbed and roved with the Starwolf squadrons until a quarrel with a comrade had resulted in a fight, and a dead Varnan, and Chane fleeing into exile to avoid the vengeance of the dead man's clan. *And I had to pick him up,* thought Dilullo, *and turn him into a Merc, and he's been a damned good one, but all the same I'm glad I don't have the responsibility for this tiger on my hands anymore.*

Dilullo stood up. "Come on, Chane. I'll buy you a drink."

They went down the slope and into the streets of the old town, and presently sat in a cool, shadowy tavern in which time seemed to have stopped a long while ago. Dilullo ordered, and a waiter brought two bottles, and he shoved one of them across the table.

"Orvieto abboccato," said Dilullo. "The best wine in the whole galaxy."

"If it's that good," said Chane, "why are you drinking whiskey?"

Dilullo answered, a little embarrassed, "The truth is, I've been away from here so long I'm not used to wine any more. It upsets my stomach."

Chane grinned, and drank his wine, and looked

around, at the old wooden furniture, at the smoke-blackened ceiling, at the open doorway outside which twilight was coming to the street.

"It's a nice town," said Chane. "A real nice place for a man to retire and live quiet in."

Dilullo said nothing. Chane poured himself more wine and said, "You know, you're lucky, John. When the rest of us are out there beating up the starways, in trouble up to our necks on some faraway planet, why, you'll be sitting here and drinking and taking it easy, real peaceful-like."

He drank and set his glass down and added, "I'd sure like to settle down in a place like this myself when I get old."

"Chane," said Dilullo, "let me give you a bit of advice. Never try to needle people, to cat-and-mouse with them. You don't know how, as you're not quite all human yourself. Now say what you want to say."

"All right," said Chane. He poured more of the straw-colored wine for himself. "John, do you remember that when we came back from Arkuu, we heard the Singing Suns had been stolen?"

"I'm not likely to forget it," said Dilullo. "The greatest art-treasure in the galaxy robbed away by the Starwolves. You must have been real proud of your people."

"I was," said Chane. "Just six ships, slipping in to the throne-world of Achernar and snatching the Suns out from under their noses. Achernar has been screaming bloody murder ever since."

They had, Dilullo knew, and he didn't blame them. The Singing Suns had been their almost-sacred treasure.

They were not really suns. They were synthetic jewels, created long ago by a master craftsman, and the secret of their creation had died with him. Big, varicolored, glorious, the jewels represented the forty biggest stars of the galaxy, revolving in a mobile. And the jewels sang, each one differently . . . the deep and somber note of Betelgeuse, the soaring sweet tone of Altair, the thrilling sounds of Rigel and Aldebaran and Canopus and all the others, blending together into a true music of the spheres.

Chane was still smiling. "They talked of sending a war-fleet to Varna to get the Suns back. But that couldn't be done, for all the independent systems in Argo Spur, where Varna is, wouldn't let their sovereign space be violated by a fleet going through them."

"I've said before," said Dilullo disgustedly, "that it's a damned immoral arrangement. Those Argo systems protect the Starwolves from attack because they profit from the Starwolf loot."

Chane shrugged. "Anyway, the government of Achernar, as a last resort, has offered a two million credit reward to anyone who'll go in there and bring back the Singing Suns."

Dilullo made a harsh sound that was not quite laughter. "They'll get far with that! Who is there in the whole galaxy that's going to try to recover Starwolf loot?"

"I thought some of us might," said Chane.

Dilullo stared at him. He seemed completely serious, but with Chane you never knew.

"Go to Varna? Take something away from the Starwolves? There are easier methods of suicide!"

"The Suns aren't at Varna, John," said Chane. "Do you think the Varnans would just keep them and admire their beauty? I know the Starwolves, and I can tell you they don't care a tinker's damn about art, no matter how great. No, they'd break up the Suns, sell the jewels separately in the thieves' market worlds of Argo Spur."

"Break them up?" exclaimed Dilullo. "Of all the vandalistic, blasphemous things ever heard of. . . ."

Chane shrugged again. "That's what they'd do, John. A thousand to one, the Suns are right now on certain worlds of the Spur. We figure we could get hold of them and claim that two million."

"Who are 'we'?" demanded Dilullo.

"Why, Bollard and Janssen and some of the others have agreed to give it a try," said Chane.

"How did you convince *them* where the Suns are?" said Dilullo. "You couldn't tell them about your Starwolf past."

"I just lied to them," Chane said shamelessly. "I told them I grew up in the Spur and knew a lot about its worlds." He added, grinning, "And so I do, too . . . but from going with the Varnans to barter our loot."

Dilullo was too used to Chane's lack of conventional morality to be surprised. He said, "That Spur is murder. There are more nonhuman- than human-peopled worlds in it, and on nearly all of them you can get killed just for the clothes you're wearing. Supposing that you can locate the Singing Suns there—"

"I can locate them," Chane said. "I know just where loot like that would be sold."

"So you locate them," Dilullo finished, "then how do you figure to get hold of them?"

"Take them," said Chane.

"Just like that? Good old-fashioned Starwolf stealing?"

Chane smiled. "This wouldn't be stealing, John. You forget that the Singing Suns rightfully and legally belong to Achernar, and whoever has them knows it. If we get hold of them, by cunning or force, we're only recovering stolen property for the owners. All legal and honest."

Dilullo shook his head. "Legally, you're right. Even ethically, you're right. But I don't want to hear a Starwolf talking about honesty!"

He added, "Anyway, how do you and Bollard and the rest figure even to get to the Spur? It takes money for an expedition like that, and nobody would advance you a nickel on a venture into that hellhole."

"We all have some money from our Arkuu job," said
Chane. "And that's where you come in, John."

"I do, do I? In what way?"

Chane explained brightly, "You got a hundred
thousand for your share of that last job. You could help
finance this one and take a leader's share if we make it."

Dilullo looked at him across the table for a long time
before he spoke.

"Chane," he said, "you're a marvel in one way. You
have the most brass of anyone in the universe. You know
bloody well that hundred thousand is for my house."

"I didn't figure you would ever build that house," said
Chane.

"Why did you figure that way?" asked Dilullo, his
voice dangerously soft.

"Because," said Chane, "you don't really want a house.
Why have you sat around here for weeks without starting
one? Because you know that when the first nail goes into
the house it's going to nail you down here and you'll
never see the stars again. That's why you've put it off and
put it off. I knew you would."

There was a long silence, and Dilullo looked at Chane
with a look that Chane had never seen before. Chane
tensed himself, ready to spring back out of the way if
Dilullo struck at him.

Nothing happened. Nothing except that Dilullo's face
became slowly bleaker and that a haggardness came into
it. He picked up his glass and drained it and set it down.

"That's a bad thing for you to say to me, Chane," he
said. "And the reason it's so bad is that it's true."

He stared down into the empty glass. "I thought it
would all be the same here, but it hasn't been. Not at all."

He sat staring into the glass and the lines in his hard
face were deep. Finally he stood up.

"Come along," he said.

They went out of the tavern. It was dark, but the moon
was bright on the streets of old white buildings. Dilullo

led the way, along a street that went twisting out of town, with the whisper of the sea vaguely audible on their left. Dilullo walked with his shoulders sagging like those of an old man, and he neither looked at Chane nor spoke to him. He finally stopped and stood staring at nothing . . . nothing but a vacant lot between two old stucco houses. He stared silently for a long time.

"This is where my first house was," he said.

Chane said nothing. There was nothing to say. He knew all about that house and how, long ago, Dilullo's wife and children had perished in its burning.

Dilullo suddenly turned and grasped Chane by the arm, so fiercely that even Chane's iron Starwolf muscles felt it.

"I'll tell you something, Chane," he said. "Don't ever go back and try to live things over again. Don't ever do it!"

Then he dropped Chane's arm and turned away. "Ah, let's get the hell out of this place," he said. "Let's go to the Argo Spur."

II

The galaxy wheeled through infinity, a vast, spinning, lens-shaped storm of stars. Out from its central mass trailed mighty spirals, and one of these spirals was isolated, sweeping far out into space. It had a dim, tarnished look compared to the other vast arms of the galaxy, for beside its myriad suns this spiral contained many dark nebulae and an unusual number of dead stars. It was often called the Dark Spiral, but its other name was the Argo Spur.

Beauty and horror, riches and danger, worlds of men and many more worlds of not-men, were in the Dark Spiral. None knew that better than Morgan Chane, as he sat in the bridge of the little speeding ship and looked and looked, his face dark and brooding. What he looked at in the viewscreen was not an actuality but an accurate simulacrum, for they were in overdrive and in non-space direct vision is impossible.

The fabric of the ship was shuddering and shaking around him. It was an old ship and its overdrive was not very good. It did what it was supposed to do, it hurled them across extra-dimensional space toward the spiral at its highest speed, but it trembled and creaked ominously all the time it did so.

Chane disregarded that. He looked at the spiral in the simulacrum and his eyes were fixed on a tawny yellow star blazing deep in the wilderness of the Argo Spur.

And how often I've come this way, he thought.

The superb tawny-gold sun was the primary of the planet Varna, the most hated world in the galaxy.

And this vast, far-flung spiral of stars ahead was the old road of the Starwolves. Through it they had come and gone on their way to raid the systems of the main part of the galaxy. And through it Chane had come and gone with them, so that there was little about the tangle of suns and dead stars and dark nebulae that he did not know at least something about.

The little ship hurtled on, still trembling and whispering uneasily. There was nothing for a pilot to do when a ship was in overdrive. All that was needed was a man in the bridge to keep watch on the telltales of the overdrive units. Chane was the man now, and he did not at all like the way the telltales quivered.

After a time, Bollard came into the bridge. He looked at the instruments and shook his head.

"This ship is a dog," he said. "A worn-out old dog."

Chane shrugged. "It's the best we could lease for the kind of money we had."

Bollard grunted. He was a fat man, so fat that his paunch bulged out his coverall, and he had a moonlike face with crinkles around his eyes. He looked slobbish, but Chane, who had been out twice with him, knew that Bollard was strong and fast and tough, and that in a fight he was about as slobbish as a swordblade.

Bollard touched a switch, and a simplified star-chart was projected into being. He looked at the blip of their ship, now well into the base of the spiral.

"You said you had an idea about where we'd drop out of overdrive," he said to Chane. "Where?"

Chane indicated with his finger a small area marked in red.

"There."

Bollard stared. "That's a Zone 3 danger area. Do we *have* to go into it?"

"Look," said Chane, "we've been all over that. We'll

be scanned from the time we enter the Spur and we've got to look like the drift-miners we're supposed to be, which means that we have to go where drift-miners would go."

"We could skirt around the area and make like we are mining without going into it," said Bollard.

Chane smiled. "That's a real clever idea. Only, when we get to Mruun, we've got to show some reason for coming there, and some valuable ores to sell would be a good reason."

Bollard seemed unconvinced, and Chane added, "You don't know the Spur. I do, for, as I told you, my parents were Earth missionaries who moved from one of the Spur systems to another when I was growing up . . ."

He thought that the first part of his statement was true, even though the rest was not. His parents had indeed been dedicated missionaries, but Varna alone had been the scene of their mission, and they had lived and worked and failed and finally died on Varna.

". . . and I can tell you," Chane finished, "that on some of the Spur worlds, just one whisper, one breath, of suspicion will get you killed quick."

"I still don't like this idea," grumbled Bollard. "It's all very well for you; you were a drift-miner before you joined the Mercs. But I've never been a rock-hopper."

Chane said nothing. He had told them he was a drift-miner to cover up his Starwolf past, but he had never been one and he thought he had a tricky time ahead of him.

He thought it even more when, finally, the blip of their creaking ship had moved quite near to the red patch of the danger area. Dilullo, sitting in the co-pilot chair beside Chane, studied the chart.

"We'd better drop out of overdrive here," he said.

"We can go a little closer," Chane said.

They went closer, and Dilullo began to fidget. Presently he said decisively, "That's close enough. Drop out."

Chane shrugged, but obeyed. He pressed a button that gave the alert signal throughout the ship, and set up the controls.

Chane moved a switch, and they dropped out. And Chane, who had done this hundreds of times, thought again that it was something like dying and then being born again. From the extra-dimensional space in which they had been traveling, he seemed to fall through vertiginous abysses. Every atom in Chane's body felt shock, his senses whirled, and then they came out of it.

And now the viewscreens no longer presented a simulacrum. The glory of the Argo Spur was revealed and there smashed in upon them the light of ten thousand suns.

A series of ear-piercing shrieks came from the drift indicators. At the same instant, Chane saw great and small bulks hurtling by the ship.

"*Knew* we were getting too close!" yelled Dilullo.

Chane saw death looking him in the eye. Their little ship had dropped into space right inside a colossal stream of stone and metal. And they couldn't go back into overdrive until the unit recycled.

"This damned drift has changed since I last saw it!" he exclaimed. "Sound the hooter!"

Dilullo pulled a lever and the hooter alarm yelled stridently through the ship.

An odd-shaped mass of stone was bearing down on them. Chane hit the controls and stood the ship on its tail. There was a rattling of tiny particles on the hull and he hoped they weren't holed. Dilullo was shouting something, but between the hooter and the constant shrieking of the drift-alarms he couldn't hear what it was.

Radar and sight both informed him of another weird-shaped mass coming at them, tumbling over and over. He hit the controls again.

Then the Starwolf surged up in Chane. They were trapped in this bloody cataract of drift and they probably weren't going to get out of it alive, and all the careful maneuvering in the world wouldn't do them any good now. He took the Varnan way, the way he and his old comrades would have taken had they been in a bind like this. He held steady on the steering and smashed his free hand down on the power and sent the ship hurtling blindly ahead at full normal speed.

Gamble your ship and your life. It was better than trying useless dodgings and turnings and getting killed anyway.

Chane's teeth showed in a mirthless smile. He had had a good life as long as it lasted, and if it had to end he was not going to claw like a frightened old woman against the inevitable. No.

Dilullo was still yelling at him, but he paid no attention. John was a good man but he wasn't a Starwolf, and he was getting a mite old.

A monstrous face of stone whirled past them. A face with bunches of tentacles instead of eyes, and a protuberant trunk-like mouth, and nothing human about it.

The ship slammed through particle-drift again, and past another face that had no relation to humanity, and then past a mighty tumbling statue of a thing with the same tentacle-eyed face and too many arms and legs.

Faces, figures, a phantasmagoria of nightmare shapes . . . and of a sudden the scream of the drift-alarms shut off. They were out of the cataract of meteoric drive and into clear space.

Chane took a long breath. The gamble did pay off, sometimes. He turned around and looked at Dilullo with a bright smile.

"What do you know?" he said. "We made it."

Dilullo started to curse deeply. Then he shut it off. "All right, Chane," he said. "I thought we had taken some of that Varnan out of you. I see we didn't. I'll remember that."

Chane shrugged. "You've got to admit, it was no place to hang around in."

Dilullo said, "Those faces . . . those figures. What the devil is this place?"

"Some sort of nonhuman cemetery, I think," said Chane. "Long before there were ever men in the Spur, there were other races. They made meteors into memorials."

"Nobody's ever mined this drift," Chane explained. "At least I don't think so. You see, everybody's superstitious about it. I figured this would be the best place to pick up some precious ores, before we head for Mruun."

Dilullo shook his head. "I might have known it. Robbing a galactic graveyard. Only a Starwolf would think of that!"

III

Chane, in his spacesuit, cuddled up against the gigantic, unhuman stone face and prepared to commit mayhem upon it. His analyzer had told him there was a rich palladium ore-pocket in this sculptured shard of stone. He thought, from his readings, that if he cut out the ear of the thing he could easily reach it.

Stars above, around, and below him, the bright pitiless face of infinity. The great river of stones, some of them sculptured in awesomely alien busts, others stark and untouched, flowed serenely on through the void. These meteors and broken asteroids moved at the same pace but they did change position in regard to each other, so that one had to be wary of a bulk of stone slowly and majestically approaching and grinding one to powder.

Clinging like a fly to the monstrous face, Chane hauled around the ato-torch that hung from a sling hooked to his suit. It fouled with the sling of the analyzer and he tugged at it impatiently.

"Chane!"

The voice came from the receiver in his helmet, and it was the voice of Van Fossan.

"Chane, you're not going to cut into one of the heads? Remember John's orders."

Chane muttered a curse under his breath as he turned and saw the spacesuited figure angling toward him, using an impeller to drive himself forward. Van Fossan was a young and eager-beaver Merc, and he would show up just at this time.

Chane remembered very well what Dilullo's orders were. Before they left the ship, which was now cruising outside the meteor stream and keeping pace with it, Dilullo had said, "The people or not-people who carved those heads have been gone a long time. But a memorial is a memorial. I wouldn't want strangers prospecting for ore in my tombstone, and neither would you. Leave them alone."

Chane had made no objection to what he considered Dilullo's sentimentality. But he had never meant to be bound by it. It was his bad luck that Van Fossan had come up on him.

"I just stopped to untangle my slings," Chane said. "You go on ahead."

He waited until Van Fossan had gone, a small figure against the backdrop of an infinity of suns, angling away across the majestically flowing river of stones.

When he was out of sight, Chane unshipped his cutting laser and began to slice into the edge of the monstrous ear.

"*Stranger . . .*"

Chane stiffened, his head swiveling, his eyes glaring around him for the one who had spoken.

"*Stranger, spare us our pitiful immortality. . . .*" Chane suddenly realized that the words were reaching his mind, not his ears, and that they were not words at all but thoughts. Telepathic speech. "*If you are here at all, you are a lord of the starways. We were lords of the starways . . . and of all our might and magnificence only these stone faces are left. Leave us this much. . . .*"

Chane rebounded with a galvanic kick of his feet from the huge stone head. He floated near it, and then he laughed.

So that's why these heads have never been mined, he thought; *a telepathic record set in each one.*

He told himself that both superstition and sentimental appeals were lost on him; but if the telepathic bit still worked, there might well be other and nastier things about the monuments that still worked.

Chane switched on his impellers and went away from there. He angled through a shoal of fine drift, feeling it rattle like hail against his tough suit and helmet. The light of the Argo suns glanced down on him, and by it he saw other Mercs in the distance, swimming like dark men-fish amid the drift, searching and going on and pausing to search again.

He too swam and stopped and searched and searched again, using the analyzer. It told him nothing. He began to get irritated by his failure. It seemed to him that the eyeless stone faces sneered at him as they went by.

A queer uneasiness came upon Chane. For a time he did not understand what caused it. Then he remembered. The last time he had moved like this, in his spacesuit, alone in the drift, it had almost been his death. He had been wounded, exhausted, with the Starwolves hunting him, and he had seemed to float all solitary in the universe with the bright eyes of the suns of Corvus Cluster pitilessly watching him. Only the fact that his signal had brought Dilullo's Merc ship had saved him.

"To the devil with it," Chane muttered to himself. "That's past history."

He forced himself to shrug off the feeling, to get on with his job, to impel himself deeper into the drift, keeping clear of jagged meteors and unhuman stone faces that bore down upon him. But wherever he pointed his analyzer, it seemed that there was nothing any good.

"Chane," said Dilullo's voice inside his helmet, startling him.

"Yes?"

"Return to ship."

"John, I haven't got hardly a thing," said Chane.

"The others have," answered Dilullo. "Come on back."

Chane, as he forsook the search and cut in his impeller to highest power, was not sorry to lift up out of the majestic never-ending parade of stone faces that moved forever through the drift.

As he shot in front of one of the great faces that was bearing down on him, he turned and made a disrespectful sound toward it.

In the hold of the ship, he put down the small chunks of ores he had brought along in his net carrier.

"You got less than any of us!" Sekkinen said loudly to him. "You, the professional rock-hopper."

Sekkinen was a tall, rawboned man who had the habit of saying emphatically just what he thought. He did not much like Chane.

Chane shrugged. "You just had beginners' luck. I didn't. That's the way it goes."

He looked around at the haul, glistening chunks of stone and metal, frosty with the utter cold of infinity.

"It's not very much," he said.

"A good chunk of terbium, some palladium, and a few of the rare C-20 ores," said Dilullo. "No, it doesn't amount to much. But we'll get more as we go on."

They went on. The little ship crept perilously along the coast of one of the dark nebulae that dimmed the Argo Spur. Its main analyzer probed ahead, seeking treasure. Nothing.

They crept on and on, still coasting that enormous cloud. Finally there came a time when Bollard, who handled the big analyzer, said sourly, "I've got it . . . but you won't like it."

They didn't like it. It was a dead star, with a pocket of rare transuranic element on it, such as a burned-out sun sometimes creates during the long aeons of its dying.

When they had landed and were sweating in their special heavy-gray suits to cut the ore, there was a grumble from Janssen, ordinarily the lightest-hearted of the Mercs.

"I don't much like this place."

Chane agreed. To a spaceman, the great suns were the blazing, radiating life of the universe. It was an oppressive thing to stand upon the corpse of a star.

The vast dark cindery plain, rising into low ridges of slag, was somber and sad beneath the starry sky. They cut away with the ato-torches, but even with the mechanical-assist devices built into the heavy-grav suits every move they made was toilsome. Chane was used to heavy gravity, but nothing this heavy. Through the helmet-intercom he could hear Bollard puffing noisily.

"Chane," said Bollard, "this is a pretty clever plan you dreamed up, collecting precious ores to take with us to Mruun."

"I thought it was pretty clever," Chane said.

"Just do me a favor," said Bollard, "and next time don't get clever at the expense of my aching back."

They finally got the ore into the hold and left the dead star. Again they coasted the enormous dark nebula, using the probe of the analyzer on every likely-looking mass of drift within range, but with no result.

They angled away from the cloud and soon made passage through a mighty triplet of blazing suns, two of them yellow and the third a yellowish green. Chane knew them well, for they were a famous starmark on the old Varnan road.

Chane had told Dilullo about a freak star-system beyond this triplet, and they pulled cautiously toward it. It was one of the curious systems found here and there which mothered comets instead of planets. A bewildering shoal of elliptical comets spun about the white star, looking like brilliant moths around a flame.

The ship drove through them. Comets were a large

bunch of nothing, except for a possible nucleus of meteoric material, but they could play the devil with instruments. Dilullo took it cautiously, and finally set them down on one of the asteroids, the nearest thing to a planet this sun possessed.

No rock-hoppers had been here, and the first sweep of the analyzer located terbium and tantalum. In a comparatively short time they had what they needed in the hold and Dilullo was feeling his way back out through the comets.

"And now," he told Chane in his cabin later, "Mruun. And it's up to you to find the Singing Suns."

Chane looked at him. "You don't much like this one, do you, John?"

"Let's say," answered Dilullo, "I don't much like the Argo Spur. Its name is a stink and an abomination in the galaxy, and not only just because the Starwolves lair there."

It was on the tip of Chane's tongue to ask why he had come if he felt that way, but he did not ask. He knew why Dilullo had come.

"Well," said Chane, "it may cheer you up to hear that while we'll all be in danger at Mruun, I'll be in a special added danger."

"At the moment, that does sort of cheer me up," said Dilullo.

Chane grinned. "I thought it would."

IV

In the steamy, suffocating night of Mruun, the big city throbbed with life and sound. Going through its crowded streets with Chane, Dilullo thought that although he had been on many queer worlds, he had never seen anything like this before.

The Mruunians themselves might have been human once. . . . Earthmen had discovered when they first got the star-drive that they had had predecessors, a forgotten star-traveling human race that in the remote past had seeded much of the galaxy with humanity. But time and evolutionary pressures had changed the original stock in many ways. The natives of Mruun were now gray-skinned, Humpty-Dumpty types with big pot bellies, small short legs and narrow faces. They were extremely polite as they waddled through the streets, and their faces had a calm malice in them; Dilullo did not like them at all.

But the gray natives were only a part of the incredibly motley crowd that thronged under the lurid orange lights of these bazaar streets. Beaked and feathered men strode along, regarding everything with unwinking yellow eyes. Bulky, white-skinned creatures with elephantine legs smiled blandly as they went along. There were some who wore cloaks and hoods as though they did not want to show their bodies at all. Then over the buzz and hum of the street came an outburst of yelping laughter as a bunch of furry near-men who looked like big bear-dogs walking erect swayed drunkenly into a tavern.

"They're from Paragara," Chane said. "Not a bad lot but not very good with spaceships."

"They look to me," said Dilullo, "like a lot of country boys who have come to the wicked city and are about to be taken for all they have."

Chane nodded. Dilullo noticed that as Chane went along, carrying their sack of ore samples easily with one hand, his eyes kept shifting here and there over the throng, his dark face wary and alert.

He remembered what Chane had said to him when they had left the Merc ship at the spaceport.

"I'm known as a Starwolf on Mruun, John. Not only by old Klloya-Klloy, to whom I've sold a lot of loot, but by others here, including off-worlders. That's why I don't want anyone but you with me, or the Mercs are likely to find out all about me."

It had taken all Dilullo's authority to keep the others confined to the ship, but he had managed it by his assertion that they were needed to guard the ship and its equipment on this thieves' market world. Looking at the faces of this crowd, faces human and nonhuman but nearly all steeped in the wickedness of the Spur worlds, Dilullo felt that his assertion had not been far wrong.

Drinking places from which loud voices spoke, barked, or howled, cook-shops from which drifted odors that were partly delectable and partly nauseous, brothels where God knew what went on . . . the place made any of the Star Street quarters of the main galaxy look like a kindergarten. He was glad when they got into a less crowded section of large shops. They were mostly shut at this hour, but their barred windows displayed silks and jewels and outlandish sculptures, loot of many raided worlds sold here quite openly.

Chane casually turned down a narrow and dark side way. He glanced around as they went, but there was no one in sight. He darted suddenly off the dark street into a still darker area behind the buildings that housed the shops.

Dilullo, following him, said, "And what the devil are we going to do here?"

"Keep your voice down, John," whispered Chane. "I am going to engage in a bit of burglary and you are going to wait for me, that's what we're going to do."

"Burglary? That's nice," said Dilullo. "Do you mind telling me what you're going to steal?"

"You promised to let me run this operation," Chane said. "All will be explained to you. But to ease your conscience, stealing is considered the highest form of art on Mruun, and nearly everything in all these shops is stolen property."

He hunkered down and in the darkness Dilullo could see that he was fishing something out of the sack of samples. It was a small cylindrical object which Chane fastened to his coverall by a clip. He touched it and it began a faint, almost inaudible buzzing.

"An alarm-damper," said Chane. "Every one of these places is guarded in ways you can't imagine, but I think this will take me through the first beams without setting them off."

"So this is what you were so busy making on our way here in the ship?"

"This and a couple of other things," Chane said. "But there's one instrument I can't possibly make, and that's what I have to steal here. You see, this shop specializes in highly sophisticated instruments of crime."

With that he was gone, moving like a shadow through the darkness to the back of the low building. Dilullo examined his stunner, and then sat down on the edge of the sample sack to avoid sitting on the damp ground.

The air was oppressive, like a steam bath. There were few sounds here except the murmur of the distant

uproar in the main streets. Dilullo mopped his face and
wondered why in the world he should be sitting in this
damp hellhole when he could have been taking his ease
in Brindisi.

Well, he knew the answer to that one and there was
no use thinking about it, and he had better just sit and
hope Chane didn't set off something that would get
them both killed.

After a few minutes he heard a low sound from the
dark building, like the sound of a voice abruptly cut off.
Dilullo jumped erect and stood with his stunner in his
hand.

Nothing happened. He stood there for what seemed
quite a long time, and then a shadow came toward him.
He could not identify the figure in the dark and he did
not want to raise his voice in a challenge, so he just
gambled that it was Chane coming back.

It was. Chane held in his hand a cubical thing that
looked like some kind of instrument. He squatted down
with it, and rummaged in the sample sack until he
found what he wanted and dragged it out. It was a sheet
of palladium, and Dilullo remembered how, on the way
to Mruun, Chane had hammered on a sample of the
metal to make that sheet.

"If I'm not interrupting you . . ." Dilullo said
politely.

"No interruption at all," said Chane. "What is it?"

As he spoke he was bending the sheet of palladium
and wrapping it all around the cubical thing he had
brought out of the dark shop.

"Were there guards in there?" Dilullo asked.

"There were," said Chane. "Two of them. And to
answer your next question, I didn't kill them. I was a
good little Earthman like you said, and only stunned
them."

"Now what?" said Dilullo.

Chane, working away in the dark, did not look up as
he answered, "We want to know where the Singing

Suns are. All right. There's only one merchant on
Mruun big enough to buy them from the Starwolves,
and if he didn't, he'll know who did. That's
Klloya-Klloy, and he'll need a little inducing. That's
what this instrument is for. You could call it an
inducer."

He finished wrapping the palladium sheet completely
around the cubical box, and then put the thing down
into the sack of ore samples and stood up.

"You see," said Chane, "we'll be scanned from the
moment we go into Klloya-Klloy's place. We'd never
get past the first gate with this thing. But with the
palladium wrapped around it, the scanner-rays will see
it as just another ore sample."

Dilullo shook his head. "Do you know, Chane, I'm
kind of glad I came with you on this. It's educational.
That's what it is, real educational."

He expected Chane to lead him to one of the big
shops in the bazaar, but instead Chane went through
more dark side streets into an area of large villas. One
of these had a high wall around its extensive grounds,
and a gate in the wall with two enormous yellow men
standing guard.

Chane spoke to them in galacto, the lingua-franca of
the galaxy. "We've something to sell. These are
samples."

"Weapons," said one of the guards, extending his
hand.

Chane handed over his stunner, and Dilullo followed
his example, though he did not like doing it. He was
sure from what Chane had said that from somewhere in
the gatehouse beside them they and their sack were
being thoroughly examined by scanning rays.

A voice spoke a word from inside the guardhouse,
and the yellow guards stood aside to let them enter.

"Fallorians," said Chane as they walked toward the
villa. "Real tough men. Klloya-Klloy has a lot of
them."

"You know," said Dilullo, "I'm beginning to wonder where my brains were when I came along with you."

The villa was a big mansion, and there was the loom of even bigger warehouses in the grounds behind it. They went into a lobby that was garishly decorated with fabulous-looking art pieces from many worlds, all in utterly conflicting styles. A couple more of the huge yellow men lounged here, and a young Mruunian sat behind a desk.

He said, "Ore samples, eh? I hope you have enough of the stuff to make it worth our while to bother."

Chane said, "I'll talk that over with Klloya-Klloy."

The Mruunian tittered maliciously. "Rock-hoppers wanting to deal personally with the master. What will we have next?"

Chane smiled and reached across the desk and grabbed the Mruunian up out of his chair. "Tell Klloya-Klloy that Morgan Chane the Starwolf wants to see him, or I'll drive my fist right through you, little pudding."

"Starwolf?" The Mruunian looked shaken. "Now I remember you. But—"

A voice came from the communic on the desk. "I heard that. Let him in."

A door opened at the far end of the lobby. Chane picked up his sack and Dilullo followed him into a surprisingly small office. The door closed silently behind them.

In one of the dish-shaped things that passed for chairs on this world, an amazingly fat Mruunian sat, his whole obesity shaking with his laughter. But his small eyes remained cold.

"Morgan Chane," he said. "Well, well, I heard that they ran you out of the Starwolves."

"They did," said Chane. "And I took to prospecting, with some friends. And I found something big."

"It would have to be big," said Klloya-Klloy. "You know me well enough from the old days . . . . I never touch anything small."

"Wait till you see this," said Chane.

He took out of the sack the square,palladium-wrapped object. He set it down on the desk before Klloya-Klloy. With his two hands he tore the palladium sheathing suddenly away, revealing a cubical instrument from which there extended a cord whose bifurcated tips ended in flat black metal disks.

The instant he saw the instrument, Klloya-Klloy reacted violently. His chubby arm darted toward a row of buttons on the desk.

Chane .was too fast for him. With one hand he covered the Mruunian's mouth, and his other arm encircled the obese body and pulled it, chair and all, away from the desk.

Dilullo, utterly astonished, stood goggling. Chane hissed to him, urgently.

"Quick, get the deherer disks over his head. One on each side. *Quick!*"

V

Dilullo grabbed the cord and applied the disks to each side of the struggling Mruunian's head. The disks were connected by a spring that held them in place. Then, at Chane's direction, Dilullo snicked on the two switches in the side of the small cubical instrument.

At once Klloya-Klloy stopped struggling. He sat stony still in the dish-like chair and his narrow eyes became glazed and expressionless.

Chane let go of him and stepped back a little. Dilullo said, "I've heard of these things, though I never saw one. It's a shorter, isn't it?"

Chane nodded. "It is. Shortcuts the will completely and makes truthful responses mandatory."

"And the things are illegal on every world," said Dilullo.

Chane smiled. "Nothing is illegal on Mruun. Now stand by."

He turned and spoke to Klloya-Klloy. "Did the Varnans bring the Singing Suns to Mruun to sell?"

Klloya-Klloy answered tonelessly, staring blank-eyed straight ahead. "Yes."

"Did you buy them?"

"I did not buy them. The sum was too great. I acted as agent."

"To whom did you sell them?"

"Eron of Rith, six. Iqbard of Thiel, four. Klith . . ."

He named off several names and the number of Suns purchased until they were all accounted for, ending up with, ". . .and the Qajars, ten."

"The Qajars?" Chane frowned. "I never heard of them. Who are they? What is their world?"

"A planet in the dark cluster DB-444 beyond the Spur."

Chane's frown deepened. "There's no inhabited world in that cluster."

Klloya-Klloy remained silent. No direct question had been put to him, so he made no answer.

"Where is the cluster?" asked Dilullo. He was asking Chane, but Klloya-Klloy heard the question.

"Celestial latitude and longitude are . . ."

He began to reel off figures and Dilullo noted them down. But Chane still scowled.

"There are no people out there rich enough to buy ten of the Singing Suns," he muttered.

"Look," said Dilullo. "We've stuck our heads into the lion's jaws to get this information . . . though I'll admit this character looks more like a turnip than a lion. Hadn't we better get out of here?"

Chane nodded. "I think you're right."

"How do we do it?"

Chane shrugged. "We just walk out. The shorter will keep him sitting here until someone comes in and takes it off his head."

They walked out. They went through the lobby, loftily ignoring the young Mruunian at the desk, and out of the big building. At the gatehouse, the yellow Fallorian guards gave them back their stunners.

They went down the dark street twenty paces, and then a screeching, hell-roaring siren let go behind them in the villa grounds and Chane said, "*Run!*"

Dilullo could not run with Chane's Starwolf speed but he stretched his legs and did his best. Chane reached an arm to help him along and Dilullo struck it angrily aside, and Chane laughed and said, "Your pride is going to get you killed one of these times, John."

When they got into the crowded bazaar streets, Dilullo's hopes picked up. But then he looked back and saw a low car with the big yellow Fallorian guardsmen in it turn into the street.

The motley mob was too dense for the car to get through. The Fallorians piled out of it and came after them, plowing massively through the throng.

Dilullo, glancing back, did not watch where he was going and collided with a large furry body. The bunch of bear-dog men whom Chane had called Paragarans had just come out of a drinking place. They were now very drunk indeed and the one Dilullo had careered into went off his feet, and Dilullo with him.

Chane reached down and yanked Dilullo erect. The bear-dog men milled around, staring at them in a fuddled way.

"We've had it," said Dilullo.

The Fallorians had overtaken them and were roughly pushing aside the bear-dog men to get at them.

It proved to be the wrong thing to do. The bear-dog men were drunk enough to fight anyone who pushed them around. With barking howls they threw themselves at the yellow guards.

The Paragarans were almost as big as the Fallorians and they were ferocious fighters. They went in with their jaws seeking for holds and their arms whirling like furry maces. Chane jumped in with them, using all his Starwolf strength against the Fallorians and not caring who saw him.

The thing became a swirling brawl. Dilullo stood apart from it, with his stunner in his hand. There was no chance to use the weapon, the combatants were so closely mixed. Chane seemed to be enjoying himself hugely. He used his fists, his elbows, his feet, his knees, and the butting surface of his head, all with equal agility. It seemed to Dilullo that only a few moments went by before the thing suddenly quieted and the Fallorians were lying insensible or twisted up and groaning.

The dog-like Paragarans slapped Chane on the back with immense, drunken joviality. Then one of them, looking owlishly wise, spoke to the others in a husky, barking voice. They all started away from there, weaving a bit and sort of leaning against the crowd. The crowd made way for them very rapidly.

Chane, mopping his brow, grinned after them. "They think they had all better go back to Paragara," he said. "I know a little bit of their language."

"I think they're right," said Dilullo sourly. "And maybe we'd just better emulate their example and get back to our own ship. I'd like to get the devil out of here—if we still can. Your friend Klloya-Klloy may have alerted the spaceport security officers."

"That's the beauty of a world like Mruun," said Chane. "No security officers. No law. If you've got anything valuable you hire guards to look after it for you. It's up to you, completely."

"A nice kind of world," said Dilullo. "For a Starwolf, that is. Wait a minute. . . ."

He had spotted one of the furry Paragarans, lying senseless in the street not far from the yellow guards. He raised his voice and yelled after the Paragarans who were receding into the darkness.

"Come back here!" he yelled in galacto. "You've left one behind."

"They don't hear you," said Chane. "Too drunk."

"What will happen to this one?" asked Dilullo, frowning down at what ridiculously resembled a gigantic teddy bear dropped by a passing child, only the child would have to be ten feet high.

"I expect the Fallorians will cut his throat if they catch him," said Chane, quite unconcerned.

Dilullo rapped out an oath he rarely used. "No. We'll take him with us. Pick him up."

Chane stared. "Are you out of your mind? Why should we bother with him?"

Dilullo got a wintry edge to his voice. "Every now

and then, Chane, I have to remind myself that you're not altogether human. Well, I am. And anyone who fights on my side, I don't leave behind to get killed. Not even a damned Starwolf."

Chane laughed suddenly. "You've got me there, John. I remember back on Arkuu when that damned fanatic Helmer had us pinned on the mountainside, you came chasing back up to see if I was dead or living."

He picked up the unconscious Paragaran and slid him across his shoulders. He winced as he did so.

"He's big and heavy," Dilullo said. "Let me give you a hand."

"It's not the weight, it's the stench of him," said Chane. "This critter smells like a one-man tavern."

He started forward down the street, and on Mruun, where everybody minds his own business, nobody even looked at them. They reached the spaceport road and went along it under the light of the Spur stars.

Dilullo kept looking back but there was no more pursuit as yet. He began to think that with luck they might make it.

Chane, as he stumped along with his furry burden in the steamy dark, uttered a low laugh.

"Fun and games," he said. "Isn't this better than sitting on your backside in Brindisi?"

Dilullo made a sound indicative of disgust. Chane continued, "You know, John, I've often thought of Arkuu . . . and that girl Vreya. I'd like to go back and see her one of these days."

"Leave her alone," said Dilullo. "She's far too good for the likes of you."

The spaceport lights came up and Dilullo kept his hand on the hilt of his stunner, but nothing at all happened.

They went into the ship and Bollard greeted Dilullo with a sweet smile on his moon-fat face.

"Did you have fun?" he asked. "While we were all sitting here with our thumbs up our noses?"

"We had fun," said Dilullo. "There'll be more of the same and enough for all if we don't get off Mruun as fast as we can."

Bollard shouted an order and the Mercs scattered to their posts. Then Chane came in behind Dilullo and dumped his unconscious burden on the deck. Bollard stared at it.

"Who the hell is that?"

"A Paragaran," said Chane. "We sort of got mixed up with him and John felt we couldn't leave him behind."

The hooter sounded as the lock doors slammed shut. They got into the chairs and the little ship went skyward, fast. By the time acceleration eased off and they got out of the recoil chairs, they found that the Paragaran had apparently been revived by the shock of takeoff. He stood up, looking puzzledly around him and swaying gently with an unsteadiness that had nothing to do with takeoff. His gaze lit on Chane and his hairy face split in a pleased grin.

"A damned good fight," he said in galacto in a roaring, husky bellow. He clamped Chane on the back with his great paw. "And you're a good fighter. You brought me out of there?"

Chane shook his head. "Not a bit of it. I'd have left you lying there." He pointed to Dilullo. "But my friend John here is the loyal comrade type. He brought you to save your neck."

The big Paragaran turned and stared at Dilullo with red-rimmed, glazed eyes, and then stepped unsteadily toward him.

"I'm Gwaath," he bellowed. "And I'll tell you this: anybody does Gwaath a favor like that and he's got a friend for life!"

His furry arm went around Dilullo's neck in a crushing embrace. He looked into Dilullo's face with drunken, doggy affection, and uttered a mighty belch.

Dilullo reeled.

VI

The ship, in overdrive, went farther and farther into the vast wilderness of Argo Spur. It went over great drifts of dust-choked suns whose haggard witch-fires extended for many parsecs. It passed dark shoals where dead stars had long ago collided and filled space with wheeling debris. It skirted a huge tornado-like whirl of dead and living stars that spun ever faster in a mad maelstrom that had a core of neutron stars.

The old Starwolf road, thought Chane, and he knew every star and swarm and dark nebula along the way. And far ahead, on the simulacrum in the bridge, the sun of Varna was a tawny eye watching him, and he looked at it and dreamed.

Presently, over the creaking thrum of the faulty overdrive, Dilullo spoke from behind him.

"I've got half a mind to give up the whole thing and go back to Earth."

"Losing your nerve?" said Chane.

"I've told you before, don't try to needle people. You're no good at it. I've got more nerve than you when the chips are down."

Chane thought about that and then said seriously, "I believe you're right. I can do anything as long as it's fun doing it, but you've got some kind of repression and drive. . . ."

"Call it the Puritan conscience," said Dilullo. "And I

342

don't need any amateur psychoanalysis, either. How much chance do we have of getting the six Suns that Eron of Rith has?"

Chane shrugged. "I've never been to Rith but I've heard about it from Varnans who were there. Eron is a tough character.. He'd have to be, to live on that planet. . . . It's nothing but storm all the time, they say."

"Nice," said Dilullo. He was about to add something sour, but Gwaath came lumbering into the bridge.

"Oh, for God's sake," muttered Dilullo in English.

"He loves you," said Chane. "You saved his life, remember? That's why he keeps following you around all the time."

Gwaath's large form seemed to crowd the whole bridge. He patted Dilullo on the shoulder in breezy camaraderie, almost knocking him to the deck.

"How's it going?" the Paragaran asked, in English. "How's everything, old boy?"

Dilullo stared at him. "So you've been picking up things?"

Gwaath nodded, then switched to galacto to explain. "The men down in the crewroom have taught me a little of your language. Listen to this. . . ." And in English he started off a stream of expressions that made Chane grin and brought from Dilullo a hasty demand to stop.

"They *would* teach you things like that," said Dilullo.

"Why, man, children know stronger language than that on Paragara," said Gwaath. "On Paragara—"

Dilullo interrupted. "Look," he said desperately. "Are you sure you don't want us to set you down on some world here in the Spur? Some world where you could get a message to your ship? Then your friends could pick you up."

"I told you before, they're no friends of mine anymore," Gwaath rumbled. "They deserted me there on Mruun, left me to be killed." He added, with an air of ultimate indictment, "They were *drunk*."

Chane did not laugh. The Paragarans might look like big fubsy bear-dogs, but their renown as fighters had gone all through the Spur and they were quick to take offense.

"No," Gwaath was saying, "I'll stick with you till we hit some world where I can get to Paragara on my own. Where do you touch first?"

"Rith," said Dilullo.

"Hell of a place," said Gwaath. "If it isn't raining it's hailing or lightning and it usually does all three together."

"You've been there?" asked Dilullo.

"Two—three times," said Gwaath. "The people of Rith buy some herbs that are raised only on Paragara. When the herbs are dried and then burned, they do very strange things to the mind."

"Who is Eron of Rith?" asked Dilullo.

Gwaath stared. "The ruler. They don't go for all that stuff about democratic government on Rith. One planet, one boss. Eron is it."

Dilullo looked inquiringly at Chane. Chane knew what he meant, and nodded.

"I'll tell you what, Gwaath," said Dilullo. "We're going to Rith on a kind of risky mission. And I think you ought to know what it is before you go along with us."

He told Gwaath about the Singing Suns. The Paragaran made a sound of admiration.

"And the Starwolves got them? Just what I'd expect. Ah, those Varnans are bastards but there's no more bold and clever thieves in the universe. Even on Paragara we're just as glad the Starwolves let us alone."

"From what Klloya-Klloy told us, Eron of Rith has six of the Suns," said Dilullo. "We want them all, and his six come first."

"How are you going to get them?"

"Take them," said Dilullo. "This Eron knew bloody well they were stolen property when he bought them. If we can return them to their rightful owners at Achernar, there's a huge reward waiting for us."

Gwaath's small bright eyes began to gleam in his furry face. "It sounds like fun," he said. "The Rith are a tough lot. Not as tough as the Starwolves or the Paragarans, but tough enough. Even so, it might be done."

"You know Rith, we don't," said Dilullo. "If you want to join in on this there's a share of the reward for you at the end." He added, "Of course, the Mercs have to vote you in first."

The Paragaran did not take long to decide. He shrugged massive shoulders and grinned a grin that showed formidable teeth.

"I might as well," he said. "My ship's gone without me. We were going to become fighters for a kinglet on a Spur world whose subjects are rebellious. Probably there's no more risk looking for the Suns."

"All right," said Dilullo. "I was wondering what excuse for landing we'd make when we set down on Rith. But this takes care of it . . . we're setting down to put ashore a Paragaran crewman we picked up from a world where he was beached."

"Fine," said Gwaath. "What's your plan for getting the Suns away from Eron, once we're on Rith?"

"Yes, John, what is your plan?" asked Chane, straightfaced. "I've been waiting to hear it."

Dilullo gave him a slightly nasty look. "You'll hear it when I'm ready to tell you. Come along with me, Gwaath. I want to ask some questions about the setup of Eron's city."

Gwaath cleared his throat. "Well, you see, I was pretty drunk each time I visited the place and I might not remember things so clearly if I was cold sober. I mean—"

Dilullo interrupted. "Two drinks, that's all." He added, surveying the massive figure, "I'll make them large ones, considering your size."

When the ship finally came out of overdrive near Rith, Chane was piloting. The blue-shining sun of this system was a small one, and Rith itself was not a very large world. They could not see much of it because the surface was blanketed under heavy clouds.

Janssen gave Dilullo the readings which gave the location of the radio beacon at Eron City starport.

"At least, I *think* it's the location," said Janssen unhappily. "There's the devil and all of a thunderstorm covering that whole region, and most of what I got was in little bits and pieces."

He went back into the radar room. Dilullo studied the readings. Then, instead of handing them to Chane, he spoke into the intercom.

"Sekkinen, you come up to the bridge for pilot duty."

Chane looked around at him. "I'm perfectly capable of taking her in."

Dilullo nodded. "I know you are. But it's going to be tricky in that storm and I'd just as lief not have a Starwolf type of pilot who thinks hell, let's take a chance, and slams us right into the middle of the city."

"John, you remember things too well. You ought to learn to take it as it comes."

But he made no other complaint, and yielded the pilot chair to Sekkinen when he came.

Sekkinen was a born complainer. He complained now about the fact that it was not his turn at duty, about the injustice of asking a man to home in on fragmentary radar readings, and about the fact that he hadn't been allowed to finish his dinner.

He went on and on, but while he complained his hands were moving swiftly and surely and the little ship went down into the cloud-masses and the storm.

They were descending toward the night side of the planet, but the incessant sheets of lightning made it frequently brighter than day. The winds, as registered on the board, were terrific; they would have known that anyway from the buffeting. The flaring atmospherics broke and distorted the sensor rays of the ship's instruments so that it lurched about half blind. Sekkinen kept complaining and all the time his hands kept moving skillfully. Presently the lightning-flares showed a small starport rushing up toward them, and when they bumped down onto it Dilullo sighed with relief.

"Listen to that," said Chane, when the power had been turned off.

The ship was being smashed at by rain that fell in great solid chunks rather than as drops. The drumming roar of it was deafening.

"We can't go out into that; it'd knock our heads off," said Dilullo. "We'll wait."

They waited. The drumming downpour continued. It was well over an hour before it suddenly stopped.

"All right," said Dilullo. "Just Bollard and Gwaath and me, for now. Crack the lock."

They went out into chill, damp darkness. Dilullo saw the lights of what he took to be starport administration and started toward them. The other two followed, Gwaath's big feet splashing in the puddles.

Suddenly they were washed by a fierce glare of spotlights from ahead of them. At the same moment a hard voice spoke to them in galacto from an amplifier.

"There are four heavy lasers trained on your ship," it said metallically. "Every man aboard is to come out, without weapons, and walk in this direction."

"What is this?" demanded Dilullo loudly. "We're an Earth prospecting craft, and we only set down here to land a stranded Paragaran. . . ."

"Just keep walking, my innocent Earthman," said the harsh voice. "Eron wants to see you. He knows exactly why you have come to Rith."

VII

It is not often, Dilullo thought, *that you see a thoroughly happy man. It does your heart good to see one.*

Eron of Rith was a happy man. He strutted back and forth, a small man with a tough, faintly red face and bristling black hair, looking for all the world like a falcon turned human. He laughed and slapped his sides and laughed again, looking toward the table where Dilullo and Chane and Gwaath were sitting.

"It's so damned *funny,*" he said in galacto. "You just don't realize yet how funny it is."

Dilullo drank a little, not much, of the fiery Rith liquor they had been served. He said mildly, "Let us in on the joke. What makes it so funny?"

Eron shook his head and laughed and kept striding back and forth. He was small, but he threw a big shadow across the stone floor of the great barny banqueting hall.

Men stood around it here and there at a respectful distance, well out of hearing. Red-skinned men of Rith, powerful runts with lasers and stunners. Their eyes never left the three men at the table.

The room was cold and utterly unwelcoming. On its walls in a sort of palimpsest over blurred old paintings of gracious blue people in gardens were daubed crude, violent figures of small red men carrying weapons in war. Once there had been a gentler civilization here, Dilullo

348

knew, and then the fierce outlanders or outworlders had come. It was an old story; one met it all over the galaxy.

Eight girls danced, almost naked, at the far end of the long shadowy hall. None of them were of the red Rith people; they were of various colors, tall, and they danced with a lazy, sinuous grace to the twanging of hidden musicians. Nobody watched them. They were a decoration, not a performance.

Dilullo waited, saying nothing more. Eron was so full of himself and his triumph that he would sooner or later start talking. In the meantime, the Mercs were all under guard in an upper wing of this sprawling old palace, and only he and Chane and Gwaath had been brought here.

Gwaath was pretty happy himself. Lots of the fiery Rith liquor had been set before them and the Paragaran had quaffed it in truly heroic quantities. He sat in a bit of a daze, his furry face leering foolishly at Eron, like a schoolgirl admiring a hero. There was something so ridiculous about his expression that Dilullo felt like laughing.

There was nothing about Chane that made him feel like laughing. Chane had got pretty drunk, and this was a surprise. Dilullo had seen him drink a good bit at times, but it had always seemed only to deepen the mocking irony in his dark face. But Chane looked black as a thundercloud now, and the exquisitely measured deliberation of his movements told Dilullo how drunk he was.

Homesick, thought Dilullo. *He's got back out here to the Spur, and Varna is not too far away as galactic distances go; but he can never go back there and it's eating on him.*

"Didn't you ever dream," said Eron, "that Klloya-Klloy might send messages to all of us who bought the Singing Suns, to warn us that Mercs were out to get them?"

Dilullo shrugged. "We thought of the possibility. We supposed that Klloya-Klloy would not want to advertise the fact that we'd come right into his headquarters and twisted his nose. It wouldn't be good publicity for a famous receiver of stolen goods."

"You were wrong," said Eron. "Klloya-Klloy doesn't care whether it's good or bad publicity. He was so angry he just wanted you caught and punished."

Dilullo nodded. "It figures. But I'm leader of the mission. Why bring Gwaath and Chane up here for your gloating?"

Eron said, "As to the Paragaran, I'm just curious as to what he's doing with you. You might say he's just for laughs."

Gwaath responded to this by a tipsy smile that split his formidable face open and showed his gleaming teeth. It was a sort of I-love-you-too smile. Then he put his head down on the table and snored.

"As for the man Chane," Eron continued after a moment, "Klloya-Klloy mentioned him. Morgan Chane, the Starwolf. How can an Earthman be a Starwolf?"

Chane drained his goblet and set it down. He said, "But I'm not a Starwolf."

He got up and stepped around the table toward Eron. The little red men around the hall raised their weapons a trifle. The naked girls continued to dance to the twanging strings. On the walls the dim, gentle-faced blue people smiled from behind the striding little crimson warriors painted over them.

Chane's face assumed a sweet smile, and Dilullo thought, *For God's sake, not that. I've seen that smile before and it means trouble.*

"You see," said Chane to Eron, "I'm only half Starwolf. I was born on Varna and I grew up with the Varnans and raided with them, but I was never anything more than half a Varnan, I realize now."

And then of a sudden Chane's voice rasped like a

sword coming out of its scabbard. "But half a Starwolf is enough to merit respect from the little lesser breeds like the men of Rith!"

Rage flared up in Eron's small eyes. He half raised his hand to summon the men with weapons who were ranged around the walls of the big stone room.

He did not complete the motion. He looked at Chane with something like admiration in his face.

"You're a Starwolf, all right," he said. "Only one of those devils would say a thing like that, here where I could crook my finger and have you killed."

Chane shrugged. "I'll tell you how the Varnans see it, and how they taught me. A man can get killed any time, and in any case he can't live forever, so there's no use worrying about it."

"Why aren't you with the Varnans?" demanded Eron. "What are you doing with these Mercs?"

"A disagreement," Chane said carelessly. "I killed a comrade who tried to kill me, and I had no clan to back me up. So I got out."

"In other words," said Eron, "you ran."

"Of course I ran. Starwolves are realists. They don't want to be killed any more than anyone else does. The point is that they just don't worry so damned much about it."

Eron laughed suddenly and clapped him on the back. "Have another drink," he said. "I've got a funny story to tell you men. It's so funny you'll just about die laughing."

And here it comes, thought Dilullo, *the little surprise that has kept him so happy.*

"You came here," said Eron, "to snatch away the six Singing Suns that I bought from Klloya-Klloy."

"There doesn't seem to be any point in denying it," Dilullo said sourly.

"That's where the joke comes in," said Eron. "I do not have the Singing Suns."

Dilullo stared at him. "But you just admitted that you bought them from Klloya-Klloy."

"I did," said Eron. He had to stop and laugh again before he went on. "But I don't have them. You see, the joke is not only on you, but on Klloya-Klloy too. And to think he took the trouble to send me a warning . . ."

He was off into mirth again. Dilullo had a fair bit of patience but it was beginning to wear thin.

"If you don't mind," he said, "I'd like to hear the point of this wonderful joke and then I can laugh along with you."

"The point," said Eron, "is that all the Singing Suns were bought by one purchaser. The Qajars. They used the rest of us as purchasing agents. If they'd bid for all the Suns, Klloya-Klloy's price would have been like the ransom for a star. So they only bid for some of them and had the rest of us—all that list of buyers the old merchant gave you—buy the other Suns in piece lots. We delivered them and now the Qajars have all the Singing Suns."

Chane, despite his dark and bitter mood, laughed aloud. "A neat trick. They foxed the old spider of Mruun very nicely."

"Neat is the word for it," Eron agreed cheerfully. "So you can understand why, when Klloya-Klloy rushed me a warning and you Mercs came cleverly sneaking to Rith with all sorts of plans to take my six Suns, I thought it was really funny."

"It's so funny I'm speechless," Dilullo said. "So the Qajars have all the Suns? Who the hell are the Qajars, anyway?"

"People," said Eron. "Very odd people. They're aesthetes, probably the greatest lovers of beautiful things in the galaxy. They are also extremely clever with weapons. And they have no bowels of mercy in them. You think we Rith are tough and ruthless—"

"I don't," said Chane.

Eron shot him an irritated look, but then went on. "Besides the Qajars, we're tender as maidens. I just can't figure them out. They have the most beautiful and valuable objects ever heard of and they love them the way a man loves his newest slave-girl. I could understand their wanting to defend them. But their weapons are not built just for efficiency. They're deliberately designed to torture as well as kill, and the Qajars delight in using them."

"They sound like charming people. And they have all the Singing Suns?"

"They have all the Singing Suns."

"Where is their world?"

Eron smiled. "I've been there often. Last time I took the six Singing Suns. And you know what . . .?" He had to stop to laugh again. "I landed on their world and I took tridim pictures of all their treasures and they never even knew it. They'd have killed me if they had, they're so secretive."

Chane looked at him. "The man asked you a question. Where is their world?"

"Ah," said Eron, "of course you want to know that. I thought you would. And maybe I'll tell you. Maybe. You see, the Qajars have kept themselves and their treasures utterly hidden. I'm one of the very few people who could tell you about them."

"I seem to smell some kind of deal coming up," Dilullo said sourly. "All right, get to it."

"We have heard," said Eron, "that the government of Achernar is offering a two million credit reward for the return of the Singing Suns. That reward is what you Mercs are after, isn't it?"

"I don't see any point in denying that, either," said Dilullo.

"You haven't got a prayer of getting to the Qajars and the Suns on your own," said Eron. "You don't know where their world is, and even if you knew, your ship would never reach it. They've got defenses like you never heard of."

Dilullo eyed him and said, "Go on."

"But," said Eron, his small eyes very bright, "I could direct you straight to them. I could lend you a small Rith scout that would fool them into letting you land. My tridims would show you just where the Suns are. All this I would do . . . for half of those two million credits."

He added, "Of course, a Rith scout is small. Only three or four of you could go in it. The rest would be my guests here . . . and a guarantee that you'd return."

"In other words," said Dilullo, "having foxed Klloya-Klloy as an agent for the Qajars, you are now willing to betray your employers to us."

Eron grinned. "That's it."

"At least," Dilullo said, "you do put a high price on your loyalty." Then he asked, "Will you tell me . . . is there a single honest man in Argo Spur?"

Eron stared. He turned to Chane and said, "Did you hear that, Starwolf? He's looking for an honest man in the Spur!"

And both Chane and Eron roared with laughter at the idea.

VIII

A small cluster of dead, dark stars, with only a few nearly extinct suns showing a dull red light. . . . It was a lonely and desolate spectacle as the tridim projector showed it in the shadowy hall.

"I know that cluster," said Chane. "It's clear outside the Spur, in a nadir-westward direction."

"Right," said Eron.

"But there's no inhabited world in there."

"Wrong, this time. The Qajars live there, on the planet of one of those dying suns, deep in the cluster. They call it Chlann."

Chane looked incredulous. "Nobody, not even the Varnans, has ever heard of it."

Eron smiled. "That's because the Qajars want it that way. They're one of the richest peoples in the galaxy and because of that they remain carefully hidden."

"Rich? What is there in that mess of dead suns and frozen worlds that would make them rich?" demanded Dilullo.

"There's radite," said Eron. "The rarest transuranic element of all. There are tremendous deposits of radite on their world, which is why they came there originally. You know the price that stuff brings."

Dilullo still looked skeptical. "How the devil could they sell it and still keep their existence secret?"

"Simple," said Eron. "They use a few selected

people in the Spur as their agents. I have been one of them. We go into the cluster and pick up the radite, which is our pay for bringing them back the things they want. And the things they want are always costly, and beautiful, and difficult to steal."

"I'll be damned," said Dilullo. "They sound worse than that thieves' race on Mruun."

"The Qajars are a lot worse," said Eron. "I'm convinced they're more than a little mad . . . that the emanations of radite have had a genetic effect on their minds. They never leave that hidden world. They stay there and fondle their treasures and invent ever more ingenious and unpleasant weapons with which to guard them, and all the time they acquire more and more of the rarest art-treasures in the galaxy so they'll have more to guard. And if that isn't madness, what is?"

Chane mentally pricked up his ears. "It sounds like a fine place to loot."

Eron nodded. "Exactly why they've kept themselves a secret. But nobody would get their treasures easily. The Qajars are infinitely cruel and very cunning, and they have many defenses. Like the Lethal Worlds."

"The Lethal Worlds?"

Eron pointed to the pictured dark cluster. "The Qajars say they have mined many of the dead planets in that cluster with sufficient charges of radite to explode them like huge bombs. They could destroy any fleet that came against them."

Chane said contemptuously, "It sounds like a bluff to scare people away."

"I wouldn't count on it," said Eron. "I know myself they're absolutely without scruple or mercy. In fact—" He hesitated. "In fact, I had a feeling that after they got all the Singing Suns together the Qajars would start doing away with the agents who procured them, so no one would ever know. I wouldn't go into that cluster again!"

"But you're suggesting we go in," said Dilullo.

Eron grinned. "That's different. If you get hurt I won't feel it."

He made a signal and the tridim picture changed. They seemed now to be hanging above the surface of a nearly-dead planet. Black, arid plains swept away to low, dark mountains, all the landscape illumined dimly by the feeble red rays of the dying sun.

At one point on the plain rose a small city. Its buildings were of glittering metal. They were of no great size, most of them, but the center of the city was a round open area, and around this plaza there rose a ring of soaring metal towers. Over the whole place brooded a glow of blue radiance that seemed quite sourceless.

"That halo gives them light and warmth," said Eron. "They have radite enough to maintain a thousand like it."

Dilullo noted the ships parked on a big starport. "I thought you said these Qajars never left their world."

"They don't," said Eron. "Those are all warships, for defense."

"Are those tall towers their treasure houses?" asked Chane.

"You've got a Starwolf's eye for loot, all right," said Eron. "Yes, they are. I've never been allowed inside them, but my concealed tridim camera, using sensor rays, got pictures of the interiors."

The picture changed to the interior of a big room whose walls were softly-burnished metal. And there were people in this room.

The Qajars. Tall men and women in white robes. They had pure white faces, almost beautiful, and slender hands. Their eyes were dark and wide and calm. But there was a chilling inhumanity about the unnatural placidity of those cold faces.

"I see what you mean about them," muttered Dilullo. "They do look as though progressive genetic change and isolation have twisted them."

Chane was not looking at the Qajars. He was looking at the objects that crowded the room, glittering treasures that drew his gaze like a magnet.

Diamond, pearl, chrysoprase, fire-rubies from the worlds of Betelgeuse, shimmering lightstones from Kharal, the sea green gems that are brought up from under the oceans of Algol Three, gold, silver, electrum, all put together into incredible vases, chairs, panels, and other things he could not even define. They all had overwhelming grace and beauty, but it was not that which made Chane draw in his breath sharply.

"Makes you drool, doesn't it?" said Dilullo. "All that loot."

"And we of Varna never even dreamed of it," muttered Chane.

"I told you the Qajars are masters of cunning," said Eron. "Wait till you see into the other treasure houses."

Mobiles, statuary, tapestries woven of tiny gems, monstrous planetary idols in gleaming precious metals, strange symbols from far stars whose stones flashed like fires, great books of gold whose leaves were silver illuminated with designs in tiny jewels.

And through these rooms, between these stunning objects, walked the men and women of the Qajars, looking with calm gaze to the right and then to the left, inspecting their hoard, drinking in its beauty, savoring it in some strange deep way that other men could not even guess at.

"And that's all they do?" said Chane incredulously. "Gather together all that stuff and then just sit and admire it?"

"I told you they're a little mad," said Eron. He added, "Now look at this."

The final tridim pictures showed first a certain tower, and then the interior of a room in it. It was a big, circular room whose whole interior was black—ceiling, floor, the silken hangings on the walls—black as outer space. And in it, as in a shrine, were the Singing Suns.

Incomplete. There were only twenty-eight of them, not forty. Yet they paled everything seen before. They were varicolored, like stars. Pale green, cold blue, warm gold, dull red . . . gleaming glories that slowly revolved as a group, and also around each other. The whole group of them were only four feet across, and they were contained inside a force-shield above a thick four foot base which contained the power unit for the shield. And the beauty of their shining brought a sigh from Dilullo.

"You can't hear them," said Eron. "Not in this picture. But they say if you can hear them as well as see them, you never want to leave them. Anyway, they've got all forty of them now."

Chane looked and looked at them, and there rose strongly in him the Starwolf lust for loot. "We've got to have them," he muttered. "But how?"

"How about my deal, before I go any further?" demanded Eron.

Chane gestured toward Dilullo. "Talk to him. He's the leader."

Dilullo thought for a while. Then he said to Eron, "The deal is on . . . but only conditionally. There are three steps to this operation: getting there, getting the Singing Suns, and getting out again. What can you provide that's worth a million credits?"

"I can provide you with Step One . . . without which there will be no more steps anyway. On Step Two, I can give you the exact location of the treasure room that holds the Singing Suns, the approaches thereto, and what I know or can guess of the obstacles you'll face." Eron smiled, glancing at Chane. "Once you're down you're on your own. And in the matter of thievery, I bow to the master."

Chane showed the hard edges of his teeth. And Dilullo said, "Let's hear it."

Eron said, "You'll go to Chlann in a Rith scout, using my charts. You will message that you're coming in with a shipment of *ara* root."

"*Ara* root? What's that?"

Eron nodded toward the snoring Paragaran, who still sprawled with his head on the table.

"They grow it on Paragara. About the only place it will grow. It's some kind of stimulant; I don't know exactly what. Anyway, the Qajars love it. They buy it, but not directly. They never do anything directly. The Paragarans bring it here and we take it to Chlann."

Dilullo remembered what Gwaath had said and nodded. "So we go in a Rith scout, with a message about *ara* root. What then?"

"The Qajars will demand identification before they permit you to land. Visual identification."

"And the minute they see our faces we're dead," said Chane. "Nothing could make us look like Rith. How do we get around that?"

Eron smiled, the small delighted smile of a man charmed by his own cleverness. Again he nodded, indicating Gwaath.

"He does it. He makes the visual identification, and he tells them that he's come on from Rith to inform them that there's been a disaster in the *ara* root fields and there won't be any more of the stuff available for a couple of years . . . except maybe a very small supply for very special customers at, naturally, a very special price. It's the price he wants to discuss with them. The Qajars will be worried enough to let you come in."

"*If,*" Dilullo added, "they haven't got sensor equipment that will scan the whole interior of the ship. If they see us that'll blow it, as Chane said."

Eron shrugged. "I can't guarantee that they don't have such equipment, I don't know. But they've never full-scanned a Rith ship. They're used to us. So I don't see why they'd bother this time."

"Sounds like a fair gamble," said Chane.

Dilullo grunted. "I like a little shorter odds, myself. However . . ."

Chane said, "Let's hear about the treasure room."

Eron told him, partly with the aid of the tridim pictures, partly from memory, partly from shrewd guesswork. When he was through Dilullo looked at Chane and said, "Well?" and Chane nodded slowly. His mouth smiled and there was a kind of light in his eyes. *Wolf-light*, Dilullo thought, and fought down a cold cramping of the guts.

"What about the deal?" asked Eron.

"We'll have to talk it over," said Dilullo.

"All right," said Eron. "But don't take too long. I might change my mind."

"One thing," said Dilullo. "None of my party except me knows that Chane was once a Starwolf. I don't want the others told that."

Eron shrugged. "That's no problem as far as I'm concerned."

Chane said, "Thanks for the solicitude, John."

Dilullo looked at him bleakly. "I'm concerned about the others, not you. If any of them found out the truth they'd refuse to work with you, certainly, and might very possibly kill you. Which would break up the whole job." He nodded toward the snoring Paragaran. "Pick up my friend and bring him along."

"He's got to stop this," said Chane, as he slung the sleeping Gwaath across his shoulders. "It's getting to be a habit."

The other Mercs were in a big barrack-like room two floors up in another wing of the palace. The single door was guarded by several of the little red men with lasers. A few of the Mercs were sleeping but the others were aware and anxious.

Dilullo told them. Their faces fell, a million credits' worth, and Bollard shook his head emphatically.

"It's too risky, John. Two, three men in a little scout—what chance would you have against all those Qajar weapons?"

"Maybe more chance than you think," said Dilullo. "From what I heard, the Qajars have been immune so long that maybe the last thing they'd expect is three men making a sudden raid on their treasure houses."

"Who would the third man be?" demanded Bollard.

"Chane," said Dilullo.

Bollard got belligerent. "Why Chane, instead of me?"

"Because," said Dilullo, "it was Chane who thought up this whole idea of going after the Singing Suns. If I run into a first-class disaster, I'd sort of like him to share it with me."

"I don't blame you," said Bollard, looking without love at Chane. "All the same, I think you're doing something harebrained."

Chane thought that Dilullo's reason for taking him sounded good enough, but it was not the whole reason, even though there was doubtless much truth in it. The real reason was that this was a Starwolf job and Dilullo needed a Starwolf to do it.

"Look," Dilullo was saying to Bollard, "has it occurred to you that we may not have any choice? Eron is being nice right now because he figures to use us as cat's-paws to take the Suns. If we refuse, I can't very well see Eron waving us a sweet goodbye and wishing us a pleasant trip home."

"You may be right," muttered Bollard. "But if you pull it off and bring the Suns back, can you see Eron allowing us to leave with the Suns to get the reward from Achernar to split with him? If he's got the Suns, why should he split at all?"

"Let's not think of that just now," said Dilullo. "We've got trouble enough right ahead without worrying about what comes after it."

IX

The little cluster was a graveyard of stars.

Dead suns, ashen hulks black and cold forever. Almost-dead suns, with little tongues and wreaths of fire on their stony, dark surfaces. Dying suns, red and ominous, most of their planets wrapped in everlasting ice. Such worlds had no interest for Starwolves.

But they had been wrong, Chane thought. The Qajar treasure houses, as he had seen in the tridim pictures, had been enough to make a Starwolf go mad. He thought that if the Qajars had been cunning enough to conceal all that for so long, they would be no mean antagonists.

Dilullo sat in the pilot seat of the fast little scout. Gwaath had claimed loudly that he could handle the ship, but when they gave him the chance his piloting had been hopelessly sloppy.

And Chane had said to Dilullo, "I told you the Paragarans aren't much good in space."

He used English but Gwaath caught the critical tone and snarled, "Use galacto! What did you say about me?"

"I said how lucky we are to have a Paragaran with us to fight, if we get into trouble."

Gwaath glared at Chane with his small red eyes. "You're lying. You can't fool me. You may think I'm stupid—"

"What," Chane interrupted blandly, "would give you that idea?"

Gwaath began to roar, and Dilullo raised his voice to tell them both to shut up.

The little scout went on, and they slept, and took turns at the controls, and ate, and swore at the monotony.

And finally they dropped out of overdrive.

A sun far gone into the dusky redness of age glared at them like a huge bloodshot eye. Around it swung a dark planet that seemed nothing but a barren ball of rock. Chlann. The Qajars. The Singing Suns.

Chane quivered a little, like a hunting animal that sees its prey.

"If what Eron told us about these people is true, we'll be challenged very quickly when we go in to make worldfall," said Dilullo.

He was in the pilot chair. He had set up the audio-visual communic so that its view comprised only a limited area of the interior of the scout. Gwaath was seated in front of the little screen of the communic.

"Are you sure you've got it?" Dilullo asked him.

The Paragaran said emphatically that he was good and damned sure. Dilullo hoped he was. They had drilled him in his speech until he ought to be able to repeat it in his sleep.

"Remember," he said, "you're not to move from that seat. The Qajars must not see either Chane or me."

Chane was giving a final check to the laser controls. The heavy lasers were mounted in the prow of the scout, in deep ports.

"If we can get down into that open circle in one piece," said Chane, "these will open a quick way into the treasure room."

"Tell me again," said Dilullo, "what's going to keep the Qajars from clobbering us the minute we set down. It sounded good when you said it, and I need comforting."

"Two things," said Chane confidently. "One, our lasers trained on their beautiful buildings—they'd rather

lose one treasure than lose all. Two, they'll be warned
that our power unit is set to blow if the ship is hit. If
they destroy us, they destroy their own buildings."

Starwolf reasoning, thought Dilullo; *Starwolf cheek.*
He hoped Chane was as good as he thought he was.

"Even so," said Chane, "it'll be touch and go,
getting in and getting out with the Suns."

"Keep remembering that," said Dilullo. "And don't
get tempted to linger for any more of that dazzling stuff
we saw, or you might just linger forever."

They were low over the dark, forbidding planet when
a voice spoke sharply from the communic.

Dilullo nodded to Gwaath. Gwaath switched on the
visual circuits of the communic. In the small screen
appeared the pale face of a Qajar, an elderly man with
unnaturally smooth skin and the calm icy eyes of his
kind peering from under the cowl of his white robe.

Gwaath spoke in galacto, giving the whole
carefully-coached story about blight in the *ara* root and
how Eron of Rith had told him he should deal directly
with the Qajars and lent him a Rith scout to do it in. He
talked about shortage and price and future deliveries,
and Chane thought that he was the clumsiest liar he had
ever heard in his life. But when he thought about it, the
Paragaran wasn't so bad after all. There was a certain
disarming, not to say stupid candor about him that
made it difficult to doubt him.

The Qajar in the screen seemed to consider for a
moment. Then he said, "This matter is without
precedent. Put your ship into stationary orbit, while we
consider."

Gwaath said he would do that. He asked, "Can I shut
off the visual till you call? It consumes power."

The man in the screen nodded contemptuously. He
said, "My name is Vlanalan. You will receive our
decision very soon. Until then, any attempt to land will
result in instant destruction."

Gwaath switched off the visual. Then he turned

around and looked at Dilullo with a did-I-do-good? expression.

"That was fine, Gwaath," whispered Dilullo. "Just sit there and wait. . . . I'll put the scout into orbit."

He did that, and they waited. And thought about the next move, the descent toward the starport, the sudden diversion and landing in the open circle among the treasure houses, the thing done so swiftly and unexpectedly as to catch the Qajars quite by surprise. They hoped.

They waited for permission to land. And waited. And as the minutes went by a strange feeling, an uneasiness, came over Chane.

He could not define it. It was not a sixth sense. But Starwolves had their five senses honed to a keenness far beyond normal. And this was the same kind of feeling he had had on Allubane, in the dark jungle before the Nanes jumped him. Something was not quite right.

"I think . . ." he began to whisper.

Dilullo held up a hand sharply to silence him. The auditory channel of the communic was still open, and Dilullo was signaling that they must not be heard.

More minutes went by, and the little ship went on around the dark planet, and the bloody eye of the dying sun looked down at them.

Like a bolt of lightning, pain ripped through Chane's nervous system. His nerves were afire, electric with agony. He tried to dart to the controls, where Dilullo had suddenly crumpled in the chair with his shaking hands over his face.

He could not make it. He was Morgan Chane, the Earthman who had grown up a Starwolf; he had strength and stamina and speed beyond any man of Earth, beyond any non-Varnan in the galaxy. He was very strong and nothing could stop him.

But now he was a baby, weak, shuddering in agony. He fell on his face and lay with his mouth against the cold deck, his tortured body rippling in long slow rhythms of pain.

He rolled around in a vain attempt to get up, and then sobbed as the agony increased. He saw Gwaath, his red eyes wild, rise and stagger and stumble and then crash into a corner. After that Gwaath got to his knees and swayed back and forth uttering hoarse animal sounds.

Dilullo did not even try to get out of the pilot chair. Dilullo seemed to shrink and shrivel, as though a fiery breath of absolute pain was burning him up.

Chane tried to force himself to act. He was bathed in hot agony, but he had felt agony before. What he had to do was get to his feet, get to the controls, and send the scout out of orbit away from Chlann before they all died or went completely mad, which was going to happen very quickly now, in minutes, perhaps seconds.

Summoning all his fierce Starwolf resolution, he got to his feet. And fell down on his face again.

"Fools," said a cold, remote voice. "Did you think we would let your ship approach without searching it by sensor rays? Especially after we had been warned that Earthmen were trying to take the Suns?"

It was the voice of Vlanalan, speaking from the communic. It lashed them with icy, scornful tones.

"You could have been killed at once, of course. But that is not our way. You must suffer until you realize the blackness of your crime in attempting to steal things of beauty from the Qajars. A ship will come. You will be boarded and brought in to us for further examination. In the meantime, your punishment begins."

As though a switch had been turned, the pain that shredded Chane's nerves was stepped up. Dilullo just sagged farther in the chair. Gwaath started to roar insanely and throw himself against the wall. He did that twice and then fell and lay struggling feebly.

Chane whimpered. He was tough, he had taken pain before, but nothing like this. He lay with his face against the deck and he was not a Starwolf any more; he was a hurt puppy.

"Do you like it?" asked the voice of Vlanalan. "Like it, strangers. For there is more, much more."

A terrible hatred grew in Chane. He had been hurt in conflict and borne no grudge, for getting hurt in conflict was natural and if you did not want to risk it you avoided conflict entirely. But this relentlessly applied, scientifically calculated torture, the cool taunting voice, made him feel a hatred he had never felt for an enemy before.

Chane nursed his hatred. It fought back the pain. He hated Vlanalan and all the Qajars. He would pay them back for this. And that meant that he must survive. . . .

Survival first, and then revenge.

Survival . . .

They must get away from here before the Qajar ship came.

He fought to clear his mind of the daze of agony. He could never make it to the controls; he knew that. The force that brought the pain to his nervous system had stunned all his motor centers. And there was no hope in Dilullo, who sagged in the pilot chair and seemed not to breathe.

Was he dead? *Oh God, did I bring him here to die?* What, then?

Gwaath rolled on the deck, howling. The feeble twitching had become a wild flailing. His hands and feet struck the deck plates.

Chane looked at him through pain-misted eyes.

The force that tormented them was attuned to human bodies, human nerves. Gwaath was humanoid but not human, bred of a different stock. He was suffering but he could still move, still howl.

Chane waited until Gwaath's head was near him, beating on the deck like a hollow gourd. He had to wait so that his croaking whisper, which was all the voice he had, might be heard.

"Gwaath. Gwaath . . .!"

Gwaath continued to roll and flail his hands about.

"The controls, Gwaath. Throw us . . . out of orbit. Escape . . ."

He kept saying *controls escape Gwaath,* or trying to say them, but the words did not seem to have any shape to them and Gwaath seemed to be beyond hearing in any case. Then it seemed to him that Gwaath's rollings and flounderings and howlings were moving him closer to the control board, and he watched, thinking how strange everything looked when you saw it through your own blood and tears, forced red and watery to burst the eyeballs. The distorted shape of Gwaath moved in the redness. . . .

Howled suddenly.

Flung itself sprawling upon the control board.

The voice of Vlanalan said something shrill.

The ship roared out of stationary orbit. And the agony was doubled, tripled.

The unseen net was reaching now to kill them before they could get away.

X

Chane was surprised to wake up. He had been sure, when that last blast of unspeakable pain had knocked him into darkness, that he was dying.

He still lay on the deck. The fiery anguish had left him, but all his nerves crawled and twitched and rippled with the memory of what had been inflicted on them. For the moment he was incapable of movement; his motor centers appeared to have burnt out. He wondered if it was permanent.

He lay there and thought of the Qajars. How clever they were, with their sensor rays and their probes of pain. How ruthless they were, those calm-faced lovers of beauty, delighting in tormenting those who might threaten their treasures, drawing a man's soul out of his body as slowly as possible and enjoying his suffering. He could imagine what would have happened to the three of them if the Qajars had got them on their world.

Gwaath bent over Chane, bringing his furry face down close and looking inquiringly at him with red-shot eyes.

Chane made a great effort of will and spoke. One word.

"Dilullo?"

"Not dead," said the Paragaran. "But not awake, and nothing wakes him."

"Help me up," said Chane.

Gwaath did so. He did it three times before Chane finally got his legs under him and stayed up, with only a little help. The big Paragaran still looked a bit groggy but otherwise was nearly normal. His humanoid body had endured that last blast of agony pretty well. But Chane himself knew that he had been very near to death when the scout sped out of orbit and out of range of the force.

And Dilullo?

He thought, when Gwaath helped him to the pilot's chair, that Dilullo was dying. His eyes were closed, his pulse slow, his whole body slumped and shrunken. Dilullo was a lot older than he, Chane thought, and the thing had hit him harder.

He had Gwaath open down one of the folding bunks and carry Dilullo back and put him in it. Chane sat down for a few minutes, trying to get his shocked nerves back to normal so that he could move without falling over.

The scout was in overdrive. Gwaath had set a course toward Rith, but the course was not quite correct. Chane reached out a shaking hand and reset the course. After a time he got unsteadily to his feet and went back to Dilullo.

Dilullo still lay with his eyes closed, his breathing spasmodic, his face gray. Little shudderings of his limbs and body were evidence that his nervous system was suffering the same aftereffect that Chane had felt.

Chane massaged nerve centers, while Gwaath looked back anxiously from the pilot's seat. Finally, to Chane's immense relief, Dilullo opened his eyes.

They had a dull, glazed look, and when he spoke his voice was thick and slurred.

"We burned our fingers that time, didn't we?" he said.

"We did," said Chane, and told him how Gwaath had got them out of orbit.

"Well, we did right to bring Gwaath along," said

Dilullo. "I guess we're lucky to get out of this one with our lives."

Chane said bitterly, "I'll show the Qajars some bad luck if I can ever get back at them. Damn them!"

"I've seldom seen you so angry," Dilullo said. "Usually you just take it as it comes."

"You didn't get the full blast of it," said Chane. "You passed out quick. But I got it all, and I'll pay them for it when the time comes."

"Forget it," said Dilullo. "Think instead about what's going to happen when we come back to Rith emptyhanded."

Chane thought about that, all the long time it took the scout in overdrive to cross the Spur. He could see big trouble ahead and he did not like the shape of it at all.

But he worried more about Dilullo. Dilullo had not completely snapped out of it. His face was thin and drawn, his body still occasionally twitched as the nerves remembered their torture. Chane thought he would lose these aftereffects in time but he was not sure. And his own bitter hatred for the Qajars, for the cool voice that had mocked them as it applied the agony, deepened.

When they dropped out of overdrive and came in to Rith, they were surprised to find a watery sunshine on its daylight side. But beyond the black stone city, vast masses of dark cloud brooded sullenly, promising more tempest for this storm-ridden planet.

Rith officers met them and escorted them to the barny palace of Eron. Nothing was said except a few politenesses until they reached a chilly stone room where Eron sat. The bantam-sized red ruler looked at them accusingly.

"You didn't get the Suns," he said.

"Ah, so your men have already searched the scout and called you," said Dilullo. "No, we didn't get them. We were lucky to get away alive."

"For your lives I care nothing," said Eron angrily. "Nothing, you understand? What concerns me is your failure."

Dilullo shrugged wearily. "You can't win them all. The Qajars were just too much for us. You said they wouldn't full-scan, and they did."

He told what had happened and the cocky little ruler strode back and forth nervously, his tough face getting darker and darker in expression.

"It comes to this," he said finally. "You used a Rith scout. You tried to deceive the Qajars and failed. Suppose the Qajars ask me how you got that scout?"

"Tell them we stole it," said Chane.

Eron glared at him. "You think it's that simple? You still don't comprehend all the powers of the Qajars, even after they showed they could handle you like children! Suppose they find out you're here and demand that I surrender you to justice—their justice?"

"Are they likely to do that?" asked Dilullo.

"I don't know," said Eron uneasily. "Nobody knows what the Qajars are liable to do because nobody knows the extent of their powers, how far they can see, what weapons they can wield. I know one thing: I don't want them as enemies, and I don't want to lose them as profitable customers in trade."

"What you're leading up to," said Dilullo, "is that if the Qajars ask for us, you'll throw us to the dogs."

"If necessary," said Eron harshly. "Only if necessary. But you will have to stay here until I'm sure the Qajars are *not* going to demand you."

"Fine," said Dilullo. "A fine loyal partner you make."

Chane said nothing. He had expected this.

"Nothing here will harm you," Eron went on. "I've given a small wing of the palace to your men and they've been quite comfortable. So will you be."

"In other words, we're prisoners till you find out which way the cat jumps," said Dilullo disgustedly.

"Yes," said Eron. "You will go now."

He gave an order in his own incomprehensible language and one of the officers and four armed Rith came forward. Chane noticed that they were armed, not with stunners, but with lasers.

It was no time to make any resistance, he decided. He and Dilullo went along with the Rith as meek as milk. They went up through stairs and corridors, poorly illuminated, where the gentle blue faces of the old race had not been painted over. The faces looked down at the captives as with vague pity.

The men halted at a guarded door. A Rith officer searched Chane and Dilullo very efficiently, taking everything they had in the pockets of their coveralls.

Then the door opened. The ugly, grinning little red man gestured to them with a sort of mock politeness. They went through and the door clanged behind them.

There was a long ill-lit corridor and there were doors off it. Some of them were open, and from one they heard the sound of voices. They went that way.

Most of the doors opened onto small sleeping rooms, but the one from which the voices came was a bigger common room. The windows of all these rooms were mere ventilation slits, too narrow to admit anything larger than a cat.

Janssen sprang up from the group that was sitting around and drinking Rith liquor in the common room.

"What do you know?" he exclaimed delightedly. Then his face fell as he looked them over. "You didn't make it, did you?"

"We didn't come within a mile of making it," Dilullo said. He went over to the table and sat down in a chair, and Sekkinen poured him a drink of the fiery liquor from a slender flagon.

Gwaath reached for the flagon, and it was a measure of Dilullo's weariness that he did nothing to stop him. The big Paragaran tilted the flagon and drank with a gurgling sound and put it down and wiped his hairy lips.

"We were knocked silly," said Gwaath.

Chane was not all that tired but he sat down. He saw Bollard scrutinizing Dilullo's worn face by the light of the lamps that were set in brackets around the walls.

"You know what, John?" said Bollard. "You look like hell."

"So would you, if you'd been through the wringer we went through," said Dilullo. He drank again, and then he told them all about what had happened.

"It was a nice idea," said Dilullo. "Real nice. Only it didn't work. And now we're in a bad jam."

They all sat and thought about that. Nobody said anything for a while. Gwaath reached for the flagon again, but Chane got up and took it from him and poured himself a glassful of the liquor. Then he handed the vessel back to the Paragaran, who emptied it in a long gulp.

"We've done a lot of things," said Dilullo. "We've pulled it out of the fire a good many times when nobody thought we could. But no matter how good a man is he's going to fall on his prat sooner or later. This is where we did."

"Then we kiss the whole job goodbye?" said Janssen.

"What do you think?" asked Dilullo.

Neither Janssen nor anyone else had an answer to that. After a moment, Sekkinen said, "Then the only thing left is to make a break and get the hell off this planet and go back to Earth?"

Chane spoke up. "It won't be easy. We might break out of this place, but when we landed at the starport I noticed that they've got enough guards around our ship to hold onto it. Also, there are heavy lasers trained on it."

"I don't know," said Dilullo. "I just don't know."

Bollard looked at him keenly. Then the fat Merc got up and said decisively, "One thing for sure. We're not going to do anything tonight. You need some rest."

A tremendous banging of thunder punctuated his words. Lightning flared outside the window and thunder rumbled again, and then there was the crashing sound of rain.

"Give us this day our hourly storm," muttered Janssen. "What a planet."

"Come on, John," said Bollard. "I'll show you where you can sleep."

Dilullo got up and followed Bollard out of the room and down the corridor, a man in a daze. Chane went with them, not liking the look of Dilullo and afraid he might keel over at any moment.

Dilullo made it into one of the rooms and onto a bed. He was asleep before he hit it.

Bollard bent over him, loosening the neck of his coverall, taking off his shoes, putting a blanket over him. From the little window came the hiss of the rain and the turmoil of the storm, and Chane thought, *Janssen's right; what a world!*

Chane went out of the room with Bollard. But in the corridor, after he had closed the door, Bollard suddenly stopped. His round fat face was not at all good-humored and moonlike now. It was dark and angry, and he reached out his hand and caught the front of Chane's coverall and pulled him closer.

"Are you happy, Chane?" he demanded.

"What the devil are you talking about?" Chane demanded.

Bollard did not let him go. "Are you satisfied, now that John is about half dead from the job that you thought up for him?"

Chane began to understand. "So that's it. The job is blown, we're in a mess, and now you're crying because it was my idea. Look, you're all grown men. You could take it or leave it. When I proposed to go after the Singing Suns. You took it."

Bollard nodded. "We did. And none of us are crying. But with John it was different. He'd retired. He had

money. He was going to build him a house and live
easy, after all the hard knocks he'd taken across half
the galaxy."

A dangerous light came into Bollard's small eyes.
"But you wouldn't let him be. You had to drag him
back into space. You went after him and talked him
into it, and now where is he? His money's gone, he's
half dead, and he's liable to be all dead before we're
through. And you did this to him, Chane!"

Chane's anger surged up and he raised his arm to
send Bollard crashing back into the wall.

He did not do it.

He could not answer the accusation.

It was all true.

XI

In the middle of the night after the third day of his imprisonment, Chane lay unsleeping. A dark and bitter anger had been growing in him.

His anger was directed partly at himself. He had done an evil thing, by his own code. To a Starwolf, a debt was something that must be paid. He owed Dilullo his life, yet how had he repaid him? By cajoling him back into space, to be subjected to an agony that had now made him only a shadow of his former self.

And why had he done this? The others might think it was because of greed for the great reward offered for the Suns, or because of sheer lust for adventure. But Chane knew the truth. He knew that it was the chance to get back to the Spur that had driven him. His nostalgia for the world of the Starwolves had become such that even to look at Varna and its sun from a distance had drawn him like a magnet. He had talked the others into this reckless mission chiefly for that.

And John must have suspected it, thought Chane, *but he never said a thing.*

But he also had another anger, one mixed with bitter hatred, and that was directed at the Qajars. Those calm-faced, beauty-loving men who had savored such quiet delight in torturing Dilullo and Gwaath and himself.

If I could make them pay, he thought. *If I could*

*smash in there and loot away their treasures and leave
them wailing . . .*

It was just his anger and hate speaking, he knew.
There was no way to do that. They were prisoners here
on Rith, and if the Qajars demanded them they would
be turned over, to be tormented until they died.

The Qajars had weapons of unguessable capacities.
There was no power in the Spur able to beat them
down, and forces from the main galaxy were not
allowed to come into the space of the Spur worlds.

No power in the Spur? Chane's pulse suddenly
leaped. There was one power that could do it . . .
maybe.

Varna.

The Starwolves would go anywhere, and fight any
fight, for loot. They would have raided the Qajars'
gloomy world long ago if they had dreamed of the
immense loot there.

And what if he, Chane, told the Starwolves about
that loot . . . and proved it to them? Ah, what then?

Chane uttered a mirthless whisper of a laugh. It was a
fine idea. Fine, except for just one thing: if he went to
Varna, he would be killed before he could tell
anything. The clan of Ssander still hungered for his
death.

He dismissed the idea that had been born of anger
and desperation. He lay in the darkness, watching the
tiny window that was lit to a white flare every few
minutes, listening to the distant thunder as another of
the incessant storms approached. Between the rumbles
and bangs he could hear the heavy breathing of Van
Fossan and Sekkinen and Janssen, who shared the
sleeping room with him.

But his wild idea would not go away. He kept
thinking about it, even though he knew it was all folly.
How could he land on Varna without having to face
Ssander's clan one by one in single combat, as Starwolf
law demanded?

Gradually, a possible way crystallized in Chane's mind. It was only the shred of an expedient, and it was almost sure to fail. But it *might* be done.

Chane sprang up silently from the bunk. He would not think about that possible expedient any more. If he did he would see its hopelessness. No, he would act upon it. Any action was better than being cooped up here waiting for doom.

He would act now. This minute.

But how escape this prison?

The walls were of blocks of solid stone. The windows were too small to get through. There was only one entrance and Riths armed with lasers stood outside it. This was, obviously, a detention wing.

Chane thought and thought. He could see only one possibility, and that seemed a pretty thin one.

Don't think! Act!

He took his coverall and turned it inside out. The stout cloth had an inch-wide tape border over all the seams. The tape was not cloth, though it looked like it. It was a woven plastic stronger than anything except steel. And it could be detached.

Chane detached it, and it came away in one unbroken length. It was doubled, and when he had undoubled it, it formed a thin rope over thirty feet long.

Bad fixes were habitual with the Mercs, and over the years they had worked up a good many little things like this tape to help get them out. Chane now proceeded to another of those things.

He turned the coverall right-side out again and put it on. Then he unsnapped the broad button that held the flap of the upper right-hand pocket. The button was a miniaturized ato-flash with good intensity for its size, but with a capacity of less than a minute's duration.

Not enough, thought Chane. *Not nearly enough.*

He moved silently around the room, picking up the coveralls that belonged to the three sleeping Mercs and robbing them of their buttons.

Then Chane went quietly out of the little sleeping room and down the corridor to the common room. There was no provision for sleeping here, nothing but a few bench-like chairs, so the room was deserted.

Lightning flashes from the advancing storm lit the room. Chane went to the window. He removed the plastic shield that kept rain out, and by the light of the recurrent flashes he studied the window carefully.

In the stone-block wall, one block had been omitted to make this opening for light and air. Not the thinnest man could wriggle through the small opening. But his examination convinced him that there might be another way.

Chane took one of the miniature ato-flashes and turned its minute flame of force upon the thick mortar around the block immediately beneath the opening.

In forty seconds the flash went out, its charge exhausted. He used another one, and another. Then he studied his handiwork by the lightning flares.

The mortar was deeply cut all around the block. But how deeply? Enough?

There was only one way to find out. He got his arms out through the small opening of the window and took a grip from the outside on the block.

Bracing himself, he put all the Starwolf strength Varna had given him into a mighty heave.

The block moved inward, with a grating noise that sounded as loud as the crack of doom to Chane's ears. Luckily, one of the frequent rolls of thunder from the approaching storm masked it.

He had pulled the block no more than an inch inward, but now that he knew the mortar was cut through he had no further doubts. He kept heaving and pulling in little jumps, each time waiting for a clap of thunder before he did it.

The block finally came clear. His muscles were now so numbed by effort that he almost let the block go crashing to the floor of the room. He managed to

prevent that by pressing with his body against the block,
holding it against the wall and slowly easing it to the floor.

He stood up, panting and sweating. The small window,
now that the block beneath it was also out, had become
just big enough for an average-sized man to wriggle
through if he held his belly sucked in and didn't breathe.

And then what? Chane thought of an old Earth
proverb that Dilullo used: *Out of the frying pan into the
fire.*

He shrugged. Maybe it would prove so. But he wasn't
even out of the frying pan yet.

He moved one of the heavy benches, as silently as he
could, to a position just beneath the opening. He got up
on it and stuck his head out and peered downward. Some
of the windows below showed light, and he remembered
the way they had come well enough so that he was able to
tell which one was a window of the big throne-room
where Eron had talked to them and shown them the
tridim pictures.

It was not directly beneath him. It was the second
window to the left, two levels down.

Chane estimated distances by the lightning flashes. He
did it as carefully as he could, for everything depended on
his estimate.

When he felt sure, he took his long tape and tied one
end to the heavy bench. About two-thirds of the way to
the other end he tied a loop big enough to get his foot
into. Then he dropped the tape out of the window.

There was one more thing to do before he went. On a
table lay the deck of cards which the Mercs had been
allowed to keep, alone of all their personal possessions,
and with which they beguiled their captivity.

Chane took a card and, with the tongue of his
belt-buckle, scratched white letters on the colored back.
Only a few words, telling Dilullo that he was going in an
attempt to help them get out of this, and that he would be
back.

No more than that. Another Merc than Dilullo might

read this first. He put the card down conspicuously
apart from the pack and then went back to the window.

By the flashes he tried to see if there was anyone in
the wooded grounds of the old palace. He could see no
one and he hoped he was right because he was about to
show up as clearly as a fly on a white wall. He twisted
his shoulders into the enlarged opening.

He thought at first he was not going to get through.
He backed off and tried again, letting one shoulder go
first. This time he made it, barely. He grabbed the
tape, drew out the rest of his body, clamped his feet on
either side of the tape, and then slid slowly down until
his feet felt the knot of the loop.

Chane got his right foot into the loop. He would have
liked to pause for another breather but he was too
conspicuous hanging up here in the glare of the
ever-increasing lightning-flashes.

He began to swing himself, gripping the tape to pull
it in and then letting go of it. He swung parallel to the
wall and so close to it that his fingers, gripping the tape,
rasped painfully against the stone. Chane swore but
kept swinging. He thought with grim amusement that
he would be a damned outlandish sight if anyone saw
him.

Lightning washed the wall every half-minute now.
The thunder had become deafening. He hoped that the
close approach of the storm would have discouraged
anybody from being out of doors.

He swung wider and wider until at last he was
swinging just below the edge of the window he wanted.
Chane gripped the stone sill with his fingers and then
slowly drew his head up to look inside.

The window was a good-sized one, there being no
need for precaution as in the detention wing. The
plastic pane was closed against the coming tempest.

It was the right room, the big barny stone room
gauded with tasteless trappings that was Eron's idea of
an audience chamber. It was softly lighted, and two of

the runty, red-skinned men bearing lasers strolled to and
fro in it.

Chane had expected that. It seemed that Eron kept
some of his treasures in this place, and he would not
leave them unguarded.

He waited, hanging onto the windowsill, until both
guards had their backs to him. Instantly Chane drew
himself up until he crouched in the deep window-
opening.

He braced his feet against the stone. With all the
Varnan speed and strength he possessed he hurled
himself forward, and the light plastic pane went flying
into the room.

The two Rith guards swung around. They were fast but
no one was as fast as a Starwolf, and Chane reached them
as they first began to raise their lasers.

He hit one man with a clean punch, saw him drop, and
kept on without stopping his movement. The second
man had got his laser almost to the firing position.
Chane's fist opened, became a hand, grabbed the barrel
of the laser and slammed it upward with tremendous
force into the guard's face. It hit the man's forehead like
a hammer. He let go his end of it and fell down.

Chane examined them. They were both unconscious.
He tore strips from one of the florid hangings and
carefully bound and gagged them. It seemed a waste of
time, but he could not kill these men. He would be
leaving Dilullo and the other Mercs captive here, and if
he killed any Rith, John and the others would suffer for
it.

And there was no question, there never had been any
question, that he could take the others with him. One
man, himself, alone, might make it out of the palace and
to the spaceport without being caught, but not the whole
mob of them. If his plan worked, and worked in time, he
might save them. If it did not . . .

No use worrying about them now. Chane sprang to the
cabinet from which Eron had taken the tridim pictures.

It was locked, and the lock was strong and good.

A swiftly-gathering roar came from outside as the rain arrived. Chane set his teeth and forced himself to work calmly and deliberately with the lock. He had to have those pictures if his mission was to have any chance of success. They were the only means of proving at Varna that his whole story of the Qajars and their treasures was true.

He was clever with locks; nearly every Starwolf was. He found the combination, opened the door, and a moment later had the thick little plastic pictures in his hand. He stuffed them into his pocket, ran to the window, and started to slide down the rope to the ground.

The rain smashed him with solid masses of water. He had seen Rith rain before, God knew, but he had never felt it. Its pile-driver blows knocked him down along the rope like a toy monkey on a string. He hit the ground with a bang.

Chane had thought that the rain would be an ally, keeping people inside and helping to hide his movements. He found out now that with an ally like this he did not need an enemy.

The rain pounded him, trying to inlay him into the muddy ground. He breathed incautiously and got solid water up his nose. He snorted it out, shielded his nose with one hand, and finally managed to get to his feet and stand shakily erect under the downpour. It was like standing under a waterfall.

He could see almost nothing. Only the fact that the wall of the palace was against his back told him it was there at all. He clung to it, orienting himself, he knew the direction in which the spaceport lay but he was afraid that when he let go of the wall he would lose all sense of where he was.

Still, he could not stand here shivering. He had to make his try. He fixed his mental compass reading and started walking.

A man could not go far in this. It was a battle to stay on his feet, a battle to move at all. Sometimes he went on all fours until some chance shelter let him rise again. He was blinded, deafened, dazed, strangled. The only thing that kept him moving was his Starwolf pride. *A man would give up,* he kept saying to himself, *but not me, not a Varnan.*

He bumped into a stone wall. He was in a street now, and it seemed, as far as he could guess, to lead in the direction he wanted. He staggered along it like a blind man in the stunning rain, one hand trailing along the building walls of the street side.

He was never able to tell later how long he had struggled forward. When the guiding wall ended he knew that he was out of the small capital of Rith. But which way now?

There would be lights at the starport but he could not see them. He could not see anything. He thought he might as well take a chance and go on in what he thought was the right way.

He did, and got nowhere except to a growing realization of failure. His head was so dazed by the impact of the downpour that when it began to lessen he did not at first realize it.

The rain slacked off until it was no more than a heavy cloudburst on Earth. And he caught the watery gleam of lights not far away to his left.

His knees went weaker still with relief. It was the starport, only a few hundred yards away.

And now he had to hurry. If the storm slackened any more he would be caught flat out. He took a deep breath and began to run.

He went straight onto the starport, running. He might be tripping a warning beam, but it had not seemed to him that the Riths were as hipped on security as all that, and anyway, he had to take the chance.

He heard no alarms. And suddenly out of the sheets of rain there loomed a vague but familiar outline.

Their Merc ship, with its typical Terran eyebrow bridge. He could not see anyone around but he sheered away from it even so. He knew the ship was guarded; the guards would be inside now, sheltering from the storm.

The Merc ship gave him his bearings. He angled away, passing the vague bulks of other ships, until he came to a much smaller craft: the scout in which he and Dilullo and Gwaath had made their ill-fated journey to the Qajar world.

He had thought it would still be here, knowing that it would take at least a couple of days to service it. He opened the airlock and went inside, ready to attack if anyone was there.

Nobody was. There was no particular necessity to mount a guard here, and it had not been done.

Chane closed the lock and got the lights on. He shook himself like a half-drowned dog, and got busy.

The scout had been serviced. Good. He got into the pilot's chair, sitting with runnels of water dripping from him to the deck.

He took the scout up and away from Rith as fast as it would go, giving not a damn for any precautions. He came up into clear space and set his course. Far away but bright, ahead of him, shone the tawny star of Varna.

He had tried to be a good Earthman with the Mercs. But he was not a good Earthman.

He was a Starwolf, and he was going home.

XII

He would know, he thought, within the next twenty-four hours which it was to be—life . . . or death.

The scout had dropped out of overdrive and the great golden sun blazed huge before him, and the blue and copper ball of Varna came around it toward him, as though to welcome him. But what kind of welcome would he find there?

He knew the watch that was kept and he was expecting the challenge which at a certain moment came from the communicator.

He answered, "Morgan Chane, coming into Krak starport, in a Rith scout."

There was a long moment of silence and then a shocked, astounded voice said, *"Morgan Chane?"*

"Yes."

Another slence, and then the voice said, "All right. Come on in . . . if you want to!"

Chane smiled grimly. He might not last long on Varna but it seemed that he was going to be a sensation while he did.

He drove the little scout downward and it seemed to him that he fell swimming in a cataract of the tawny golden sunshine. Of a sudden he felt unbeatable, unconquerable. He knew that this was only the euphoria of coming home and he laughed at it in his own mind, but he could not help it.

It was spring on Varna and the great arid planet had a surface of pale green instead of the usual burnt gold and brown. And there came up the metallic-looking oceans and the green lands, and finally the far-scattered sprawl of dull red stone that was Krak.

On the broad starport the neat squadrons of small, needle-shaped ships were drawn up, glinting in the golden sunshine. It was all as it had always been.

Only it was not. . . .

All the feeling of long nostalgia left Chane. He became wary and cold. It was all very well to come back home, but there were those at home who wanted very earnestly to kill him, and he must forget emotions if he was to live.

When he had landed and cracked the lock he stepped out into the hot dry sunlight. The heavy gravitation of Varna grabbed him and almost staggered him. He had been away from Varna for quite a time and he had to get used all over again to the drag which had so nearly killed him as a child. It reminded him that he had no advantage here, that he was merely one Starwolf among many, and not the strongest.

He stood there beside the Rith scout, listening to the cracking sounds as it cooled.

Then he saw a man striding out toward him.

Berkt, he said to himself.

All of the Starwolves walked proud, but none in quite so tall and proud a way as Berkt. He was one of the greatest of the leaders, who had raided more worlds than Chane had seen.

He came closer, tall and mighty, the light golden down of his body hair glistening in the sun with only a leather harness to cover it. His slanted, uptilted eyes, pale as agates, bored into Chane's.

"I didn't believe it," he said. "I was seeing to the refitting of my ship, and I heard it, but I didn't believe it."

"Hello, Berkt," said Chane.

Berkt disregarded the greeting. He looked at Chane and he said, "Now understand me, Morgan Chane. I don't particularly care whether you get killed or not."

Chane nodded.

"But," said Berkt, "I feel I should tell you that almost the whole clan of the Ranroi, Ssander's clan, is on Varna right now. If you want to live, take your ship and go."

He added, "I think you know why I'm giving you this warning."

Chane nodded again. He knew.

Berkt was years older than he was. He had never particularly liked Chane, though he had had no particular dislike for him.

But Chane could remember the time when he was a small boy; when his father, the Reverend Thomas Chane of Carnarvon, Wales, Earth, and his wife had still been living.

Two rather small people who had come to Varna as missionaries, to reform the wicked Starwolves. They had, of course, got nowhere at all. Nobody came to their pathetic little chapel except curious Varnan children. The mature Varnans just ignored them.

Except Berkt. He had not had the smallest shred of religion, any more than any of the Varnans had. But he was, even in those days, a leader of great courage and renown. And Berkt had seen courage in the slight, small figure of the Reverend Thomas Chane. This little Earthman, who with his wife was slowly dying from the heavy gravitation of Varna, but who would not give up, who would not go away, held to his mission until they both were dead.

The most unlikely of friendships, Chane had thought of it later. The mighty young Starwolf lord, and the frail little man who had come from Earth to preach. He could remember, from his boyhood, his father's glowing face as he talked, sitting on the bench in front of the little chapel, and with a tall young Berkt sitting

beside him, gravely listening, not pretending to agree
but never contradicting.

"You've got your father's courage," Berkt was
saying. "And I see you have his stubbornness. What
the hell are you doing on Varna?"

"It's a rather long story," said Chane.

Berkt said, "You don't have that long. You're a dead
man if you don't go away."

"I am not going away," said Chane. "I have
something to tell the Council."

"Fine," said Berkt, looking disgusted. "Well, I'll
give you a drink or two before you're killed. Come
along."

Chane walked with him across the starport. It was a
long walk, because this main starport of Varna was a
big one. For this was the home nest from which the
falcon ships of the Starwolves raided out across the
galaxy.

A roaring thunder echoed from the brassy heavens,
stretching far away across the starport. Big, powerful
machines were hammering and probing at ships that
had come back from raids with wounds in their sides.
Power units throbbed, raged, and sometimes coughed
and died, as they were repaired and tested. Heavy
truck-carriers rumbled between the ships, taking
supplies. There was a deafening roll and crash across
the sky as a squadron of five needle-shaped ships came
in for landing after a test flight. . . . He knew it was a
test flight from their formation and from the fact that
none of them had scars on their sides.

There were hundreds of ships, thousands of Varnans,
on this port, and all of the men were busy at their work.
The work of the Starwolves was robbery, the far-flung
raids across the galaxy that had made them famous and
infamous, and they loved their work and toiled as
industriously as bees to make sure that when they went
forth on a job of stealing by force, none of their ships or
equipment would let them down.

But the work slowed, almost stopped, where Berkt and Chane walked between the ships. Chane was, and always had been, a standout here, for his dark, compact form and his coverall garment were quite different from the gold-haired, harness-clad figures of the Varnans. They knew him when they saw him; there were not too many on Varna who had not heard about the Earthman Starwolf, and it seemed also that they knew what had happened to him, for they stared at him in incredulous wonder.

"They just can't believe," said Berkt, "that you were crazy enough to come back."

Chane shrugged. "I'll admit it must look that way to them."

Berkt looked at him curiously. "Where have you been all this time, anyway?"

"With the Mercs," said Chane. "They picked me up when I was about half-dead from the wound Ssander gave me, and I joined them."

"Then they didn't know that you were really a Varnan? They couldn't have known, or they'd have hung you."

"One knows," said Chane. "Not the others."

"I've heard of these Mercs," said Berkt. "Are they any good?"

Chane turned and looked at him as they walked. "They're not as good as the Varnans; they haven't got the Varna-bred bodies for it. But they're good. Good enough to outfox a Varnan squadron in Corvus Cluster."

They came out of the starport, and Berkt had a car. It was not like the cars of Earth, soft-riding and smooth and silent. It was a vehicle as tough as the Varnans themselves, and it went over the rough roads outside the starport—What? A Starwolf labor on roads?—with a jolt that Chane remembered and enjoyed.

They went up and down the rocky, craggy hills. Varna was a poor world, which was why its sons, when they had attained starflight, had gone out to loot the rest of the galaxy. The golden sun was declining and its rays lit the harsh landscape. Down there below the hills was the city, Krak, but there was not much of it. A great market-square with buildings of dull red stone around it, but the Varnans, who had the freedom of the stars, did not much enjoy living crammed together.

The lords of Varna, such as Berkt, had their keeps and strongholds of stone set well apart from each other, preferably on the tops of the rocky hills. It was the lesser ones and the young men who lived in the city, as Chane had once lived in the stone barracks down there.

The car jolted on and approached a stone wall. They went through its gateway, and before them was the rambling pile of reddish stone that was Berkt's home.

A tall golden woman came out to greet the noisy approach of the car, and then she forgot her husband to stare at Chane.

"Nshurra," he said, and smiled.

"The little Earthman," she said. "Oh, no, it can't be."

There had only been two people on Varna who could call Chane a little Earthman without a fight. Both of them were women, and Berkt's wife was one of them.

"Did you bring him back here to be killed?" she demanded of Berkt.

"Bring him back?" said Berkt. "He *came* back. He's tired of living; he wants to die. At least that's the only reason I can see."

Nshurra came and grasped his hands. "Chane, we thought you were dead. Everyone thought so."

She had always liked him. Chane had always thought that her liking had been born of pity, for she was older than he and could remember him when he had been an Earth-descended child struggling to move, to breathe, against the crushing gravitation of Varna. He could remember Nshurra picking him up and helping him along, when he was a child. But always when no one else could see, so that he might not lose face and pride.

They stood under the stone portico, with the tawny blaze of the sun almost level on their faces. Chane, feeling for the first time a real sense of homecoming, turned to Berkt.

"May I kiss her?"

"If you do, I'll break you in half," Berkt said casually.

Chane smiled, and kissed the golden cheek. He went with them into the place, and it was cool and shadowy and as he remembered it. Presently they sat on a balcony and watched the sun go down. They drank the Varnan wine, wine so strong that it was said it would kill anyone but a Starwolf. It did not kill Chane, but made his head ring as though with golden bells.

"All right, Chane," said Berkt. "Tell me."

Chane told him. Of Dilullo, ill and trapped on Rith along with his comrades, and the fault all Chane's. Of the treasure of the Qajars. Of his hopes to get part of that treasure, and with it to pay Dilullo the debt of life he owed him.

He told him everything, except one thing. He did not tell of the Singing Suns being in the possession of the Qajars.

Berkt was silent for a while, and then poured more wine. The sun had gone down and the great ragged blaze of the Spur stars was across the sky. The smell of Varna came up to Chane, and it brought old memories.

He wished that he had been born to be Berkt. How would it be to sit here and look at the stars, and know that you would presently go out and raid them of riches, and return, and drink your wine, and know yourself one of the lords of Varna? He had thought that one day it might be so, with him.

Berkt finally broke the silence. "I'll tell you something, Chane. Nshurra was always fond of you, because she helped you when you were a child. I never admired you."

"I know that," said Chane.

"Then, know this," said Berkt. "For throwing away your life—and almost certainly that's what you're doing—to help your friend, for that I do rather admire you."

Chane took the little tridim pictures out of the pocket of his coverall . . . all except the one that showed the Singing Suns. That he had put into a secret pocket.

A viewer was brought, and in the dusky room the glories of the Qajar treasures were shown.

"How could we ever have missed a hoard like that!" Berkt exclaimed.

"They're clever people, the Qajars," said Chane. "Extremely clever, and very subtle, and a little mad. They've got practically a world of radite and they've used it to pay thieves to bring them all the things they set their hearts on. They've also used it to keep themselves hidden, and to set up powerful defenses. It was one of their defenses we ran into."

"And you want revenge for the torture they subjected you to? Is that it?"

"For that, and for what they did to Dilullo," said Chane. "But also, I want very much to get my hands on some of the Qajar treasure."

"And so you came here with those pictures, to drum up a Varnan raid on the Qajars," said Berkt.

Chane nodded.

"It's not a bad idea," said Berkt. "Not bad at all, except for one thing. The one thing is that you won't live long enough to see this through."

Chane smiled. "That remains to be seen."

Berkt refilled his glass. "Chane, I'd like you to tell me something: How did you come to kill Ssander? You two were good friends."

"I thought we were good friends," said Chane. "We'd grown up together here. He used to bat me around when we were boys, because he was stronger and wanted to prove it. Once in a while, I'd manage to bat him around. All very natural."

He drank and put his glass down. "We raided Shandor Five, and Ssander was sub-leader. We did well, and Ssander took a sub-leader's share of the loot, and that was all right with me. But then, when it was all divided, he saw a jewel he fancied in my share, and he said, 'That's mine, too.' "

Chane poured himself more of the wine, and drank, and Berkt watched him with his piercing eyes.

"I thought it was like when we were boys together on Varna," Chane said. "I struck him. I batted him back, and said, 'You've had your share.' And he looked at me and said, 'You damned Earthspawn, you struck me.' And he grabbed his laser and shot me in the side. I shot back, and killed him. And then his brothers were coming, and there was nothing for me but sudden death if I stayed, so I jumped into one of the ships and took off."

Berkt nodded, after a time. "I thought it was something like that. You know, Chane, you're a bit unfortunate in feeling like a Varnan but looking like an Earthman."

A communicator inside the room purred softly, and Berkt went in and spoke briefly into it. When he came back he said, "That was Chroll calling—you remember him? He tells me that several men of Ssander's clan are at the starport, watching your ship. Just watching, to make sure you don't go away in it."

He added grimly, "You're in the trap, Chane."

XIII

The blue-black night skies of Varna lit to silver and then to silver-pink, as the two different-colored moons chased up into the sky. They lit the road that went down into Krak, and Morgan Chane followed it, finding a certain satisfaction in the solid way his heels hit the ground. He thought that Varna was a harsh mother, big and bony with rock and dragging at its children with its heavy gravitation, but still it was his mother world.

The air was cool, with a faintly metallic smell to it that came from the not-too-distant ocean that ran up onto the stony beaches in long, furious tides. Down there ahead of him the warm and ruddy lights of Krak beckoned, and all was as it used to be. Or nearly so.

Chane left the road by the first bypath, and continued to work his way down toward the city by little-used paths, and then into the city by obscure streets well away from the lights and noise of the great marketplace. In that market, rich goods looted from all over the galaxy were bought and sold; there were always many people there, and it was no place for a hunted man.

If I can slip around to the west and reach the Hall, he thought, *I may just pull it off.*

If the clan of Ssander—the clan-name was the Ranroi, after a revered ancestor—caught him before then, it was all up and his gamble of coming to Varna would have failed.

He was not, of course, afraid of being suddenly shot down. The clan of Ranroi had great honor, and he would be given the normal challenge and the fight would take place at the appointed place, in the way that was perfectly legal on Varna.

"They know you're in my house," Berkt had said. "They won't bother you here, of course, for that would be starting a feud with me. But they'll wait patiently, right from the first, for you to come out. You might just as well try it now."

Chane had thought so, too, and here he was, slipping along a dark little street which he knew perfectly well, with the great stone bulk and lighted windows of the young men's barracks a few blocks away on his left.

He heard from one window the sound of voices raised in a chorus. The Starwolves sang in a way that made you think of lions singing. He could not distinguish the words but he knew the tune of it and had many times himself sung the song, which was a highly disrespectful one about a great Starwolf lord who was constantly rushing off on foolish raids because he could not endure to stay home with his shrewish wife.

Chane grinned, and slipped on. He had learned these dark streets very well indeed, in times past when he and Chroll—and, yes, Ssander—had stayed out later than barracks law permitted, and had had to return unseen.

Two or three times he saw people moving ahead, and each time he went down a crossway, not ducking stealthily but staggering and throwing his arms around as though very drunk, so that the difference in his figure might not easily be perceived.

He finally stood behind the Hall.

The big, square, and unlovely mass of stone was the only center of government the Varnans of this region had. They were a highly individualistic people who wanted as few laws as possible. A Council of twenty decided all issues beyond the individual. The Council was unique in that, though its members were chosen by vote, only Varnan men who had taken part in at least five raiding missions were allowed the vote.

Chane thought that it was unlikely that any of the Ranroi would be here. They would not be expecting him to come to the Hall, not having as yet any idea why he had come to Varna.

Still, he went around the more shadowed side of the massive building as carefully as a hunting cat. He reached the corner of the front facade and peered around it.

Nobody was in front of it.

Chane went fast, then, to the tall open door. It was always open, and there was always an official here to hear appeals.

The official sitting now at the wide desk was old, for a Varnan. Few Starwolves, by the nature of their hazardous profession, lived long enough to get gray, but this old man had white in his hair and shaggy eyebrows, making him look like an aging tiger.

The old man said nothing, but his upslanted eyes narrowed slightly as Chane walked toward him. He knew perfectly well who Chane was—everybody in Krak knew about Chane—but he nevertheless asked.

"Your name?"

"Morgan Chane."

"You have completed five missions?"

"Many more than five."

The old Varnan opened a section of the desk and touched studs. Presently a card popped out. He looked at the card.

"Verified," he said. "What is your purpose?"

"To make an appeal to the Council," said Chane.

The cat eyes narrowed a trifle more. "The nature of your appeal?"

He thinks I'm going to ask Council to have the Ranroi restrained, thought Chane. *As though the Council would ever take away a clan's feud-right!*

"My appeal is for a hearing in which I will propose something that could enrich all fighting Varnans," said Chane.

The old man's eyes widened a little in surprise. But he reached for a book and opened it, and wrote briefly in it.

"Your right of appeal is legal and is granted," he said. "You will be notified when Council will hear you."

Chane bowed to him, with the respect of a young fighting-man to an old one with also a touch of *To hell with you!* in it. He thought that the shadow of a grim smile came into the old Varnan's face, as he turned and walked out of the Hall.

He was outside, his appeal had been granted and witnessed, and now what? Back to Berkt's? No, not yet.

Violet lightnings had begun to play in the west, out over the sea. Varna had thunderstorms that made the thunderstorms on Earth look childish, but Chane, from long familiarity, decided that this storm would not come inland.

He walked the streets now, not caring who saw him. Varnan men and women stared at him, and to those he knew, he bowed. They greeted him, with a sort of startled air.

He had walked like this, in the lights and the crowds of tall Varnan people, in years gone by. He had realized quite well in those days that he was behaving like a cocky bantam, simply because he was a bit smaller, and, on the whole, a bit weaker than these tall golden folk.

He walked like that now, not caring much where he walked. And then he found himself in quieter streets, and when he began to realize where he was, he realized that old-time habit had betrayed him and had taken him to a place where he had not really wanted to go.

A quiet street, with rather small houses. He wanted

to turn around and leave it, but somehow he could not quite do so. He did not stride arrogantly now, he plodded. And his slow steps took him to a small, old house that had snarling masks carved on its rainspouts, and that had next to it a vacant lot with a few tumbled stones lying about in it.

The distant lightning flared, and washed out the light of the silver and pink moons. Chane went into the lot and looked around.

His father and mother had lived in the small house, and on this empty lot had been the chapel, long fallen to ruin, where the Reverend Thomas Chane had preached.

Chane thought, *Just like Dilullo. Does everyone have a vacant lot, a lost something or someone, in their past?*

He walked to the back of the grass-grown space. His father and mother had been buried behind the little chapel where they had striven so valiantly for their creed.

The violet lightning far out over the ocean flared and he saw the two small tombstones. They were clean and well cared for, and he could even read the lettering, for it was in the fire-stone that was Varna's hardest mineral.

"The Reverend Thomas Chane, Carnarvon, Earth. . . ."

And he remembered the old man in bleak, windy Carnarvon who had said, "The Reverend Thomas was a fine man and a strong preacher. I do not doubt that he converted many out on that distant world before the Lord took him."

No, he had not. The Reverend Thomas had converted no one. But he had made at least one friend. Chane had no doubt at all that it was Berkt who had kept the graves cared for. He remembered the funeral, and he remembered Berkt taking him, a boy trying to restrain his tears, and shoving him into the door of the place where young Varnans learned their skills, and saying to him, "Go in there, and find out whether you're fit to be a Varnan or not. It's not what your father would have wanted, but there's nothing else for you on Varna."

Well, there was no use at all in thinking about it now. But even Starwolves mourned their dead.

He heard a sound and swung around. There was a man near him, a tall, dark figure.

Then the distant lightning flared again and he knew the man.

It was Harkann, the oldest of Ssander's brothers.

XIV

"I thought you would come here," said Harkann.

He was years older than Chane, and he was one of the Starwolf lords, not as great a one as Berkt, but a famed leader of raids.

He towered over Chane, and in the shadows Chane could see the livid scar across his forehead from an old wound, where the Varnan down would never grow again. Underneath that scar, the slanted eyes seemed to glow in the dusk as he looked down at Chane.

"I'm glad you came back to Varna," said Harkann. "Very glad."

Chane smiled. "I rather thought you would be."

"I have told all the Ranroi not to challenge you," said Harkann. "I have wanted the pleasure of this all for myself."

Chane said nothing. After a moment, Harkann added, "It will be tomorrow, then? You know the place . . . it is still the same one."

Yes, Chane knew the place, the rocky gorge not far outside Krak where feuds could be settled fairly and with no danger to anyone else. And Harkann would be there, with his weapons, and if Harkann did not manage to kill him in fair fight, it would be the turn of Thurr, the other brother of Ssander, to try to do so. And if Chane killed Thurr, then one by one any others of the clan of Ranroi could challenge him. It was a big clan, whereas Chane had nobody at all: his only kin on Varna lay beneath the two fire-stone markers.

"I have claimed the Council right," said Chane.

Harkann's head jerked with astonishment. "The council right? For what reason?"

"I have come to Varna with something for the Council to hear," said Chane.

Harkann was silent for a moment, his big catlike body hunched forward as he glared at Chane. Chane could guess his frustration.

No feud could be pressed against a man who had claimed the Council right, until the Council had heard that man. It was unbreakable law, designed to prevent one litigant from challenging and killing another litigant before the Council could hear the case.

"It's a trick," Harkann said. "But it won't save you, Chane. You murdered Ssander—"

Chane interrupted sharply. "Ssander tried to murder me. And he damn near succeeded. I only drew my weapon after he had used his on me."

"Murder, self-defense . . . it doesn't make one bit of difference to us of the Ranroi!"

"I never thought it would," said Chane. "But I want the record straight."

Harkann said between his teeth, "The record will very soon be closed for you, Chane."

He turned away. After a moment Chane left the place also but he went another way.

He headed westward, toward the place where the sea came nearest Krak. There, on a cliff above the ocean, towered one of the lordly castles, arrogant in the light of the flying moons. As he went forward toward the building, he could already hear the thunderous booming of the great tides beating against the base of the cliffs.

A woman came out into the moonlight from where she had been sitting on a carven stone bench beneath a tree.

Chane smiled. "So you were so sure I would come that you were waiting for me, Graal?"

"You were mad to come back to Varna at all, Chane!" she said. "Do you know that right now the Ranroi are looking for you?"

"I know," he said. "I've met them. But there's a delay in their plans, for my Council right."

He stood, admiring her. Graal was taller than he was, and her splendid, golden-down covered body was very little concealed by the garments she wore. With her glowing chatoyant eyes, she looked like a beautiful panther.

"Why did you come back, Chane?"

"To see you, of course."

"Liar," she said. "Tell me."

He told her. She shook her head. "But after the Council hears you, you'll have to fight the Ranroi, one after another."

"I have an idea about that, too," said Chane. "But we won't talk about that, but about you. Berkt says you are not yet married."

"I am not," said Graal. "I like fun and men too much to tie myself to any lord yet."

"I know." He nodded. "I used to get quite furious with you about that."

"And you're not furious now?" She moved closer to him, in a way he remembered. "Perhaps you have met outworld girls more attractive?"

"One," he said. "On a world called Arkuu."

Graal burst into laughter, and then put her arms around him and kissed him. It was something like being kissed by a tigress.

"That's my little Earthman, always trying to make me feel jealous."

Chane grinned. "It's true."

"Then you shall tell me about her."

They walked beneath the trees, in dappled pink-silver moonlight and shadow. Graal seemed already to have forgotten her worry for him. She was a fine, generous, merry-hearted girl, but she was a daughter of Varnans, and a Varnan's business was fighting.

The sea boomed, and the wind had hints of metallic-tasting spray in it. The moons glided on and their shifting radiance poured down, and it was good to be again on the world of his youth and with Graal's arms around him.

"I'm sorry if I'm interrupting," said a man's voice.

Graal only laughed, but Chane turned angrily. Then his anger left him as he saw the young Starwolf who stood with an amused look on his handsome, reckless face.

Chane went to him and gripped his arm warmly. "Chroll!" They had been comrades on many a raid, and both remembered.

"Would you mind if I take him with me, Graal?" asked Chroll. "I'm trying to get his neck out of the noose into which he has run it."

"Then take him," said Graal. "I don't want my little Earthman hurt, if it can be prevented."

She gave Chane her mocking smile as she said that, but he only smiled back at her, and then went with Chroll.

As the car started down the hillside, Chroll talked fast. "I heard about your claiming the Council right, Chane. But that won't protect you for long. Old Irrun, the head of the Ranroi, is one of the Council and will see that you get a hearing fast. And after the hearing, you'll have no Council right to protect you."

Chane said, "I've got an idea that might still restrain the Ranroi after the hearing."

He told Chroll his idea, and Chroll said that he did not think much of it.

"Irrun will try his best to quash any such proposal as that," he told Chane. "And if he succeeds, then what? You'll have to face one after another of the Ranroi until one of them kills you."

He swung the car from the base of the hill, toward the lights of Krak.

"I can get you off Varna, Chane, but it will have to be tonight. If we can get unnoticed into my ship . . ."

"No," said Chane. "I bring no other man into my private feud. That's the way I was taught here, and that's the way it will be."

"Damn Ssander!" muttered Chroll. "I never did like him, though I know you did."

"Besides," said Chane, "just escaping from Varna is not what I want. I came here to do something, and just to go away without even trying to do it would be a stupid waste of time."

"Berkt told me of your plans," Chroll said, after a moment. "I can't say that I blame a man for loyalty to his comrades." He added, after a moment, "By the way, Chane, don't say anything to Berkt of my offer to get you away, will you? He wouldn't consider it quite honorable."

"You're still as much in awe of Berkt as when we were boys, then?" said Chane, laughing.

"Yes, I am. And so are you."

Chane did not deny it. Chroll asked, "Do you want to go back now to Berkt's?"

"What would you want to do if it were your first night on Varna for a long time?"

"I'd want to raise a little hell," Chroll said.

They did. They went to the huge tavern by the marketplace that was the favorite drinking place of the Starwolves.

The place roared and blazed. The red-colored lights did very little in the way of illumination, but they were sufficient to enable a man to find his glass. None of the great Starwolf lords were here; they were far too proud and dignified for that. But the junior officers, the fighting men, the men Chane had known, were here in great numbers.

They hailed him in good friendship. Obviously the word had got around that he had returned to Varna. Three of them, who were of the clan of the Ranroi, got up and somewhat ostentatiously left. But nobody paid much heed to them. These young blades didn't give a curse for feuds, but they had raided with Chane, they knew him as the poor little Earthman (none of them dared use that phrase to his face) who had had a hard time growing up on Varna but who had made it; they liked him, and they bought him wine.

The strong wine went down and Chane's head rocked and rang, and he thought, *This is not very well advised, but damn it, it's part of what I came back to Varna for,* and he drank it down and went on from table to table.

Talk, talk, good talk, talk about the last raid to the Hyades, talk about Sarn and how he got himself into a lot of trouble off Deneb: he thought he had a fat lot of loot just sitting there waiting to be picked up, and did he get a nasty surprise! Talk about Aranso, and how he ran right through the triple crown, the three stars whose gravitic tides were murder, but he did it. And Chane bought a large cup of wine for Aranso and complimented him, and Aranso insisted on his sharing the cup. Aranso was rich with loot, and in a drunken, happy mood, and at this moment he loved Chane like a brother.

"And where have you been, Chane? What have you been doing with yourself?"

Chane was pretty exhilarated by now, and enjoying it greatly, and he poured himself more wine and stood on a table.

"Do you really want to know?"

"Of course we do!"

"I have been with the Mercs," he said. "Nearly all of them Earthmen."

"Back to your own, is that it, Chane?"

Chane drained the cup, and then looked at them and said gravely, "You are my own, you miserable, misbegotten sons of Varna."

Laughter and cheers. Most of them were getting a bit drunk by now, and they enjoyed the insult.

"What are Earthmen like, Chane?"

Chane considered. "They're stupid, for one thing.

They have all sorts of vague, cloudy ideas about morals and laws and doing good for people."

"Like when they first came to Varna and taught our people how to build starships?" shouted someone, and the whole great room rocked with laughter.

That was a famous and favorite story on Varna. How the Earthmen, who had discovered the principle of the stardrive—rediscovered, really, since it had been known ages ago by the race who had seeded the whole galaxy with humanity—had come and innocently offered to show the Varnans how to build starships, so that they might engage in honest trade in the galaxy.

And how the Varnans of that day had demurely said, yes, they would very much like to have starships so that they could engage in honest trade and be good men. And, having thus gulled the Earthmen, they had learned how to build starships, and had been the raiders and robbers of the galaxy ever since.

"Yes, they're stupid," said Chane. "They clog up their minds with nice ideas that somebody thought up. But, my brothers—"

"Yes?" said someone.

"They are a goddamn tough lot," said Chane. "They can't move in space the way we do; their bodies aren't up to it, for Earth isn't a heavy-grav world. But . . . they are tough."

He thought, as he spoke, of Dilullo and Bollard and Sekinnen and the others, and of the things they had done together.

"I was on Earth," said Chane. "I went back to the place where my parents came from. And there was a young man there who taught me a song, and the song he taught me was an old Earth battle-song. That song might tell you what the men of Earth are like. Do you want to hear it?"

"Sing it!" they cried, and Aranso sent him up another cup of wine, and he drank it off and now his head was really ringing, but nevertheless he still remembered the

song that tall young Hayden Jones had taught him in
the little bar at Carnarvon.

He sang it, the old war-song of the men of Harlech,
and the Starwolves listened fascinatedly, and then they
began to sing it too, the great, tall cat-eyed
golden-furred men who scourged the stars, singing of
Saxon bowmen and Saxon foemen as though they had
just come out of the dark marshes of Wales with their
swords and spears in their hands.

The idea made Chane stop singing to laugh. And as
he stood laughing among the roaring chorus, a hand
plucked his knee, and Chroll was there, offering him
another cup of wine.

"Having a good time, Chane?"

"I am having a good time."

"That's good, Chane. That's very good. Make the
most of it. For old Irrun worked fast, and the Council
will hear you tomorrow, and it may be your last good
time for a while."

XV

They were the greatest of the Starwolf lords, and they sat like kings behind their wide table at the side of the dusky stone hall.

Chane, standing facing them, thought fleetingly, *Dilullo would call them a royal bunch of robbers.*

From one point of view that was true, for raiding and robbing were the life of Varna. These nine men represented the greatest Varnan clans, but also they were famous for the great Starwolf raids they had led in bygone years.

Khepher, who had led the great raid on the Pleiades that had brought home such loot as Varna had never seen before; Somtum and Yarr, who had hit the throne-world of Canopus, looting for the first time the royal treasury of a system so huge and powerful that it had never feared attack; Berkt, sitting there and looking as though he had never seen Chane before, who had struck halfway across the galaxy to lift the legendary Terbium Ten and fight his way home with them again; Vonn and Martabalane and Munn, who had taken the treasured jewels of Betelgeuse Four away from their spidery owners by a triple-play feint and attack that was a classic of Varnan history; Hof, who with only twelve ships had bagged the richest convoy in the galaxy's history; and Irrun, who had privateered all along the north-zenith edge of the

411

galaxy and had come home with ships heavy with plunder long after he had been given up for lost.

They were all looking at Chane, and the regard of Irrun was a piercing one. The head of the Ranroi clan was a massive man well past middle age, who sat with his wide shoulders hunched forward as he stared at Chane. He had been Ssander's uncle, and he would be the main difficulty in the way of Chane's proposal.

Khepher, who had the seniority of the Council, spoke formally to Chane.

"Very well, Morgan Chane. The Council will hear you."

Chane braced himself. If he failed here, Dilullo and the other Mercs might never leave Rith.

"My appeal is for the right to present a plan that could bring vast riches to Varna," he said.

They looked surprised; Irrun's eyes narrowed and he looked as if he was going to interrupt. But Khepher said, "You have leave to speak."

Chane pointed to the compact projector-device he had brought with him. "Can I, before speaking, show a few tridims relative to what I will say?"

Khepher nodded.

Chane turned on the device, with its controls set to reproduce a three-dimensional image of life size.

The first Qajar treasure room sprang into vivid, almost solid-seeming glory in the shadowy hall: jewels heaped up in golden jars, jewels woven into tapestries, weird statuettes that were each cut from a single blazing gem . . . all with such reality that the astonished Starwolf lords, except for Berkt, leaned forward as though they would grasp these things with their hands.

"What foolery is this?" snarled Irrun.

"I am showing you the treasures of the Qajars," said Chane. "There are more."

He changed the tridim and another of the incredible treasure rooms came into being. And as he showed room after room, the slant eyes of the Starwolves gleamed with lust for plunder.

When the last tridim had been turned off, Khepher leaned forward. "Where are these things?" he asked. "*Where?*"

"On the planet Chlann, of a people called the Qajars," said Chane. "It lies not far outside the Spur."

"The whole galaxy would have rung with the news of such a treasure, if it existed!" said Irrun.

"The Qajars," said Chane, "are a clever people. Oh, very clever. They have gathered together the most beautiful and costly things in the galaxy, having paid thieves to steal them. They have kept all this secret and have kept their world secret, and very well defended. I know; I nearly died trying to get to their treasure."

He paused, and then added, "I can guide you there. I can lead a Varnan squadron through their defenses, although I cannot guarantee that there will be no losses. I will do this, if I may have my pick of any single item of the Qajar treasures."

"You are bold to come and make terms with the Council," snapped Khepher. "Is there anything else you want, perchance?"

"One thing more," said Chane coolly. "Council right to protect me, until the squadron returns to Varna."

Irrun leaped to his feet, his face raging. "A trick!" he roared. "This man killed my nephew and has incurred the feud of my clan. He asks the Council right so that he can escape our rightful revenge."

Chane stared at him, as though not in the least impressed by Irrun's position and fame.

"To escape your clan-feud," he said coldly, "I needed only to remain away from Varna."

Berkt laughed. "You will have to admit that young Chane has a point there."

Irrun said fiercely, "It is well known, Berkt, that you had a friendship with this outworlder's father!"

Khepher's voice rose sharply. "There will be no bickering between members of the Council! We are here to listen to the man Chane, and then later to decide."

He turned his attention to Chane. "Describe what you know of the defenses of the Qajars."

Chane did so. He stressed that he was the only one who could lead a Varnan squadron with any safety whatever into that cluster of dead suns and worlds.

"These so-called Lethal Worlds that you describe," said Khepher; "you went safely between them and back again. Could you lead an attack squadron that same way?"

Chane shook his head. "Not possibly. The Qajars just did not think it worth while to use such huge weapons against my small scout. But against a squadron, they would use them. My suggestion is that we sacrifice a number of old ships, unmanned and on automatic pilot, sending them in ahead of us to blow enough of the Lethal Worlds to make a passage."

He went on rapidly: "The Qajars have powerful radiation defenses; I felt them. Anti-radiation helmets should help us there. And they have a fairly powerful squadron of battle cruisers, though none of them heavies. But I feel we could handle those, if we could get through the Lethal Worlds."

"The strategy would have to be debated later, by those fit to do so," said Khepher in cold reproof. "But if we smothered the Qajar defenses, you could lead us to the treasure chambers?"

"I could," said Chane, and added in his mind, *All except one, where I'll never lead you. I'll give you one of the biggest hauls Varna ever had, but not the Singing Suns.*

The examination went on, others of the Council flinging sharp questions at Chane. These were men who had a lifetime of raiding behind them, and who knew about every danger interstellar space could hold, and they were not going to take anything for granted.

"It has not been explained," said Irrun sharply, "how these Qajars could have acquired sufficient of the highly rare radioactive substances that would be required to convert dead planets from their Lethal Worlds."

"My information from Eron," said Chane, "was that there are tremendous deposits of radite, one of the rare substances you mention, on the world Chlann. It is the source of the Qajars' wealth, with which they've bribed thieves to steal treasures for them."

Chane added, "Eron felt sure the Qajars are a bit mad. They've nested there behind their defenses, gloating over their treasures and avoiding direct contact with most of the galaxy. If anyone approaches them uninvited, they kill him by torture. I say that this thief-spider nest should be broken into, and their treasures taken by more suitable owners—namely, the Varnans."

Some of the Council lords smiled at that: it was exactly the kind of talk to be expected from a cocky young Starwolf.

"The matter will not brook sudden decision," Khepher told Chane. "It must be further examined. The tridims must be gone over by experts to make sure they are not fakes. Our records concerning that cluster must be examined to see if they contain any contradiction to your statements."

Chane bowed. Khepher concluded, "You may go for now. You will in time be notified of our decision. Until then, you continue to have the Council right."

Chane would have liked to say more but this was an arbitrary dismissal, so he bowed again and left the Hall.

Two nights later he sat in the moonlit gardens behind Berkt's keep, drinking wine with Chroll and Graal and Nshurra. He knew very well that Nshurra had never liked Graal and her free-and-easy ways, but she had been smilingly hospitable to her.

For two days Chane had awaited the Council decision. In those days he had had a fine time reliving old days with Graal . . . and nearly getting drowned by her when she held him under water as they swam the great tides of the beaches beyond Krak.

"Relax, Chane," said Chroll. "It'll be decided soon, one way or the other."

"What do they think of Varnans on that old world of Earth, Chane?" asked Nshurra. "You said you were there."

"Savages," said Chane. "Wild, hellroaring savage robbers of the whole galaxy." He looked at Graal and added, "They say the Varnan women are even fiercer than the men."

Graal promptly threw her wineglass at him, and he ducked just fast enough to let it go past his ear.

From far away at the distant starport beyond Krak, there was a series of three twanging sounds and three bolts of light flashed up into the sky.

Chroll smiled. "A small party of very young Varnans, going out to try their luck. They'll probably come back empty-handed. But you remember, Chane?"

"I remember," said Chane. "Very well."

There came the jolting grind of one of the heavy Varnan cars ascending the hill, and Chane tensed. He tried not to show it.

None of them spoke until the grinding stopped, and presently Berkt came around into the garden.

"Well?" said Chane.

"I won't keep you in suspense," said Berkt. "After all this argument, the Council has decided to sanction the raid on Chlann, and the clans have pledged in all some seventy ships."

Exultation soared up in Chane. He could almost feel his hands on the Singing Suns.

"But before you get too happy about it," came Berkt's dry voice, "there is a condition attached to the sanction. It was attached by Irrun and his supporters on the Council, otherwise they would veto the raid."

Chane stiffened. "A condition?"

Berkt nodded. "Irrun's nephew Harkann commands the raid. And, as pilot, you go with him in his ship."

"So the Ranroi are not going to let me out of their grasp?" muttered Chane.

A rage grew up in him. Damn the Ranroi and their feuds! He would go with Harkann, but if one of them had to perish, it was going to be Harkann.

XVI

A great horn bellowed brazenly across the city Krak. And at that signal, other mighty horns took up the clamor, echoing and re-echoing off the stone walls until the whole city was buffeted by waves of brassy sound.

In long ago days the Varnans had been a fighting race, and the battle horns had sounded when the clans went out against each other. And though centuries had gone by, and though they had become highly sophisticated in the technology of star travel which Earthmen had unwisely taught them, the old custom remained and when a Varnan expedition set forth to raid for loot, the great horns all sounded.

Out from the red stone buildings broke the brilliant flags of the different clans. With cheers and waving of hands, the tall golden people along the streets honored the cars that were filled with fighting men, and that rolled and jolted away in the direction of the starport.

Chane, riding in one of the cars, thought, *On Earth, they'd do this for a defending army going forth, but never for a band of pirates going for loot.*

But it was the way he remembered it, and the brazen roaring of the great horns sent a hot thrill through him as it always had in the past.

There was a brightness in the eyes of the Varnans riding with him. They might be going to sudden death between the stars, but there would be excitement and

fighting and maybe a shipful of rich plunder to bring
home, and this was the way a Varnan liked it.

It made Chane think of the very first time he had gone
out on a raid, how he had tried to conceal his excitement
as the horns bellowed, how he had tried to look cool and
haughty and as unexcited as the veterans around him.

To the devil with nostalgia, Chane thought suddenly.
Nostalgia will get me killed.

No raid he had ever gone on would be as dangerous for
him as this present one, and he had better stop dreaming
and keep alert every moment.

The hot golden sunlight poured down on the cars as
they rumbled out onto the starport and between the long
lines of needle-shaped ships. Beside the ship that was
starred with the symbol of the leader, the figure of
Harkann towered above a group of captains. Harkann
gave Chane an icy look, but did not otherwise greet him.

"You all know where the dropout point will be," he
said, and they nodded. Chane had calculated that
dropout point, and experts in stellar navigation had
confirmed it. Harkann went on, "You know the order
and timing in which we'll drop out; you have the full
schedule. So there's nothing more to talk about."

The captains went away, all except Harkann and
Vengant, who was his second officer. They turned and
went into the symbol-starred ship, and Chane followed
them.

The ships of the Starwolves were small ones, with a
crew of eight to ten each. The fighting men of the ship
gave no greeting to Chane. They were all of the Ranroi
clan, and knew him. Vengant took the controls, and
Harkann and Chane the chairs behind him. They looked
out through the broad bridge screen, and nobody said
anything.

From far away they could hear the brassy echo of the
horns of Krak bidding them farewell and good looting.
Then a new sound began.

It was less a sound than a vibration, and it grew until

the tarmac under the ship was quivering with it. A deep and awesome thunder, the thunder of the first division of ships as their power units came on.

"Time," said Harkann curtly, and as he spoke, the first division started skyward, with a lightning-bolt sound of splitting atmosphere.

Thirty needle-ships, heading halfway up the zenith. But these were not proud Varnan craft. They were old, corroded, their sides scarred by battles out in distant space from which they had limped home long ago. They had been furnished with enough repairs and power to get them into space again, and had been manned by skeleton crews. They were the expendables, the sacrifice to deceive the Qajars. With them went five sound ships to take off the skeleton crews when the moment came.

The roaring thunder of their takeoffs died away, and Harkann sat silently watching the chronometer. Finally he said into the communicator, "Second Division, five minutes to offworld."

The chair in which Chane sat began to quiver as the power units back in the stern compartment began their muted roar. The five minutes went by.

An explosion of power hurled the ship skyward, and smashed Chane deep into his chair. His guts contracted agonizedly, and he felt his vision darkening as an unseen fist battered his head, and he thought startledly, *I've been too long away from Varna; I can't take this many gravs now!*

Then his belly muscles tightened up, and his vision cleared, and he knew that he had not lost the strength that the painful years of childhood on Varna had given him, that he could still endure.

The ship kept rising on an acceleration schedule that would have paralyzed an Earthman. That was why the Starwolves were so hard to beat in space. The heavy gravitation of massive Varna had bred into them a strength and resistance that made them able to take G's which no other spacegoing race in the galaxy could take.

Chane took it, and liked it. This was the speed at which he had been used to traveling in space until the time he forsook Varna. The slow speeds of the Merc ships had sometimes seemed intolerably sluggish to him.

They went away fast from Varna. Out in the brilliant sunglare, on either side of the flagship and behind it, shone bright, winking little points of light that were the other ships of the squadron. Starwolf forces kept tighter formations than ordinary men could dare, since they could if necessary alter course with sudden changes of speed and direction that would crush the guts out of an Earthman.

From the golden glare of Varna's arrogant sun they went out into the blackness and the starshine, driving headlong toward the predetermined drop-in point.

"Time," said Harkann, and Vengant hit the controls and went into overdrive.

The vertiginous feeling of the fall into extra-dimensional space came and went. Without a pause, the ship hurtled on, and all the ships that were behind it.

And still none of the Ranroi had said a word to Chane.

Chane remembered what Berkt had said, before he left Varna. Chane had been saying goodbye to Chroll, who had signed long before for another raid and was not going against the Qajars, and who was unhappy about it.

"Don't feel too badly about not going with Chane," Berkt had grimly advised Chroll. "Wherever Chane is on this job, there's going to be the worst danger."

"You don't mean that the Ranroi will try to kill him out there?" Chroll had exclaimed. "No, they wouldn't. . . . He has Council right until the raid-squadron returns."

"There's a good many of the Ranroi I don't like, but they're not dishonorable," Berkt said. "They—or most of them—wouldn't break Council right. But there'll be fighting out there, and Harkann can give Chane the most dangerous spot in it without violating his right."

Later, after Chroll had left, Chane had looked at Berkt and had said wryly, "Thanks for the encouragement."

"You know it's true, don't you?" said Berkt, and Chane nodded.

Then Chane hesitated. Something bothered him.

"You've been a good friend to me, Berkt," he said.

Berkt shrugged. "Partly for your father's sake, and Nshurra's."

"I haven't told you the whole truth," said Chane. "It's not that I've lied about anything, but I omitted a bit of the truth."

Berkt said nothing, waiting.

"The thing I'm after on the world of the Qajars," said Chane. "The one item of treasure which, by the Council terms, I'm permitted to select for myself. Between us, it's the Singing Suns."

Berkt's upslanted eyes opened wide, and a look of incredulity crossed his cruel-planed, haughty face.

"But the Suns were broken up!" he exclaimed. "After Morrul and his clan stole them from Achernar, Morrul sold them to Klloya-Klloy on Mruun, and Klloya-Klloy broke them up and sold them to several buyers."

"The several buyers were all agents of the Qajars," said Chane. "It was their trick to keep down the price of the Suns."

Berkt stared, and then suddenly broke into a burst of homeric laughter.

"That's the damnedest thing I ever heard! Then that's what you and your Merc friends came to the Spur for?"

Chane nodded. "To get the Suns and collect the two million credit reward for them when we return them to Achernar."

"*Return* them?"

Chane said defensively, "Earthmen are queer fish, Berkt. Even the Mercs, who are pretty tough, won't do anything that's against their particular ideas of honesty. I'll admit it seems pretty foolish to me."

"If Harkann and the others see the Suns, they won't much like your taking them," warned Berkt.

"I know," said Chane grimly. "But the Council agreed that I could take any single treasure-object I wish. And I'm going to do just that . . . if we get that far."

"Which is a big if," Berkt said. "Harkann's a good raid leader, whatever else he is. But from what you told me, you're going up against some pretty nasty stuff. Well, good luck!"

Remembering that now as the ship flashed on in overdrive, Chane thought he would need the luck. Now and then he caught the eyes of Harkann, cold and deadly, watching him.

It did not exactly frighten him, but all this inimical silence on the part of everyone began to bore him. When he had finished a trick at the navigation instruments, he went back to the tiny bunk room and stretched out.

He wondered what Dilullo and Bollard and the others were doing, if they still lived. He grinned as he thought what they would say if they could see him now, out with the Starwolves.

Well, the devil with worrying, he thought. *I've made my gamble and I'll follow through with it, and there's no use thinking any more about it.*

They went on, angling across the whole width of Argo Spur. They stood their tricks, and checked the ship weapons, and ate and slept and watched the simulacrum viewscreen that showed their squadron passing between the nebulae and stars.

A tenseness grew in them as they neared the edge of the Spur. Beyond it the screen indicated empty space, the great ocean that washed the shores of the galaxy.

And out in that space showed the dark cluster that

Chane remembered, the little cluster of many dead suns and worlds in the heart of which the Qajars had their stronghold.

There came a time when Harkann said, "The first division, right now, should be *here,*" putting his finger on the screen on a point two-thirds of the way out to the dark cluster.

Chane was sure that they would be right where Harkann had indicated. They had to be, to make the whole attack plan work.

Starwolves, contrary to general belief in the galaxy, did not rush bullheaded into an attack when they raided. It often looked that way, but actually the dreaded Varnan raiders planned their major raids on a finely-calculated schedule.

It had to be that way for a raid to succeed. The Starwolf squadrons were never very big. Given time, almost any planet they hit could bring up overpowering forces against them. So the Starwolves never gave them that much time. They dropped out of overdrive at the precise right moment, used their unmatchable speed in space to make a lightning swoop, grabbed their loot and went away again as fast as they had come.

Chane felt the familiar feeling of tenseness, excitement and eagerness he had always felt when a raid mission neared its climax.

He thought, *Dilullo would be disappointed in me. After all his efforts, I'm still a Starwolf!*

When they had approached almost to the edge of the dark cluster, as shown on the simulacrum, Vengant said sharply, "Dropout time for One!"

Harkann, studying the screen, nodded silently. Some distance ahead of them in space, not far from the actual edge of the dark cluster, the fleet of thirty old ships that were to be sacrificed would at this moment be dropping out of overdrive.

Chane could visualize it. The skeleton crews of the old ships, now that they were in normal space, would be swiftly setting the controls on their automatic, prediagramed courses. Then those crews would be picked up by the five sound cruisers that had gone along with Division One for that purpose.

The chronometer showed a figure, and Vengant said, "Time."

"Drop out," said Harkann.

They came out of overdrive next moment, with the dizzying, spinning sensation you never got used to.

On the viewscreen, now that they were in normal space, they could see far to their left the vast coast of the galaxy, sweeping away in cliffs of stars. The tarnished plume of Argo Spur was behind them. Ahead there was only the darkness of space, in which the dark cluster could not yet be seen visually.

But the radar screen showed the little cluster sharp and clear. It showed five blips outside the cluster, the ships that had taken off the skeleton crews. And it showed thirty other blips, racing at highest speed toward the cluster and soon to enter it.

Harkann spoke into the communicator, to the whole squadron.

"Be ready for the signal."

It seemed to Chane, as it had always seemed to him at this penultimate moment before an attack, that as the squadron waited it was quivering to be unleashed.

XVII

The thirty sacrifice ships flew fast toward the dark cluster. The ships were not bunched together, but were spread out in a broad line. The course to be followed through the dark worlds and dead stars of the cluster had been carefully programed for each one of them.

"If your Lethal Worlds exist, we should soon see some evidence of them," Harkan said to Chane.

They peered at the viewscreen, which had now been set to give a close-up view of the cluster.

"Nothing," said Vengant, contemptuously.

Blinding light flashed from the viewscreen as a small, dark planet exploded into a colossal flare. The flare of force engulfed several of the robot Varnan ships, but the others raced on.

"It seems," said Chane, "that the Qajars keep a good watch on their monitors. And that the sight of Varnan ships has upset them."

Another body in the cluster, a big planet that swung far out from its dead and ashen primary, flashed into a parsec-wide flare.

"Seven more of the robots got it," said Vengant. He began to swear. "Who are these crazy people, anyway, who explode worlds as a weapon? It's sheer madness."

Chane shrugged. "They've got the worlds to spare. . . . This cluster is just a graveyard of dead suns and planets, with no life on any of them. And they've

426

got the radite. A big charge of it, when it's set off, transforms a great mass of the planet into unstable atomic compounds, and it blows. It's easy for them."

Another mined planet blazed up, and then two more almost at once. All the dead suns and icy worlds of the dark cluster sprang into visibility in the unthinkable glare that was the pyre of planets.

"All thirty of the robot ships gone," reported the man at the scope.

"How near did they get to Chlann?" demanded Harkann.

The man punched a key, and then read off the figure.

"Pretty near," muttered Harkann. "But there might be a few more explosive worlds yet."

Chane shook his head. "Too near Chlann for that, I think. They would hardly want a backblast from their own weapon." He added, "Well, the robot ships have made a path for us through the Lethal Worlds. Are we going in?"

"We'll go in," said Harkann, and spoke the signal, and the whole Starwolf squadron dashed forward in a long, narrow column.

It was a poor fighting formation if the Qajars came out to fight, thought Chane. But only a narrow column could follow the gap made by the robot ships through the Lethal Worlds. And maybe that gap wasn't wide enough, maybe they would catch it in a planet-flare; but if that was so, they would never know what happened, so why worry?

They had put on the anti-radiation helmets that had been prepared at Varna, and Chane thought that they all looked oddly like ancient soldiers. But the helmets should keep out the worst of that mind-shattering attack weapon the Qajars used. He hoped.

The Starwolf column flashed into the cluster, following exactly the middle of the path that the sacrificed robot ships had taken. *The old Starwolf swoop,* thought Chane, *that all the galaxy feared.* But they might have bitten off too much, this time.

A hellish flare blotted out the whole universe on their

right. A small planet had gone to glory there, but when their dazzled eyes recovered, they saw on the radar screen that the column had not been touched and was driving ahead.

Now other dead worlds and moons let go, and all space seemed filled with the gigantic flares. The circuits of the ship faltered, lights went out, the craft rocked and went dead and then picked up again, but all the time their roaring momentum kept them going in.

It was like running a gauntlet of world-destroying fires, thought Chane. Harkann sat like a rock, looking doggedly at the viewscreen, his massive shoulders unmoving.

He's my enemy and I'm probably going to have to kill him, thought Chane, *but he goes into battle like a Varnan.*

Shaken, quaking and shuddering, the Starwolf ships rushed on. Dead planets far too distant to harm them sent up their mighty flares as they exploded.

Chane thought that the Qajars must be afraid indeed of the Starwolves, to try to frighten them back with this holocaust of worlds. But it took a good deal to frighten a Varnan.

The last flares fell behind them, and their stunned eyes began to recover.

A needle of pain went through Chane's brain. It was like the time when he and Dilullo and Gwaath had been tortured, but not a tenth of that agony. It gimleted into his head, and seemed to twist and turn.

Some of the Ranroi crew had uttered exclamations, and Vengant was swearing. Harkann had half risen from his chair, and then he turned and looked at Chane with a question on his hard face.

"This is one of their weapons," said Chane, nodding. "The helmets keep most of it out, but not all. We'll have to stand it."

"We'll stand it," said Harkann harshly. "But curse people who use such a weapon."

"They're clever, the Qajars," said Chane. "I'm hoping that soon we can make them pay for their cleverness."

The squadron rushed on toward the dark world that still was not visible to them. But now Harkann gave an order, and smoothly the squadron shifted from the long column to a new formation, which looked like an irregular swarm. There was nothing at all random about the casual-looking formation: every Varnan ship had its place in it.

"*Damn* this thing that gets into your brain!" said Harkann, shaking his head.

"Be grateful you've got the helmet on and aren't getting the full blast of it," said Chane.

The probing finger of pain in his skull made him remember the ordeal that he and Dilullo and Gwaath had gone through, and his lust for vengeance sharpened.

"Will they come out to fight?" demanded Harkann.

"I think they have to," said Chane, "when they see that neither the Lethal Worlds nor this pain ray is stopping us."

"They're coming now," said Vengant, and pointed to the radar screen.

Harkann and Chane studied the screen tensely, estimating the blips on it that now moved toward them.

"At least eighty ships," said Harkann. "Coming on in a concave formation. Figuring to box us in and give it to us from all sides."

"*Very* clever," said Chane. "But they haven't fought with Varnans before."

And he and Harkann both smiled grimly.

The swarm of Starwolf ships kept going straight ahead, and the Qajars half-moon formation flew toward them, so that the Varnan swarm would be caught between the horns of the semicircle, and be the target of concentrated fire.

They went on, and were actually between the horns

of the Qajar half-circle, before Harkann rapped an order to his captains.

"The left horn. Up shields. All right, let's take them."

The whole Starwolf squadron suddenly turned sharply left. The turn was an impossibly abrupt one, for anyone but Varnans. Even though Chane expected it, and had braced himself in the chair in which he sat at the controls of a missile-launcher, the blood drove into his head and the pressure crushed him as with a giant hand.

The Qajars had indeed never fought Varnans before, and the swiftness and speed of the swerve took them by surprise. Before they could alter formation, the Starwolf ships were swarming around the cruisers in the whole left horn of the formation.

Two or three Varnan ships attacked each one of the Qajars, having here a local numerical superiority. The missiles began to flare and Qajar ships went up in destruction as their shields were overloaded, before there was even any firing back.

Chane kept the radar of his launcher locked onto a Qajar ship that was in plain sight against the stars. Two other Varnans were pumping missiles at it, and the strain became too much for its shields. The Qajar ship blew, and they turned to another prey.

"Hit them! Hit them before the others form up!" Harkann was shouting to his squadron.

The whole middle and right horn of the Qajar fleet was milling confusedly. They could not loose missiles at the Starwolf ships without hitting their own ships that were at death-grips with the Starwolves.

"Faster! Don't give them time!" Harkann cried, as Vengant drove their ship down toward a Qajar craft already engaged with a Varnan cruiser.

The vault of space was dancing with missile-flares, and Chane saw that the Qajar ships of the left horn were already mostly destroyed. The unexpected swiftness and savagery of the Varnan attack had taken a deadly toll.

Even as their immediate enemy's shields failed, and their missiles got through to it, Vengant gave a yell from where he sat at the controls.

"Harkann, look at them! The others!"

Chane turned to glance over his shoulder at the radar screen, as Harkann swung also to see it.

The remaining two-thirds of the Qajar force had not come into any formation. Suddenly, without any attempt to form an attack pattern, the whole formless mass of Qajar ships flung itself headlong toward the Starwolves.

"They must be crazy, to attack without formation!" exclaimed Vengant.

Chane remembered that Eron had said the Qajars were more than a little mad, and now he believed it. Only a sudden maniac fury could have impelled them to such an unplanned attack.

"Crazy or not, we've got them!" bellowed Harkann. "Cone out! Cone out!"

It was at this point that the Starwolves' unique ability to take the tremendous pressures of quick change of direction was brilliantly displayed. The metal of the flagship screeked in protest, and the blood drove again into Chane's skull, as the needle-shaped ship whirled away.

Every Varnan cruiser drove to its assigned position in one of the maneuvers that only Varnans could endure, and which they had practiced so many times that they almost do them in their sleep. With incredible quickness, the Starwolf ships formed into a gigantic conical pattern right in front of the onsweeping Qajar ships.

The Qajars could not react with the same swiftness, and their disorganized mass drove right into the giant cone. And the concentrated fire from all around them, the hail of missiles, shot half of them out of space.

"They're breaking!" cried Harkann. "Pour it on!"

Chane, loosing missiles as fast as he could get them off, saw the remaining Qajar ships turn wildly away, smashing clear of the cone of death. Three Varnan cruisers perished in head-on collisions.

And then the surviving Qajar vessels, no more than twenty-odd, were fleeing back in the direction of their world.

"After them!" ordered Harkann. "Three columns."

Chane saw things through a bloody haze, the pressure effect still clouding his vision.

It was only now, as they began the pursuit, that he realized that the probing finger of pain was still inside his skull.

XVIII

Thirty Starwolf ships flew low over the surface of the shadowy planet Chlann. The other ships of the Varnan squadron were orbiting in detachments around the planet, wary lest the survivors of the Qajar fleet should return. But so far, none of them had returned.

Chane piloted the flagship now. He was supposed to be an expert on the Qajar world, he thought ironically. Fine. All he knew about it was the location of the city, the location of the treasure houses, and the fact that he had been clobbered real hard the last time he had been here.

"Stand by," he said. "I think we'll be coming up on it pretty quick."

It was dangerous flying starwhips this low over a planet. But the Varnans were used to it—it was part of their regular raid technique—and also they were used to danger.

"Looks like mines of some sort," said Vengant, peering down at the face of the planet as it whirled beneath them.

The primary of Chlann, the old, red, dying sun that was one of the few stars in this cluster with any life left in it at all, cast a dim, bloody light on the surface of the planet. Dark, stony, arid, lifeless, the world below appeared.

But Chane too had caught the glint of the ruddy light on great constructions of metal that rose out of the rock.

"Automated mines," he said. "I told you, this planet has enormous radite deposits, and that's where the Qajars got their wealth. There may be several cities, but I only know of the one, and it's coming up fast. Stand by."

Up over the horizon of the planet came a soft glow. He knew it at once, although he had only seen it in the tridims Eron had made.

The city of the Qajars. The glittering metal buildings, the domes and towers and minarets, all of them bathed in the blue glow that seemed to well up from the ground itself, a sourceless illumination that strangely enough did not seem to conflict or clash with the dusky light of the dying sun.

From the city, a bolt of white lightning shot up toward the advancing Varnan ships. Only it was not lightning at all, but a tremendous laser ray that ripped the air close in front of them. And then other laser batteries joined in, and their ships were flying into a forest of laser lightnings.

"Stunpower projectors on," said Harkann's hard voice, speaking through the communicator to the whole squadron.

A droning began back in the stern of the ship. At the same moment, two laser bolts caught a Varnan cruiser just behind them and sent it tumbling out of the sky.

"On," said the voice of their engineer.

The thirty Starwolf ships were flying in a broad line. And now from every one of them the fans of invisible powerful forces went down.

The force was just the same as that which was generated by the small hand-stunners they all wore in their belts. But instead of being generated by a small portable power pack, it was created by the mighty power units of the Starwolf ships, and it swept the whole terrain beneath them with a paralyzing, stunning force.

And as they flew over the streets of the glowing

metal city, they saw the hurrying robed figures down there fall and lie still as the fans of force caught them.

It was the old Starwolf raiding technique. If you came in to a world using your missiles and laser full on, you could kill a lot of people but you would also destroy most of the loot you were after.

They went on over the city and the lasers that had been striking up at them from it fell still. A moment later, with a sense of immense relief, Chane felt the probing finger of pain in his head fade away.

Harkann uttered a rough oath. "So we got whoever was operating that damned pain ray! I'm only sorry we won't have time to hunt him out and kill him."

"*Look out!*" said Chane.

They were nearing the starport and from it there stabbed viciously an unexpected cluster of laser rays. Chane automatically spun into an evasive course, and the rays went by them.

Another Varnan ship was hit. Its shields were penetrated, and it tumbled downward. Harkann uttered a curse, and then they were past the starport, and its laser battery fell silent.

"Damn these people!" said Vengant. "I'd like to kill them, not just stun them."

"We haven't enough power for lethal, on the broad range we're using," said Harkann. "Otherwise, I agree with you."

Chane shrugged. "I don't mind their lasers, although I can't say I love them. But when I remember how they took my brain apart with that ray, I agree with you too."

"All right," said Harkann. "Come about and land on that starport. There may be some down there we didn't knock out, but we should be able to handle them."

He gave that order to the rest of their force, and then called up to the ships on watch in orbit. "Anything?"

"Not a thing," came the answer. "They've had the fight taken out of them and have landed and holed up somewhere."

"All right," said Harkann. "Let's go down and get the plunder."

They came down on the starport in a rush, and landed there in semidarkness under the black starless sky. They tumbled out of the ship fast, and all across the starport the big golden Varnans were coming out of the ships, the smell of loot in their nostrils and their eyes shining. And to Chane it was all as it had been since the first raid he had ever made, and what better life was there in the whole galaxy than to raid with the Starwolves?

"Break out the sleds," ordered Harkann. "And move!"

The starwolves prepared for their raids in a careful manner. When they hit a world they wanted to take what things they could there, and get away fast. For this the sleds were invaluable.

They were not really sleds. They were narrow, oblong flat hover-craft that nested together in a space just inside the hull of the ship. Chane helped pull them out and separate them.

Then Chane jumped onto the front end of one of them. He unfolded to an erect position the medium-heavy laser there. He opened the controls, and the sled rose several inches above the starport surface, its lifting-jets spuming up the dust underneath.

Vengant remained as ship-guard but the others now urged their sleds toward the city. Nobody among them waited to follow a leader; they raced across the starport in the semidarkness in any sort of order, shouting and laughing to each other.

Chane felt the high, fierce excitement he had always felt on these dashes. But he restrained it. He was now fast approaching the crisis of his whole struggle.

"This way!" bawled Harkann from his racing sled, pointing toward the blue radiance that rose beneath the dark, red-tinged sky.

They approached the smaller outer buildings of the

city, gleaming metallically in the blue light. The air
became perceptibly warmer as they entered the blue
radiance. They whirled on toward the tall towers that
glittered brightly in the center of the little city. And
now Chane let his sled fall behind the others a bit, without being too obvious about it.

They had the lasers on the fronts of the sleds, and
wore their stunners in their belts, but there was no need
to use them. The Qajars lay where they had fallen, in
streets and buildings. They looked quite neat, sleeping
in their long robes, and the sleds racing over them
cleared them and did not disturb them.

Chane wished he had time to look for the Qajar
named Vlanalan, who had tortured Dilullo and Gwaath
and himself.

*But taking their stolen treasures will probably be
revenge enough,* he thought.

The Varnans poured into the metal towers. And
quickly they started coming out, laughing and shouting
and bringing the first of the loot.

Jewels, precious metals, priceless statuary, all the
costly and superb treasures which the Qajars had had
thieved for them from worlds far across the galaxy. The
big Starwolves, their strength immense on this smaller
planet, bundled these treasures together higgledy-pig-
gledy into the carrying-nets they had brought, and
lifted it onto the sleds, and went back for more.

Chane unobtrusively steered his sled around the
plaza toward the smaller, less-impressive looking tower
he remembered from the tridim pictures. So far, it had
been ignored. He ran up its steps, his heart beating rapidly, flung open the wide doors, and burst into the
round, lofty room that he remembered.

It was the room of the tridim picture, with walls of
black hung with silken black hangings, all of it designed
to highlight the one thing that was in the room.

He looked at the Singing Suns, and now he heard
their music.

XIX

A long time ago on Earth a man named Plato had looked up at the planets of heaven and dreamed that in their stately movements they made each a glorious music.

Many centuries later, on a world far across the galaxy from Earth, a master artist had looked up at the stars and had the same dream. And because he was a master scientist as well as an artist, he had created the Singing Suns. His world was in decline and his arts lost and he himself long dead before the wider galactic life touched there, and nobody would ever create such a thing again.

And they do sing, thought Chane, standing with more of a look of awe on his dark, wild face than anyone had ever seen there.

There were forty of them, forty jewels that represented the forty mightiest stars. They had been synthetically created, but in their flashing splendor they made all natural gems look dull. Into each one had been built a tiny miniaturized generator that was fed by an almost unaging supply of transuranic fuel. And these generators powered the matrix of invisible force that held the Suns together, guided their movements, and produced the electronic sounds that made their music.

The jewels moved in an intricate pattern, a star-

dance that was too complicated at first to follow. Red,
green, golden yellow, bright blue, they wove their
unhurried ways in a design of mathematical perfection.
The whole mobile of the Suns was only some four feet
in diameter, but its splendor to the eye was the fact that
it was always changing, now one dark red star-jewel
passing two golden ones, now an ethereal blue-white
gliding above a greenish one.

And the jewels sang. From each one came its
individual note of pure sound electronically produced,
rising and falling in a lilting mode. And like the pattern
of their movement, the pattern of their sound changed
perpetually. Yet by the miracle that a master of both
art and science had wrought, the changing web of
sound was always music.

Chane stared, fascinated. No one who had roamed
the starry universe could remain unmoved by this
brilliant, changing, singing simulation of the great stars.
There were the great suns that he knew well, the
mighty red glare of Betelgeuse, the white blaze of
Rigel, the golden splendor of Altair. It was as though
he saw the whole changing, blazing galaxy in miniature,
and the siren music of its components reinforced the
sensation so that he seemed to fly as a disembodied
spirit through the galactic spaces, rather than to stand
looking at a mobile.

A Varnan shout not far outside the building startled
Chane out of the spell. On Starwolf raid, there was no
time for dreaming!

*And when they see what I've got, there'll be something
like a Starwolf riot,* he thought.

He hurried out and brought the sled right through
the opening of the great double doors. Then he grasped
the base of the mobile.

The thing was heavy, but his strength was quite
sufficient on this lower-gravity world. He managed to
tip and walk and work the base of the Singing Suns up
onto the sled and fasten it securely. And even as he

sweated at this task, the jewel-Suns only inches from
his eyes continued their smooth, mazy motions and
their music thrilled his ears.

When he was done he ripped down one of the black
silk hangings from the wall and used it to cover the
Singing Suns. Then he backed the sled out of the
building and went away fast.

Under the blue radiance of the halo, the Qajar city
was a strange scene. The Starwolves, intoxicated by the
loot they were loading on the sleds, shouted and
laughed at each other, big bawling golden figures
gutting the treasures of the Qajars.

And the Qajars still lay sleeping in their robes, as
the beauty they had plotted and stolen and tortured
to obtain was taken away from them forever. Remembering the agony they had inflicted on him and
his two comrades, Chane was fiercely glad.

He drove the sled out of the city at its highest speed,
toward the starport. He passed out of the blue radiance
and was again in the semidarkness beneath the
mourning black sky. Now he met sleds returning from
having loaded a first cargo of loot aboard ship, going
back for more. Their drivers waved to him elatedly.

When he reached the starport and threaded his way
between the little Varnan ships he saw loading still
going on at some of them. With reckless speed, in the
semidarkness, Chane drove on toward the flagship.

Outside the ship, as though waiting for him, stood
two tall Varnan figures, dark in the shadows.

Vengant.

And Harkann.

Instantly Chane knew that there was going to be
trouble. Harkann should not be here; he should be
back in the city supervising the operation.

Chane stopped the sled and got off it. And Harkann
said in a harsh voice, "I was curious, Chane. I found
you'd slipped away and I wondered what it was you
were after."

Chane shrugged. "The Council gave me the right to

select one single treasure for myself—whatever I wanted. And why are you worried about that? Haven't I brought you to the greatest plunder Varna has taken for years?"

"The plunder is fine indeed," said Harkann. "So fine that I wondered why you would pass it by and go after something else. What have you got on the sled?"

Well, Chane thought, *it would have had to come to the pinch sooner or later, so it might as well be now.*

He reached forward with both hands and pulled the silken black hanging toward him.

Both Harkann and Vengant stared, astonished, at the glorious thing on the sled. "The Singing Suns," said Harkann slowly, and shook his head as though not believing what he saw. "They were broken up and sold, but here they are . . . for the second time in Varnan hands."

Chane, still holding the silken hanging idly, corrected him. "In my hand. I claim the Suns by Council right."

Harkann slowly turned his stunned gaze from the singing jewels to Chane. His face became passionate, his upslanting eyes flaming like embers.

"Oh, no," he said. "No outworld bastard is going to take this all for himself."

"The Council right—" began Chane, and Harkann raged, "The hell with the Council right. We Ranroi would have had your life anyway when we got back to Varna, and it might as well be now!"

Chane triggered his stunner. He had drawn it gently from his belt behind the black hanging he was holding, while the others were staring at the mobile in amazement and greed. The thing buzzed nastily and the force of it went through the cloth as easily as through air. Harkann and Vengant stiffened and toppled over.

Chane dropped the concealing cloth. He muttered to the two still forms, "I should have used it on lethal, but I've got enough feud with the Ranroi without that. Sleep for a while, my friends."

He glanced swiftly around. Some of the Varnan ships

being loaded from the loot-piled sleds were not too far away, but in the noise and cheerful confusion and the semidarkness nobody seemed to have noticed.

He bent down and dragged Harkann and then Vengant some little distance from the ship and threw the black hanging over them.

The air lock doors of the ship were open, and they were very wide doors, wide enough to admit a sled. When the Starwolves departed a planet with a load of loot they wanted to depart in a hurry. Chane ran the sled up the gangway and into the ship and maneuvered it to the rear of the main compartment. There were clamps there to lock sleds fast, and in a moment he had his cargo secured. The Suns glittered and sang and wove their dance serenely.

Chane jumped to the pilot chair, hit the lever that sealed all locks, and got the power unit started. When the power unit had built to a barely sufficient level, Chane took the little ship off in a steep climb.

As he shot toward the starless sky he looked down and could see startled faces turned up to him. It would not be long, he thought, before somebody stumbled over Harkann and Vengant. But it would take quite a time to bring them around, time enough, he hoped, to get away with the Suns.

A sudden wild emotion filled him as he sent the little ship arrowing out headlong from dark Chlann. He had snatched the Singing Suns away from the damned Qajars and from Harkann both.

He had not planned at all to do it this way. He had supposed that he would have no choice but to go back to Varna with Harkann, and then try to slip away with the Suns before the Ranroi could finish him off. He had never had the slightest intention of going through single combats with one after another of the Ranroi until inevitably they got him. He considered that too damned unfair, when there were hundreds of them and only one of him.

But Harkann had changed the plan by his sudden access of rage, and Chane like a good Starwolf, had changed his tactics in mid-leap.

Fine, he thought. *This is much better . . . so far. But what if they track me?*

That was a problem he would have to face, but not now. His first job was to get out of the dark, crowded cluster and into overdrive.

He headed the ship through the clutter of ashen suns and stony black planets, toward the Spur but not toward Rith. Instead, he laid his course for Varna.

They would be ranging him, back there on Chlann, wondering why the devil a Varnan ship had taken off prematurely, and where it was going. He had better try to deceive them as to his course, though he knew in his heart that no Starwolf would fall for such a clumsy trick. At the moment, it was the only one he could think of.

It was dangerous to go into overdrive too near to a celestial body of any size. It had been done, but not very often. More times than not, the gravitic field had flawed the overdrive reaction and made wreckage out of the ship.

Chane was always willing to take chances but it did not seem to him that there was any real need to risk suicide. He urged the ship to its highest speed, thinking as he looked at the view-port that he never wanted to see this cursed little clutch of dead suns and mourning planets again.

He broke clear of the cluster at last, and now in the distance ahead stretched the immense coast of tarnished fire that was the Argo Spur. When he was at a marginally safe distance from the cluster, he set up the overdrive controls.

Before switching on he looked back at the rear range screen. There were four blips showing, and he knew then that he had overestimated the time it would take to bring Harkann back to consciousness.

"That's what I get for playing it soft like John is always telling me," he muttered. "I should have used lethal."

The pursuers were after him.

XX

It was a dead, dark, airless world, infinitely desolate and useless, but it was a hiding place. And Chane was hiding.

He had got well inside the Spur when he decided that he had best go to ground. He knew the bitterness and rage with which Harkann and his Ranroi would sweep and quarter after him, waiting for the time when he would have to come out of overdrive, when they could spot him and pounce.

He could not fight four cruisers, or one cruiser. He was only one man, not a crew, and while he could keep the ship going he could not possibly fly it and fight it both. A hiding place was his best chance, and this dead planet of a giant red star looked like the best one he could find in time.

There were no telltale blips on his screen as yet. But he knew better than to linger.

He had dropped out of overdrive on the back side of the dead planet, so that the mass of the world itself served as a screen against their radar. Then he began a quick and frantic search for metal deposits. When the analyzer showed him one of a size and content to meet his needs, he landed the ship at once.

It was a hazardous landing, in the bottom of a narrow gully between glistening rock walls. The ship took a banging, but endured. Chane got into his suit and helmet, cracked the lock and clambered out. Climbing up the side of the rock wall, he used one of the portable lasers he had brought to dislodge a shower of small fragments and he hoped that he was not going to dislodge a big boulder that would crash down and do an evil to the ship. He did not. He played the laser with skill, and presently the upper part of the ship's hull was dusted thickly with particles of rock debris.

It was a pretty faulty protective coloration, Chane thought, but it would have to do. The debris, containing heavy metal deposits, should blend the ship more or less indistinguishably into the background. The Ranroi would do a search sweep with their analyzers, but Varnan analyzers were not fine scientific instruments; they were, rather, simple affairs designed to detect ambushed ships and the like. With luck, they would simply note an area of metal-bearing rock and go on.

With luck. . . .

Sitting in his camouflaged ship and watching the screen, Chane grinned to himself. Luck. "If we have luck they'll go away." That was what Nimurun had said years ago when their Starwolf party had raided the Pleiades and nearly been caught, and they had had to hide their ships in the ghastly metal ruins of a war-destroyed world. Well, they had had luck that time, and all he could do now was hope it would repeat, and in the meantime drink some of the Varnan wine and watch the screen.

Nothing, yet. But he was sure they would be along. They could be very patient, very thorough in their search.

He turned and considered the Singing Suns. Here in the confines of the ship their music was louder, but still soft. It changed and changed in infinite permutations of melodic phrases, always singing of the glory of the great suns, the majesty and burning splendor of the mighty stars that lorded space.

And the Suns moved in their endless glittering mazy dance, and when he looked at them long enough it was as it had been when he first saw them on Chlann: he seemed to be drawn among them and they became, not singing jewels, but flaming giants whose mighty star-song filled the whole of space.

An hypnotic effect? He did not think so. The Suns had no need for such tricks as hypnotism. Their beauty of sight and sound held one imprisoned in a dream.

He had better not get too imprisoned, he thought, and turned to look again at the screen.

He tensed sharply. Two blips moved across it, two ships orbiting this dead world at high speed, moving in the familiar search-sweep pattern. Chane knew that their analyzers, tuned to detect metal, would be probing with broad fans of force, seeking a metal ship on the desolate rock.

The blips came around fast and Chane whispered, "Nothing down here but a metal outcrop, boys. Go right on."

They did. Had the metal outcrop fooled them, or would they come down to investigate?

The minutes went by. The Suns sang softly, of cosmic beauty and strength, of beginnings and endings, of the life of stars which men can never know.

The two blips came on again. They were continuing the search pattern southward. They were not coming down. Chane exhaled pent-up breath.

He continued to watch as they completed their sweep of the planet. Finally the two blips left the screen entirely. They had gone.

Chane did nothing. He continued to sit there and pour himself the golden wine and listen to the singing of the Suns.

He was not through with the Ranroi yet.

Harkann and his little squadron would shake out this whole part of the Spur before they left. That was certain. For Harkann would not want to go back to

Varna and admit that his clan-enemy the damned
Earthman had foxed him, used his mission as a
cat's-paw to take the Singing Suns, and gone off with
them in Harkann's own ship. Even though the raid
would have brought home plunder rich beyond even
Starwolf dreams, Harkann would not want to face that.

How Berkt would laugh if he heard that, thought
Chane. *How all Varna would laugh!*

But the laughter would never come if Harkann could
prevent it. He and his Ranroi ships would hang to the
search like grim death.

Should he leave this planet, try to slip away before
the search swung back? Chane thought not. It was
exactly what they were looking for; this preliminary
sweep was designed to flush him out, urge him to run so
that he could be spotted and chased. He had made his
gamble when he hid here, and he would push that bet
all the way.

He drank, and ate, and slept, and waited. He did not
once go outside the ship. Nothing must be disturbed in
any way.

Days went by before two blips again came onto the
screen. The two ships made exactly the same
search-sweep over the planet as before. And Chane
knew that the analyzers would be probing again while
their little tape-banks chattered through Comparison.
If one small object did not correspond exactly with the
record of the first sweep, the ship would land and
investigate.

The two ships finished their search and went away
again. But still Chane made no move. A section of the
Spur was a big place to search, and the Ranroi would
likely be around for quite some time yet.

Chane hated waiting and doing nothing; all
Starwolves hated that. But they could be very good at it
when they had to, for there were times in their
dangerous trade when it was necessary.

The Suns sang on. It seemed to him, as he watched

and listened day after day, that the rising and falling
music spoke words, not faulty words such as humans
use, but the pure and perfect language of stars.

What did stars talk about, in that silver-singing
speech? Of the birth of the universe, when they first
exploded into being? Of the mighty rivers of force that
ran between them, of the darkening and dying of old
comrades, of the dreadful and glorious fate of novae, of
the thin, far-off messages that came from brother giants
remote across the intergalactic void?

Chane dreamed of these things, but this time he did
not let his dreaming interrupt his careful watch on the
screen. And there came a time when he saw five faint
and distant blips moving away in the direction of
Varna.

Chane laughed. "So you finally gave it up, Harkann?
I'll gamble that your crews made you do it."

Chane knew the Starwolves, and he knew how it
would be with those crews, how eager they would be to
get back to Varna and celebrate one of the richest raids
in history, and to hell with Ranroi vengeance and
Harkann's private feud until after we've had a time!

He waited for a safe interval and then got busy. He
put on the suit and helmet, unclamped the sled which
bore the Suns, and maneuvered it out through the big
air lock into the vacuum outside.

The fierce glare of the red giant illuminated the floor
of the narrow rock valley. Chane drove the sled along
the valley, mile after mile, until he found the place he
wanted.

It was a deep cave in the base of one of the enclosing
cliffs. It could not have been formed by erosion—this
world had never had an atmosphere from its looks—but
bursting gases when the planet was formed had created
this bubble. High above it on the steep cliff-face was a
place where the rock bulged outward.

Chane drove the sled deep into the cave. He took the
Singing Suns off the sled and set them on the rock. In

the darkness here they still gleamed with supernal beauty, but in the soundless vacuum he could not hear them.

He left the Suns there and backed the sled outside. Then with the laser mounted on the sled he attacked the bulge of rock high above on the cliff. The laser flashed and flashed, quite silently, cutting deep. Finally a section of the cliff tumbled down and effectively sealed the entrance to the cave.

Chane made careful note of the exact location and then turned the sled back toward the ship.

When he was ready he took the ship off with a bold rush. It was an almost suicidal risk to take off from a cramped place like this valley, and he wanted to make it fast or not at all.

He made it. He came up off the dead planet and swept past the glaring red sun, laying his course for Rith.

XXI

Storm was sweeping across the night side of Rith where the little capital of Eron lay. Chane had counted on the frequency of the storms here, and he had not brought his ship toward the planet until he was sure another of the interminable tempests was raging.

The ships of the Starwolves were unmistakable because of their small, needle-like shape that had been designed to endure the sudden turns that gave the Varnans their big advantage in space. And when a Starwolf ship arrived at any planet other than Varna it would pretty surely be met by a hail of missiles.

Chane had had experience with the way the great thunderstorms of Rith played the devil with radar and scanners, and he was hoping to get down on the starport without being scanned.

He got the ship down all right, and the solid downpour of water prevented visual observation. But also his own instruments being aborted led to his making such a bad landing that he was glad no one had seen it.

He worked very fast now, before the storm should cease. He set up the automatic controls so that in three minutes the ship would take off on a course laid for Varna, with the automatic trips set to detour around all celestial obstacles. He was damned if he was going to let a Varnan ship and its secrets fall into enemy hands.

He was grinning as he cracked the lock and started out of the ship.

"How sheepish Harkann will be if his ship comes wandering home empty-handed after him!"

The rain smashing in his face took the laughter out of him. He started struggling through the hellish downpour, and he only heard in a muffled way when the ship he had just left took off. He hoped he could make it to one of the starport administration buildings before he was flattened.

Two hours later, Chane sat in the big cold barny room he had burglarized not too long before. Two of the runty red guards watched him. He thought they must be the same two he had knocked out and tied up, the murderous way they watched him.

Eron and Dilullo came in. Dilullo gave Chane a sour look that had no warmth in it.

"So, we've got you back again, have we?" he said.

"Thanks for the welcome, John," said Chane. "From the way you look, and from the fact you've recovered your usual sunny temper, I take it you're normal again."

Eron had folded his arms and was glaring at Chane in what was intended to be a crushing manner. But when Chane did not look at him, the little red king suddenly roared, "You stole one of my scout-ships! Where is it?"

Chane smiled at him. "It's far away. I don't think you'll ever see it again."

Eron began to curse. "The men at the starport said they thought a ship landed you and then took off again. What kind of ship?"

"A Starwolf ship," said Chane.

That made Eron's eyes pop. But Dilullo looked at Chane and for this once, at least, a warm light came into his eyes.

"Chane, then you went home to Varna? And you got back alive? How was it?"

"It was wonderful, and it was dangerous," said
Chane, "and I'm damned glad I did it."

Eron broke in, raging. "You Mercs have been
nothing but bad luck to me since you came here. This
settles it—when the Qajars demand you you'll all be
turned over to them. I don't care if they put you over a
slow fire."

"Relax, Eron," said Chane. "It will be a long time
before the Qajars bother you or anyone else. Those
nice, crazy, torture-happy, beauty-loving people have
been most thoroughly smashed, and their world has
been most thoroughly looted, and I don't think anyone
will hear anything from them for a long time."

"Smashed? With their defenses?" cried Eron. "Lies,
lies. Who could do that?"

"The Starwolves did it," said Chane, and his teeth
flashed. "And I led them there." And he turned to
Dilullo and said, "We didn't really kill hardly anybody
there, John, but we did strip them clean, and that pays
them off for the fun they had with us."

"Those treasures!" cried Eron. "And the Singing
Suns? What became of them?"

"I got them," said Chane.

Eron began to shout again. "Lies, lies! You had
nothing, nothing at all, when you landed on Rith."

Chane nodded. "Of course. Do you think I would
bring the Singing Suns here, so you could grab hold of
them and then boot our behinds off this world? Little
man, I'm not that foolish!"

Eron stared at him, and then burst into a bellow of
laughter.

"I knew," he told Chane, "the first time I saw you
that you were a bastard of a Starwolf!" He came up to
Chane and grabbed his arm. "So you did it, eh? Tell me
how?"

Chane told him, Dilullo, listening, watched Chane's
face and said nothing. But Eron again and again rocked
with crowing laughter.

"Wonderful, wonderful!" he cried. "But where, actually, are the Singing Suns?"

Chane patted him on the shoulder. "You're a nice little king, Eron, and I rather like you in a way, but please don't insult me with questions like that."

Eron shrugged. "Well, I can see your point. It happens that I'm the soul of honor, but you couldn't be expected to know that. Just tell me how and when you'll turn over my half of the two million credits' reward. That was our deal, you remember."

"That *was* our deal," Chane said. "But if you recall, that deal went sour when your information and your ship didn't get us anywhere near the Suns. The deal was off, and you were going to feed us to the Qajars if they wanted us. I broke loose, and now we have a new deal."

"What kind of deal?" asked Eron, looking black but crafty.

Chane smiled. "I'm generous to a fault. When the Suns are taken back to Achernar, you get one-tenth of the reward."

"One-tenth?" Eron began to curse in his native language and Chane said, "Put it into galacto, if you want me to get it."

Eron lost his good humor completely. His face became stony and dangerous. He glared at Chane.

"All right," he said. "I've tried to be nice about this. But you've hidden the Suns somewhere and now you come swaggering in here and think you've got the upper hand. You forget that I've got you right in the hollow of my hand. Just a few hours of Rith working-over and you'll be babbling all you know about the Suns."

Chane shook his head. "It won't work. Nobody ever got anything out of a Starwolf by torture. And you know why? It's because, to protect the secrets of Varna, every Starwolf who goes on a raid has a drug capsule under his skin. All I have to do is press my skin in a certain place and then my body is completely anesthetized and you could carve on me all day and I'd never feel it."

Eron stared at him, startled. "Is that true?"

"No," said Chane. "It's a great big bluff and a lie."

And he broke into laughter, and Eron roared with him.

Dilullo sprang up from his chair. "God save me from getting into any deals with people who think everything's funny."

"Relax, John," said Chane. "I think Eron and I understand each other."

"Sure we do," said Eron, going hail-fellow-well-met again. He clapped Chane on the back. "Bluff or no bluff, nobody's ever made a Starwolf talk. Let's sit down and bargain this like gentlemen."

They sat down at a table. Eron called for flagons of the strong Rith liquor, and then more flagons. Dilullo drank it, but looked like a thundercloud.

As time went on it was evident that Eron was trying to get them very drunk. But it was not working very well. Dilullo would not drink that much. Chane tossed it off goblet for goblet with Eron, but he had the stronger head. He kept shaking it at Eron and turning boredly away to watch the decorative dancing-girls who had appeared.

"Fifteen percent," Chane said finally. "The absolute last offer. Look, better fifteen percent of something than nothing."

"Twenty-five, or I'll have you all lasered before morning," said Eron.

"Not one percent, not one hundredth of a percent more," Chane told him, and poured more liquor into the goblets.

"Look," interrupted Dilullo, "my head aches, my rump aches, I'm sick of all this haggling." He said to Eron, "Twenty percent, or let the whole thing go."

Eron considered. "Four hundred thousand credits.

Well . . ." He suddenly added, "But I have the price of my stolen scout ship as well."

Dilullo said, "All right, that seems fair enough. How do you want it?"

"Not in galactic credits," Eron said. "We don't trust that currency in the Spur. Bring it in jewels. I'll give you a list."

He added, "One more thing. Just so you remember to come back again with my share, I'll keep your friend Chane here with me. He's a good drinking companion."

"I was pretty sure," said Chane, "you would insist on some such little condition. All right." He looked at Dilullo. "I'll tell you in the morning where the Suns are hidden, so you can take them to Achernar."

"By all means wait until morning to tell me," said Dilullo. "You're in no condition to tell anyone directions to anything right now."

In the morning, after Chane had given Dilullo the location of the Suns on the dead world of the red giant, the Mercs took off in their ship.

Chane remained. He was a guest, an honored guest, and little red men with lasers watched him day and night.

He did not find it unpleasant. Eron insisted on trying to drink him down every night, but each time it was Eron who ended up with his head on the table. Nearly every night, after that, Chane tried to make a connection with one of the dancing-girls, who were attracted but also afraid.

The days, the weeks, the perpetual storms went by, and Chane was beginning to get just a little bored by the time the Merc ship called in for a landing.

Dilullo alone came from the starport to the pawky palace and put a package down in front of Eron.

"There it is," he said. "You can look the jewels over if you like."

Eron told him, "I can tell when I can trust a man, so there's no need. However, since you suggest it . . ."

The hours went by while the jewels were examined by Eron experts. Then the little red monarch exclaimed, "All there."

"I may add," Dilullo said, "that there are no jewels, no credits, nor anything else of value on our ship, so that it will not profit you to detain us."

"As if I would!" said Eron. He clapped Chane on the back. "Well, I'll miss you, Starwolf. Good luck."

"Good luck to you, Eron," said Chane. "You just might find some good pickings left at Chlann, now that the Qajar defenses have been broken."

"I hate to break up these affectionate leavetakings between fellow robbers," grated Dilullo. "But if you don't *mind* . . ."

He and Chane, at the starport, walked out together toward the waiting Merc ship.

"So you went to Varna, and you raided again with the Starwolves," said Dilullo. "How was your homecoming, Chane? The same as it was with me, at Brindisi?"

Chane considered. "Not quite the same. Most of the people I knew were still there. But . . . I can't go back there again."

"Well," said Dilullo, "you're younger than I am, and that's what made the difference."

Then he added, "The devil with all this nostalgia. A starman's home is space. Let's go."

They went.

MORE SCIENCE FICTION!
ADVENTURE

BEST-SELLING
Science Fiction
and
Fantasy